THE DARK LORD

By Jack Heckel

The Dark Lord
The Pitchfork of Destiny
A Fairy-tale Ending
Happily Never After
Once Upon a Rhyme

THE DARK LORD

JACK HECKEL

HARPER
VOYAGER
IMPULSE

An Imprint of HarperCollins*Publishers*

EPub Edition NOVEMBER 2016 ISBN: 9780062359339

Print Edition ISBN: 9780062359346

10 9 8 7 6 5 4 3 2 1

To Taba, Isaac, Heather and Carleigh
and everyone who ever role-played with us

"'I think you are a very bad man,' said Dorothy.

'Oh, no, my dear; I'm really a very good man, but I'm a very bad Wizard, I must admit.'"

—L. Frank Baum,

The Wonderful Wizard of Oz

PROLOGUE

Hello, my name is Avery, and I am the Dark Lord.

If you have ever read any other accounts of dark lords or, gods forbid, been under the thumb of one yourself, your first thought should be, "What is a guy named Avery doing being a dark lord?"

At least, that's what I was thinking as I watched the final battle in the War between Light and Dark from the highest balcony of the tallest tower of my Fortress of Despair. Far below, on the poisoned steppes of the Plains of Drek before the bloodred gates of the stronghold, men, elves, and dwarfs united against all the forces of evil: me and my army.

All day the Army of Light had been advancing inexorably, but every inch of progress came at a terrible cost in blood and death. It was awful to behold, and I wanted nothing more than to turn away, but I wouldn't let myself. Since this war, for better or worse, was being fought at my bidding, I felt the least I could do was bear witness. And so I did, though I was not sure how much more I could take.

The worst of it was the smell. No matter how hard I tried to abstract myself from what was happening on the battlefield, the smell would not let me. It was a mix of something burning and something metallic, something sweaty and something rotten. It got into my mouth and made me want to spit.

Gods, what could make such a smell?

The images that formed in answer to my unspoken question made my stomach lurch and my hands begin to shake uncontrollably. I grasped the rough wall of the parapet to still them, and reminded myself again that this was necessary and that good would come of it. The reassurance had worked well at one time, but over the past few months it had grown threadbare with overuse.

I was brought back to the present as the stone beneath my hands shuddered violently. Looking down I saw that the Army of Light had fought its way to the very walls of the fortress and even now were battering at the gates. My defeat seemed certain. I mouthed a prayer of thanks and was about to retreat to my throne room to await the inevitable when I heard voices drifting up from a balcony below.

"Cravock," a familiar voice roared. "What news?"

I peeked over the edge of the parapet and saw Morgarr the Slaughterer, the merciless general of the Army of Evil, and his sniveling reptilian servant, Cravock. Morgarr was standing in full battle armor surveying the carnage of the battle with an imperious glare. Cravock squirmed and prostrated at his heal. Morgarr should have been down with his men. Those were my orders. But I couldn't blame him for disobeying. I wouldn't have wanted to be out there either.

"Your Great Wickednessss," Cravock hissed, "the enemy isss at the gatesss. You mussst do sssomething before it isss too late."

"I must?" Morgarr roared. The hell-forged plate that encased him rippled as it tried to contain his rage. He hefted Death Slasher, his black double-headed battle-axe, and pointed its curved blade at the half-lizard, half-man. But while Morgarr's attention was on Cravock, and Cravock's attention was on Death Slasher, the living eye embedded in the handle of the battle-axe was staring up at me with a burning hatred. It was hard to say if the Army of Dark was more afraid of Morgarr or that battle-axe, but for me there was no contest. Death Slasher was terrifying.

I ducked back out of sight while Cravock whined, "Pleassse forgive me, Great Dessstroyer. I meant no insssult. It isss only that I thought—"

"I do the thinking, toad," Morgarr shouted. "You do my bidding. Order out our reserves, the blood orcs, the twelve-headed rage demons, the viper dragon—empty the fortress if you must!"

I almost felt bad for Cravock, because I knew he wasn't going to be able to do any of those things.

Earlier this morning I had given orders to ensure that the blood orcs were led into an ambush and destroyed. Last night I had painstakingly removed each of the twelve heads of each of the twelve-headed rage demons. And a couple of days ago I'd freed the viper dragon from his magical enslavement with the command to fly off and never return.

Cravock hissed, "Your Wrathfulnessss, we have no reservesss. The blood orcsss have been routed, the rage demonsss dessstroyed to the lassst head, and the viper dragon hasss not been ssseen sssince the night before lassst. All that we had hasss already been deployed. Only the power of the Dark Lord himssself can sssave us now."

"That displeases me greatly," Morgarr said quietly. "I must have an audience with my master."

That was my cue. I left the balcony and made my way down to the throne room. As I descended, the Fortress of Despair shook with the impacts from siege engines and explosions from magical spells. I could hear distant shouts of triumph. The enemy had breached the gates, and from the number of abandoned guardrooms and barracks I passed, my army had been broken. Even the murk-scaled kobolds and mindless gibberlings that normally lurked about in the shadowy corners of the keep had fled. The forces of good would face no further resistance. A vast weight lifted from my shoulders.

When I reached my inner sanctum, some signs of normalcy returned. Flanking the entrance were my ever present gaunt-fiend honor guard. They snapped to attention and I swept between them as the doors closed behind me. I mounted the stairs of my dais of skulls and arranged myself atop my throne of skulls to wait the end. To pass the time I pulled out a small notebook and began chronicling my last day as the Dark Lord. Everything had to be properly documented if I wanted to have any chance of including this in a later publication.

I had barely begun recording my impressions of the final battle when there was a loud boom and the doors to the chamber were thrown open. Morgarr stood in the vaulted doorway, bowing, his great multihorned helmet tucked under his arm. I gave him a negligent backhanded gesture. He ducked his head and ran forward, prostrating himself before the stairs to my throne. He remained there at my feet not daring to meet my gaze, though I could not say the same for his cursed battle-axe. Its red eye glared at me knowingly.

"Rise!" I commanded, and then realized that I was still holding my notebook. Hastily, I shoved it under my seat and tried to assume my most diabolical expression.

By the time my gaze was properly ominous Morgarr had already begun to plead. I cleared my thoughts and tried to focus on the behemoth of a man before me. ". . . I have done all that I can, Dark Lord. The enemy has breached our defenses. The legions of undead have been shattered. The beastmen and brigands have fled like dogs. The blood orcs are no more, the rage demons have lost their heads, and the viper dragon has abandoned us. The Heroes of the Ages will be here in moments. There is nothing more that we can do. We are lost without you, my master. You must unleash your powers to save us . . ."

I will spare you the rest of what he said. Suffice it to say there was a lot of blame shifting, minimizing, and justifying going on. When he finished I fixed him with one of my well-rehearsed, pitiless stares.

Several days ago I had decided that when this moment came I would have to kill him. Not that I wanted to. Left to my own devices I would have preferred for someone else to deal with him, but I'd done a back of the envelope calculation and knew that if I left him to the Heroes of the Ages there was a pretty good chance that he would take one or two of them out on his way to the grave. That I couldn't have. They had an important role to play in rebuilding the world after my defeat and I was already down to five so I didn't have a lot of them to spare.

I need to make it clear that my hesitancy in killing Morgarr wasn't about whether the man deserved what he was going to get. He was the most loathsome creature I had ever met. He was a cold-blooded killer and a fiend, and had been since long before I came to this world. Still, I'm not that good around blood and death, and had made it a point up till now not to kill anyone myself. Sure, I made certain everyone thought I was a mass-murdering psychopath—you kind of have to when you're trying to be the

Dark Lord—but usually when I had to give a public demonstration of my power I simply transported my victims somewhere on the other side of the world. The melting bodies and horrific screams that accompanied this were nothing more than illusion and good stagecraft.

I sighed. Having committed to do this I was determined to follow the proper forms. I rose silently from the throne, letting the full length of my great dark robes spill around me. With the added height of my boots and the advantage of the pile of skulls on which the throne was built, I towered over the kneeling Morgarr. I gazed down on my general in silence; a single thought filled my head.

I'm not going to have to wear this ghastly makeup after today.

"You have failed," I hissed in a terrible rasp that I had spent several weeks with a speech coach to perfecting. It was theatrical and absolutely wrecked my throat. I made a mental note that I needed a good tea with honey after all this.

I raised my left hand with a flourish, twitching as I stretched my fingers as wide as possible. I had begun to unleash the spell of obliteration when Morgarr did something unexpected. He flinched. It was the only hint of humanity I think I'd ever seen from him, and it made me hesitate.

He's Morgarr! I reminded myself. *How many has he killed in your name!* "How many more will you kill if I leave you alive?" I asked aloud as I stared down at the man.

He met my eyes; they were remorseless. "As many as I can, my master," he vowed.

"As I thought," I whispered hoarsely, and purple bolts of energy flashed from my shaking fingertips consuming his flesh. Morgarr the Slaughterer was dead. Only the bones and the armor were left, and the battle-axe.

The eye of Death Slasher was fixated on me. I cursed it and wished, not for the first time, that I had a spell that would destroy it, which is ironic because I had created it. Unfortunately, invoking it out of existence was impossible. I'd done the research and there was simply no way to resolve the cosmic morality term without it. Something about evil balancing good. I'll admit, subworld physics was never my strong suit. To simplify things you can think of the battle-axe as the remainder on a nasty long division problem: irritating, impossible to ignore, and always leaving you with the sneaking suspicion that you messed up the arithmetic.

I put aside the finer points of arcane mathematics, strode over to the battle-axe and stared down at it. It studied me in return behind its unblinking eye. I dropped my Dark Lord voice and said, "Don't look at me like that. He deserved it, and you'll get yours too. One day. Somehow."

The eye seemed to grow even more malevolent. I picked it up with a shudder, and quickly dropped it into a folded piece of reality: a useful thing, about the size of a large wallet on the outside, but that opens onto an extradimensional space inside large enough to hold a studio apartment's worth of furniture—at least that's as much as I'd ever put in there.

I was wondering what to do with the rest of Morgarr's remains when I heard the sound of clashing weapons and shouts of battle from the hallway outside. I was running out of time. I rushed to my throne, scooped my notebook into the extradimensional space, folded it, and tucked the whole thing back into my cloak. I had only retaken my seat when the doors to the chamber flew open again, and the Heroes of the Ages stepped in.

Finally.

I had been waiting years of their time for this meeting. I recognized them all through the tales of their deeds, of course. There was Feldane the Archer, scion of the elves; Mad Jarl of the Dwarf Mechanism with his living armor (it was a bit squatter than I thought it would be); St. Drake the Suffering (the gibberlings and I liked to call him St. Dork the Insufferable); the masked rogue known only as the Weasel; Mystia, sorceress of the Enigmatic Isles; and Valdara.

How to describe Valdara without coming off as a creep . . . she was a warrior woman. Oh, forget it, there is no way to do her justice without being a creep. Valdara was tall and long of leg, with gorgeous bronze flesh and red hair that fell in curls over her shoulders. Even in the guttering torchlight of my chamber her green eyes shone, and I couldn't help but admire the curves of her body and her taut bare stomach. After the horror of the last few days it was wonderful to look on someone so beautiful, even if she was here to kill me.

It was Valdara who spoke, which was good because I really didn't want to look away. She pointed her gleaming blade at me. "Dark Lord, for all the evil you have wrought, for the suffering and pain you have caused, the free people of Trelari call you to justice."

I watched every syllable escape those red lips of hers. I wanted to explain everything, perhaps over a nice dinner and a bottle of wine, but that was not to be. This was my final data point, and my entire research project, not to mention the future of these people, depended on me.

"Foolish mortals! You would dare defy me? Come! Show me what the 'Heroes of the Ages' are capable of," I said, adding an evil rattling laugh to the end.

They did their best—arrows and magical energies flew at me, some kind of superheated steam from the clanking armor blasted me—but it was no use. My power was far superior to theirs. After all, I literally held the key to their reality. Well, I should say that I wore it around my neck on a silver chain. There wasn't much that I couldn't do.

I laughed again, but with less rattle because my throat was starting to hurt a lot. "Your power is as nothing compared to me. Now you face the fury of the endless abyss itself!"

I raised my hands to the sky, letting a little power trickle over my fingertips for show, then I unleashed enough of it to convince them I was trying without risking injury to anybody. Blackness swirled about Mystia and Feldane on the wings of flapping phantasmal ravens, blinding them and driving them to their knees in terror. A great wind tore across the room toppling Jarl's mechanism. With a crack, a rope of infernal magic whipped out and ensnared the Weasel as he or she (or it?) tried to slink behind me through the shadows. Only Valdara and St. Drake were still standing. They struggled against the buffeting, trying to reach me.

Bracing himself against my magic, St. Drake held aloft a staff that blazed with a mystic light. "Dark Lord," he shouted, "Your defeat is at hand. We come bearing the Mage Staff of Mysterium," he shouted.

I let the swirling darkness diminish. "No . . ." I rasped, putting an emphasis on my pause as I stepped back. "Not the Mage Staff. It isn't possible. I sent it into the void myself." I gurgled out the last bit and held up a quivering hand. I was worried that I was overacting, but they didn't seem to notice.

"You're a fool, Dark Lord," Drake shouted, and then intoned significantly, "Even you cannot destroy that which is eternal."

I cringed at the truism. I'd written it into the world's pattern to add a bit of color, but it wasn't my best work. The staff on the other hand was a stroke of genius and cheap to make. It was nothing more than a plain wooden rod onto which I'd affixed a shard of purple glass that I'd charmed to emit a muted glow. It was a constant source of amazement to me the nonsense you could get people to believe if you cloaked that nonsense in mystery and burnished it with antiquity.

I thrust my arms forward as if to send more waves of magic against them. All I was really doing was making sure that Drake wouldn't be able to reach me. According to my simulations, if St. Insufferable defeated the Dark Lord this world would end up a theocracy. For reasons that involve having attended a Catholic boy's school as a child, I didn't want that. Besides, I knew who I wanted to defeat me. Valdara was going to make a great queen. She was just, wise, and would look much better as a statue.

With a flick of my fingers I sent a single, sudden and violent burst of air against St. Drake. He tumbled backward and was pinned to the wall. He struggled and prayed to the Seven Gods, but my power was too great. "Valdara!" he shouted. "I can't reach him. I haven't the strength. You must take it."

Valdara threw herself across the room and took the staff from his hand. "As long as I have breath in my body, it will be done," she said, and kissed his brow.

It was all going exactly as I had hoped. I lessened the winds around her, letting her push toward me. Step by agonizing step she made her way across the room and up the stairs of the throne dais.

"This isn't possible!" I roared, and widened my eyes in feigned confusion.

At last she was in front of me. I fell to my knees

before the glowing staff. I held up a quavering hand and rasped, "Even if you destroy me now I will be reborn, and should your people grow weak, I will rise again."

"We will never allow your evil to return, Dark Lord. Never!" Valdara shouted.

Make sure that you don't, I thought.

She spun the staff and, as required by the legends I'd written, and called upon the mystic energies of the Seven Gods to help guide her blow. Her eyes burned with the fire of victory. I wanted to put on a good show for her, but found that I couldn't muster even the fake anger necessary to glare back. It was time to go. I was tired, and it was time to go. I readied the spell of exit.

With a wordless roar Valdara thrust the staff at me. It struck me in the chest, right above my heart. There was no pain, but I screamed like a drama queen as I completed the spell of exit.

A light flashed and I watched as Valdara and Drake and then the world faded from sight. I was gone. The forces of Light had triumphed and the Dark Lord was defeated. I had saved them all, and my dissertation was complete.

CHAPTER 1

MYSTERIUM, MYSTERIUM!

With a flash of blinding light and a jarring sensation, best described as the feeling you might experience if your brain was yanked out through your ears, I materialized in Mysterium, or to be more specific, in experimental circle closet 12B in the basement of the Magus Nicholas Reingold Subworld Studies building on the campus of Mysterium University. I held my breath as the smoke from the ionized fazestone powder dissipated and felt the weight of true reality wrap around me like a blanket. I was home. I let out a deep and unexpectedly bittersweet sigh of relief.

What is Mysterium?

I have no idea. The truth is you would either have

to be a scholar of obscure magical history or an etherspace physicist to even attempt an answer. Mysterium is and, as far as I know, always has been. I can tell you that if you think of all the infinite worlds and subworlds in the universe as points in a great spinning pinwheel, Mysterium is at its center. To be honest, that's as much as you need to know unless you are fond of headache-inducing complexity.

Being the focal point of the universe, Mysterium's reality is highly concentrated. For this reason, all true wizards and magi, come from Mysterium or those thirteen worlds that lay directly on its borders. People from these places are called "innerworlders" or "Mysterians." By contrast, those worlds at the edge of my imaginary pinwheel have less concentrated realities. People from these far-flung realms are called "subworlders" and are, for the most part, never discussed in polite company—sort of like an embarrassing aunt.

I am an innerworlder from the same place you likely live, Earth. This is not because there aren't other innerworlds you could be living in, but is more a reflection of the fact that my publisher hasn't agreed to do an otherworld run of this volume. Not that I'm bitter or anything.

If you are from Earth you might be asking at this point, *Wait, why don't I know about Mysterium?* You actually do, though you aren't aware of it. If you have ever read great (and sometimes not so great) fantasy or science fiction literature, then you have read the echoes of works by some of Mysterium's greatest magi: Bradbury, Zelazny, Heinlein, Wells, Clarke, Le Guin, Rowling, and, of course, Tolkien.

Their original writings on magical theory and practice, history, zoology, biography and so on have been transformed and propagated across the realities by subspace entanglement, and are usually mistaken for works of fiction. There was a Thom Briddle, and he did try to discover the secret of immortality, but splitting his *soul* seven times to do it? That's nonsense. The spell he created did require him to cut off bits of his body—for some reason he picked fingers—and his friends had him institutionalized after number four. On the other hand, Pratchett's works describing the cut-throat world of tenure at magical universities are chillingly accurate.

Another natural question is, *Why are some people able to cross from the innerworlds into Mysterium?* My honest answer is that I don't know. Not to get all mystical, but people don't find Mysterium; it calls to them. I myself had been three years studying in Oxford—Anthropology—and was walking down New College Lane, just passing under the Bridge of Sighs, when I noticed a little black door in the wall of a completely unremarkable red brick building. It is not that I had never seen this brick building or its black door before—there is an alley that runs along one side that leads to the Turf Tavern, which I am very familiar with—but I couldn't say that I ever *noticed* the building or the door.

Whatever the reason, on this day I *noticed* the black

door. Not only did I notice it, but I felt compelled to go up to it, open it, and go through it. And I found myself in Mysterium. More accurately, I found myself in Mysterium University's admissions office, which is like most admissions offices in any world: puke-green walls, lots of cubicles, and filled with an atmosphere of stale paper and crushed dreams. Although the administration denies it, I think this is one of the tests for entry. If you can find the door, make it through the bureaucracy of the admissions office, and pass the requisite reality weigh-in (more on this later), then you're in. It's as simple as that.

Nor is the door off New College Lane the only way into Mysterium from Earth. I met a woman that found the door next to a pizza joint across the street from Yale's Sterling Memorial Library. At least two of my friends found the door at various places along Bancroft Way in Berkeley. And one professor swears that he found the door to Mysterium in the bathroom of a bistro near the Ècole Normale Superieure in Paris. The only common threads seem to be proximity to a university and obscurity.

Now that you know how I got here and where we are in relation to where you are, I have to tell you that I'm not a big fan of my home world. I haven't been back since winter break of my second year of novice school when I had a screaming row with my parents over my decision to piss away a perfectly respectable career in anthropology for magic, a position, which doesn't seem unreasonable given the existence of "magicians" like David Blaine and Criss Angel. Frankly, I'm not sure that anyone in my family ever believed that Mysterium existed even though I brought home my letter of admission, my transcript, and my dirty laundry. The result is that I spend my breaks and holidays on campus or traveling the other innerworlds, and I don't see myself returning to Earth unless compelled by a death in the family or expulsion.

And who am I?

My name is Avery Stewart, I am a fourth-year adept. An adept is the third and highest level of student at Mysterium University. And though I know a great deal of magic, I am still not a full magus, as my faculty advisor often reminds me. The magi say a novice does not know that he knows nothing, an acolyte thinks he knows everything, and an adept knows he knows nothing.

As for my major, I am a scholar of subworld evolutionary sociology, which is the study of subworld societies, and their creation and quite frequent destruction. And before you ask, I was standing in the middle of a magic circle in experimental circle closet 12B because I had just completed—successfully, I hoped—the last experiment in my dissertation study on "Subworld Self-Stabilization Through Extraworld Feedback Implantation." Title notwithstanding, it would be a real page-turner with monsters, magic, and beautiful female warriors if not for the behavioral formulae, which really muck with the storyline.

I started to step out of the circle and stopped short,

my foot inches from breaking the invisible plane of my runic cage. I considered the glowing field around me with suspicion. It would be just like one of my "friends" to alter the circle or put some trigger spell on the floor so I would turn green for a week, or break out in weeping boils, or have my hands replaced with beer steins. (I swear that last one actually happened to a fellow I know, and it was three days before he could eat solid food.) Perhaps it isn't fair to generalize, but, center of the universe or not, Mysterium is full of pricks—good-humored pricks, but pricks nonetheless.

Needless to say, I took a moment to study the little stone room and the magic circle that had been my umbilical to reality for the last . . . "Damn, how long have I been gone?" I asked aloud.

I tried to remember while I gazed about the room by the light of my still-glowing transport circle, and mumbled my calculations to the stale air. "I was . . . a year altering the histories and planting all the items . . . two trying to find someone as twisted as Morgarr to lead the Army of Dark . . . another five years gathering the hordes of monsters infesting Trelari together into an army . . ."

There was precious little space in here for anyone to hide. The whole room wasn't more than ten foot to a side, and apart from the semi-pornographic graffiti that successive generations of acolytes and adepts had left on the walls, it was barren. A lopsided desk littered with half-used sticks of fazestone chalk and old diagrams of containment circles sat against one wall next to the door. From where I stood I could see that the lunch I'd been eating when I left was still there, which, along with the acrid smell of the lingering smoke, would explain much of the sour odor that seemed to fill the room.

". . . three or maybe four years for Morgarr to capture the Eastern Hinterlands and the Amber Plains and begin his westward march toward the Golden Woods and the Jeweled Lands . . ."

Images sprang, unbidden, into my mind of what Morgarr's armies had done to those beautiful lands and their peoples in my name. I shook them away, as I had so many times before. Experienced subworld magi will tell you that chaos and destruction in subworld is inevitable, and that allowing yourself to feel for the people is pointless and self-indulgent. They are probably right, but my hands were shaking again.

I distracted myself by considering the only other piece of furniture in the room: a much-abused wardrobe where I had stashed my regular clothes. The thought of *my* clothes—my boxers, jeans, and sneakers—reminded me of how uncomfortable the heavy dread cloak and six-inch platform boots were. I felt a sudden compulsion to be out of this costume and out of this room. I discarded caution and stepped out of the circle.

Despite my resolve, I tensed as I felt the brush of the containment spell pass across my body. My foot touched the floor. Nothing happened. Maybe my classmates weren't as bad as all that. Maybe they'd taken pity on me. After all, I had been off-world for at least fifteen subworld years, which meant what in Mysterium time? I stared up at the ceiling and tried to remember the conversion factors.

Trelari, otherwise known as subworld 2A7C in standard Zelaznian coordinate space, is 10,876 worlds away from Mysterium. That meant I needed to apply a time conversion factor of . . . carry the three . . . 018, which in turn meant . . . "Three months!" I exhaled.

It had felt much longer, but the fact is I had completed my experiment with two weeks to spare. Something that might even impress my advisor, the very hard to please High Magus Eustace K. Griswald.

I crossed the room to the wardrobe and yanked open the door, feeling the warning tingle of power against my fingers too late. There was a flash of red light followed by a muted pop, and wisps of smoke began leaking out of the crack around the edge of the wardrobe door. Sighing deeply, I rested my head against the wooden cabinet.

"Damn."

Of course they (whoever "they" were, and trust me, I would be making a list) had cursed the wardrobe. It was such an easy and obvious target. I was an idiot, a naïve idiot. I pulled the door open to inspect the damage. A cloud of dark thick smoke spilled out of the interior like vomit from a drunk. When it finally cleared, all that remained of my things was a light dusting of ash and a piece of unblemished white parchment floating in empty space on which was written:

BOW DOWN!
BOW DOWN, MYSTERIUM!
THE DARK LORD RETURNS!

Like I said before, they were pricks every one of them.

I snatched the piece of paper from the air and crumpled it into a ball. With a snarled curse, I whipped it across the room and into the circle where it disappeared in a flash of green and white light.

Had I been in my right mind, I might have contemplated the implications of this particular message making its way back to the subworld, but I was pissed, and the piece of paper, the circle, and Trelari had all been forgotten. My entire focus had turned to getting out of this damnable closet, getting back to my room, and getting drunk—and not necessarily in that order. I fumbled in my cloak for my reality fold, being careful to avoid touching Death Slasher, and pulled out the key to the solid-steel, triple-enchanted door to the closet, which has an ensorcelled lock to prevent people coming in and tampering with your experiment, but which is useless because the jerks in charge of the storeroom can be bribed to give out the spare keys for a pizza and a six-pack of beer.

I unlocked the door and stormed out, ready to unload my most colorful language at whoever was unfortunate enough to be standing there, but the hallway outside was empty. I looked up and down its dimly lit length. Nothing but gray and beige in both directions. Nobody was here.

I paused and listened.

There was a stillness that bespoke either a Mysterium-wide apocalypse, or the week before final exams. I turned to look at the chronometer mounted on the wall next to my door. It counted down the days, hours, and minutes left till my experiment was officially overdue, at which point Griswald would have had to come down into the bowels of the Subworld Studies building and yank me back into reality. Which, by the way, would also have been the moment my hopes of being raised to a magus would have officially ended. The glowing dials indicated seventeen days, six hours, and thirty-seven minutes remained. For a back of the hand calculation, I hadn't been that far off, and it meant that I'd returned smack in the middle of exams.

"What a lucky break," I announced to the empty hall.

Exams meant that all the novices and acolytes would be locked in their rooms feverishly studying and praying that they would be able to advance a year, and all the adepts, like myself, would be at the bars complaining about all the whiny novices and acolytes that were pestering them at study hall. In other words, as long as I avoided the libraries and bars, the grounds would be deserted.

"Who knows," I mused aloud, "I might make it across campus with minimal humiliation."

I reached out to zero the clock, which would signal that I had returned, but my hand froze in place. I drew it back and considered. If I was officially logged back into Mysterium, Gristle (we all call Griswald that if we think he's not around) would want to go over my matrix implantation experiment right away. His interworld grant was up for renewal in a few weeks and he would be waiting on my results to complete his report. This would mean days spent sitting in his office going over my notes and having to listen to his asthmatic imp, Harold, wheezing away.

It would also mean reliving my time as the Dark Lord in detail, perhaps even under the compulsion of one of Gristle's searingly thorough memory recall spells. For some reason, the thought of the inquisition to come made my insides churn and the gorge rise in my throat. I took a couple of deep breaths and let my stomach settle while I considered my alternatives. I could take a few days to go over my notes, maybe deal with the ax, and revive myself with some much needed diversion.

"What would be the harm?" I asked aloud to the empty hall. "And who would be the wiser?"

The decision was made in the time it took me to relock the closet. I tucked the key in my reality fold, and snuck out a little used side door and into the cool dark of a lovely fall evening.

Once outside, I dispensed with stealth in favor of speed and aggression. I decided that a six-foot-five man (remember I still had those damned boots on) wearing, conservatively, twenty yards of dread cloak, and sporting a face that can only be described as equal parts hideous and gruesome would be noticed less if he was striding purposefully down the middle of the sidewalk than he would be skulking around the shadows.

I needn't have worried. The grounds of the university were nearly deserted. The few people I did pass were either too engrossed in their books or too drunk to notice me. I used the unexpected solitude to enjoy the sights by the light of Mysterium's triple moons.

I suppose I should take this opportunity to try to describe the world I call my home. Mysterium rises out of the mists of a folded rocky land of indeterminate dimension. It is difficult to say where the university ends and the countryside begins, or, for that matter, where the countryside ends and another reality begins. All that one can say for certain is that at the heart of Mysterium lies the university: a chaotic jumble of buildings and towers and campanulas and plazas and amphitheaters and statutes of every imaginable size and shape, crisscrossed by a dizzying maze of broad avenues and narrow cobbled alleys and dead ends and tunnels and bridges, and woven through with galleries of ancient, soaring trees and vast lawns and sweet-smelling gardens, and hidden courtyards with trickling fountains. It really is a remarkable place.

When was it built? Who built it? I can't say. I have never seen a building under construction or undergoing repairs. Perhaps they grow out of the land itself. An organic origin would make the most sense, because the architecture of the place defies rational explanation and good taste. This is not to say that the buildings lack traditional form. In fact, nearly every architectural school from any era is represented, but no matter what "style" of building, every one of them incorporates certain Gothic elements, even where those elements are wildly inappropriate. Take for instance the gargoyles that sprout wart-like from the otherwise clean lines of the art deco Novice Health Center, or the stained-glass windows that sheathe the twenty-story steel tower of the Theoretical Metaphysics building, or the absurd flying wings that unnecessarily buttress the severely modernist concrete block that is my own Subworld Studies building. Still, even when a building seems hideous, everything fits into the tapestry of the whole so admirably that one cannot imagine replacing the monstrosity with anything else.

Speaking of monstrosities, I had arrived at one—McKinley College, my home in those rare instances that I am not studying or working. McKinley College is a seven-story block of prestressed concrete that looks like a very tall cheese grater onto which someone has unartfully pasted what have charitably been described as cubist interpretations of randy seraphim in flight. The place radiates despair. I stared at the building and imagined a smoking crater. Maybe the campus could be improved by some selective demolitions.

I had managed to escape recognition thus far, but peering through a window into the lobby I saw that the front desk was being manned by an acolyte in my year who was most definitely a prick. I thought briefly about trying a side door, but was too tired. I pulled out my student ID, took a deep breath, and stormed into the building on a head of steam I hoped would see me straight past him and into the stair with no questions asked.

Again, my concern was misplaced. He never looked up from whatever book he had his nose buried in, proving once again that hiring students to serve as monitors of anything is like asking a two-year-old to pilot a jumbo jet. You might save a lot of money on salary, but the death toll is enormous.

I skipped the elevator and six flights of stairs later found myself, at long last, at my door. With a sigh of relief I grabbed the handle, gave it a twist, and it came off in my hand.

"Really?" I muttered. "Away for three months and it's still broken!"

I was home.

CHAPTER 2

ELDRIN

Let me be clear at the outset, the handle falling off was not another exotic prank by some mischievous classmate. My door had been broken for the better part of two months—five months now.

For us, by which I mean my roommate and me, fixing such a thing was quite out of the question. I am an evolutionary subworld sociologist. My roommate is an etherspace physicist. Practical magic is not something we do. Nor do we have any skill with screwdrivers, hammers, or, well, anything practical. Adding to our general uselessness is the fact that, as the result of a series of unfortunate and nearly unforeseeable circumstances, we could not call a maintenance wizard. And so, the handle was and would remain broken.

I pounded on the door. "Eldrin, open up."

There was no response.

"Eldrin, I know you're in there. Get up and come open the door. It's me, Avery, your roommate, remember?"

There was a sudden burst of noise from the far end of the hall and a group of six adepts spilled out of a room in a haze of noxious blue smoke.

Damn.

The last thing I needed was for the reprobates in my dorm to see me in my Dark Lord gear. I would never live it down. You see, I live in the worst housing college in Mysterium University. Drugs, illegal conjurations, and vile necromancies are part and parcel of life in my building—especially on my floor. My roommate and I tended to avoid our "colleagues," and had survived in McKinley by keeping the door locked and avoiding the common areas. It was while contemplating the puzzle of the handle and my impending humiliation that it suddenly dawned on me that this might all be part of one of Eldrin's elaborate practical jokes.

First, he ashes my clothes so I'm stuck as the Dark Lord, and then he strands me in the hall for maximum exposure. Bastard.

It all made sense. It was perverse and evil, but it made sense, or would have if he had ever pulled a prank on me before. Looking back I can see that I was being paranoid, but at the time it all fit together so neatly, which is characteristic of paranoia, I suppose.

Frantically, I jammed the handle back onto the door. I glanced down the hall; of course the mob was coming in my direction. If it weren't for the narcotic fog of smoke that surrounded them they'd have seen me already.

I mouthed a prayer and gingerly turned the handle. The latch finally drew back and I slipped inside. I caught a brief glimpse of six shocked faces as my floormates passed by, and then I slammed the door closed and threw the dead bolt into place. Maybe they hadn't recognized me, maybe they were too stoned, or . . .

The slow soft drawl of my roommate's voice broke my train of thought. "Hey, Avery."

I glared across the room at him. What can one say about Eldrin Leightner? To start with, he's from the innerworld of Hylar . . . which I realize means nothing to most of you.

It means he's elfin—you know, oddly elongated ears, delicate features, prone to making flower chains and writing bad poetry. He, like me when I'm not wearing six-inch platform boots, is of average height and build, but that is about the only similarity in our appearance. While my hair is cut short and night-black, his is shoulder length and of an incandescent chestnut, and while my eyes are of a faded blue, his are dark, like a pair of onyx jewels shot through with floating specks of blazing silver that comes from staring into etherspace for too long. He also has that maddening kind of shimmery bronze skin so common to his race, and so popular with the ladies. What can I say—he is objectively gorgeous and I am not, not that I would ever admit that to him. Despite our differences, we are two of a kind, which is probably why we have remained roommates the last three years. I'd like to say he's a prick, but he's not.

Having said that, in the moment I was not being nearly as charitable, and not just because I suspected he had ashed my clothes, but also because he was indulging in one of his most odious vices. He was seated on the floor in the middle of our tiny room, his head bent low over an enormous parchment map covered in a kaleidoscope of multicolor hexes, the vast majority of which had been filled with stacks of impossibly tiny wooden circles—some white and some black. He was completely consumed in fishing more of these little pieces out of a box and did not even bother to look up, so my glare and therefore my anger went unnoticed.

I tapped my foot on the floor and said, "Well, aren't you going to admire your handiwork?"

He didn't, instead carefully straightening the little stack of black circles between his fingers and, with maddening precision, placing the stack on one of the few unfilled hexes on the map. Only when this task was complete to his satisfaction did he look up. There was a moment's pause as his eyes traced up the leather platform boots, along the death-shroud cloak to the macabre make-up, and then a big grin stretched across his face. "A little dramatic for a Friday night, but I am nothing if not open-minded."

"Don't play innocent with me," I spit. "I know damned well that you had a hand in burning up my clothes, and it isn't funny."

He cocked his head to one side and considered me for a second. "No, not funny at all."

The answer doused my anger a bit, but then I remembered my favorite T-shirt had been in that wardrobe and rallied. "So, you deny it?"

"It's not really my style," he said patiently as he picked more of the little pieces from the box. "I won't deny I considered playing a prank on you, but my plan was to alter your transport circle to filter out your clothes and then have it chain transmit so you would appear stark naked in the magi lounge. But, to be honest, I didn't think you be in the joking mood when you returned."

At that moment there was a loud sucking noise from the corner behind Eldrin and a section of the wall disappeared. A chill passed through the room as the cold night air rushed in. After about thirty seconds the wall reappeared, the noise vanished, and the breeze died away. Neither of us reacted to this extraordinary event, but by mutual and unspoken agreement we suspended our conversation. Eldrin used the time to lay down another stack of black pieces, and I used it to consider the implications his prank would have had on me. I blanched.

Right about now some of you may be asking yourself, *What just happened there, Avery? And why were the two of you not freaked out when a chunk of your wall disappeared?* Remember those unfortunate and unforeseeable circumstances I mentioned earlier? Well, to be completely honest, my roommate and I had attempted a bit of extradimensional remodeling early in the school year and had melted the reality lines in one of the corners of our room. As a result, a three-foot section of the exterior wall kept phasing in and out of existence. If someone from Mysterium Facility Services ever found out we'd be sure to lose our deposit. So, rather than dealing with the problem, we pretended it didn't exist.

Whether it was the wall (which always depressed me) or the lack of any gloating on Eldrin's part, the anger had gone out of me. It's hard to have an argument with someone as mellow as Eldrin, and I didn't have the energy to carry the whole thing off myself. I sat heavily onto my bed, unhooked the cloak from around my neck, and started yanking at the massive boots. When at last I was free from wearing the Dark Lord's clothing, I threw the lot of it into my wardrobe and pulled on a pair of boxers. It felt amazing.

I sat back down on the bed and crossed my legs. Eldrin had stopped what he was doing with his game and was staring at me. I gave him a few seconds to say something and then asked, "What?"

He closed his open mouth and said, "I missed you. I mean . . . how did the experiment go?" With a shake of his head he turned back to the board and began moving the little pieces about again. "You're seventeen days early, so it must have gone well."

A colorful curse leapt through my mind. He'd either been charting my return the whole time, or he'd done the time calculation in his head in the millisecond between the "you're" and the "seventeen." Sometimes I found his competence really irritating.

At my growl of disgust he looked up and peered uncertainly at me through the fringe of his bangs. "It did go okay, right? I see you've lost some weight."

"Yes. Maybe. I don't know," I mumbled.

I now had Eldrin's full attention. He sat up and fixed me with his star-flexed eyes. "Spill it, Avery. Something's wrong."

"It went fine," I said, which was true, but oddly felt like a lie. "Gristle will be happy. Can we talk about something else? I'm tired of thinking about Trelari. What have you been up to?"

A frown crossed his face and he looked back at his board. "I've been in the etherspace observatory for the past two weeks watching an outer subworld going nova. Fantastic explosion. Wonderful colors." He punctuated this statement by simulating little firework bursts in the air with his wiggling fingers.

A shiver went down my spine at the thought that he had been happily watching the death throes of a world much like the one I'd been inhabiting. I decided to change the subject again. "What's the game?"

He said nothing, but became suddenly fascinated

by the state of his nails. This lack of an answer immediately piqued my interest, because there is nothing that Eldrin likes to talk about more than his hideously complex games, which he insists on calling simulations. "The game?" I asked again.

He cleared his throat. "It's called the Fall of the Dark Lord. It simulates the rise and fall of . . . of, well, of you."

I stared down at the board and saw that it was true. There were the mountain ranges and plains and forests of Trelari reproduced in miniature. "How did you . . . ?" I asked.

"I was experimenting with subworld scrying."

"You spied on me?"

"Only a little bit . . . at the outset," he said quickly. "If I had observed you the whole time it might have biased my simulation." He tapped one of the black pieces on the board with the tip of his finger. "Out of curiosity, how did the Heroes stop Morgarr?"

"I disintegrated him," I said with a depressive sigh.

"Oh!" He looked back to the board. "That explains a lot. According to my results the forces of good should have taken longer to win. I didn't expect you back till tomorrow. I was going to grab some of that tea you like from the magi lounge in the observatory. Anyway, if you're up for it, I'd love to go over a few points of my simulation with you." He pointed at a thick tome sitting next to him.

"No."

"Why?"

"Your rule book is longer than my dissertation," I said flatly. "And it's about a subworld I've been stuck in for the past three months Mysterium-time."

Something about my tone must have convinced him I was serious, because he sighed deeply and went back to his game.

What I didn't say was that seeing the map of Trelari and the pieces aligned against each other was bringing back unwanted memories of watching the final battle from atop the battlements of the Fortress of Despair. The undulating lines of black and white as the two armies clashed, the screams of the dying, the smell of blood and burning flesh. I felt my hand begin to tremor in my lap.

I had to get out of this room and clear my head. What I needed—what we both needed—was a night of frivolous diversion. The problem would be getting Eldrin to come with me. His idea of a perfect night would be the two of us listening to music, playing his game, and talking bullshit together till dawn. Even if I refused and he had no chance of playing his game, he would still sit there and set out those pieces for hours, stare at them, and then spend most of the day tomorrow putting them away again. Like I said, it was an odious habit.

I determined to overwhelm him with brute enthusiasm. I braced myself and then said with authority, "We are going out tonight and see if we can't find some girls to flirt with."

His body seemed to deflate at the idea. "Not tonight."

I made my way to my wardrobe and began digging through my clothes for something decent to wear—sniffing and discarding the worst. Between shirts, I asked, "And why not tonight?"

"I thought the two of us could hang out," he mumbled. "Besides, I'm busy with—"

"With that bloody game?"

"Well, what's wrong with that?" he asked.

Finally, I found a long-sleeved gray sweater that was relatively clean. I pulled it over my head before answering. "First, I lived through it and, frankly, am not anxious to relive the experience. Second, and more importantly, you know all that will happen if we stay is that you'll spend the next two hours finishing the setup, then you'll stare at the board for fifteen minutes doing . . . whatever it is you do when you stare at those things, and then you'll take it apart. Besides, you said you've already figured out how it'll turn out."

He raised his chin in defiance. "I enjoy setting up games. And I haven't completed all the scenarios. I even found one where you won . . . kind of . . ."

The thought that there was even a remote chance that Morgarr and the Dark Lord might have won made my head swim. "I . . . I don't want to hear another word about your game."

"But—"

"No buts. You should be at a bar hitting on girls. Dammit, Eldrin! You're a Hylar. Women love the shimmer of your skin, and your accent, and the way you'll unselfconsciously recite poetry to them—even if it is in a language ninety percent of them can't understand."

He shrugged, which had become his go-to response whenever I broached this topic. It was genuinely puzzling, because before we met he'd gone out a lot and even managed to maintain relationships with one or two women long enough that they began calling themselves his girlfriend. Since we'd moved in together, all I got was a shrug.

"A shrug won't cut it tonight," I said. "Give me one good reason you can't come celebrate my first night back with me."

"I don't have any money," he whined.

"I'll pay," I said, overriding his nascent rebuttal as I finally managed to pull up my trousers.

His mood brightened considerably at this offer. "You'll pay?" he asked, already standing and smoothing his hair. "Is dinner included?"

I sat back on my bed with my shoes in hand and studied him. Lack of money was a problem we shared, because he, like me, got very little support from home. This inevitably led to a lack of food, particularly toward the end of the semester. Without my own paltry funds to bolster his, it must have been a very lean couple of months. It was entirely possible that he had not eaten in a week or so. He was Hylar and could get away with it for a while, but not forever. Being hungry was also something we didn't talk about.

"Fine," I said in mock seriousness, "dinner first, but you better put out."

The tips of his ears turned bright red. I laughed. "For a Hylar you can be such a prude." I jumped up and clapped my hands together. "All right, if that's settled, let's go."

He shook his head and grabbed his toiletry bag. "I need to get ready." I sat back down on the bed with a groan.

If you don't understand my reaction, then you've never had a Hylar roommate. Thirty tortuous minutes, two shirt changes, three different colognes, and both a brushing and a combing of his hair later we were ready to go.

I paused at the door and smiled back at Eldrin. "I feel lucky tonight. Nothing is going to get me down."

I grabbed the handle of the door and turned. It came off in my hand. Eldrin stared at me and cocked his head to one side. "By the way, did you want to go out looking like that?"

I turned to the mirror. A hideous reflection stared back at me. I still had the Dark Lord make-up on. There was a loud sucking sound from the corner of the room and a blast of frigid air rushed in.

Defiantly, I restated, "Nothing is going to get me down."

CHAPTER 3

A HOLE IN THE WALL

Forty minutes, three boxes of tissue, and innumerable expletives later we were finally on our way, marching through the crisp night toward a well-deserved drink. After several outfit changes, Eldrin had settled on something light, loose, and flowing. Just looking at him made me cold, but then he had the elvish habit of paying heed to neither weather nor fashion sense. I shivered and buried my hands deeper into the pockets of my trench coat.

We walked in silence for a time. I was enjoying wearing jeans and soft-soled shoes, and not thinking about my research project. I was so wrapped in the thrill of these pleasures that it took Eldrin two tries to get my attention.

"Avery? Are you there?"

"What?" I asked.

"Your research. It worked? You were actually able to create a self-perpetuating construct that operates to stabilize your subworld's reality matrix permanently?"

Sorry, but Eldrin talks like that sometimes. Forgive him, because if you don't I certainly never will.

"I suppose," I answered without much enthusiasm. This was exactly what I hadn't wanted to do: rehash my time in Trelari. I decided to keep the conversation theoretical. "I proved that the spell I wove into the pattern of the world was able to generate sufficient force from within the subworld itself to prevent a collapse. I wouldn't go much farther than that though. The 'self-perpetuating' aspect relies on a sociological construct, based on the mythological archetype of the Dark Lord and the continuing threat of his rise. One day someone will need to go back and make sure the spell is capable of addressing future reality collapses with no additional intervention."

"Someone?" Eldrin asked in surprise. "I thought you wanted to handle the follow-up work. A project like that could easily justify a half-dozen multiyear research grants. Your own lab. Your own army of adepts to do all the grunt work. You'd be set for life, or at least past your thirties, which is pretty much the same thing."

I shrugged away the question, and to his credit he didn't press me. The truth of it was, he was right. How many times had he patiently listened to me late at night laying out my master plan to become the next Magus Griswald. Using the spell construct I'd developed for Trelari, I would travel the universe experimenting on a dozen different subworlds, varying and refining my technique until I became a legend. That had always been the dream, but now I wasn't so sure.

I hadn't lost faith in the magic. I was certain that absent my spell the strain on Trelari's reality would have fractured the world in another century or so. Now it would be stable for millennia. The magic worked, what I had begun to doubt was whether I had what it took to be a true subworld magus.

Eldrin remained silent and let me wander through these thoughts at my leisure. He is very sensitive to ruminating and daydreaming, because he is prone to those practices himself. It was one of the things I liked best about him.

After a time and apropos of nothing he said, "Still, it's a little disturbing."

I was familiar enough with Eldrin's convoluted thought processes to know that there would be a logical connection if I gave him enough time to reveal it. Today I was in no hurry. "What is disturbing?" I asked.

He glanced at me and I watched the moonlight trace crazy patterns in the flickering spots of silver in his eyes. "The results of your study," he said. "If it's possible to stabilize subworlds using sociological constructs, then half the theories about how and why subworlds work are wrong."

I opened my mouth to say something, but Eldrin had the bit in his teeth, and there was no stopping him.

"For years there have been two schools of thought," he explained, ticking them off on his fingers. "The deterministic school, which is supported by etherspace physicists like myself, that says subworld creation and collapse can be understood in simple physical terms in accordance with fundamental principles that can be expressed mathematically, and the organic school, supported by arcana geneticists and other cranks, that says subworlds are like cells or organisms that have natural, if unpredictable, life cycles. If you're right, wouldn't it seem to indicate that the societies and even individual beings on those worlds decide their own fates?" He flung his arms wide. "There would be no meaning to . . . to anything."

I dismissed his concerns with a chuckle. "Trust you to find deep water in shallow pools. I've only studied one subworld. That's hardly proof of a universal truth, much less a scientific law. I wouldn't worry about it."

His eyebrows drew down close around his eyes, and he bit his bottom lip. "I don't know. Your theory verges awfully close to Jordanian creationism. What about the Van Dorn Apocalyptic Postulate? Does your theory explain why subworlds become unstable in the first place?"

"No," I confessed. "Like everyone else, I know the symptoms that lead to subworld collapse, but not the cause. It's like . . . gravity. It is easy to see how it affects things, but wrapping your head around the fact that it curves space either requires an enormous quantity of mind-altering drugs or being Einstein."

He snorted at my analogy. Eldrin had never been impressed with the state of science on Earth. "What does Griswald say?" he asked.

His mention of my mentor brought me up short. He walked a few paces more, and then, noticing I had stopped, turned back to me. We were in one of the many parks on campus, and the path we were following was meandering its way uncertainly through a thick grove of trees. The world was quiet and dark.

"Where were you thinking of going tonight?" I asked as nonchalantly as possible.

"To the Cove, of course," he said in a puzzled tone. "Why?"

Covenant House, the Cove for short, was *the* place to go for faculty and students of the Subworld Studies Department. If I showed my face there it would be sure to get back to Gristle would be sure to hear about it, and then my little subterfuge about when I got back would come out. He would crucify me. I shivered again, but this time it had nothing to do with the cold.

"Um," I started uncertainly, "let's go someplace else tonight."

"But we're almost there."

"I know, but . . . I don't feel like going there tonight."

"Why?" he pressed. "I thought you'd be all keyed up to tell everyone about your brilliant success."

Normally he'd be right, but I actually wasn't, and not only because I was playing truant. Rather than try and tease out the many threads of my jumbled emotions with Eldrin right then, I decided to lie. I mumbled, "It's nothing. I just don't feel like going there tonight."

He tilted his head to one side as he studied me. "What have you done?"

"What? Nothing."

"Come on, out with it," he pressed. "What is it that makes you so keen to avoid a place where people might know you?"

I sighed with the realization that I would have to confess—at least partially. "It's nothing, really. It's just that—technically—I'm not back yet."

His eyes narrowed. "You aren't experimenting with split-worlding, are you? That is really dangerous. I knew a guy that tried it once so he could moonlight as a bartender in an off-world pocket reality during the semester, and he ended up losing half his small intestine."

I shook my head. "It's nothing like that. Hell, I wouldn't know how to do that if I wanted to. I just didn't log my return."

"So your circle is still going?"

"Mmm-hmm," I said in the hopes of staving off the more difficult questions he might ask.

Without another word, I set off down a side path that would take us away from Covenant House. He fell into step beside me. A moment of silence passed and I almost relaxed, but then I heard a sharp intake of breath from him.

"Wait. You don't still have 2A7C's reality key with you?"

I ignored the question and kept walking, but he grabbed my arm and turned me around to face him. His eyes were wide with alarm. I decided blunt honesty was the best course. "Of course I have the key, Eldrin. I couldn't check it in, could I? The bastards in the storeroom would have immediately logged me back into Mysterium."

He was staring at me like I had sprouted a second head, not that such a thing was entirely out of the question in Mysterium, but you get the point. I pulled out of his grasp and started walking again. "It isn't that big a deal," I said.

He lurched into a half jog to keep up with me. "Not a big deal!" he shouted, and then lowered his voice as he heard his words echo back to him across the empty campus. "You literally have the key to a reality in your pocket. If you were to lose it—"

"I won't," I said, cutting him off. "It's perfectly safe." I patted the chain around my neck to reassure him. "I want one night of freedom before I report to Gristle. You know that once he and his imp get their claws into me, it'll be two solid weeks of working around the clock before I see the sun again. And Harold hates me. He's always trying to bite me when Gristle isn't looking."

"But . . . think of the risk. If he finds out he'll throw a fit."

"Who, the imp?"

"No, Griswald!" he hissed. "And quite trying to change the subject. What are you going to do about the key?"

"Nothing," I said, and set off again. "Tomorrow morning I'll officially return, but tonight I am going to have a little fun. I'd advise you to do the same."

By this point we had reached the object of our journey, a little hole in the wall frequented by members of the School of Magical Ethics and Mystical Literature. (I mean, literally there was a round hole in an otherwise featureless wall with a lamp hanging next to it illuminating a sign that read ARDA HALL.) From what I'd heard, the beer was supposed to be good and the girls cute. It was perfect for tonight, because I could almost guarantee that no one else from Subworld Studies would be there.

"Arda Hall?" Eldrin said at my heel. "Why are we going here? It's full of ethics majors. They'll be talking Tolkienian philosophy all night, and you know I can't stand dualists."

"Stop whining, Eldrin," I said. "We are here to have a few drinks and maybe, if we are lucky and you don't start going on about post-Donaldson relativism, meet a girl or two."

He sighed in resignation. "All right, at least the food is supposed to be good."

"That's the spirit." I pushed him through the hole.

Arda Hall looked a bit like an Oxford pub on the inside, with a low beamed ceiling, a broad stone hearth set with a crackling fire, and a long polished bar that stretched along one wall. Sprinkled here and there were tables and a couple of secluded booths. The place was full, but not crowded. In the far back they had cleared a space for a stage on which a quasi-Celtic singer, backed by a fiddle, a flute, and a bodhrán, was going on about losing her true love in a meadow or something.

I don't know that I believe in love at first sight, but I can say that the moment I slipped through that hole in the wall, my eyes fixed on one woman, and I couldn't tear them away.

She was sitting at a table near the fire talking with a dark-haired girl who had her back to me. I know it's cheesy, but it was her eyes that first got my attention. They were almond shaped and of an extraordinary aquamarine blue shot through and ringed in gold.

It is cliché that you can tell a lot about a person from their eyes, but for a magus it happens to be true. Magic always leaves a mark on the caster, and for Mysterium mages, the mark is left in the eyes. Eldrin's eyes are silver speckled because he works in deep etherspace; my once bright blue eyes have faded nearly to gray from spending so much time travelling in subworlds. Gold rings meant she was a seer, or more likely a student in the Department of Divination and Prognostication, or something like that—it's a mouthful. What ever she was, it was fascinating to wonder whether she saw something in my future that made me so interesting to her, because she had been staring at me since I came in.

I stared unabashedly. She was willow thin and small-busted, and had a pretty face, slender and rounded with a creamy complexion that made me think of the pale light just before dawn. A wavy curtain of corn-silk blond hair fell down her back to just below her shoulders. I watched as she brushed a few loose strands back behind her ear. Then she leaned forward, briefly shifted her gaze to her friend, and whispered something. The other girl turned and looked at me. With a roll of her eyes she picked up her drink and headed toward the back of the pub. I barely paid any attention to her leaving, because those blue-gold eyes were back on me. I was mesmerized. I think I would have gone straight to her without a word to Eldrin had he not grabbed my arm.

"Where do you think you're going?"

"Over there," I said, not taking my eyes from her.

"No, you're not. I'm not going to let you abandon me to starve in this wretched dive so you can go hit on, and likely get rejected by, the first girl you see. You promised me an evening out, including dinner."

I reached into my pocket, pulled out some notes, and thrust them into his hand. "Here," I said with a grunt.

Eldrin started to say something, but after looking back and forth between the two of us he must have thought better of it. With a roll of his eyes and a shale of his head he let me know with perfect clarity the disdain he felt at that moment for the shallowness of humans. Without another word he wandered off to the bar.

I took a couple of deep breaths to steady my nerves and walked over to her. On the way I came up with a dozen devastating lines, but when the moment came to say something all I could manage was "Hi, I'm . . . may I . . . um . . ?"

"Hello, Avery," she said in a soft musical voice. "I've been waiting for you."

CHAPTER 4

VIVIAN

Only after I sat down across from her did the implications of what she said hit me. She knew my name and knew that I would be here even when I had not. A rush of warmth passed through me as I contemplated all the other things about me she might know.

She raised a golden eyebrow and said, "Well, aren't you going to say something?"

My throat was suddenly dry, and my tongue didn't want to work. Still, through a supreme effort I managed to force out, "Hi, uh, I'm . . . Avery?"

She drew her lips together in an enigmatic smile and said, "Yes, I think we've established that. And I'm Vivian. Nice to meet you."

The barmaid put a beer down in front of me. Vivian smiled. "I hope you don't mind, I ordered for you."

I sat down across from her and took a sip—a Hylar pilsner. "My favorite!"

She laughed. "I know."

I nodded stupidly in reply and took a long drink to try and cover my continued inability to speak. To be fair to me, it is pretty intimidating to talk to a beautiful woman under any circumstances, but try it with one that seems to know what you're thinking when you're thinking it, and what you're going to say before you say it.

"I'm an acolyte in the School of Portents and Augury," she volunteered, and when I still said nothing, she continued. "My specialty is future shaping. It's based on the theory that, if one knows the future in sufficient detail, it should be possible to 'shape' that future by manipulating events in the present. For example, let's imagine that I knew the barmaid was going to trip over the bodhrán player on her way back to the kitchen and drop her tray . . ." Wetting her finger in the condensation on the outside of her glass, Vivian drew a circle on the center of the wooden table with the moisture. "That would be the target event."

She had beautiful hands, long and tapered, with delicate nails that shone with a pearly glow in the firelight.

"Are you paying attention, Avery?" she asked.

I tore my eyes away from her delicate wrist. "Of course. Future shaping. Fascinating."

She pursed her lips, but continued. "Well, one could focus one's mind on that event and try and trace back—" fishing an ice cube from her glass she used it to draw a series of ever smaller circles to the right of the first and interconnected them with arrows "—the cause to some event that could be altered, and then—" she drew a new arrow that bypassed the original circle "—shape the future to avoid the accident. It's all part of some pioneering work by Magus Herbert. I've applied to join his group for my adept-level studies."

Vivian raised an arm and signaled to the barmaid. She had been about to take a tray of dirty glasses back to the kitchen, but instead put it down and came over. I started to order another beer, having surprisingly found that I had finished the first. Vivian stopped me and asked, "Can we get the check, please?"

The barmaid looked between us and gave Vivian a knowing smile. "No problem," she said, and went to retrieve the check.

It took me a moment to realize what was going on. When I did I spluttered, "You're leaving? I had hoped to . . . I mean, I was having such a good time."

She leaned across the table and dropped her voice. "I thought you might walk me back to my college. It's late and, unlike you adepts, we acolytes have exams to take. Besides, it's too loud and I want to hear all about you." She dropped her hand onto mine. "Interested?"

Rarely had I been as interested in anything as much as I was in her at that moment. I wanted to say something appropriately dashing in response, but as I have noted my brain was not properly engaged and all I managed was a stupid grin and a grunted, "Sounds great."

The barmaid came back and placed the check down on the table, then went back to the bar to pick up her tray. At that moment, there was a loud crash as the bodhrán player, who was clearly in his cups, toppled backward off the stage and slammed into the wall next to the kitchen door. A good-humored "Huzzah" erupted from the audience and several patrons rushed over to help push him back into place.

I had the unshakable feeling that I was missing things, repeatedly, but Vivian was rising to go and there was no time to sort it out. I paid the bill and glanced about to see if I could find Eldrin. He was in a little booth beside the stage holding court with the dark-haired girl Vivian had been talking to when we entered. I pointed at them. "I see my roommate has met your friend—poor girl."

Vivian glanced in their direction as she wound a fawn-colored scarf about her. She studied Eldrin critically. "Is he a cad? Should I fear for my friend's virtue?" she asked as she fanned herself with the back of her hand in a mock swoon.

I chuckled aloud at the thought. "Eldrin? No, not unless she's into etherspace optics or obscure subworld simulations. His idea of a good time is reading dry academic articles on subether particles and higher order ritual math."

"Well, I'm afraid your friend is unlikely to find his

soulmate in Dawn," she said shaking her head in exaggerated sadness. "She is an almost insufferable proponent of proactive magical ethics, with an emphasis on the 'active' part."

I shrugged myself into my trench coat and said, "I think we should leave them to it, then. Perhaps opposites will attract."

Vivian grew still and stared at them, the gold rings in her eyes glowing brightly in the dim light of the pub. After a few seconds, she blinked and said, "I don't think so. She'll probably leave in a huff when he casually dismisses some important point of moral ethics she's trying to make, and then he'll spend the rest of the night wondering why she didn't fancy him."

My mouth fell open and she blushed ever so slightly. "It's just a guess," she said, and then added with a wink, "Mostly."

We both laughed.

The sound of her laughter and the smile she gave me as I helped her into her coat made me a little light-headed. Either that or the beer she'd bought me was stronger than I'd realized. Whatever the cause I enjoyed the buzz as we made our way out of Arda Hall.

It is a grand feeling to step out of a bar with someone you've just met. Your mind thrums with possibilities. I savored that feeling as Vivian directed me down a path toward her college. She slid in beside me and tucked her arm through mine. The night had deepened the bite in the air, but the feel of her touch and the subtle scent of spice that hovered around her banished the cold. I felt no pain.

I did have a lot of questions though. Had she been joking about waiting for me? If she had been telling the truth, why had she waited? I was self-aware enough to know that I didn't have a chiseled physique or roguish good looks or a way with the ladies. I considered her and these questions as we strolled along.

After only a little thought, it came to me that there was one logical reason for her to stalk me: she needed help on an end of term project. She was an acolyte, and it's exactly the sort of thing an aggressive student might do to ensure a better grade. The likelihood that she was not interested in me, but instead in what I could do for her, was a bit of a letdown, but I decided I would prefer to live in this moment even if it was illusory.

After a minute or so she pulled away from me and said, "I'm waiting."

"Waiting?" I asked, afraid I had missed some sign that she wanted me to kiss her or, well, something. I was glad it was dark, because I blushed at the "somethings" that ran through my mind.

"Yes," she said. "I've told you all about me. I want to know about you. What are you studying?"

"Oh," I said, disappointed. I had a feeling that reality was about to intrude itself on my blissfully illusory evening. I tried to change the subject. "It isn't that interesting. You would be bored."

"You don't think I'll understand it. You think I'm

nothing but a silly acolyte." She crossed her arms and fixed me with an exaggerated pout.

"Not at all. It really is boring. I promise."

I was still clinging to the hope that maybe she wasn't only interested in me as a potential tutor, but beyond that I simply didn't want to talk about my research. I didn't want to find out that all she wanted was insight on subworld dynamics because she was failing a class, but I definitely didn't want to have to think about Trelari or Morgarr or anything else that had happened. What I wanted was to talk about silly things, like what she liked to do on the weekends, and what kind of music she enjoyed, and whether or not she was going to let me kiss her good night. And, the big question, would she see me again.

"It can't be that bad," she said.

"Trust me, it is, and I should know. I've been living my research for the past three months."

"What do you mean?" she asked, and, much to my relief, slipped her arm back through mine.

I thought about how I could explain my research without being tedious or getting into the specifics. I looked up at the moons and said, "It isn't a very good analogy, but have you ever watched someone blowing bubbles and wondered why some last longer than others?"

"Sure," she said. "I guess everyone wonders that when they're children. Well, when they aren't trying to pop them."

I laughed. "This may be a better analogy than I

thought." I reluctantly untangled my arm from hers and held my hands out in the air before us, my fingers spread wide. "Imagine subworlds are bubbles floating through the air. At any moment some bubbles are forming and some are popping . . ."

"I don't think the people on those worlds would like this analogy," she pointed out.

"I suppose not," I agreed, but as that was heading into conversational territory I was determined to avoid, I abruptly pivoted. "The important thing is that magi have been studying the 'why' of subworld existence for years. Some of them, like my roommate, believe that subworlds really are like bubbles, and that if you could understand the physics and mathematics of how they're created, then you could determine when they'll cease to exist. Others think of subworlds as organisms that live and die and get sick just like any organism."

She frowned.

"See," I said, "I'm boring you. Let's talk about something else."

"No, you're not boring me," she said with a shake of her head. "It's just that it's awful. All these worlds full of people. There must be a way to stop them from dying."

"Exactly," I said, clasping my hands together. "And that's what I've been working on."

"How?"

There was newfound warmth and intensity in her voice. Despite my suspicions about her motives and my discomfort talking about my work, I puffed up at her attention. "Well, I believe that the reason subworlds cease to exist is that they become unbalanced. I don't care if this 'imbalance' is framed as ether particle expansion or a reality matrix virus, but at some point it rips the world apart."

I glanced at her to make sure she was still interested. The focus I saw in her eyes was almost unnerving. I didn't want to disappoint her, so I continued. "If my assumption is correct, then the next question is, can you fix this imbalance? What subworld sociologists have found is that the destabilization of subworlds usually accompanies or is accompanied by an increase in sociological upheaval within the native population: war, famine, wide-spread destruction. Sometimes the societal chaos is resolved and the instability reverses, and sometimes not. It's like—" I tried to think of yet another good analogy "—like when you kick an anthill. And all the ants scurry about. If you watch them, sometimes they reconstruct the nest, and sometimes they simply walk away."

Vivian frowned more deeply and folded her arms across her chest. "Awful."

I found her reaction interesting. I didn't disagree, but it was unusual. Almost from our first day of admittance, the magi of Mysterium teach us not to get sentimental about subworlds or their inhabitants. It isn't that we are encouraged to abuse or demean them, but their lives are so short and uncertain that it is difficult for Mysterians to build a real attachment to anything except the larger arc of their histories. I wondered if this was Vivian's first exposure to the reality of subworld existence, or if her disgust was directed at my admittedly crude analogies.

I wished again that she would let me change the subject, but absent that, I decided to move the conversation onto safer ground. "It is very bad. The good news is that I believe I have come up with a way of stabilizing unbalanced subworlds—potentially forever."

Vivian's face lit up in a way that made my heart flutter. "You've done this? How?"

I smiled at her as I answered. "It's complicated, but in essence, I overlay a carefully designed spell construct onto the subworld's reality matrix that operates to rebalance the world in the event of a destabilization."

I had been so caught up in walking with her that I had not been paying attention to where we were going. With a start I realized that we were approaching the Subworld Studies building. I was surprised, because the SSB was on the opposite side of campus from the acolyte colleges. A notion began to grow on me that she might be taking a long way home to extend our night.

She interrupted my pleasant musing with a rush of words. "And once the spell is cast it'll stay that way forever?"

"Not exactly. The idea that you can stabilize a subworld is not new. Many Mysterium mages have intervened in collapses over the millennia—Le Guin,

Moorcock, Eddings, and so on. While all of these magi were able to stabilize the subject worlds for a time, the imbalance they initially cured later returned and with greater virulence. Another intervention was required, leading to another imbalance. Each time the imbalance would grow larger and larger until finally the world—poof—ceases to be. Magus Jordan spent his whole life and published fourteen volumes on the problem—three of which had to be issued posthumously."

"If it's so hard, and people have failed so often, how are you able to fix these subworlds where they can't?" Vivian asked.

She had stopped walking, which was unfortunate because we were now standing directly in front of the SSB. All those dark, empty windows seemed to be staring down at me and judging. An uneasiness twisted at my insides. I tried to pull her further along the path, but she wouldn't move. "Because," I said quickly and in a low voice, "I don't try and impose a solution from outside. Using the power available within the world, I create a safety valve that operates to release the pressure of an imbalance before it can grow too strong."

I was simplifying things enormously at this point, skipping over a lot of the messier bits of the magic and the social engineering needed to make my solution work, but I could feel a panic attack building. I wanted to be anywhere but here. Unfortunately, she was not taking my hints.

"Tools?" she asked.

"The people," I said impatiently. "I use the people and the creatures of the world as a source of positive force. I create legends and histories so that they'll know the signs of an oncoming imbalance and then my spell construct guides them, or at least a select group of them, to defuse the imbalance before it gets out of hand." I tugged at her arm again. "Can we move on a bit? I'm . . . I'm getting a little cold."

"In a second," she said sharply. "So, this works? You've actually observed the people in one of these worlds 'fixing' one of these 'imbalances'?"

There was something funny in her manner, like she was seeking a specific piece of information, but didn't want me to know what it was. I let it pass. I needed to leave. In my mind's eye I could see Gristle bursting out of the front door of the building to snatch me up.

"Yes," I answered in a hissing whisper. "But only the initial imbalance. It will take millennia of subworld time before another imbalance arises. Until then I can't be certain of the 'perpetual' part of the spell."

At last I succeeded in moving her past the front of the building, but she stopped again as we reached the side door from which I had made my escape earlier that evening.

"Show me," she said.

"What?" I asked.

"Show me," she said again, and pulled me toward the little door. "I want to see it . . . see where you work."

I shook her arm off mine and studied her as I would a subject of one of my experiments. Her face was flush, her eyes glinted and gleamed; her whole body seemed coiled with excitement. Then it struck me, this was what the entire evening had been leading up to for her. Maybe I was an extra credit project, or maybe this was all part of a seer study she needed to complete, but there was a purpose to her actions that went far beyond an acolyte looking for some extra tutoring.

Noticing my hesitation, she came back to me and took my hand in hers. "Please."

I smiled at the smooth, soft, feminine hand in mine and made the decision to find out what it was she wanted before I sent her away. Besides, there would be no harm in letting her see the circle. It was a fairly standard magical construct.

With an arched eyebrow, I raised the back of her fingers to my lips and gave them a light kiss. "Of course,."

I put my palm against the small of her back—that was nice—and directed her to the side door. The building was still deserted, but I wanted to give her a good show, so I made a little production of checking the corridors before each turn, and a larger production of ensuring that she remained as *close* to me as possible as we made our way down to the basement. When we arrived at the door to the closet all was as it had been. There was no Gristle waiting to ambush me, just the empty hall and the clock diligently counting down my return. I smiled at the irony.

I pulled out my reality fold and reached inside for the closet key. As I groped about for it my hand brushed against the smooth steel of the battle-axe. A momentary shudder passed through my body that left my head spinning. I drew my hand back and frowned at the numbness in my fingertips. I had always put down my hatred for Death Slasher to its general creepiness, and to the fact that it was Morgarr's weapon and had done untold evil, but it suddenly dawned on me that perhaps the root lay deeper than that. Doubt and his constant companion, fear, began to gnaw at me. Nothing that was happening right now was a good idea and in my heart I knew it. I needed to ditch Vivian and spend the rest of the night in consultation with Eldrin, trying to figure out how to rid myself once and for all of my experiment's remainder: Death Slasher.

I spun around to tell Vivian that, nice as it had been, the night was over. At the same moment she stepped in close behind me. We found ourselves in each other's arms—her chest, her body, her warmth pressed against me, her lips mere inches away. I am ashamed to admit that all thoughts of the battle-axe vanished from my mind.

A second passed, and then her eyes widened and she stepped back. "Sorry," she mumbled. "It . . . it's a little creepy down here."

I know it's cliché and terribly archaic, but I'm afraid I said something like, "You have nothing to fear, Vivian. I'm here."

She arched an eyebrow, but otherwise said nothing. The fact that she didn't call me on my bullshit right then and there should have been an enormous red flag, but I wasn't thinking straight. It isn't an excuse, but it is the truth.

I unlocked the door and walked in. I was back, and being back brought all those fears to the surface again. Everything reminded me of my professional indiscretion, and that Gristle and the battle-axe and all the other complications in my real life were still waiting to be dealt with.

"Well," I said with a deep exhale, "this is where the magic happens."

It was an old joke and poorly delivered, but her response was still not what I expected: silence.

Actually, it was worse than that. She ignored me. Vivian paced about the room and wordlessly studied the circle for a minute or so. I took the time to discreetly scrape the trash off the worktable and dump it in a bin.

"I don't get it," she said at last. I'll admit, I hadn't been expecting that response either. "This is a simple transport circle," she said, gesturing to the glowing ring. "Granted, it's a lot more complicated than any transport circle I've ever seen, but how could it—"

Seeing where she was going, and that it was so far off track, I couldn't help interrupting. "No, no," I snapped, as I would during office hours to some annoying underclassman. "The circle is just a circle. All the subworld manipulation has to be done *in situ*. That's what makes my method fundamentally different. I don't impose an external magical framework onto the subworld."

She held up a hand to stop me. "If you aren't using Mysterium magic, then how do you do anything?"

It was a great question, better than she knew, but rather than give her the truth, which was messy and embarrassing, I simplified things. "I use the reality key."

"What are you talking about?" she asked. "The key to the closet?"

I shook my head and pulled the chain from around my neck. Though they are quite common in my area of study, for excellent reasons the existence of reality keys is not widely circulated. It is not that they are officially classified, but everyone in the field agrees that it is for the best to keep the majority of mages ignorant of them. Nevertheless, I found myself explaining the use of one to her like I might the beverage function of a microwave to my grandparents.

"Every subworld has a reality matrix. If you know how, and the mages at Mysterium know how, you can imprint this matrix on an item. I can't explain that part of the process. Eldrin could, but you would likely want to claw your eyes out by the time he was finished. Anyway, for some completely unknown reason, the reality matrices are mapped onto keys—one for each subworld. This is the one for Trelari, where I conducted my experiment."

She reached out her hand and held it just above the key's surface—seeing if she could feel a radiant power field around it. I knew that she wouldn't, but said nothing.

"It doesn't feel magical," she said, staring at it like it was a cross between a pretty jewel and a venomous snake.

"It isn't," I said. "Not here. Here it's quite ordinary, but in my subworld it has the power to remap reality itself. There is nothing . . . well, almost nothing you can't do with it when you are in the world."

"Nothing?" she said, and tore her gaze from the key to smile at me.

That smile made me feel all those possibilities stirring again. "Nothing." I left off the "almost" part this time.

She trailed the end of her fingernail up my hand to my arm. "I'd like to see that. Take me."

It was an absurd suggestion and I laughed aloud at it. "That's not going to happen, Vivian."

"That's where you're wrong, Avery," she said, and the gold rings in her eyes blazed to life. "I happen to *know* that you and I are destined to return to your world tonight."

Something about her certainty unnerved me. Whatever this was, it was no longer an amusing diversion. I opened my mouth to tell her that it was time to leave and felt a stabbing pain in the bend of my arm. Looking down I saw that her forefinger was capped by a black metal thimble inscribed with dozens of magical runes. A needle extended from the thimble's end and she was pulling its sharp point from my skin.

In the time it took the pinprick of blood to well from the puncture, I felt the sleep spell, for that is what it was, pulling me under. I tried to draw power for a counterspell, but already my mind couldn't focus on a pattern and the magic slipped away.

"Please, don't try to fight it, Avery," she pleaded. "It's a very powerful casting. I stole it from one of my professors."

"What . . . what have you done?" I slurred as my tongue grew thick and clumsy.

"I've put you to sleep, Avery," she said calmly. "I am going to take the reality key and return with you to your subworld. Don't worry, I will bring you back. But I need time to learn how to use the key, and if I leave you here there's a chance someone may find you and come after me before I'm ready."

The full horror of what she was saying took a moment to filter through my sleep-addled brain. When it did, I tried to draw away from her, but my legs weren't working. The room tilted on its side. I stumbled and pitched forward, clutching the reality key to my chest. Only Vivian's outstretched arms prevented me from cracking my skull on the stones of the floor. She lowered me to the ground and rested my head in her lap. Even if I'd wanted to fight her my limbs would no longer move. I gazed up at her with blinking eyes.

"I'm sorry, Avery," she said, and I heard the regret

in her voice. "I wish this could have turned out differently, but it's the only way. You never would have taken me to your world willingly, and I need to go. Your experiment is more important than you know. It could change everything, but it won't unless I'm there. I don't know what I'm meant to do. I can't see beyond tonight, but I know that I need to be there. I hope you can understand."

I tried to answer, to beg her not to do this, to warn her of the danger, but the words wouldn't come. My eyes flickered closed and only my thoughts remained. *She is taking me back.*

I felt a wetness on my face and knew that I was crying. Vivian's soft fingers wiped them away. The smell of her swirled around me. I realized she was saying very softly, "I'm sorry, Avery, I'm sorry." She repeated it over and over again almost like a meditation until even her voice faded away and I heard no more.

CHAPTER 5

MORNING HAS BROKEN

I awoke from a dream I couldn't recall with a screaming headache. I was in my room, in my bed, which isn't that unusual except that I couldn't remember coming home. The last thing I could recall was stepping out of Arda Hall with Vivian on my arm. I smiled at the memory and instantly regretted it as a stabbing pain shot through my temples. I clutched at my head and groaned.

"So, you're finally awake," Eldrin said in a voice that reverberated in my skull like thunder.

I glared at him through slitted eyes. He was sitting on the floor, his back against his bed and a book propped on his lap. A dozen more open books were arrayed around him like an audience. "Shhh," I hissed.

"My head feels like Dave Lombardo's drum kit after a concert."

He cocked his head to one side and pursed his lips, which was what he did when he didn't get one of my earthly references.

"It hurts like hell," I clarified. "Vivian and I must have gone on one hell of a bender last night. I can't remember anything."

"Night?" Eldrin said with a snort. "Try two nights and a day."

He was obviously trying to put one over on me, but I was in no mood. "Don't, Eldrin. I'm really not feeling well."

"Don't what?" he asked sharply, his ears twitching with irritation. "You abandoned me Friday night to go off with *that* woman, and now it's Sunday afternoon."

Maybe it was that his voice seemed to be trying to bore a hole through my skull, or maybe I was just pissed that I couldn't remember the epic debauchery that must have contributed to my current state, but I didn't want to get into it with Eldrin. "Seriously, stop it," I grunted. "It's not funny."

He closed his book with a sharp snap that made me wince. "You really don't get my sense of humor, do you?" he said, and seemed to be genuinely aggrieved that I didn't. "Let me make myself clear—you have been gone almost two full days. What I want to know is the censored version of what the two of you were doing, and where you were doing it, because when you didn't come back yesterday, I tried to find you and, at least as far as every divination spell I know is concerned, you weren't in Mysterium. Although I'll admit that the state of scholarship in the field is atrocious." He gestured about at the mass of books as if to confirm this fact.

My forebrain was still trying desperately to claw its way out of my head. I closed my eyes and decided to delegate the higher thinking to Eldrin. "That doesn't make sense. All I did was walk her back to her room—I think. Anyway, I don't have the stamina to do two days of drinking . . . or anything else for that matter."

Funny thing though, I couldn't actually remember even making it to her room. Not exactly. I opened my eyes and looked at Eldrin. He had on his angry expression. *Shit.*

He shook his head. "You're not getting what I'm saying. You weren't anywhere in Mysterium. You must have gone off-world, which is totally irresponsible considering what you were carrying around with you. What were you thinking?"

I raised an eyebrow.

He blushed. He'd been doing that more and more lately. I wondered again if he had a bit of a puritanical streak in him, which would be unusual for a Hylar. They are typically very . . . open-minded.

"Never mind," he mumbled. "I guess no harm was done. It was still damned stupid though."

"You weren't there," I said smugly, which earned me a very elven eye roll. I didn't want to admit that with as little as I remembered, I might not have been there either. I sat up. The movement made my brain knock about in my head. I needed coffee and aspirin and a plate of greasy eggs and bacon, but first I needed to know how I got here. I yawned. "My memory is a little hazy. How and when did I get home?"

Eldrin shrugged. "I don't know. I found you propped against our door this morning when I went to take my shower. There was a note pinned to you." He gestured vaguely at my desk. "And before you ask, I didn't read it. I have some boundaries."

With an enormous effort, I reached over and plucked a bit of old-fashioned parchment from the desk. It had been folded and the edge sealed with a rough circle of black wax into which had been pressed the image of a climbing rose. The note was written in an elegant hand I didn't recognize.

Dearest Avery,

I'm sorry to leave you like this, but it is the only way. I have so much still to do here in Trelari, and you did not seem happy to be here any longer.

When you get this you are going to want to panic, and you are going to want to come for me. Don't. I promise you, there is a GOOD reason for everything. The world has begun to speak to me, and every day my path becomes clearer. I know now what I am doing. More importantly, I know what I will be doing and what I still need to do.

You are the most extraordinary mage I have ever

met. I hope one day you will forgive me and that we can meet again under happier circumstances and talk of all those silly things you wanted to talk to me about.

Yours,

Vivian

P.S. Sorry about the headache; repeated sleep and compulsion spells will do that, I'm told.

P.P.S. Please tell Dawn that I am okay.

I read the letter twice through, hoping that it would change. When it didn't, I sat, unmoving, with the paper in my hand, listening to the blood pumping through my brain.

"What does she say?" Eldrin asked over the roaring in my ears. "If it's explicit don't read it to me. I like to keep a bit of mystery between us."

His words washed over me, heard but not registered. Then full weight of what she had done hit me. My nerves began to burn like my body was on fire. My hands shook violently. I dropped the paper and clawed at my neck, searching for the chain that was always there. It was gone. I leapt from the bed and tore at the pockets of my trench coat and then my pants. I was in the process of dismantling my desk and the books on my shelf when I felt Eldrin's hand on my shoulder.

"Avery," he said quietly.

Oddly, it was the calm in his voice that pushed me over the edge. I felt my knees give out beneath me, and Eldrin guide me back to my bed. I knew he was saying something to me, but it took a while for the words to filter through my panic.

". . . a deep breath. You're as pale as chalk. You've got to calm down or you're going to pass out."

He knelt down so his eyes were level with mine. "It's the key, isn't it, Avery? She's taken the key to your subworld."

I nodded. "She's there now, in Trelari."

I saw a mixture of sadness and disappointment pass over his face. He picked up her letter and began pacing back and forth across our room as he read it. I watched him and hoped that he was going to come up with a plan, because at this point I was beyond rational thought. He stopped with a shrug. "Well, the only thing for it is to go and get her."

This made sense and sounded simple. "Right," I said. "We can use the circle to go to Trelari and find her."

He looked at me with an expression that made my stomach sink again. "It would only be that simple if she wanted to be found," he said patiently, "but from her note it seems clear that she doesn't. And if she doesn't want you to bring her back, then you'll be trying to compel someone with absolute control over reality. Remember what it was like to be the Dark Lord?"

I lay back on the bed and groaned. "I don't understand. Why did she do it? What can she want with my subworld? It's only special to me because it was the one Griswald assigned me to study."

Eldrin started pacing again, folding his hands in a distinctly Eldrin-esque way. "In her letter she mentions 'knowing what she will be doing and what she still needs to do.' Do you know what she's talking about? What does she *need* to do?"

I shook my head and mumbled, "I have no idea."

"Do you remember anything about her, or about what you did with her?" he asked, his jaw clenching and unclenching in frustration.

"No," I wailed. "I . . . I remember meeting her in the bar, having a drink with her, and then leaving, but nothing after that."

"What did you talk to her about in the bar?" he asked.

I wrinkled my brow in concentration as I tried to reconstruct the evening. It was like trying to watch a movie through a thick mist. Everything was obscured and diffused. At last I said, "I think we talked mostly about her. She told me she was an acolyte seer and that she'd been accepted into a research group and was going to be studying . . . something . . ." I snapped. "Future shaping! That was it. She went on and on about how she was going to join Herbert's group and study future shaping."

Eldrin's eyes widened and he crouched down in front me. "This is very important, Avery. Did you tell her about your experiment?"

I started to shake my head, but then stopped as an image of Vivian and me standing in front of the Subworld Studies building crystalized in my mind. "Yes!" I said. "She was very interested. She wanted to know all about what I was studying, and got very excited that my method might be able to stabilize subworlds permanently."

We both looked at each other and Eldrin said, "She thinks she can predict the outcome of your experiment." I nodded. "But that's going to be a disaster," he said, his voice rising. "She's going to get all sorts of bogus visions, and if she tries to future shape in a subworld, well . . ."

"The whole place might unravel around her," I supplied.

"Dammit, Avery!" Eldrin shouted. "Why did you have to keep that key with you? How could you be so stupid?"

I didn't even try to muster a defense. "I don't know," I whispered, and I didn't. Why had I been so unhappy and reckless that night? How could I explain something to him that even I didn't understand?

We sat on our beds, staring at the narrow gap of floor between us, both lost in our own thoughts. I was considering alternate career paths and trying to remember the lyrics to a certain song when Eldrin jumped off his bed in a sudden burst of energy and went to his desk.

"No use sitting about," he said with forced brightness. "I'll do some quick calculations to see how best to insert ourselves into the subworld. We can probably reuse your old circle with the right modifications."

As he sat down at his desk, the sucking sound of our wall dissolving echoed across the room. Eldrin glanced over at the corner with a sigh and went back to his books, his pencil beating a rapid staccato as he thought through our options. I stared at the wall, and considered my roommate.

"You know it was my idea to try and build an extradimensional closet in our room," I mused aloud.

If Eldrin heard he didn't respond. He was engrossed in sketching a series of incredibly complicated runes and waved my words away with the eraser end of his pencil. But the thought was stubborn and kept bothering me. The fact was, most of the bad ideas we'd had over the years had been mine, and this was no exception. I suddenly knew what I had to do. I stood and braced my feet so that they were solidly set on the floor. I hadn't performed magic of this sort since my third year of acolyte training, so I made sure I had the pattern of the magic set in my mind very carefully before I started. Then I began.

I gathered my energies slowly and steadily. There was no reason to alarm Eldrin unnecessarily. When I was certain I had enough magic stored up for my purposes, I focused it through the pattern and willed him to sleep. It was not until the first tendrils of power touched him that he reacted. He began to turn, but by then the spell was already beginning to take hold. His movements began to slow, I saw his mouth open as if to say something, and he slumped forward—unconscious.

I dressed quickly and turned to leave. There was another sucking sound from the corner, and the passing wind fluttered the papers on Eldrin's desk. I examined the sketch he had been working on. It was brilliant, of course. I slid the paper out from under his arm and tucked it into the pocket of my trench coat. He stirred in his sleep.

"Thanks, Eldrin," I said and, grabbing the pillow from his bed, I laid it beneath his head. "Sweet dreams."

Outside, with the warmth of the midday sun beating down, it all seemed so impossible. Adepts were playing plasma Frisbee and touch football on the greens; even the acolytes and novices had emerged mole-like from their study holes to enjoy the brilliant weather. Nothing could be wrong on a day like today. Still, impossible or not, there was a clock outside a door in the basement of a building that was ticking down the days to the end of my career. I had two weeks to bring Vivian back, and each minute that passed for me would be hours for her. I started running.

Before I could figure out exactly how much subworld time I might have to chase down and subdue a woman with the power of life and death in her hands, I was standing in front of my closet door breathing hard. I reached for the handle and paused. Had she remembered to lock it? If she had I would be sunk. The only way to get into the shielded room would be to get the spare from the stores, at which point my deception would be known and Gristle would get involved. Even if I survived the fallout, Vivian never would. Stealing a reality key meant expulsion at a minimum.

I closed my eyes, whispered prayers to a dozen deities at once, and twisted the knob. It didn't budge. I rested my head against the cool hardness of the metal and muttered profanities to the same gods I had moments before pleaded to for help.

I was considering my very limited options when I heard the sound I'd been dreading—footsteps. They were coming, fast, and their echoes rebounded down the tile corridors like miniature thunderclaps. I only had a few seconds to act. Hiding in the empty and featureless hallway was out of the question, but every ten feet or so was another door letting on to another circle closet—most of which would not be in use. I opened the nearest one and ducked into the darkness of room 13A.

I had just enough time to pull the door closed when whoever it was turned the corner. I gave the gods one last try and begged for their intervention. *Please keep going, please keep going.* Of course the unwanted interloper stopped right outside my room. Gods can be such pricks.

I heard a key turn in a lock and the sound of a door opening. It must be my closet, which meant it had to be Gristle. *He must have seen me come in*, I thought, followed quickly by the silent whine, *Why me?*

I was in the process of coming up with some truly inventive excuses when Eldrin's whispered voice broke the silence. "Avery?"

The relief at knowing it was him, or at least not Griswald, was exquisite. I fumbled for the door and came spilling unsteadily out into the hall. "Eldrin?!" I said in a half shout. Then more quietly, "How are you here? You are supposed to be—"

"Asleep?" he said in an injured tone. "You think a third-year charm is going to keep me out of commission? What sort of poser do you think I am, and what the hell were you thinking anyway?"

I smiled at him. "I was thinking that you can't come with me, Eldrin."

"Why not?" he asked, and this time the hurt in his voice was real.

"Because this is my problem, and I won't have you risking your career to help me fix it."

"But—" he began.

"No," I said firmly. "Not this time. If you won't stay clear of it, then I am going straight to Gristle's office and turn myself in."

A sinister smile crept over his face. "You forget I am already in it." He waved the spare closet key at me. "I had to check this out. They will know I went to your closet."

I shook my head. "No dice. You know as well as I do that the storeroom guys give those things out to anyone that will slip them a cold beer. All you have to say is that you were playing a prank on me. I am going alone."

He frowned deeply. "You are committed to this?"

"Yes, and if you don't mind I'd like to get started. I only have—" I glanced at the ticking clock "—crap, less than fifteen days now."

"All right," he said reluctantly, "but I want you to take something with you."

He reached into his pocket and pulled out a coin made of a silvery metal that seemed to be simultaneously dull and shiny depending on how the light fell on it. On one side it had a silhouette of a face in profile, and on the other a magical circle of immense complexity inscribed in minute detail.

"What's this?" I asked impatiently.

"It's a transtemporal subworld communicator," he said with a look of immense satisfaction. "I've been working on it for months now. I was going to test it next time you went subworld hopping."

"What the hell is a trans . . . that?" I asked, pointing at the coin.

"Well . . ." he began.

However Eldrin might have explained the device he never got the chance, because at that moment we heard the heavy tread of hard-soled boots coming along a side passage. This would have been frightening enough, but my blood froze as I heard the unmistakable muttering of Magus Eustace Griswald, and the wheezing of his imp. Eyes wide, I looked at Eldrin. If I were as pale as he was, we must have looked like a pair of ghosts standing there.

Eldrin moved first, thrusting the coin into my hand and shoving me through the door. "Start modifying the circle," he hissed. "I'll hold the old man off as long as I can. Oh, and, Avery, good luck and come back safe."

With that he pulled the door shut and twisted the key in the lock. The sound of the bolt falling into place seemed final and dreadful. For a moment I stood there dumb, but then I heard Eldrin's voice raised to an unnatural volume. "Magus Griswald, what an unexpected surprise."

I could not hear what my mentor said in response, but Eldrin replied, "What am I doing here? Well, you see, sir . . . That is to say . . . What I was doing was just . . . checking on his progress."

Gristle must have moved a little closer, because now I could hear the indistinct baritone rumble of his voice filtering through the door. When Eldrin answered whatever Gristle had asked, his voice was alarmingly high-pitched. "The other key has been checked out, you say? Yes, I have it."

Knowing that Eldrin was only a few feet away talking to the one magus in all Mysterium I wanted to have nothing to do with drove me into a flurry of action. I ripped the paper with Eldrin's diagram from my pocket, grabbed a stick of fazestone chalk from the desk, and bent to the circle. As I drew, I reflected that this type of subterfuge was not a strength of Eldrin's, and that that I probably didn't have long before Gristle got annoyed enough to demand the key. I needed time. The modifications were essential or when I returned I would materialize on the Dark Lord's old throne, which would be both awkward and potentially fatal as I had designed my stronghold to turn to dust and scatter itself with the wind on the dawn after my defeat.

Outside, Gristle barked something sharp and short to which Eldrin replied, "Into the room, sir? Did I go in? Well . . ."

Keep it together, Eldrin.

I was working in a clockwise direction, adding a rune here and altering a mystic symbol there. Under normal circumstances the changes would not have been that difficult to make. They were subtle and intricate, but well within my skill. However, these were anything but normal circumstances. My heart was beating so hard that I feared it might seize up altogether. Plus, hearing Eldrin's one-sided conversation with Gristle had my nerves in such a heightened state that my hand kept trembling. I was having to use my off-hand to steady it.

At that point Gristle must have stepped right up to the door, because I could make out what the old man was saying. "You wouldn't be here to play a prank, would you, Mr. Leightner?"

"Of course not, sir," Eldrin squeaked.

"I wasn't always a magus, Mr. Leightner, and I have never been a fool," he said, this time in a growl that contained significantly more menace. "Open the door."

My hand froze for a second at his request, and then I returned to the last figure. It was a fiddly thing, like a bisected spiral. I took a deep breath to steady myself and began.

"Yes, sir!" Eldrin said.

I heard the key fumble against the lock and then a

metallic clatter as it fell to the ground. Gristle gave a muffled curse. "Dammit, Leightner, that was my foot. Just stand still. I'll get it."

I was done. I dropped the chalk and stood. Normally I would have examined the new markings to make sure I'd done everything correctly, but there was no time. I stepped into the circle as the key went into the lock. I felt the familiar but never pleasant sensation of my insides briefly exiting my body, and then nothing. For better or for worse, I was gone, and all Griswald would find was an empty circle closet. I thanked most of the gods most profusely.

When I materialized it was not triumphantly on the steppes of the Plains of Drek as I had planned, but with a splash in a mire of mud and manure in a nondescript stable yard somewhere in Trelari. I let loose with a most profound blasphemy.

"Amen," a ragged voice said from my right.

CHAPTER 6

SERIOUSLY WRONG

I looked around, trying to figure out what was going on. It was night. The stable yard I'd landed in was narrow and surrounded by high walls that cast everything in deep shadows. Once my head stopped swimming from the transport spell and my eyes adjusted to the dark, I peered at the disheveled heap that had spoken. I use the word *heap* advisedly, because the speaker was so covered in filth that it took me a moment to realize that it was a man at all. He was propped against a nearby wall surrounded by a half circle of empty bottles, and even over the stomach-churning stench of the place, the miasma of bad wine that clung to him made my head spin.

I started to ask the man who he was and where we

were, but at that moment the moon came out from behind a cloud and bathed the stable in light. I stared into the face of the beggar and my mouth fell open. There was no mistaking that long, aquiline nose, or the coal-black hair, dark eyes, and dramatically arched eyebrows. Dirty and degenerate as he was, this man was St. Drake, one of the Heroes of the Ages, and the most pious man in all of Trelari.

He seemed to recognize me also, because for a second his eyes cleared and went wide; he extended a shaking finger toward me, and gasped, "The Dark One has returned!"

He started to topple backward and I grabbed the front of his robes to keep him upright. "What are you talking about? The Dark Lord was destroyed. You helped destroy him. Don't you remember?"

St. Drake stared at me for a moment, then his mouth split open into a rictus grin and he began to laugh hysterically. It was hideous, and I was relieved when his eyelids fluttered shut and he began snoring. I stood there, dripping mud, staring at the passed-out-drunk man in disbelief.

This was St. Drake, the Unselfish.

On their way to confront me, the Heroes had been forced to march for two weeks over the Wasteland of Grolm. My spies, which were many, informed me that St. Drake had refused all food because the Weasel claimed he need extra nourishment to fight off a bout of hypothermia he'd been suffering. Hypothermia? On a burning waste?

This was St. Drake, the Pure.

The rumor making the rounds with the gibberlings back in the day was that he allowed nothing to pass his lips that had not been sanctified in a purity ritual (of his own devising) that took about a day and a half to complete. This explained why the Heroes needed nearly two weeks to cross across the Plains of Despair, which were, at most, thirty miles wide.

The point is, this wreck of a man snoring at my feet was St. Drake. His presence in this place and in this condition violated everything I knew about him and everything that was supposed to be true about Trelari. Something was wrong.

As if to affirm this fact, my name suddenly began reverberating through my brain. "Avery . . . very . . . very . . . very . . . very?"

Fortunately, I recognized the voice. "Eldrin? Why does it sound like you're shouting into a cave?"

"Damn . . . amn . . . amn! Let . . . let . . . let me . . . me . . . me adjust . . . ust . . . ust the . . . the . . . the gain . . . ain . . . ain." There was a short, sharp crack that nearly ruptured my eardrums, and he said, "Is that any better?"

"Much," I answered, and yawned around the pain in my head.

"It works!" came the unmistakable voice of my roommate. "This is so cool! Can you believe that we are communicating across subworld space and we have chronal calibration?"

"Yes, it's great and normally I would celebrate another one of your achievements, but we have problems. The transport didn't work right. I'm standing in what smells like a pigsty next to one of my Heroes, and he is in a state that defies every standard of decency."

He didn't answer for a few seconds and I tapped at my ear and asked, "Is this thing still working?"

"Yes," he said hoarsely. "I need to confirm. Are you telling me that you just appeared in the subworld this very moment?"

"Of course, what did you expect? You must have called me immediately after I left."

"No, I didn't," he said in a voice like the one a doctor would use to tell you that you have terminal cancer. "It took me two hours to get away from Griswald and back to our room to make the call."

I heard the words, but they didn't make any sense. Eventually I said, "That's impossible. With the time dilation factor between Trelari and Mysterium I should have been here a couple of days at least."

"Try nearly a week," he corrected.

We both fell silent. I shifted in the mud, too afraid to ponder the meaning of this discovery. At last I asked the question I was dreading the answer to. "What's going on, Eldrin?"

"I don't know," he answered in a stunned whisper.

That's when I got scared. It took me a few moments to be able to focus on his words again. When I did, he was muttering to himself and, from the sounds in the background, emptying his shelves of his extensive personal library volume by volume.

"There's got to be an explanation," he mumbled. "Maybe there's something in Adams's *Observations on Galactic Improbabilities*? No . . . besides all his proofs collapse down to the same value." There was a loud thud as a book hit the ground. "Asprin's treatise on dimensional transactions is interesting at a general level, but the deveel is in the details . . ."

In between Eldrin's mutterings I had a flash of inspiration. Eldrin was not an expert on this world, nor was Adams or Asprin. I was the world's greatest expert on Trelari, and there was a several hundred-page guide on the shelf above my desk that might have an answer as to why the transport spell had gone so badly off target and even an explanation of the strange time jump I'd experienced. As a bonus, I had written it.

"I may have the answer."

He was reading books, so of course he ignored me. "Baum? No, and besides where would we get ruby shoes?"

I began massaging my temples. It wasn't that I had a headache, but knowing how my roommate reacted in these sorts of situations, I knew it was an inevitability. I said a bit louder, "I know what we need to do."

"Lewis is just as useless," he groused, still oblivious. "Who goes subworld traveling with a full-sized wardrobe anymore?"

"Eldrin! Listen to me!" I yelled.

"Why are you shouting at me?" he asked in hurt tones.

I opened my mouth to say something snide and thought better of it. "Sorry."

"It's okay," he said quietly. "What is it?"

"Look on the shelf above my desk—right-hand side."

"Your collection of graphic novels?"

The headache had arrived. I rubbed at my throbbing forehead. "I meant left-hand side, and don't touch my graphic novels—those are first editions. On the left, you should find the Dimensional Macrocosm Guide I wrote for subworld 2A7C."

"Your DMG?" he asked in a voice high enough to seriously imperil any nearby windows. "Don't make me look in there."

"How do you think I feel Eldrin?" I asked. "I'm literally standing in a shit-hole, and if I don't get out of here soon I'm going to pass out. But unless you have a better idea, can you please consult the only book ever specifically written for this world?"

I heard the unmistakable sound of flipping pages, and he groaned.

Now, before I go on, let me explain our dismay. A DMG is a manual of sorts (in official parlance a detailed log of experimental requirements, parameters, and procedures) that has to be written by every Mysterium researcher that wants to conduct an experiment on a subworld. In theory, nearly any question about the world (its people, geography, religion, climate, etc.) can be found in the researcher's DMG. However, the comprehensive nature of the document means that its utility is almost entirely dependent on how well it is organized (how thoughtful the table of contents is and how thorough the index). I wrote those key portions of my DMG in a mad rush about twenty-four hours before I was due to start my experiment, a fact Eldrin was keenly aware of.

Eventually he stopped flipping pages. "Did you know that, according to you, on your subworld a long sword has the potential to do 'eight damage' against small and medium creatures, but up to twelve against large creatures? What does that even mean? What scale are you using? This book makes no sense."

"Eldrin, focus."

"I mean, why should the damage of a sword increase by fifty percent simply because the creature is larger? A sword is a sword—"

"ELDRIN!"

"This may take a while," he said. "There are dozens of important tables in here on the subworld's cosmology and what not, but they are strewn haphazardly through the book. And it's like that with everything."

"It's a first edition. I was meaning to do something more concise later. Why not look in the table of contents or the index for 'time dilation' or 'transport failure'?"

"The table of contents?" he asked incredulously. "The table of contents you drafted gives no idea of what each section is about, and the index only seems to catalog the least important terms in the book. There are entries in here for different poisons and exotic diseases, locations for charts on weight limits and travel times. You even obsessively indexed the treasure possessed by various mystical creatures that are probably all extinct, not to mention the weather and terrain in dozens of different ecozones. Is there a single reference to the Dark Lord?"

"Yes?" I said weakly.

"No!" he shouted.

I began muttering a dozen curses to the sky, with several rather clever invectives directed specifically at myself.

"This is *not* my fault," he protested.

"I'm not cursing at you. I'm cursing at me," I said in disgust, and began pacing back and forth across the stable yard. "Do you honestly think that I don't understand how profoundly I've screwed things up? Why didn't I take the time to write up a better DMG? Because I'm lazy. Why didn't I close out the circle and return the reality key when my experiment was complete? Because I'm irresponsible. Why did I take an unknown girl into my still-running circle closet?"

This last question stopped me in my tracks. My immediate thought was that the answer was obvious and had more to do with libido and psychology, but I knew that those weren't the real reasons. "Why did I need that night and her so badly?" I whispered.

There was a long silence.

"Um," came Eldrin's voice. "I didn't catch that last part. I think you may be cutting out. Which reminds me, I should probably warn you that this communication link will only work while we have direct etherspace line of sight between the subworld and Mysterium."

"Good to know," I said, still distracted by the question of Vivian. "How much time do we have left?"

"Let me see." I could hear the scratch of his pencil on paper as he made the calculation. "Five minutes."

"Five minutes!" I exploded. "For the love of . . . never mind. Let's discard the question of transport and time for the moment. It would be great to know how much time has passed, but I can probably get that from St. Drake—if he ever wakes up. For now, I am here, for better or worse, so I might as well get on with finding Vivian. Please tell me you have some idea about what I'm supposed to do next. Does the DMG say anything helpful about how I can find and stop her?"

"How could it?" Eldrin replied. "Not to state the obvious," he said, stating the obvious, "but you are off the map, my friend. I'm checking the DMG for rules about how you can blend in with the natives. You know, local dress, dining habits, trade and commerce, that sort of thing."

"For the love of light!" I said in a near shout, and then remembered that Eldrin was only trying to help and I should be thankful he was willing to do that given my behavior the last few days. I took a deep breath and said in a more measured voice, "Thanks, Eldrin, but I did live in Trelari for years."

"As the Dark Lord," he said under his breath.

"Good point," I acknowledged. "But I don't think you can teach me enough in the next three minutes to make it a useful exercise."

He was silent and I heard the drumming of his fingers on the cover of the book, which was always a bad sign. "Nope, I've got nothing," he said. "Your DMG is written specifically for your experiment. Without a dark lord, it is worse than useless."

Not for the first time, Eldrin's words were an inadvertent revelation. *How could I have been such a profound idiot?*

"Hold on," I said. "Give me a second to consult with my colleague over here. I may have something."

I strode over to St. Drake. He was laid out in the mud, arms outstretched. Despite being passed out he still had a bottle grasped in each hand. I needed him to be awake. I pulled him upright and shook him. He ignored me and snored on. A trough of water stood in one corner of the stable. I lifted him in my arms, carried him over to it, and dropped him in.

His reaction was immediate and satisfying. He shot up out of the water with a shouted, "Hell!"

He was still coughing and spluttering when I took hold of his robe in my fist. I bent down so his eyes were level with mine. "You said the Dark *One* had returned, not the Dark Lord."

Eyes wide, he nodded.

"Were you being prophetic or literal?" I asked.

He opened and closed his mouth like a fish.

"One minute!" Eldrin's voice rang out.

Damn! I was either being too subtle or he hadn't sobered up enough for this conversation. Either way I had only one solution available to me. I dunked his head back under for a few seconds before pulling him up again. Before he could catch his breath to start cursing me again, I asked, "Is the Dark One really back?"

For a moment I thought he wouldn't answer, but as I began to push him under for the third time he nodded vigorously.

"Is the Dark One a Dark Queen?" I asked.

"Yes," he gasped.

I felt an eerie calm come over me. I let go of his robes and he fell back into the trough with a splash. I didn't need Eldrin or the DMG. I knew exactly what to do. This was a replay of my dissertation project, except that this time Vivian was the virus, the imbalance. That St. Drake knew this meant that my reality stabilization spell had already been activated. All I needed to do was trigger the initial conditions for Hero generation and the world would surround me with the tools I needed to defeat her.

Par for the course, Eldrin ruined my moment of inspired revelation. "Did you know there's a whole section in here on the ecology of dungeon creatures? Man, this is so messed up. How many different gelatinous polygons are there in your cosmos? Oh, ten seconds by the way."

What I needed now was a quiet place and some

time to plan. "Nice talking to you, Eldrin, but I have to go."

"Wait, what? Where are you going?" he asked.

"Table of Contents, Chapter 1."

Pages flipped in the background and there was an exhale of disbelief. "But all this says is 'A Guy Walks into a Bar.'"

"Exactly," I replied just before the connection went dead.

CHAPTER 7

A WIZARD WALKS INTO A BAR

A deafening pop, that Eldrin never bothered to warn me about, followed the end of our conversation. I still had fingers in both my ears to stop the ringing when St. Drake finally dragged himself out of the water. Sopping wet he marched to a dirty pile of straw, pulled out a long staff, and began mouthing something at me.

"What?" I asked, and removed my fingers.

"I said, do you know who I am?" he shouted.

"Yes." I shrugged. "You are, or were, St. Drake the Incorruptible, most revered servant of the Seven Gods, keeper of the Crystal of Righteousness, and wielder of the Staff of Flagellation. By the way, isn't that it?"

"What?"

"The staff." I pointed at the long carved stick he was holding.

He stared morosely at it for a second and said, "More or less."

"What happened?" I looked significantly at his filthy robes and the half-dozen empty bottles at his feet.

He sat heavily on the edge of the water trough. "I lost my faith and am now a fallen man. The Seven Gods stripped me of my powers for the blasphemy of doubt, and my order cast me out for the sacrilege of renunciation. All that remains of what I was is what you see. Now my companions are not the arm of might and the eye of truth, but the corruption of drink and the shadows of doubt."

I half listened while looking for a way out of this place and its stench. At last I spotted a gate in one of the walls. I put a hand on St. Drake's shoulder and began leading him out of the paddock. If Vivian was the Dark Queen my reality matix stabilization spell would probably be active, and would be subtly and sometimes not so subtly influencing the actions of the Trelarians. But I had to be sure, which meant I needed to find a bar.

"Look," I said to the man as we emerged onto the street. "It sounds, and frankly smells, like you've had some hard times lately." He started to reply, but I didn't give him the chance. "The point is not to dwell on your many, many lapses and failures, but to right them. And you happen to be in luck. I am going to gather a group of mighty heroes to defeat the Dark Queen. For some it will be their first adventure. For you, well, think of it as a quest for . . . for . . ." I struggled for the right word.

"Redemption?" he offered.

I completely missed the sarcasm in his voice. "Exactly! Don't you feel better already?"

I was busy trying to decipher the various signs that lined the street and so missed his mumbled reply. One had the image of a rooster in an ermine robe wearing a golden crown. I wondered what that could possibly mean when I realized that there was no one better to direct me to a bar than St. Drake.

"Say," I said brightly, "you are obviously a . . ." I nearly said *drunk*, but managed to stop myself. "A fellow who likes to enjoy a drink now and then—" he burped "—or perhaps a bit more frequently than that. Where would you go for a drink? You know, an inn or a tavern or something."

"Well, if you want a drink . . ." he began, but at that moment I spotted a promising-looking place across the street. It was not very imaginatively called the Traveler's Inn.

"Ha! There's one." I gave him a solid clap on the shoulder. He started to say something else, but I was beyond listening. I strode briskly into the Traveler's Inn, and he followed. I was in total command of the situation.

A matronly barmaid wearing an apron and carrying

a broom greeted us as we stepped inside. "Good day, gentlemen," she said sweetly, while eyeing our mud stained clothes with suspicion. "How can I help you?"

I glanced about the room. It wasn't what I had expected. There were a few groups in twos or threes scattered about eating dinner, but I couldn't see any of your classic adventuring types. These people seemed to be more farmer than warrior, more merchant than rogue. Still, it was early. Maybe the crowd got livelier as the evening wore on.

"We are adventurers," I pronounced, and swept my arm grandly about. "Famed throughout the land. We will be sitting in the back, and will buy anyone who wishes to join us on our quest for glory a bottle of their choice."

I hadn't expected a roar of affirmation, but I also hadn't expected dead silence. Nor had I anticipated the sour expression that the barmaid gave me. She pursed her lips and put a hand to her hip. "Not here, you won't."

"What?" I leaned in close and tried to give her a winning smile. "Look, if this is about the mud . . ."

"The mud doesn't enter into it," she said sternly. "This is an inn."

"Yes," I said, wondering if we weren't speaking the same language. "All I want is a table in the back and your strongest drink."

"You can have the table, you can have the drink," she said, counting off her fingers, "but the strongest you'll get here is sour milk."

"I tried to warn you, kid," said St. Drake.

"Warn me about what?" I asked.

"This is an inn!" both he and the barmaid said at once.

"What you'd be wantin' is a pub," said a rough voice from a nearby table.

I looked over and saw a man who appeared to be one continuous callus staring at me from beneath a tangle of brown hair. Before I could respond an equally rough-looking woman with a startlingly red face sitting across from him laughed violently, and said, "You're twice the fool, Amos. Everyone knows there haven't been no pubs in Blightsbury since before the Dark Lord."

"I know that, woman." The man pounded a fist on the table. "I was just sayin' that if there were a pub, then that'd be the place to get a good strong drink."

"Sure," she said, "but then if tarts were leprechauns and the sky were filled with rainbows we'd all be swimmin' in gold." The room erupted in laughter.

"Wait, there aren't any pubs in this town?" I asked.

There were a lot of shaking heads and the barmaid (who I was beginning to realize wasn't a barmaid at all) said, "No."

I turned to St. Drake. "Where do you drink?"

"Drake?" the innkeeper woman, or whatever it was she was, chortled. "He always drinks down at the Boiled Badger."

"Yeah!" roared the rough man. "Cheapest place in town. Right, Drake?"

Drake didn't reply.

"So, the Boiled Badger is a pub?" I asked, again feeling that I was losing something in translation.

"No!" the woman who would not, or could not, give me a drink shouted.

"What are ye," cackled the red-faced woman, "a half-wit?"

"But you can get a drink there?" I persisted.

"Yes!" the rough man bellowed.

"But it isn't a pub?"

"No!" the entire room roared.

Drake stepped forward and rapped his staff on the floor of the . . . the . . . well, the place where we were. He drew his thin frame upward and swept his hood back off his jet-black hair. In his dark eyes there was a fierce light, and the room grew silent beneath his gaze. "You stand in an 'inn,'" he solemnly intoned. "A term that comes from the old language and refers to a simple lodging house."

"Simple?" the innkeeper woman protested.

Drake (who I was starting to think of in nonsaintly terms) shot her a glare, but continued as though he had never been interrupted. "The Boiled Badger, which I frequent—on occasion—is a tavern, a term which is borrowed from the ancient *taberna* and literally means 'a hut,' and refers to a place where wine and spirits are sold. Coincidentally, *taberna* is also the root of the word *tabernacle*, a place I used to frequent more than occasionally, and now no longer even infrequent."

Everyone looked a bit confused at this last point.

Drake cleared his throat and plowed on. "By contrast, the term *pub* or *public house* is reserved for an establishment that is specially licensed by the crown to sell alcohol to the public. Thus, while Blightsbury has no pub, it does have two taverns."

I thought I'd heard enough, but Drake disagreed and, without even a pause for breath, said, "Much of this confusion might have been alleviated if you had asked for a 'bar,' which is the most basic term for an establishment that serves alcohol and references the counter or barrier over which drinks are passed. Both taverns and pubs have bars, although inns do not."

The entire inn (I can now safely say that is the correct term) was staring at him in rapt attention. Don't ask me why, but I felt compelled to sum up. "So, in the Venn diagram of places to get refreshments, a pub could be called a tavern, but a tavern might not be a pub, both places could be called bars, but none of them could be called an inn, which also could not be called a tavern or a pub as it doesn't have a bar?"

Drake raised one of his distinctively arched eyebrows. "Obviously. But, kid, what's a Venn diagram?"

"Never mind," I grunted.

In hindsight, I should have stopped to consider what it meant that I, Avery Stewart, self-professed expert of subworld 2A7C, had fouled up something as simple as the difference between an inn and a tavern, but I didn't. What I did was grab Drake by the elbow and march him back outside.

He shook my hand off and asked, "Where are we going now?"

"To the Boiled Badger," I said. "After the speech you just made, don't you need a drink?"

He sighed. "I suppose."

We made our way across the street to a disreputable-looking building over which hung a sign painted with a grinning badger bathing in a cook pot. We pushed our way inside. As soon as the stale, smoky air hit my nose, I knew we were in the right place, and the scene was equally promising. Along one wall stretched a long bar at which six or seven rough-looking customers were nursing drinks. The opposite wall held a hearth in which was set a blazing fire over that roasted several unidentifiable animal carcasses. Between the bar and fire were a sprinkling of tables, long and short, where a variety of gambling games were being played and whispered plots were being hatched.

I turned to Drake. "Now this is more like it!"

The barman, an enormously obese man who might have actually been trapped behind the bar, called out, "Drake!"

A number of heads came up at this and took up the call. "Drake!"

"So, how 'occasionally' do you come in here?" I asked.

He ignored my question, raised two fingers at the barman, and headed toward a table near one of the corners. I sized up the talent as we made our way across the room. There were certainly a lot of swords, staves, and knives being displayed, and each of the booths seemed to be populated by one or more mysterious hooded figures. The question was how to separate the wheat from the people who would just as soon stab you in the back as give you the time of day.

As we sat down I decided to pose the question to my companion, but as was becoming his habit, he beat me to the punch. "So, kid, what exactly do you mean you're planning to go and battle the Dark Queen?"

A serving wench cut off my answer by dropping two tankards on the table. I started to reach for one, but Drake took an ale in each hand and dragged them across the table. "Talk first. Drink second. And if you don't want a knife in your back, never baptize me again."

Judging by the look in his eyes, this was no idle threat. I realized for the first but certainly not the last time that it might take a literal miracle to reform Drake.

Drake drained one of the tankards and leaned in close. "Look, I don't know who you are, but you have no idea what you'll be facing if you go against the Dark Queen."

In many respects he was absolutely right; in other respects I may be the only person in the world that knew exactly what I was up against. At the time, I decided that projecting confidence during the recruiting process was better than admitting that everyone that went with me was probably doomed. I leaned back in my chair and laced my fingers behind my head. "I think I know what I'm up against, Drake. All I need is the right group of companions and I know I can take her down. Fact is, I got lucky stumbling onto you so quickly. With the wizard and priest roles taken care of, I only need a warrior to do the fighting, a thief to do the stealing, and a token elf and dwarf."

"Are you the wizard, kid?"

"Yes, and I'm not a kid," I replied irritably. "You aren't that much older than I am."

"It's not about age, it's about experience," he said with a twisted grin. "You look like a noble of some sort. Straight teeth. Soft hands. No scars. Like you've never seen a day of hard work or a tough fight in your whole life."

"I'm a wizard, Drake. We aren't exactly known for manual labor or fistfights."

Drake took another deep draught, draining half of the second tankard. "Maybe, but I've never met a wizard worth the title that still had all his fingers. Either way, you're wasting your time. I'm not going with you."

"Yes, you are," I said with a confidence that I'm sure baffled him. "You need to."

In response, Drake set down his empty mug and threw two fingers into the air. At this pace he would soon be useless to me. I needed to get as much information out of him as I could while he was still upright.

"Drake, let's ignore the question of you for a

moment. It occurs to me that if you're here, then you might know where the other Heroes may be. It would make it so much easier to face down the Dark Queen if I didn't have to train new heroes from scratch. So, what about it? Do you know where the others are? Like, what about Mad Jarl?"

"Mad," he responded. "Last we heard of Jarl he had become convinced that the world was an enormous hard-boiled egg, and that if he mined deep enough and far enough into its center, he would eventually get to the yolk."

He took a deep drink from his third ale, which had been delivered with a wink from the serving girl and a decidedly unholy leer from Drake.

"Well," I said as the girl went giggling away, "Jarl was always a little unstable, but how about Feldane, scion of the elves?"

"He retired. Somewhere out west," Drake slurred, and gestured vaguely over his shoulder to the north.

"Retired?" I asked.

"Yup," Drake said with a burp. "It's supposed to be nice. I used to get a letter now and then. Sounds sunny."

"That makes no sense. Elves are immortal. For them retiring is basically committing to do nothing for forever."

"All the more reason to get started early," he said, and began on his fourth ale. "How do you know so much about all of us anyway?"

"I've just heard the legends," I answered quickly,

not wanting the conversation to wander too far in that direction.

"Legends?" he said with an explosive laugh. "We aren't legends. We're failures."

"Failures?" I said in disbelief. "You defeated the Dark Lord! My only question is why the five of you aren't already going after this new maniac? You and Valdara and the rest are supposed to be the Heroes of the Ages."

He thumped his mug back down on the table and, shoving his face in mine, hissed, "Don't you get it? We're all done! Washed up! We failed. We thought we'd defeated the Dark Lord, but we hadn't. He was playing with us the whole time. Our quest, his life, his death, our victory, nothing but lies. The peace we won was supposed to last a thousand years, but less than five after we brought down the Dark Lord, a dark queen arose, a dark queen against whom we were powerless."

I was still processing that Vivian had been on world for *five* years already when he surged to his feet and shouted, "The Dark One has returned!"

I grabbed him by the sleeve and yanked him back down into his chair where he continued to mumble, "They are all one. The Dark Queen, the Dark Lord, they are all one."

Around us the tavern had grown ominously still. I fixed a broad smile on my face and said, "Charades. What can you do?"

There were several beats of uneasy silence and

then, one by one, heads bent back over cups of drink, dice games, and cards, and slowly the noise of conversation returned. I exhaled in relief, took a deep draft of my ale, and then nearly choked to death when a voice whispered in my ear, "Smooth, handsome. What do you do for an encore, dance on the tables while singing songs about your love for Morgarr?"

Coughing and trying to regain my breath, I spun about and I found myself staring into the flashing green eyes of Valdara.

CHAPTER 8

GETTING THE BAND BACK TOGETHER

In other circumstances this might have been a dream come true, but those flashing green eyes were glaring at me in a way that made it clear that, if I was in a dream, I was in serious danger of not waking up. I swallowed hard and said the only thing I was capable of saying at that point. "You're Valdara."

"Well spotted," she said with no hint of humor.

"Avery."

"What?" she asked.

"A-Avery, my name is," I stuttered. "I mean, my name is Avery."

"Didn't ask and don't care," she said. "What I want to know is what you've done to my friend, St. Drake?"

"N-n-nothing," I answered as quickly as my suddenly clumsy tongue would allow.

"Why is he acting like that?" she asked, and her eyes moved over to Drake.

I glanced at him. He was staring wildly at nothing and muttering about the Dark One and lies and death and madness. My stomach sank. I turned back to answer and felt something sharp dig into my ribs. I looked down to see the gleaming point of a dagger pressed against my side.

"Answer carefully," she added, which I can assure you was an entirely unnecessary warning.

This is probably a good time to tell you about one of the many differences between Mysterians and subworlders. Without the reality key, I could not reshape space, time, and matter at my whim, but I was still a Mysterian, which meant that the reality I was made from was a lot more potent than the reality from which Valdara was made. This meant that I was probably stronger and faster than Valdara, even though she had been training as a warrior since birth, while I hadn't seriously exercised since Oxford when I was really into Zumba. (How else did you think an undernourished adept-student like me was able to bodily lift a grown man like Drake?) This also meant that if she stabbed me with her dagger, I would probably survive. The problem is that word—*probably*—which literally means "in all likelihood," which is never a phrase you want to have associated with your own life and death.

Back in the moment, I nodded and wondered how badly things would turn out if I told her the truth. It didn't take me long to decide that the whole truth would be fatal, so I settled on an expurgated version of the truth. "I'm trying to convince Drake to join my group."

"What group?" she asked, looking around for any sign that anyone in the tavern knew me, which, of course, no one did.

"Well, it doesn't exist yet, but—" I dropped my voice conspiratorially "—between you and me, I'm going to go after the Dark Queen."

"*You* are planning on going after the Dark Queen?"

"Someone has to," I heard myself say, and was surprised to find that I meant it. Vivian or no Vivian, my spell was meant to bring the people of Trelari millennia of stability and peace. That was the bargain I'd made with myself to justify the means I'd had used. If I left the world like this, then all the deceptions and chaos and death would have been for nothing. For myself, I couldn't let that happen. As much as I'd told Drake that this quest would be his chance for redemption, it was undoubtedly mine.

Valdara must have heard something that satisfied her in my answer, because I felt the tip of the blade withdraw from my side and watched the sharpness in her eyes soften a touch. "Who are you?"

"Remember, I said 'my name is Avery,' but then you said you 'didn't ask and didn't care'? Well, my name is still Avery."

She rolled her eyes, but I thought I saw the barest hint of a smile steal across her face. Then she drove her knife hilt-deep into the wood of the tabletop. Remember that "in all likelihood" thing I was talking about before? It was moments like this that reminded me that improbable doesn't mean impossible.

"Tell me why we should join your group."

What she was offering was not lost on me, and it both terrified and excited me beyond rational thought. This was a problem, of course, because she was waiting for an answer, and despite many drunken attempts, I still hadn't figured out how to talk when my brain was not properly engaged.

"Um . . ." I began in a not too promising start and followed that with another "Um" in the hopes that repetition might improve the effect. It didn't. She raised an eyebrow and gave me a quizzical look.

This was a real puzzler. How do you tell someone that they should follow you into battle against a megalomaniacal sorceress who could reshape reality at her whim, because you were recently a megalomaniacal sorcerer who could reshape reality at your whim and so kind of had excellent insights into the strengths and weaknesses of omnipotent megalomaniacal types? I settled on, "I'm a wizard?"

"Congratulations," she snorted. "Do you know how many wizards we brought on our quest against the Dark Lord?"

"Trick question," I answered confidently. "None. Although you did have a sorceress with you, but there are some subtle differences."

She shook her head and held up two fingers.

"That's not possible," I protested. "I know for a *fact* that only five Heroes battled the Dark Lord, and none of them was a wizard."

"I'd be interested to know why you're so confident about your 'facts' when I don't remember *you* being there," she said with such relish that I was sorely tempted to tell her right then and there that I was the Dark Lord. Fortunately, many years of very expensive education had taught me enough about the permanence of death to stay my tongue. "Besides," she continued with a dark smile, "I never said that they made it to the final battle."

I took this in with an open mouth and began to wonder what else about the original quest I hadn't been paying attention to during my time as Dark Lord. I shook the thought away as irrelevant. I'd had a lot on my plate trying to rule the world and keep Morgarr's excesses in check.

"Okay," I rallied, "so you had some bad luck with your wizard . . . wizards last time. I'm better than they were. I know how to kill the Dark Queen."

"How?" she asked in a mocking voice. "With the Mage Staff of the Magi, I suppose."

A sudden anger rose up in me. She may be Valdara, but that didn't give her the right to be rude. I leaned forward and whispered, "I know you can't kill the Dark Queen with a painted stick and bit of glass."

I saw her eyes widen in shock. "How . . . how can you possibly know that?"

On the verge of answering, I froze. This close I could smell her scent—a combination of leather and wood smoke that brought to mind standing atop the battlements of the Fortress of Despair the night before the final battle, looking down on the twinkling fires of the encampments of the Army of Light and smelling that same mingling of smoke and bodies. Valdara must have been down there that night. How many horrors had I put her through, and now I was proposing to do it again. The guilt that had been sneaking around my subconscious for a while emerged in all its glory. I was torn between telling Valdara to sit this one out, and the knowledge that whether I wanted her to go or stay, if the spell—my spell—was working it would have its own opinion on the subject, and that it would have a far greater influence over her decision. I sat back in my chair no longer certain what to do.

"It doesn't matter," I said flatly. "I just know. I'm not asking you to come anyway. You and Drake did your part with the Dark Lord. No one can ask for more."

I took up my tankard and looked across its rim at her. For the first time I saw confusion and doubt in her eyes. I knew in an instant that by not trying to persuade her I had finally done something unexpected, and that without meaning to, I had said precisely what I needed to say to convince her to join me. Oddly, in that same moment I decided that I didn't want her to come.

"Don't . . ." I started to say, but before I could get the words out she responded quietly, "Yes. I will help you in your quest against the Dark Queen, Wizard Avery." I could hear the surprise in her voice at what she was saying. Without a doubt the spell was active, and it had beaten both of us.

I closed my eyes and bowed my head. And that was that, the most anticlimactic beginning to a quest ever.

We sat in silence, staring at each other across the table for few minutes, during which time Drake began snoring. Eventually she said, "Now what?"

This was funny, because it was exactly what I was going to ask her. Fortunately, I had enough sense not to admit to that. Instead, I said, "Well, we have two of the original members of the group that went up against the Dark Lord. Before Drake passed—" her eyes narrowed threateningly and I amended "—fell asleep, I was asking him what he thought our chances were of tracking down the others? What do you think?"

"Not good," she said grimly, and signaled to the barkeep for another round. "Possibly you could find the Weasel. I've heard she's been floating around some of the larger cities making a general menace of herself."

"I always wondered if the Weasel was a woman," I murmured, trying to recall what she looked like during the final battle.

"Oh," Valdara said, picking up a new mug. "I can't say for sure that the Weasel was a woman, but I always assumed so. She's far too clever to be a man." She gave me a wink and I rolled my eyes in reply. "Anyway, the rumor is that she stole something from the Dark Queen and has gone into hiding, which means you'd only find her if she wanted to be found, and she won't."

I wanted to know what the Weasel might have taken in the worst way, but that was nothing more than curiosity. It wasn't what I was here to get, because if Vivian had lost the reality key her empire would have already begun to crumble. Besides, Valdara was right, hunting for a legendary rogue who didn't want to be found wasn't likely to be the best use of our time.

"What about the others?" I asked

"No chance. Mystia's in no condition, and Jarl and Feldane might as well be dead."

"What do mean in no condition?" In answer, she made a sweeping gesture over her midsection. "What, she got fat?"

"She's with child," she said with a glower.

"Oooooh, right," I said, and then stammered, "How did that . . . I mean, of course she can't." I stopped myself before I could do any more damage and changed the subject. "So, Jarl really is . . ." I began, before realizing that I had blundered into another sensitive topic.

"Mad?" she offered. "Yes. Jarl was never the most

stable of dwarfs, but the rise of the Dark Queen and our inability to defeat her according to prophesy pushed him over the edge. He disappeared underground and hasn't been seen since. I take it you've heard about the egg thing?"

I nodded. "I can understand that Jarl may be too far gone . . ."

"That's putting it mildly," she said, and drained the last dregs from her mug.

"Okay, but what about Feldane?" I pressed. "All Drake—"

"That's St. Drake to you," she corrected.

I glanced at the passed-out man and then back at her. "St. Drake. All he said was that Feldane had gone west. Surely we could track him down."

The next round arrived and Valdara took a long drink before shaking her head in response. "You don't understand. He didn't just go west. He went into The West. It's a retirement community for elves. You have to be over four hundred just to get through the gates."

"Oh, come on, surely it can't be that hard to break into a gated community," I argued. "After all, you stormed the Fortress of Despair."

Valdara shrugged. "You can try if you'd like, but I'd rather face the Dark Queen."

That must be one hell of a homeowner's association, I thought. "All right," I conceded, "so we need to gather a few additional members, and presently Jarl, Feldane, Mystia, and the Weasel are out. How did you put your group together last time?"

"What do you mean?" she asked.

"You know, how did the five of you—"

"Nine of us," she corrected.

"Nine, really?"

She nodded and I reminded myself that I needed to review the early years of my time as the Dark Lord to see what the Heroes were doing, and what happened to all the extra members.

"Who was in your original group?" I asked, and patted my pockets looking for my notebook and pencil, and then grunted in disgust when I remembered that Vivian had them.

Valdara thought for a minute and said, "Well, at first it was just St. Drake and myself. We met in . . ." She trailed off.

"A bar obviously," I said.

"Why 'obviously'?" she asked, and her eyes grew sharp. "St. Drake was not always a drinker. He has had a very hard life."

I held up my hands in a gesture of peace. "That's not what I meant," I said truthfully, and then added a white lie to forestall any other awkward questions. "I think St. Drake may have mentioned it."

The truth was that I had simply assumed that the corrective matrix spell would repeat its original pattern, and so fully expected our adventure, including the gathering together of the group, to mirror, at least in general contours, her earlier experiences. I told her none of this, instead asking quickly, "Who was next?"

She thought for a moment. "Let's see, next there

were the dwarfs. There were two of them originally, Karl and Jarl."

I made a note and asked, "How did you find them?"

"Oh, that was easy," she answered. "Anywhere there's drink, there's a dwarf. We found them in the first tavern we stopped in." She stood and began surveying the room. After only a few seconds she grabbed at my sleeve and pulled me to my feet. "There," she said, pointing across the room at what looked to be a bright orange bird's nest surrounded by a cloud of smoke and obscured behind a hand of cards and piles of coins.

"So, how do we get his attention?" I asked, certain he wouldn't be too pleased to be interrupted, especially since he seemed to be winning.

"Last time I promised them riches and glory," she said frankly.

"Sounds like a plan to me," I said, rubbing my hands together. "Let's go try it out on him."

With a glare, she said, "Given how things turned out I'd prefer not to lie this time."

"How did things turn out?" I asked. "Didn't the Dark Lord have vaults full of riches?"

I knew for a fact he did, since I'd filled them myself, or rather the magic of the reality key did. Limitless riches are not that hard to come by when you have an item that can literally transform air into gold.

"Sure, we found piles of the stuff," she said, and threw her arms wide, sloshing some of her ale onto the floor. "Some of the mounds were tall enough that

Jarl was able to toboggan down them. But the next morning everything had turned to dust."

"That . . . that must have been awkward," I stuttered, suddenly remembering that I had designed the fortress and all the treasure to dissolve after I'd left.

"Awkward!" she shouted, and thumped her mug onto the table. "The army nearly rioted. Honestly, that was the beginning of all the bad things that have happened since. The Dark Queen still uses the story as recruitment propaganda for her new army."

I stared guiltily at the floor. There had been a good reason. I remember doing some economic simulations back in Mysterium that indicated that the release of the Dark Lord's treasury into society all at once might trigger hyperinflation. I hadn't considered the possibility that the Heroes might have been relying on that gold to pay their soldiers.

"This time," she said, throwing back her shoulders, "I'm going to get them to come because it's the right thing to do!"

"Whatever you think is best," I said with a pessimistic shrug. I sat down and took up my tankard.

I watched as Valdara stood, straightened her weapons, and smoothed her cloak. Moments ago she had been rightly suspicious of me. Now she was proposing to actively shill on my behalf. I suspected she was being influenced by my reality matrix spell, and I suppose I should have been fascinated at the opportunity to observe it in action, but in truth I found it unsettling.

"Right. Here we go," Valdara said, thankfully interrupting my chain of thought.

With an ease of grace that was breathtaking, she stepped from floor to chair to table so that she stood with her back to me looking out over the long room of the tavern. Once in place, she pushed back her hood, releasing her red hair from its confinement so that it blazed about her shoulders. Then, unbuckling a jeweled clasp at her throat, she threw her cloak aside with a swirl.

I leaned back to gaze up at her and found that I could barely breathe. She was a vision. From the ground up (which was the way my eyes traveled), she was wearing a pair of calf-hugging boots that laced from toe to midthigh and into which were thrust a set of silver-handled daggers. Above those was a pair of leathers followed by more leather armor covered in metal rings that hugged her body. On her back was a sword that was long enough for me to wonder how in the world she ever sat down. My only thought at the time (and, truth be told, I doubt I was thinking at all in the moment) was that if this is how she'd approached recruiting last time I couldn't believe that she'd only gotten nine volunteers.

The effect of her revelation on the rest of the bar was equally impressive, as a shout of "VALDARA!" rang out from the crowd.

She held up her hands for quiet and the silence that followed was nearly religious. It was only spoiled when my chair slipped from beneath me and I clattered to the floor in a tangle of limbs and a shower of ale.

Valdara looked down at me, rolled her eyes in disgust, and turned back to the crowd. "Gentlefolk of Blightsbury," she began grandly, "a great wizard has come to our land."

She gestured in my general direction, but I'm certain nobody bothered to look, which was a good thing, because at that moment I was still trying to extricate myself from beneath my chair.

"He seeks adventurers, for a quest!"

I finally got myself free and looked out at the crowd from beneath the table. I knew immediately that we had them. Every eye was on her, and in every eye you could see the desire to follow wherever she led. Unfortunately, it was at this moment that Drake woke up.

He swayed to his feet and shouted, "Where they will face terrible danger and excruciating agony . . ." I watched in dismay as eyes widened and faces paled at this pronouncement. ". . . deadly enemies will pursue them at every turn . . ."

Valdara turned to me and drew a finger across her throat. I got the message. Reaching up, I yanked the unsteady man down to the ground beside me. She turned back to the crowd and continued. "Yes, we will face enemies, but with the might of the wizard's great power, the holy hand of St. Drake, and my sword, we will drive the evil from the land and all who join us shall know that they saved Trelari and its people!"

Beneath the table, Drake and I were locked in a

desperate, albeit ridiculous, wrestling match. He was surprisingly strong and slippery for a man as ale-soaked as he smelled. Despite my best efforts, he managed to break my hold and shout, "Yes, their names shall be engraved for all time on the tombstones of the land as the worms devour their flesh and their bones turn to ash and—"

He finally shut up when I bashed him on the side of the head with my fallen tankard. However, as I climbed out from beneath the table, I saw that Drake's words had done their damage. The crowd was grumbling and casting suspicious glances our direction.

Valdara's shoulders drooped. She sighed and said in a near monotone, "And, of course, there will be riches, treasure, and glory beyond measure."

A great cheer arose from the majority of the less reputable-looking people in the tavern, but the light had gone out of Valdara. She climbed off the table, donned her heavy gray cloak, and, seizing several bottles of wine from a nearby table, settled herself into a dark booth in the far corner of the room and began to drink.

There was no longer any doubt in my mind that we had been successfully inserted into my stabilization spell's matrix. The proof was in Valdara's failed attempt to alter her previous pattern. Things were going exactly to plan, and I felt awful about it.

CHAPTER 9

HEROES EVERYWHERE

I pulled the now profoundly unconscious Drake out from under the table and propped him up in a chair. I was crouched next to him applying a wet rag to his head where a lump was forming, and trying to convince myself that the ends justified the means, when I realized that I was not alone.

Two dwarfs stood a few feet away, their noses just level with the top of the table. I rose up on my heels and peered at them. Based on my fairly limited experience they looked like standard issue dwarfs. They were both stocky and solidly built; each wore an axe on his belt, had a bottle of beer in his hand, and was staring at me with a glower in his eye. But there the similarities ended.

To start with, while they both wore plaid kilts, the patterns were of such clashing design that it was difficult to look at them at the same time without getting dizzy. And then there were their faces. The first dwarf looked a bit like a bearded snowman. His coal-black eyes, long crooked nose, and tangled beard were all arranged rather haphazardly on a head that was remarkably round and entirely bald. The second dwarf was squarer in the jaw and had washed-out gray eyes bracketed by a great mass of bright orange curly hair and a short-cropped beard of matching color.

The dwarfs both looked at me expectantly. "Can I help you?" I asked.

They bristled their brows and the bald-headed one said, "You asked for adventurers? Seamus Silversmith at your service." He bowed.

The orange-haired one glowered briefly at his fellow dwarf and then also bowed, saying, "Fergus Goldsmith at your service," in a wheezing voice that bespoke either a life of smoking, or a few years spent as the lead singer of a death metal band.

"Ah, yes." I wasn't sure exactly what I was supposed to do. I knew I needed a dwarf, but two seemed excessive. I held up a finger. "One second."

I stepped over to the booth where Valdara was sitting. She was already halfway through the first bottle of wine and her green eyes were a little fuzzy. She looked at me lazily and slurred, "Yes?"

"There are two dwarfs that want to join us."

"Told you," she replied bitterly, and took another drink from her bottle.

"Yes," I agreed, "you did. But we only need one."

"You only want one?" The thought seemed to perk her up a little bit. "That'll be interesting."

To someone else this might have seemed a non sequitur, but I recognized it as the opening shots in Valdara's next battle with my stabilization spell.

"Well, what do I do?" I asked, trying to get us back to the point.

"Let them settle it."

"I don't want a brawl or anything."

She took another drink and shrugged.

Realizing I wasn't going to get anything else from her, I wandered back to the waiting dwarfs. They both crossed their arms over their chests and said, "Well?"

"We only need one dwarf. You'll have to decide the matter between you."

The dwarfs looked at each other and then back at me. The orange-haired dwarf, who had called himself Fergus, spoke first. "If that's the way it has to be, then that's the way it has to be."

Seamus, the bald-headed dwarf, rolled up his sleeves and nodded. "We'll settle this the old-fashioned way. Prepare for the thrashing of a lifetime."

"Right," Fergus said with a drawn-out rasp.

Seamus sneered and assumed a fighting stance, but as it seemed some form of dwarven violence was about to break out, Fergus asked, "What are you doin'? I thought you said that you wanted to settle this the 'old-fashioned' way." He began to unfold a piece of sheepskin that he'd pulled from a pouch at his side. It was a playing board with sixty-four white and black squares painted on it. He slammed it down on the table and announced, "You're about to find out how I earned the name . . . Rook."

"Rook?" both Seamus and I said at the same time.

"Yep. Call me Rook," said Fergus as he wiped the back of his neck with a handkerchief.

For a moment I thought I saw my own bewilderment mirrored in Seamus's face, but in a twinkling it transformed into a malevolent stare. "Fine, if that's the way you want to play it. I'm white."

"Let's do this," Fergus growled.

I watched, mouth open, as the two dwarfs sat down and started setting up chess pieces. "Wait, what's happening?"

The dwarfs glared up at me without a word and then turned their attention back to the board. I spun about in confusion, trying to make sure this wasn't some bizarre practical joke, and found that a crowd was beginning to gather around us and that a deep silence had fallen over the bar.

I returned to Valdara's side. "Are you seeing this? Is this normal?"

She looked up blearily from between her bottles. "Does it matter? Does it make any less sense than St. Drake being drunk after spending half his life sober, or the Dark Lord being vanquished by a bit of cut glass, or recruiting people to fight the Dark Queen in a bar?"

It didn't, but a philosophical discussion with someone on the verge of blacking out wasn't going to get me anywhere. I shoved my way back through the crowd to the table, took one look at the determined faces of the dwarfs, and resigned myself to watching. I sat down and began drinking seriously.

Forty minutes of silent tension followed as the dwarfs raised eyebrows, huffed, and slammed pieces smugly onto squares. "Check!" shouted Seamus.

Fergus swallowed and studied the board from beneath bushy eyebrows. With a shaking hand he reached out and made his move.

Even though it is the "national" sport of Mysterium, I've never been particularly interested in or good at chess. I assumed that the game was nearly over when Seamus yelled "check." Tragically, I was wrong. It was at least another half hour, and I had fallen asleep, when a collective gasp from the watching crowd startled me awake. I looked at the board. There were fewer pieces, but beyond that it was nothing more than a scramble of black and white to me. However, the mood of the players had shifted dramatically. Seamus was staring at the board with a desperate look on his face.

"You know it's inevitable, laddie," Fergus said with a hoarse cough. "Ten moves."

Seamus was sweating, literally—a sheen of perspiration clung to the top of his head, making it shine.

After another couple of moves Fergus shouted, "Three!"

Seamus looked sick, but he continued to play. The people around the table were murmuring and pointing. Even I found myself caught up in the moment, though I had no idea what I was watching, or why. After moving what I thought was his king behind what I knew was his knight, Seamus slumped in his seat with a look of utter defeat on his face.

"Checkmate!" shouted Fergus, leaping to his feet. He wagged a finger beneath Seamus's nose. "You've been rooked!"

The crowd roared with approval. With a shaking hand, Seamus tipped his king over.

At once the tension between them melted away. They shook hands and then both turned to stare at me. Given the length of the game I had completely forgotten what we were doing. With a start I realized that we'd found our dwarf.

"Right," I said, holding out my hand. "Welcome to the group, Fergus."

"Hold up there, Sonny Jim," Fergus said with a raised finger, "what about Seamus?"

"What about Seamus?" I asked, genuinely perplexed.

Fergus laughed. "You can't go on an adventure with only one dwarf."

I looked over at Valdara; she was smirking at me as

she uncorked her second bottle of wine. Between her and Drake, I was beginning to think that our group might have a bit of a drinking problem.

I turned back to Fergus. "Am I hearing this right? You want Seamus to join the group also?"

"It ain't about what I 'want,' chief, it's about what's right," replied Fergus.

"And his name is Rook!" Seamus added emphatically.

I slapped my hand against my forehead. "A moment ago you were at each other's throats . . ." I paused and then amended, "At least as far as you can be while playing chess, and now you want to work together?"

They both nodded.

"Well, what was the point of all that?" I asked, gesturing at the remains of the chess table. They shared a looked between themselves and then turned back to me quizzically. "Never mind," I said. "Anyway, I don't have time for the explanation. I have to put an adventuring group together, and if we have to go through something like this with every member it'll take forever." I slumped down in my chair.

Fergus, or Rook as he was calling himself now, gave me a strange one-eyed leer and laughed. "You must be tired tonight," he said, still chuckling. I started to ask what that meant, but he waved me back to silence. "Don't worry about it, laddie. Seamus and I can handle this."

He wrapped his arm around Seamus and the two dwarfs bent their heads together in whispered conversation. When they were finished they rose and let loose two earsplitting whistles. The room grew quiet, and as if on cue, a band somewhere in the tavern that I could not see or recall having seen struck up their first notes. The two dwarfs stood in front of my table waving their arms. Then, to the rhythm of the fife and fiddle in the background, Rook sang out in a deep raspy bass voice, "Now, lads and lassies . . ."

"Elfs or elves," supplied Seamus in a baritone that seemed to surprise even him.

"Orcs or orcishes," countered Rook.

"Basically, anyone but a dwarf," I groused behind them, and then put a hand over my mouth as I realized that I'd had sung that aside in a tenor that harmonized suspiciously well with Rook and Seamus. Events were carrying me away with them just like they were everyone around me. A terrifying thought struck me: perhaps the spell was affecting me also. As a Mysterian it shouldn't be possible, but then I shouldn't have been able to sing a middle C either.

Fortunately, I didn't have much time for self-reflection. The dwarfs shot me matching evil looks, but otherwise didn't break the rhythm of their song.

"The great wizard . . ." Seamus sang, and looked meaningfully at Rook.

Rook started to sing something in reply, but then his eyes widened and he shrugged.

They both looked at me as though waiting for something. I ignored them. If this was the spell, I was determined not to be used by my own creation.

Rook leaned over the table and whispered, "Unless

you want me and Seamus to come up with one for you, laddie, I'd advise you to go ahead and tell us your name."

The threat of having the dwarfs give me a name, and the likelihood that it would rhyme, broke my resistance. "Avery."

Rook's forehead crunched together, but after a short consultation with Seamus, he said, "We can make this work."

The invisible fife player bridged back into the main melody and Rook sang again. "Avery, a wizard of great fame."

"Who goes by Avery lest his enemies discover his true name," Seamus quavered.

"Will now take petitions from those gathered here," Rook boomed.

"And who have traveled from both far and near," Seamus crooned.

"To join his dauntless fighting crew, and surely find riches and renown ere they are through," they sang in perfect harmony.

It was as though a mass charm had been cast over the tavern. One figure after another approached the table until they blurred together. Though I have studied my notes on the events over and over again, I can only remember a fraction of them. The reality is that the number of unexplained things happening were multiplying alarmingly, and I was distracted by the sudden realization that I was going to have a harder time controlling the direction of my spell and ensuring my own safety than I had originally assumed. I really needed to talk to Eldrin. Fortunately or not, Rook and Seamus had assumed the rolls of double-headed (and bearded) gatekeepers to my quest.

The first applicant I can remember was an enormous—both in height and breadth—man. He had so many muscles, and they were so corded and ripped, that his whole body seemed to be in a constant fight with itself.

"Me orc-blood. Me smash puny Dark Queen!" he bellowed.

Personally, I liked his enthusiasm, but Rook whispered, "Possible anger management issues."

"Next!" shouted Seamus.

A skinny, clean-shaven fellow in a billowing robe of impossible color stepped forward. "I am a great and powerful mage. There's nothing up my sleeves but this rabbit, which I should not have shown you and who is now trying to get loose . . ."

Rook cleared his throat and shook his head.

"Next!" came Seamus's call.

"Son, in my day, we fought three and four dragons at a time, blindfolded in the snow," said a man so ancient that his body had bent almost double so that he was addressing the floor the whole time.

"Next!" shouted Seamus before Rook could even say anything.

"My name's Sam," said an unassuming little fellow with an enormous pack on his back.

"Excellent name! Sign here," said Rook for reasons I'm not sure I understand to this day.

"Next!" shouted Seamus, cutting off my ruminations on what criteria Rook might be using—logic and consistency clearly not being involved.

An elven woman approached the table. She was wearing a robe and carrying a staff. Around her waist were belted a half-dozen knives and over her back a bow was strung. I perked up. We needed an elf. Seeing the suspicious looks Rook and Seamus were giving her, I decided to intercede. I couldn't afford for them to pass her over or, gods forbid, challenge her to a chess match.

"I see you have a bow," I said brightly. "Are you an archer?"

"I'm an elven archer sorceress rogue, but I'm not fully committed to that. Lately I've been thinking about becoming a druidess pathfinder," she said.

Having known a lot of students that could never commit to a major long enough to get past the intro-level classes, I was suspicious, but Rook gave the thumbs-up. "Good enough for us, lassie!" In an aside he whispered, "With a background like that we can fill all the eleven spots with one recruit, and then we won't have too many of them prancin' about and makin' snotty comments about how they live forever and don't need to sleep and can run all day and so on. Elves can be so aggravatin'."

Seamus was already shouting, "Next!"

So much for taking control. In fact, trying to follow what was happening was getting harder and harder. The music kept speeding up and so did the candidates. I remember little except that there were a lot of warriors and mages that had once been something else.

There was a fellow named Arthur who had been a servant of some sort until he found a stone sword in a lake. His story was compelling, but after some discussion he was rejected.

"We don't need stone-challenged swords," said Rook. "Next!"

There was a guy who had grown up working in a kitchen on a farm until he discovered that his aunt was a great sorceress. The dwarfs weren't impressed.

"If your aunt was here that would be one thing, as it is we aren't interested," said Rook.

"Next!"

An ex-blacksmith's apprentice showed enormous potential, and we'd almost agreed to let him join, but he kept going on and on and on and on about a wheel that kept turning, and ages that kept coming, and so forth.

"Next!" both of the dwarfs shouted.

A goatherd turned magician was rejected because, in Rook's words, "The smell alone will drive you mad."

It seemed like a fair point.

"Next!" shouted Seamus.

And so it went. After a couple of hours my head was spinning. "No more. We have enough people," I finally said, though I had no earthly idea exactly how many people had joined.

Rook, as I had resigned myself to calling him, cleared his throat. "So, Wizard Avery, who really needs to work on his name, now that you have a group, we need to know where you're takin' us?"

Great question. I looked over to see if Valdara was still about so I could ask her, but she was gone—probably already in bed. I had to admit, I was exhausted. I yawned. Rook and Seamus waited patiently for an answer. I hadn't the courage to tell them that there wasn't going to be one.

We stared at each other for a time and then Seamus said, "We hope you understand that normally we would have demanded a briefing with detailed maps and contracts before taking on a job like this, but with Valdara behind you we decided to give you the benefit of the doubt. Still, if we are going to provision a party as large as this one we will need to have some idea about where we're going and how long it'll take."

"How large is the group?" I asked, suddenly worried that I had missed more than I suspected.

"Eight, ten, twenty," Rook said with a shrug. "The specifics don't matter, laddie," he answered with an impressive bristling of his brow.

"I think they do," I said sternly.

"What do we do tomorrow?" he asked, ignoring the implied question and my glare.

"Yes, well, tomorrow at first light we are off on our quest," I answered vaguely.

"Yes," he pressed, "but where exactly are we goin'?"

"We are off to defeat the Dark Queen."

"Yes," agreed Seamus, "but what exactly will that entail? Where will we go to do that?"

"I will tell you in the morning," I said, and stood up so I could loom over them.

Not surprisingly, the dwarfs were used to people looming and just shifted their gazes up a few notches and kept waiting.

"In the morning!" I said gruffly.

They walked away muttering.

I understood their frustration; the problem was that I had no idea what we were supposed to do next. I knew we couldn't march off and face Vivian straightaway, and even if we tried we wouldn't reach her, because that's not the way the spell worked. It required time and the occurrence of specific events to build up its energy. We would need to quest, find treasure (perhaps an enchanted item or two), gain allies, have members of the party die (it seemed a certainty that at least one of the dwarfs wouldn't make it), and so on.

I couldn't tell them that. I couldn't tell them that, on some level, the most important decision—the only decision—had already been made: we had all resolved to go after the Dark Queen. From here on the weave of the spell would be our guide. It would encourage us when we chose to follow its path, and it would try and thwart every attempt to diverge from its plan. Nor would we be alone in our quest against the Dark Queen. There would be other groups. The spell would use all of us, building and tightening the strength of its weave as we progressed. It would discard those that fell behind, and push those that succeeded forward. All my spell cared about was getting to the end game with the tools it felt gave it the highest probability to destroy the threat to Trelari. It had no conscience, because its creator had not been worried about the what and the when.

Drake was the perfect reflection of the paradox my spell presented. How much of his current condition was the result of all the pushing and pulling it had done to him over the years? Perhaps Drake's excessive drinking was his attempt to rebel against a force that as a spiritually attuned being he could feel and hate, but not resist. If so, then my pulling him back into the spell's path was a horrible cruelty. But there was another possibility that was even more terrible. What if the spell was trying to push him out of its weave, to discard him like you would a tool that has lost its edge? In that case, coming on the quest was his only hope. The problem was it was impossible to know what was right. That was the sinister elegance of my spell.

Guilt found its way into my heart and squatted there. I tried to fight it as I always had. I told myself that if I had done nothing, if I did nothing now, Trelari would eventually be reduced to nothing more than random shards of etherspace rubble. On the other hand, the suffering of people like Drake and Valadar would be over. Which was the greater good, and which the greater evil? It was moments like this that the magi warned against: paralysis by compassion. The thing to do was to make a decision based on the facts available and act. But, not tonight.

I rubbed my tired eyes and started up the stairs, but stopped. Drake was still perched in his chair snoring. The way his neck was bent at such an odd angle looked terribly uncomfortable. I made a decision. I came back down the stairs and lifted him in my arms. He seemed a little heavier than he had before, but the burden was not too great.

I carried him up to the second floor and deposited him in one of the rooms that had been set aside for us. Then made my way down the hall to my own room. It was small and smelled of alcohol. I didn't mind. It reminded me a bit of my dorm room, except the door worked and the walls were solid. I threw myself onto the thin and vile-smelling straw mattress and felt a terrible fatigue wash over me.

"Tomorrow I will know what to do," I said to myself as I fell asleep.

CHAPTER 10

AN UNEXPECTED PARTY

The dream was a good one, but like all good dreams my memory of it disappeared the moment I woke up. I'm pretty sure it had something to do with Vivianor a really excellent club sandwich. I have a thing for club sandwiches. The point was it had been good, and Eldrin ruined it.

"Avery? Are you there?" he asked as though he'd been asking for some time.

I was instantly awake (at least from my perspective) and instantly regretted it. I may not have drunk as much as Drake or Valdara or the dwarfs or anyone else at the Boiled Badger the night before, but the pain in my head and the dryness of my mouth were telling me that I had drunk quite enough. Adding to these miseries was a general queasiness that told me it was far too early to be awake. I flicked back the curtain and looked outside. It was still dark.

I would have cursed, but Eldrin said, "I think he's asleep."

His voice had a sort of echoing quality that made me think he was talking to someone else. This was disturbing given the whole "secret" nature of my mission, and was instantly confirmed when I heard a muffled voice say something indistinguishable in the background.

"How should I know that?" Eldrin replied irritably to whoever he was talking to.

The background voice said something sharp in response.

"Well, that's your opinion," Eldrin grumped.

I felt like it was time for me to enter the conversational fray, if for no other reason than to tell Eldrin that I was still asleep. "Eldrin, do you know what time it is?" I asked.

"No, I don't!" he shouted. "As I was explaining to Dawn, calculating the actual time of day in a subworld is exceedingly tricky."

Dawn was with him? I sat up with a start.

He continued to rant. "There aren't more than three mages in Mysterium that could do it. That I happen to be one of them is beside the point. The information you get simply doesn't justify the effort involved . . ."

Dawn knew what was happening?

". . . You spend two days setting up the equations," he babbled on, "and another day sitting in the basement of the Quantum Magicks building, which is always freezing by the way, running the equation through the Hyperdimensional Aperiodic Logistan, and what do you get? A single temporally aligned chronological time for a subworld that may or may not exist in a week or so."

Who was Dawn? Why did I have the feeling that I should know her name?

My earlier fogginess was gone, replaced by the unnerving sense that something else must have gone horribly wrong. "If you are quite finished," I said, cutting short his diatribe on the increasingly irrelevant question of what time it was.

"Yes," he answered.

I took a breath to keep the rising panic I was feeling out of my voice, and said, "So we are not alone, by which I mean you are not alone, by which I mean whatever happened to keeping my little problem between the two of us?"

"I told you he wouldn't be happy," he said in response, but not to me. "No, I will not explain. You explain."

I started to beg him not to do what I thought he was doing, but it was too late. "Fine, but you're being a baby," a woman's voice said, but again not to me.

"Dawn, who are you?"

"Vivian's friend from the bar," she said.

I may have had a heart attack or a stroke or something right then, because the next minute or so was a breathless blur of roaring noise and head-spinning, stomach-lurching nausea. If she said anything to me I didn't hear it and have no memory of it to this day. When I recovered, I gasped, "Why?"

"Why, what?"

"I don't know, Dawn," I said, unable to conceal my bitterness. "Why are you in my room? Why are you talking to me? What could have possessed Eldrin to tell you what's been happening? While we're at it, why did Vivian steal my work? Why is she trying to ruin my life? Did you know she was going to do either or both? Did you help her? In short, why?"

"I am here because Eldrin was of the belief that I had nothing to do with whatever Vivian is doing, and rightly guessed that when she never came back from her 'date' with you that I would go to Mysterium security, report her disappearance, and have them track you down as a deviant maniac, which I was on the verge of doing when he knocked on my door begging me to help his friend, who he swore was a good guy even if he had done something hideously irresponsible that had put his and Vivian's lives, and possibly an entire subworld's existence, at risk."

She stopped to take a breath, and I heard Eldrin mumble something to her. She sighed dramatically and added, "Oh, and he hoped Vivian might have given me something of yours to keep, which she hadn't. That's why."

I felt that sinking feeling in the pit of my stomach

again, the one that told me something I'd done had come back to haunt me. But before I could grapple with that, I first had to take my foot out of my mouth. "I'm sorry, Dawn. I shouldn't have said that. I am pretty stressed. I trust Eldrin, and I'm grateful for whatever help he and you are willing to give me." I took a deep breath and then asked the question I was dreading. "Did Eldrin happen to mention what sort of something he was looking for?"

"No," she said sharply. "But he did tell me that it would probably be something very magical that you swore in your DMG that you never made, and the very existence of which has been warping the fabric of reality between Mysterium and your subworld. Ring any bells?"

"Can I talk to Eldrin again?"

"Certainly."

Eldrin's voice returned. "Avery, did you, by any chance, accidentally or, well, could you have, at least hypothetically . . ."

"Just ask him!" Dawn shouted in the background.

"I was," he whined, and then asked quickly, "Avery, did you happen to use a kernel of Mysterium reality in forming the matrix pattern for your subworld stabilization spell? And then did you bring it to Mysterium with you when you returned?"

Here is what I should have said: "Yes, Eldrin, I did. Was this a violation of Mysterium rules and scientific ethics? Yes, it was. Does the fact that I did this possibly invalidate everything I've worked on for the past five years? Yes, it might. In my defense, I worked for two years trying to form a reality matrix stabilizing spell purely out of subworld essence. Every time I would create what I thought was a stable spell pattern the essence would melt away, almost like it was being consumed by something. As far as I can tell it's impossible, and it was driving me mad. So, I cheated. I took something utterly insignificant, a single fork from the university cafeteria, which in my opinion was lucky to escape the food they served there. I carried the implement to the subworld and used it to forge the battle-axe, Death Slasher. I then used the battle-axe as the kernel of my spell. Finding it was what identified Morgarr to me as the focus of evil in Trelari, and the battle-axe convinced Morgarr to summon, well, me. It was and still is my belief that there should be no need for the battle-axe to exist now that the matrix pattern of my spell is in place and stable. Proving that was going to be my life's work."

What I actually said was, "Well . . ."

That was as far as I got before Eldrin shouted, "Dammit, Avery! How could you? It violates every Mysterium rule, not to mention scientific ethics, and throws into question the validity of your entire research project."

I knew a drawn out "well" would convey everything I needed to say. "Yes, I know," I replied. "But assuming I already know what a fraud I am, can you tell me why it matters?"

"Why it matters? Why it matters!" he exploded.

"Did you sleep through your entire Quantum Magical Mechanics course?"

"Yes," I answered truthfully.

"You've entangled Mysterium reality with the reality of the subworld."

"And that's bad because . . . ?"

"Do you remember your Mysterium history?" he asked.

"Better than you do," I said tartly. "You made me write all your essays."

He didn't take the bait, instead asking, "How did the innerworlds come to be?"

"Can you just tell me what I've done?" I asked, both fearing the answer and having grown tired of him being professorial.

"How?" he repeated.

"Fine, if you are going to insist," I said, and then began reciting in a fast-paced monotone. "The original race of Mysterium, for reasons still unknown and unfathomable, sent thirteen mages to the nearest subworlds and hid in each a crystal orb that was one of a pair, the second of which, if you believe the story, is kept in the central tower of the university. The orbs created a link—"

"The Palantir Effect," Eldrin corrected.

". . . between Mysterium and . . ."

I trailed off, finally realizing where Eldrin was going with this. The hair on the back of my neck stood on end as he finished my incomplete narrative. "And the link drew the subworlds inward until they stood at the borders of Mysterium. Do you remember last time we talked and I told you that I didn't know why time skipped during your first transport?" he asked.

"Couldn't forget that if I wanted to," I answered. "Just the fact that you didn't know something nearly scared me half to death."

"Well, let me finish the job," he said acidly. "I've spent the last several hours in the subworld observatory and your subworld has shifted its orbital position around Mysterium."

I was silent as my brain tried to make the words I'd heard mean something else.

"Avery? Are you still there?"

"That's impossible." It seemed like I'd been saying that a lot the last few days.

"Nevertheless," he said calmly. "Subworld 2A7C has moved closer to Mysterium by about twelve parsecs."

Any shift in the location of a subworld would be unprecedented, but because I didn't want to acknowledge that, I found myself asking, "Is that a lot?"

"Yes," he said, the lack of any further explanation confirming the stupidity of the question. "What is more, 2A7C is spiraling in toward Mysterium. If my calculations are correct, and we know they are, at this rate your subworld will be parked at the gates of the university itself in seven to ten days."

"And all this because of a stupid battle-axe?" I asked, and stopped myself from adding that it was impossible, because I was definitely overusing the word at this point.

"Yes . . ." he began, and then said excitedly, "Wait, your kernel is Death Slasher? Morgarr's battle-axe? Man, I have to up the stats on that item in my simulation."

"Oh my God, shut up about that stupid game!" I heard Dawn shout in the background. I couldn't have agreed more.

"Can we get back to the point?" I asked as calmly as I could. "You were going to explain how the . . ." *Damn!* ". . . the impossible could be happening."

"Because it's not impossible," Eldrin said. "It's amazing, it's incredible, but it's not impossible. You had the power of an entire subworld at your command when you created the battle-axe. Now that it's back in Mysterium, it's drawing your subworld to it like a magnet."

"How do you know it's in Mysterium?" I asked, desperately trying to find a hole in his logic.

"I know it's back," he answered, "because your subworld, after a lifetime of happily orbiting at an exceedingly far distance from Mysterium, has suddenly, and otherwise inexplicably, decided to plot a collision course with the place. What's more, the larger portion of this movement happened in two lurches simultaneous with your initial and then second returns to Mysterium, probably corresponding with the transport of Death Slasher from back and forth between the worlds. These sudden movements are also almost certainly the reason that time between 2A7C and Mysterium has been so unpredictable. By the way, did you find out how long Vivian's been on-world?"

"At least five years," I said in a stunned monotone, remembering Drake's surprising revelation. "Why?" I moaned. "Why would Vivian leave it behind?"

The question had been more for myself than Eldrin, but he answered anyway. "Does it matter? Whether she did it on purpose or because she didn't want to carry the thing around, the point is that it's here—somewhere."

He was right, but it was easier to argue about Vivian's motivations than it was to contemplate the consequences of what I'd done. I simply didn't want to believe I could have screwed up this badly or that Quantum Magicks was that important a subject, much less that I had the sort of power necessary to create a new innerworld. Plus, I saw one flaw in Eldrin's theory. "Look, Eldrin, even if I did create something akin to *one* of the Mysterium innerworld crystals, which I'm not granting because I'm not that good, there isn't a second one here in Trelari to complete the chain and trigger the Palantir Effect."

"I never said that *you* created the second item," he answered cagily.

"So, who created it? I hope you're not suggesting that Vivian did, because *that* is impossible," I said firmly. "It took me months of research in Mysterium and years of excruciating work in Trelari to make Death Slasher. Vivian is an acolyte, and her major area of study is divination. There's no way she has that kind of ability."

"That's what makes what's happening so amazing

and incredible," Eldrin said, still geeking out at the coolness of the magic. "If I'm right she didn't have to."

I still had no idea what he was talking about, and had a feeling that at this rate I wouldn't know for several more hours. An idea struck me. "Does Dawn understand what you're talking about?"

"I think so."

"Can you put her on for a second?"

"Okay?" he answered uncertainly.

"Yes," came Dawn's voice after a brief pause.

"Can you explain what Eldrin is talking about?" I asked.

She hesitated and then said, "As I understand it, you rebuilt subworld 2A7C's reality around this battle-axe."

"Sort of," I reluctantly agreed.

"So, when you removed the battle-axe you 'sort of' removed the core of the world's reality."

"I'm not sure if I would go that far," I hedged, but a chill passed through me as I began to spin out the implications.

"Eldrin would," she said dryly.

"But I never intended for the battle-axe to remain in Trelari," I said, and knew I was being defensive. "My plan was to remove it and let the subworld replace it with a new kernel formed from its own reality."

"Good idea, but what if the world had a plan of its own? One you'd already engraved into its pattern using your spell?" she asked.

"Let's say you're right," I said, rubbing my temples

and thinking it through. "Let's say the reality matrix my spell created was somehow robust enough to form a kernel object like Death Slasher of its own accord, which I'm not granting because that sounds crazy. Even if that were true, Death Slasher is a hybrid of subworld and Mysterium reality. To make something like it, the matrix would need some Mysterium reality to work with, which isn't exactly thick on the ground here. Where did the spell get the stuff it needs?"

Before she could respond, the answer hit me. "Oh, gods! Vivian!" I gasped.

Dawn gave me time enough to recover before saying, "We don't know if she knew the full consequences of what she was doing, but Eldrin thinks her presence gave the spell the raw material to make a twin kernel. He says that it would only take a small piece of Mysterium reality—anything really. The spell might even have taken it from her without her noticing."

"The Weasel," I murmured.

"What was that?" she asked.

"Nothing," I said. "Thanks for explaining. I really screwed this up."

"Basically," she agreed.

I deserved that, and I also owed Dawn some reassurance. "I know how little you must trust my judgment right now," I acknowledged, "but I promise that I will do everything I can to bring Vivian out of this safely."

"I know you will," she said, "but don't kid yourself—

she put herself in danger. Vivian is very good at divination, so she either knew what she was doing, or she should have known better."

Dawn meant it to be comforting, but there was another possibility that I was unable to ignore: What if Vivian had intended this all along? I pushed the frightful thought from my mind as she passed me back to Eldrin.

I needed him to believe that I still had full confidence in the plan, because I knew the moment he thought I was wavering he would insist on doing something dramatic and noble and dangerous. When I got back on, I was all business. "Tell me what I need to do."

"You need to find this new battle-axe," he answered, and I heard him flipping pages. "Give me a second."

"Are you looking through that stupid DMG again?" I asked in exasperation.

"Yes, but I've begun to index it. It's actually not bad. There's a lot of great information in here if you can find it. There's a section on artifacts, oddly on the same page as a detailed description of different types of footwear. Anyway, it says that if there is an artifact it will invariably have some strange legend behind it, usually connected with an odd name like Secna or Vaxx or, and I'm not making this up, Snaz-Furb'luu."

"Got it," I said with way more confidence than I felt. "So we go around asking about a weapon . . ."

"A battle-axe," he corrected.

"A battle-axe," I echoed, "that has a weird name."

"Yup," he answered brightly. "In the meantime, Dawn and I will be scouring Mysterium for Death Slasher."

"Sounds good, but how is any of this going to help me find Vivian or get the key back?"

"It won't, but if we don't stop your subworld from careening toward Mysterium soon, other people will begin to notice, and when that happens all hell will break loose. I've taken certain steps to protect your transport circle, but I can't guarantee that my solution, clever as I think it is, will stand up to the combined scrutiny of the faculty. If they erase your circle or, worse, modify it to destabilize your subworld . . ."

"I hadn't thought about that," I said.

"I know," he replied without a hint of conceit.

I didn't respond, because I didn't know how. I wanted him to know how much I appreciated everything he was doing for me, but I don't have that kind of eloquence. At last I took a deep breath and said, "Eldrin, I . . . I just wanted to . . . well, I want to—"

"You know you don't have to say anything," he said in his most musical voice.

"Yes, I do," I insisted.

I started to say something profound that would have embarrassed both of us when there was a knock at the door. I flicked the curtain aside and looked outside again. It was still dark.

Leaning back against the headboard of my bed, I groaned. "Doesn't anyone sleep anymore?"

CHAPTER 11

ANOTHER UNEXPECTED PARTY

"Is that someone at the door?" Eldrin asked.

"Yes, but it doesn't matter," I said, and it didn't, because even though I had a sudden strong urge to be away on my quest, this conversation was way more important to me than anything or anybody that could be standing out in the hall. "Stay on the line. I'll get rid of them."

The knock came again and more urgently. "I heard that," he said with a laugh. "Someone needs you and having me in your ear is never going to work. I won't be able to stop myself from talking, and you won't be able to help yourself responding, and you'll come away looking like a madman."

"No, wait!" I pleaded.

"Goodbye, Avery."

The connection broke with that now familiar pop. It was good that it did, because the next knock, actually a boot, was so ferocious that the door burst open. Rook stood there wearing a toothy smile. He stormed in, slamming the door behind him.

"Laddie, the group's waitin' and daylight's fadin'," he said in his distinctive rasp.

If it had not been for Eldrin's call, I'm not sure how I would have reacted to Rook's waking me up. Probably badly. As it was, I took a moment to close one eye and studied his profile.

It is a well-known phenomenon that the farther a subworld is from Mysterium, the vaguer everything can seem to be. If it was true that Trelari was moving closer to Mysterium, then everything should appear more real, including Rook. Theoretically, I might be able to tell how far the world had moved by how fuzzy he was around the edges. It was probably my pessimistic nature, but his outline looked very sharp this morning. Then again, my only comparison point was last night, which I'd spent in a smoke-filled inn . . . tavern, drinking.

I continued to stare until I realized that he was staring back, mirroring my single-eyed gaze with one of his own. In the end, the only conclusion I came to was that I should never get into a staring contest with a dwarf. Intense doesn't begin to cover it.

I blinked and Rook relaxed. "Interestin' way of looking at the world, laddie," he wheezed. "Clarifies things, don't it."

I had begun to climb out of bed, but his words (hewing so close to my own thoughts) made me misstep, and I tumbled onto the floor. "What?"

He shrugged. "When you're bleary-eyed from drinkin', closin' one of them eliminates half the bleariness."

"Oh," I said, rubbing my head from where I'd bumped it. "Where are Valdara and Drake and—" I realized I remembered no one else's name "—everyone else?"

"They are gatherin' on the outskirts of town for equipment inspection."

"Who told them to do that, and at this hour?" I asked, certain that at least Valdara and Drake would never take orders from anyone, and certainly not Rook.

He shrugged. "No one told them. They all said they *felt* it was time to go. I was standin' out in the street with everyone else when I noticed you were missin'. Didn't you *know* it was time to go?"

I shook my head, but then remembered the sudden urgency I'd felt to leave on my quest *now*. Had I not known, or had I known and not listened? My thoughts from the previous evening about the shifting world, how the spell might work to influence my own behavior, and whether those pulls would always be obvious or easy to resist, came flooding back, and I forgot that Rook was standing there waiting for an answer.

He cleared his throat, snapping me back to the

present. "Well, you're goin' to set a pretty bad example if you don't start gettin' with the program, laddie."

He was more right than he knew. If the matrix spell was going to be guiding the actions and behaviors of those around me, I had to be sure that I was sensitive to the direction it was taking; otherwise I might inadvertently interfere with its course. The weave of the spell's pattern was strong, but not indestructible. I looked back on my behavior last night and winced. Absent Rook's intervention, I might have seriously screwed up the formation of the group.

"You're right, Rook," I agreed in what I hoped was a chastened tone. "Sorry."

"Apology accepted," he said, and added sternly, "You have to have some discipline when you've got a group as large as ours."

"Have you determined how many people are in our group?" I asked, remembering that he was fairly vague on the subject last night.

"Have you determined where we're goin'?" he asked in reply.

"Yes," I said, standing and beginning to get into my clothes. "There is a weapon of great power we need to recover before facing down Viv . . . the Dark Lord."

He rolled his eyes and grunted in disgust. "I think you mean the Dark *Queen*, laddie. It would be wise to get your villains straight when you're talkin' to the others. And why would we be needin' this weapon?"

I blushed at my slip, but counted my blessings

that I'd managed to cover the much larger blunder of knowing the Dark Queen on a first name basis.

"Laddie?"

"We just do!" I snapped. "Now, out of my room. How can I be expected to answer all these questions while I'm getting dressed?"

"Aye," he said hoarsely as he walked out. "I've heard walkin' and chewin' gum is hard for some people also."

Despite Rook's insistence that I was holding everything up, the first rays of dawn were only beginning to filter over the tops of the trees when I made it to the edge of town. I was surprised to see over a dozen people milling about, most of whom I would have sworn never to have met before.

I recognized Valdara and Drake, of course. I saw Rook's companion dwarf, Seamus, busily checking people's horses and packs and shouting exceedingly confusing instructions about encumbrance of pack animals and movement rates. There were a few other nameless faces I vaguely remembered talking to in the tavern, but the rest might as well have been strangers. I looked about for Rook to ask him why there were so many, and where they'd come from, but he was nowhere to be found. Wanting someone to confirm my memory on who we'd hired the night before, I made my way over to Valdara and Drake. They were sitting atop their mounts, watching the chaos with tired expressions.

"What's going on?" I asked.

"Seamus is trying to arrange the equipment," Valdara answered with a yawn. "As usual it's taking forever."

"The ten-foot poles and fifty-foot coils of rope are always devilishly hard to strap onto the horses," Drake growled in voice that sounded like he was still recovering from last night's drink.

Valdara cocked her head to one side and said, "I never noticed before, but everytime I've started a quest everyone feels compelled to bring a ten-foot pole and a fifty-foot length of rope. How much rope can we possibly need, and what use has anyone ever made of a ten-foot pole?"

Drake said something in response, but I missed it because as he was talking the rays of the rising sun caught in Valdara's braid and the red of her hair blazed to life, framing her face and adding a counterpoint to her glittering eyes. She was startlingly beautiful.

Unfortunately, she caught me gawking. I averted my gaze and tried to cover my embarrassment by blurting, "Poles? Ropes? Very strange."

Although it wasn't, at least not to me, because all of this was written into the initial conditions of my spell. There was a table of starting equipment on some page of the DMG, and everything that was happening now was being dictated by its rows and columns. A good sign that we were on track, but disturbing to witness in real life.

At last my brain caught up to my mouth, and I remembered what I had wanted to ask. "Putting the equipment aside, which looks impossible given the sheer volume of it, who are all these people? I thought we would have eight or nine to start with. Is everyone here part of the group?"

"Group?" said a guy in a red tunic who happened to be passing by. "I was told we were a party."

"No, no, we're a fellowship," responded someone else I didn't recognize.

"Fellowship?" said a third unidentifiable someone. "A fellowship would have to have nine members. We're a company."

There was a lot of grumbling and arguing over the correct term to use for the . . . for us. Words like *league*, *order*, *society*, *guild* and *club* were thrown about and discarded. The discord was broken by a sharp whistle. Rook was standing on the back of a wagon, holding up his hands for silence. "It's okay, everyone. We are a fellowship with a few extras."

This was met by an uncomfortable silence that was filled with many covert glances from this person to that one, and from that person to this one, as everyone tried to size up who might be one of the dreaded "extras." I turned to Valdara and Drake with a questioning look. "Are you okay with the idea of taking along 'extras'? Doesn't it seem a bit morbid?"

Valdara smirked at me and said, "It's your party, or should I say fellowship, handsome. That means it's your responsibility to see that all these 'extras' make it to the Dark Queen. This time around, I'm just along for the ride."

Drake nodded in agreement. "If you don't like it I'd talk to Rook, kid. He seems to be in charge, if anyone is."

I wanted to say something about the "kid" and the "handsome," but I had way too many other things to worry about. I left them still watching the scene and approached Rook and Seamus. They were busy handing out equipment and instructing people on how to transfer items between their packs and saddlebags in accordance with a system of weight measurement that I'm sure I had dictated at one point but which I had utterly forgotten.

"Can I talk to you for a moment, Rook?" I asked.

"Of course, laddie," he said, folding up a sheaf of parchment papers he'd been consulting and putting them into his pouch. "Seamus, why don't you finish up here? Make sure everyone's got their tinder boxes and mess kits."

"Sure thing," Seamus responded. "What do I do with the little bag of sand and the small knife?"

"Sam gets those, of course," he answered as though Seamus's reasonable question was idiotic. "It goes with the ink and the paper."

"Right," Seamus said, and took an armful of items over to a skinny fellow in a billowing robe who I suppose might have been the young wizard I'd met the night before.

"Rook," I said with a warning tone in my voice. "Why are there all these extra people? And why are you holding a bell, a loop of string, and a bag full of metal marbles?"

"First," he said, holding up his thumb, "you and I both know that there are terrible dangers ahead. So I've brought on some spares to ensure that the core group survives to the end. For example, over there we have Nigel, Paul, and Cameron, or as I like to call them, our NPC crowd."

I studied the three men; they had on nearly identical outfits, which made them hard to tell apart. "Why are they all wearing the same thing?" I asked. "Did they come as a team? Are they friends?"

Rook shook his head and coughed out, "I put them in those matchin' red tunics, because red don't stain, laddie."

"That's awful," I blurted out, unable to contain my horror at what he was saying, and the matter-of-fact way he was saying it.

"We play the cards we're dealt," he said with a shrug. "We're tryin' to save a world, laddie, and that don't come easy. It'd be best to remember that."

Although cruder in phrasing, it was in essence the same thing Griswald had said to me before I'd left. I knew he meant well and that it was good advice, but I was finding it harder and harder to accept.

"As for the ball bearings," he said, throwing up a second finger, "we have a rogue in the group. Do *you*, of all people, expect a rogue to go out adventurin' without a sack full of ball bearings and a bit of string?"

I started to answer "yes" when I recalled that I had purposefully included a number of bizarre items in the initial starting equipment requirements of my spell as control variables so I could easily recognize my "Heroes" from other random adventurers. The idea was that if I ran across a group that had members with a combination of certain items, I would know that they must be under the influence of the spell—or psychedelics. "No," I said uncertainly as I tried to recall if ball bearings had been one of my controls.

"Certainly not," he said with a wheezing laugh.

I thought about my conversation with Rook earlier about "disrupting the pattern of things." I had to stop obsessing about the details, or I would break the spell's hold over us and then I'd be in real trouble. I didn't have the time to try this all again. This group . . . fellowship was my only chance. I had to get it right on the first go, which meant *not* interfering every time someone did something I didn't understand.

I left the dwarfs to their packing and retreated to my mount. If I was witnessing my reality matrix spell in action, which seemed a reasonable assumption at this point, then if taken with the proper level of detachment, the whole exercise might be quite fascinating. I gazed out over the milling group with an experimentalist's eye looking for patterns. It did not take me long to start seeing them—they were all around.

Some of the patterns were random in their specificity. As Drake had been saying, each of the horses, including my own, was burdened by a long pole, the purpose of which defied understanding.

Some of the patterns were bizarre, like Seamus's

repeated attempts to press packets of incense and a little box with a coin slot in the top on Drake, and Drake's own firm refusal to take them. Ultimately, it fell to Valdara to relieve Seamus of the items and stuff them into her own pack.

Some of the patterns made no sense. Sam, the little fellow in the big robe, was running back and forth between Rook and Seamus asking, "What about my spell book? I need it so I can write down any spells that I learn. I forget them otherwise. I also need a pouch for my components: my pins, my feathers, my glass beads, my bat fur, my . . ." His list went on and on, and when they finally found a pouch for his "components," he seemed satisfied with it even though it couldn't possibly hold everything he'd mentioned.

As I watched, I contemplated the question of free will. How much free will did the other members of my company . . . fellowship, whatever, have? Did they ever ask themselves why they were doing the things they were doing or why the things that were happening to them were happening?

I had come to no conclusion that did not make me feel guilty when Drake asked in a loud voice, "Well, Avery, where do we go first?"

In an instant, dozens of eyes were staring at me. I silently thanked Eldrin, because absent my talk with him I would have had no answer to the question, and I would have just sat there looking dumb. Instead, I rose in my stirrups. "Fellowship members, we begin our quest with a single focus. We must find a weapon of great power that mystic divinations have revealed to me is the one item that can destroy the Dark Queen."

I paused dramatically. It was a pretty good moment. I saw a few of the group members hold their breath. Then I realized I didn't have anything else to say. That was all I knew. I stood there in my stirrups looking dumb, desperately trying to find more words.

"What sort of weapon, laddie?" Rook asked with a tap of his foot. "I'm hangin' on yer every word, but my grip's startin' to slip."

"It . . . it . . ." I tried to remember everything Eldrin had said, and could only remember two things. "It's a battle-axe." I said confidently.

He had better be right about that, I swore to myself.

"The . . . the twin of Death Slasher, Morgarr's dread weapon," I said less confidently, since it probably looked nothing like Morgarr's weapon.

"What is the name of this dread weapon?" someone from the back asked with a shout. He was wearing red so I figured it was okay for me not to know his name.

"Its name?" I asked in response, and then in a flash of inspiration said, "I mean, its name is shrouded in deep mystery. To find the name of the weapon and its resting place we will first have to seek a seer who can probe the mysteries of the far ancient past. A being of such profound wisdom and—"

"Could it be Justice Cleaver?" asked the young man I was pretty sure was named Sam.

"What?" I asked.

"Justice Cleaver," he repeated.

"You know, the ancient weapon of the mythical ranger Mythran," said a young elven woman I may have recalled from the previous evening.

"I've heard of this weapon," Valdara said with surprise. "It was lost long ago . . ."

"Somewhere in the wastes beyond the Vaporous Mountains!" Seamus shouted, and he looked simply thrilled to have had something to contribute .

"Right! So we ride to the Vaporous Mountains!" I shouted, pointing dramatically down the road to the horizon.

"Aren't they to the west?" Drake asked.

"Yes," I said, and spun my arm around to point back through the village.

With that the Company of the Fellowship, as we would later become known, began its quest to defeat the most dangerous force in Trelari, a third-year acolyte student named Vivian.

CHAPTER 12

OF MOONSONG AND MADNESS

We put the town of Blightsbury at our back and headed into the woodland on its outskirts. I would like to tell you that it was pleasant to ride through the woods, with the murmur of the leaves on the trees and the birds chirping overhead, but I can't. This was not to say that the leaves were not murmuring, or that the birds were not chirping. Maybe they were, but I don't remember any of it.

You might have wondered why it is that I didn't know a lot about the details of Valdara and her original company's quest against the Dark Lord, or how it is I didn't go insane living for all those years as that selfsame Dark Lord, or why I didn't look like I'd aged fifteen years when I returned to Mysterium. The answer is the Time Dilation Trance, and it is one of the first things they teach you when you're preparing to go into a far distant subworld. The idea is that you place yourself into a bubble of dilated time so you don't have to live through all the tedious years of subworld life you would otherwise experience.

It didn't take me long on the trail—maybe an hour or so—before I put myself into one. I know that there are those who love the idea of being atop a horse with adventure ahead, but I'm not one of them. In general, being outdoors, with the bugs and the sweating and the constant rocking motion of the horse, is not my idea of fun. Also, my companions kept trying to talk to me about the quest, which I didn't want to do. First, I had very little idea about what we were doing or where we were going. And second, every time someone new came up to talk to me all I could think about was whether and when they were going to die, which is as depressing as it sounds. What snapped me out of my self-induced daydream was the music.

There I was, riding along and happily ignoring everything, when I noticed that I had this song stuck in my head. It was a soft, instrumental tune that kept intruding its way into my consciousness.

Eventually I could ignore it no longer and decided to wake long enough to ask Valdara and Drake about it, and about whether, somewhere in the back of our overly large party, there might be a bard or a minstrel hiding. I won't repeat what they said in reply, but after ripping me a new one for having not spoken a word for a week (time does fly in the TDT), both agreed it sounded like something Mad Jarl might once have complained about. I took that to mean that they could not hear it. This meant only one of two things: I was either going Jarl, or for some reason music was actually playing in my head. It was time to consult with Eldrin, something I'd been trying to do day and night since our last conversation with no success.

I reined my horse to a stop and pretended to relieve myself. Okay, the relieving myself part was real, but I did plan the timing so that when I got back on my horse I was at the rear of the company. Once I was sure everyone was out of earshot, I pulled my cloak around me and hunched over the communication medallion.

"Eldrin, can you hear me?" I whispered.

"No, he can't," Dawn responded. "And why are you whispering?"

"Because I'm not alone and I don't want to look like a crazy person," I answered irritably. "Where is Eldrin?"

"He went to the little boys' room. Do you want me to go get him?"

"Yes," I answered bluntly. "I need to know why I'm hearing music in my head."

"Riiiight, she drawled. "I'll be right back."

Dawn never came back. I was beginning to worry that we were in another one of Eldrin's communication eclipses when I realized that I was not alone, and that I was no longer in a mindless trance. The girl. The pretty elven girl. The pretty, petite elven girl with the wavy brown hair, hazel eyes, and fine features. The one with the bow on her back and the knives in her boots and whose name I could not remember. She was riding alongside me.

I knew that I'd been introduced to her the night before we left, and based on the way she fell straight into a conversation, I assumed we had spoken, or at least she had spoken to me, at some point over the past week. I was trying to sort out how to get her to tell me her name without letting on that I was doing so when she asked, "Who were you talking to just now?"

"What?" I said in response, not because I didn't hear the question, but because I needed time to invent a lie to tell her. Luckily she was way ahead of me.

"I was wondering if you were muttering spells to yourself," she answered so brightly that it made my teeth hurt. "Sam always seems to be reading that book of his and muttering. I thought maybe it was a wizard thing."

"And so it is," I answered quickly. "You know us wizards, always talking to ourselves."

"I do know," she said with an understanding nod. "I'm a sorceress myself. The Moonsong family has spellcasters going back four generations to when the land was young and the trees still spoke their dreams on the wind."

I replied to her revelation about the Moonsong family with something innocent. "Oh, I thought you were a rogue. You got the bag of marble things from

Seamus." Out of everything I had remembered this fact, because it was too random to forget.

Innocent as the comment seemed to me, I clearly struck a nerve. Her face fell and she said quietly, "I wasn't supposed to be a rogue. I keep trying to do other things, but I am always drawn back into the shadows."

I immediately sensed a story. A story I had no intention of hearing, particularly as I assumed my spell was what kept guiding her away from magic and into thievery. "That's interesting, but—" I began.

"Oh yes," she said, talking eagerly over my attempted escape. "My background is very interesting *and* detailed. Would you like to hear it?"

There was something borderline maniacal in her eye as she asked. Only a fool could fail to see how eager she was for me to hear her life's story. I was no fool. I shook my head and said, "Sorry, Moonsong, I have to go . . ."

I never got a chance to finish my apology as she began what would turn out to be a two-hour monologue about herself. And it all began with, "My name is Ariella Moonsong . . ."

That is how I learned Ariella's name, and it's about the only thing I remember from her story apart from the fact that through a series of the most bizarre incidents and coincidences she kept finding herself needing to pilfer this or that, and always for the best of reasons. Afterward, I put myself back into a trance to avoid hearing, or at least remembering, any more stories. I know it sounds cowardly, because it is, but I also know that it would have driven me mad to have become fully aware of the extent to which I had mucked with these people's lives.

I was still in my Moonsong-induced trance when Eldrin called back. "Avery?"

"Eldrin!" I shouted, and awoke to the fact that the better part of a day had passed. It was evening and we were all seated around a fire in a lovely glade.

Every head spun to look at me and I heard Ariella whisper something to Sam about the eccentricities of wizards. I made a quick apology and sprinted for the darkness of the surrounding trees. When I was far enough away, I hissed, "Eldrin? Where the hell have you been?"

"In the bathroom," he answered. "Why?"

"What are you talking about? That was hours ago," I protested.

"No, it wasn't. I . . ." he began to say, and then I think we both realized that with the different rates of time, minutes for him would of course be hours for me. Simultaneously we muttered, "Damn."

"Looking on the bright side," he said, "we can use this to give us a rough measurement of how far your world has slipped toward Mysterium. What time is it there?"

I saw that the shadows under the trees had grown considerably darker, and that what light there was had taken on a distinctly evening colored pallet. "It's almost sunset."

"Great," he said, and I heard the scratching of a pencil on paper. "I left for the bathroom right after you hung up on me, which you should stop doing by the way. That was twenty minutes ago, which means—" I heard more scratching "—Trelari has slipped again, I'm afraid."

I started to respond and then something he'd said struck me. "Wait, you were in the bathroom for twenty minutes? What the hell were you doing in there? Let me guess, you were doing your hair."

He said nothing, which confirmed it. There was only one reason for Eldrin to do his hair. "Are you trying to put the moves on Dawn?" I asked incredulously.

"We're just going to dinner," he mumbled, and then added more confidently, "to talk about the best way to find your battle-axe."

This was too good to be true. "Dinner?" I said with enough melodrama for a Mexican novella. "I can't believe you're trying to hook up with the friend of the woman that is currently in the process of ruining my life. Have you no shame?"

"I will hang up on you."

"Don't get your elven knickers in a twist," I said, and then added suggestively, "Let her do that for you."

"I'm going now."

"Wait. I'll be good," I promised, and meant it. I was actually excited that he might be interested in someone. He usually refused to do anything social unless I forced him.

"Dawn told me you were concerned about hearing music?"

I started to say "yes" when an even more bizarre paradox struck me. "Wait, if twenty minutes Mysterium time equals hours and hours here, how are we having this conversation at all? It should either take me forever to answer you, or you would have to be talking to me at an impossible speed?"

"Remember when I said transtemporal communication?" he asked.

"Yes."

"The answer is technical."

"How technical?" I asked.

He took a deep breath and said rapidly, "Well, it depends on how technical you think L'Engle tesseract constructs are, and whether you would find it complicated to use such a construct to create a five-dimensional link between your subworld and Mysterium through our medallions such that the space and time between those items no longer followed strict rules of Zelaznian subworld physics."

"So fairly technical," I replied in one of the great understatements of all time. "Let's skip it and assume that I either know enough, or am incapable of knowing enough."

"Agreed," Eldrin said dryly. "Can we get back to why you called me?"

"The music?" I asked.

"The music," he answered. "I don't think it's anything to worry about," he said, shifting into his lecturing mode. I could almost see him sitting in his swivel chair, feet up on his desk, rotating back and forth as he talked. "When you overlaid your reality pattern—"

"I call it an Averian matrix."

A pregnant pause followed this comment that let me know in no uncertain terms what he thought of that. "As I was saying," he continued, and I actually heard the sound of his feet hitting his desk as he picked up his lecture where he'd left off, "when your reality *pattern* is activated to stabilize the subworld it sets up a magical field that creates a cascading series of pattern altering events. Some of these are subtle and some not so subtle. Perhaps a king decides to invade this country and not that one, or a baker decides to make a cake and not a pie, but everyone on the subworld will be affected to a greater or lesser extent such that the combined actions of everyone in the subworld work to alter its destiny."

"I know that. I did write a book on the subject."

"A badly indexed book," Eldrin pointed out.

"Are you going to explain the music or continue to plagiarize my dissertation?"

"Good one," he said, and clapped in appreciation.

We both laughed. I couldn't believe how much I missed these friendly arguments.

I heard Dawn say something in the background. "Be right there," Eldrin replied, and then in rapid fire to me said, "The point is, this magical field sets up a resonance in the fabric of the subworld's reality. You can imagine it like ringing a bell. Anyway, the music you're hearing is the sound of the resonance in your local area."

Thinking back on my time as the Dark Lord, I did recall that there had been an omnipresent rumbling and rather oppressive rhythmic noise, but I had attributed that to the blood orcs and their drums. Mad about drums, they were.

"It can potentially be useful," Eldrin continued. "Because it should give you a rough sense of how the matrix is influencing your local reality. For example, if the music is upbeat and happy you probably don't have much to worry about."

"What if it gets spooky?"

"Run?" he suggested.

"Fair enough, but why am I the only one that can hear it?"

"Because your core reality is significantly more substantial than that of your surroundings, so rather than affecting your behavior, you experience the resonance as a simple sensory input. If the subworld continues to shift inward, you may stop hearing the music."

"That would be great," I said with a chuckle. "This tune is crazy annoying."

"No, it wouldn't, Avery. If that happens, if you stop being able to hear the music, even for a moment, you have to call me immediately." He sounded deadly serious.

"Why?"

"Because at that point you will be approaching reality equality with the subworld. It means that you will be just as vulnerable and weak as any other subworlder. The reality matrix will be affecting your behaviors and decisions just like anyone else. You may no longer be in control of your actions."

I heard Dawn calling to him again. I yearned to be back there with him . . . them stepping out for the evening.

"I need to go, Avery."

"Yeah," I said as evenly as I could. "Thanks for the information, Eldrin."

"We will get you out of there."

"I know you will. I better go too. The others are looking for me," I lied.

"Where are you heading?"

"Toward the Vaporous Mountains, I think."

"May I make a recommendation? The Village of Hamlet is in the foothills of that range and seems to be a good spot. From my mapping I think it may be near a reality nexus of some sort . . . something odd. There's a good chance an object like your battle-axe would be drawn to it. Strange name. You know a village and a hamlet are the same thing?" Dawn saw something in the background. "Anyway, gotta go," he concluded briskly and broke the connection.

After he was gone, I whispered, "I know that a village is a hamlet. I know that the town might as well be called the Village of Village. I know that it makes no sense. I'm beginning to think nothing in this world makes sense."

CHAPTER 13

WHAT ARE THE ODDS?

We rode for several more days before the trees gave way to a wide plain of deep green called the Sea of Grass, which stretched toward a distant line of blue mountains. I had stopped placing myself into a trance for fear that I would miss something significant but subtle, like the music disappearing or Eldrin calling.

And the music had changed. After we left the forest, the happy springtime song had been replaced by something sweepingly grand, like the plains before us. At first I was happy for the change, but this new tune kept building day after day as if toward some climax, and it was keeping me on edge.

The downside to taking myself out of the trance was that I experienced the full monotony of our journey. The routine was as invariable as it was awful. We awoke before dawn every day, a constant source of irritation for me and malicious joy for the dwarfs. We rode all day, stopping for lunch and little else. I was beginning to wonder if I was the only one that ever needed to go to the bathroom. We ended our ride at dusk and Ariella sang songs or recited indecipherable poetry, Sam read his book, Rook and Seamus played chess, Valdara and Drake brooded, and Nigel, Paul, Cameron and the many other random people in the company did . . . whatever they did. As for me, I spent the evenings counting my new blisters. There were blisters on parts of me that had no business getting blisters.

On a positive note, I at last got introduced to my companions in the Company of the Fellowship. But in another oddity that I assumed was my spell at work again (perhaps ensuring that each of us knew of the other's strengths and weaknesses) each member introduced themselves to me in a one-on-one instructional briefing as if they had a secret schedule that they'd worked out between them, which given Seamus's mania for organization they might. Ariella sought me out first.

"Wizard Avery? Do you have a moment? I'd like to show you something," she said one evening with a bright smile.

"Sure," I replied, not having much better in the way of a response.

I followed her about a hundred paces away from

the evening's camp. She surveyed the area. "This should be good. Do you see that squirrel beside that tree over there?"

I squinted and thought I saw a small shape some distance off. It might be a squirrel, or a rat with a fluffy tail, which is the same thing, I suppose. "Yes, I guess so," I answered.

"Excellent." With that, she drew her bow, nocked an arrow, and fired in one fluid motion.

I gasped, but then I saw the creature run beneath a branch. "You missed!"

"No, I didn't," she said with a smug expression. "I wasn't shooting at the squirrel. I'm a vegan. I hit the acorn on the branch above his head."

Sure enough, the fluffy rat seemed to be eating. At least, I thought it was.

"How could you see the acorn, and how did you know it was a he?"

"Elven vision. I can see five or six times as well as most humans, although I'm not entirely elven. I'm really a mix . . . I can tell you the whole story if you have several hours. I don't need much sleep either . . ."

Elves.

Similar performances followed for each of the company. Seamus put on a combination axe throwing, juggling, and drinking display that would have made a great stage act at a renaissance faire, all while explaining that he had been driven from his mountain home by either a dragon or a terrible orc horde—that part of the story being somewhat garbled since he was trying to simultaneously eat two turkey legs and an apple while they were flipping through the air.

The gnomes also had a story about being forced from their village in the mushroom forest. Did I mention that there were one to five gnomes in the party? I didn't? That's because to this day I'm not sure if they were real or a hallucination. They seemed to appear and disappear at random, and Rook denied having hired them. "Distrustful little beggars," I think he called them.

Even Nigel, Paul, and Cameron told me, well, I don't remember what they said . . . The point stands that they all did it, other than Drake and Valdara, who apparently felt that they needed no exhibition or introduction. Although everyone insisted on showing off their abilities, Sam had the greatest impact on me, and not for the right reasons.

In my last incarnation I had always been too busy to do an in-depth study on what passed for magic in Trelari. I knew it was a bit quirky, but with the reality key in hand I'd never had to pay attention to the mechanics. Unfortunately, I couldn't tell Sam this so he was always asking technical questions about my magic. "What school did you study under? Do you smoke a pipe? Do you think a staff or an orb makes a better magical focus? Do you principally perform invocations or abjurations?"

Had I been in my trance, I probably would have grunted or given typical wizardly answers, such as: "All things are education for a wizard," or "One must discover true magic for oneself," and even "I do what needs to be done." Out of my trance, I had a harder time known what to tell him.

Still, I managed to avoid any awkwardness until one day he cornered me after dinner and asked, "Wizard Avery, what is magic?"

I wasn't sure where this was heading, but I gave him the standard definition of magic taught in novice-level magical theory courses at the university. "Magic is magic. It is the invocation of extradimensional power and the channeling of that invoked essence into a form suitable to rewrite reality to one's satisfaction."

"So, you're an invoker!" he said, excited to have a label for me. "Did you know that my old master might have been an invoker?" Sam proceeded to discuss how he had been an apprentice/scullery boy for a great wizard who had been sucked into a maelstrom or something, leaving Sam on his own. "Anyway, that's the first part of my life, really the introduction as it were," he said, "but there's a lot more."

"Maybe you could just demonstrate some of your spells?"

What can I say, I was tired that night. Besides, that was the pattern these conversations followed. The person would talk about their backgrounds and then demonstrate their skills.

He nodded at my request and pulled out his incredibly thick spell book and studied it. I'm not sure whether he had the memory of a goldfish, or if this was the way magic worked in Trelari, but he couldn't remember a spell for more than one day even if he'd read it a hundred times.

Finally, he said brightly, "I can cast a spell to make people fall asleep."

"Well, that could be useful," I replied, trying to be encouraging. I wasn't sure how he was going to demonstrate that, but I decided to roll with it. As I looked around the camp at the others and wondered who would make a good test subject, I asked, "Can it work on anyone?"

"Yes," he said, and then thought a bit more and qualified his answer. "As long as they aren't too powerful."

"Well, how powerful is too powerful?"

"It's simple," he said, running a finger along a line of his book. "I cause a comatose slumber to come upon one or more creatures (other than undead and certain other creatures specifically excluded from the spell's effects). All creatures to be affected must be within thirty feet of each other. The number of creatures that can be affected is a function of their power level. The least powerful creatures are affected first, and partial effects are ineffective."

"That's simple?" I said, flabbergasted. "Say we were being attacked by a gibberling or a blood orc, could you put them to sleep?"

"Yes," he said, smiling, and then added proudly, "Not only that, I could affect eight gibberlings and two blood orcs or one ogre."

I thought about this for a moment. "So, if we were attacked by four gibberlings, one blood orc and an ogre? The four gibberlings and the blood orc would fall asleep, but the ogre would be left standing?"

"Exactly," he said happily, and then closed his book and started to put it back in his pack.

"But what if you wanted to affect only the ogre?" I asked. "Could you focus the effect so it ignored the gibberlings entirely?"

"It doesn't work like that," he said with a shake of his head. "It always affects the least powerful creatures first."

I was still confused. "How does the spell know to go after the gibberlings first?"

"I don't know."

"Tell me what you do to cast it. Maybe there's a clue in the mechanics."

"I move my fingers like this." He held a hand out and wiggled the tips of his fingers. "Then I hold up either fine sand, rose petals, or a cricket, and say the magic words, which I won't do now because if I did I wouldn't be able to cast it again until I rest."

The emerging magus in me was entirely unsatisfied with this answer and I loosed my frustration on Sam. "That doesn't make any sense. How can a combination of words and gestures alter reality, and if that's all it takes, why do you have to study so hard and for so long? And what in the gods' names do fine sand, rose petals, and a cricket have in common? Have no experiments been done on the differential effectiveness of the component parts of the spell? Where are your standards?"

As my rant subsided, I could see that I had gone too far. His head hung and his shoulders had collapsed in on themselves so that it looked like he'd withered to half his former size. I felt terrible.

"I'm . . . I'm getting tired, Wizard Avery," he stammered, and got to his feet. "I . . . I think I'll go to bed."

"What about the demonstration?" I asked, trying to repair the conversation. "I was looking forward to seeing your spell in action."

"I don't think you'd be impressed," he said in a small voice before wandering away.

I watched him go, and then smacked my leg a stinging blow. *Great job, Avery. How can you want to be a magus at a university and have so little skill with students? And who are you to talk about magical standards when you regularly violate your own?*

There was a lot more I wanted to say to myself, but before I could get very far into an examination of my many, many flaws, Rook shouted, "Let's set a watch."

Let me explain this ritual. Every night there would be a long debate about who was going on watch with whom, what time of night they were going to take watch, and so on. It took forever, no one was happy with the result, and thus far it had been an enormous waste of effort. Every morning everyone in the company woke up a little sleep-deprived from this "watching," but no one ever managed to do any "seeing" of anything.

Fortunately, Sam's incessant need to study his spell book had given me the perfect out. "Sadly, Sam and I must rest to restore our powers for tomorrow," I called out.

"But neither of you cast a single spell all day," Nigel or Paul or maybe Crispin complained. Although I'm not sure we had a Crispin. Could it be Charlie? I was pretty sure it started with a *C* . . .

"Doesn't matter," I said confidently. "Wizards must refresh themselves every day even if they haven't cast a spell, because . . ." I thought fast, because it still made no sense to me. "Because if they don't they will . . . will lose their connection to the mystical forces and won't be able to cast spells at all."

"So, why am I not exempt?" asked Ariella.

"Because . . ." I started, and realized that I had never seen her study magic, and yet she could probably cast as well as, if not better than, Sam. I made up another something on the spot. "You said you were a sorceress, correct?"

"Yes," she answered.

Trying my best to project a level of surety I did not feel, I said, "Well, everyone knows that the way sorcerers and sorceresses connect with magic is entirely different from wizards."

"They do?" she asked.

"Of course," I said with a superior nod of the head. "You don't have a spell book, do you?"

"No."

"There you go," I said as though that made everything self-evident.

"But you don't have a spell book either," Sam pointed out.

I opened my mouth to argue, realized I couldn't, and said instead, "Why are we arguing about watches anyway? Take a look around." I gestured to the flat barren plain, which surrounded us in all directions. I could literally see for miles. "Why exactly are we keeping watch when there is obviously no one here but us? Why don't we all get a good night's sleep for once?"

"But . . . but . . ." Seamus stuttered in disbelief. "We always keep a watch."

"It's what *they* do," agreed Rook significantly.

"And there's a good reason for that," Valdara said, stepping forward. "Most of you haven't traveled these plains, but I have." She pulled out one of her daggers and began digging furrows in the ground with it. "It may look flat and featureless, but running down from the mountains are a chain of hidden chasms. There are ravines in these grasses deep enough to hide a giant, or swallow the unaware, and they snake all around us."

Everyone, including myself, began glancing nervously at the tall grasses bordering the campsite.

"Did you all really think the only thing we had to fear on our journey was the Dark Queen?" Valdara asked derisively. "We lost three members of our original group before the Dark Lord even became aware of our existence. "During our last trip we lost one of our wizards to a band of gnolls that prowled close to this spot. It will be a miracle if we all make it across this plain alive."

"Gnolls?" I asked. "Aren't they doglike creatures? How bad could they be?"

"You want to find out?" she said with menace in her voice.

"All right, lads and lassies!" Rook said, stepping between us. "Who wants first watch?"

No one said anything. Valdara gave a grunt of disgust and said, "I'll take first watch."

"Okay," Seamus said. "Who's on watch with Valdara?"

Half of the group volunteered. I did not, but it wasn't because Valdara's story hadn't impacted me. I stood up and walked toward the edge of the camp. "Eldrin!"

Thank the gods he answered immediately.

"Avery? I'm in the middle of something fairly delicate right now. Can it wait?"

"No."

I heard him sigh. "Fine, we have five minutes—tops. After that my silence spell will fail and I'll have a hell of a time trying to explain why I'm stalking around the faculty lounge."

"You're what?"

"Dawn and I have a theory about Vivian and where she might have hidden Death Slasher," he said in a voice that was way too calm for my liking.

"It had better be a good theory," I said, more nervous for him and his continued academic career than I was for my own chances against gnolls.

"Man, is it ever!" he said with a chuckle. "If I'm right—"

"Normally I'd love to hear your conspiracy theory, Eldrin," I cut in, "but I only have four minutes, and I need to know whether or not you calculated the odds of us running into any monsters in the Sea of Grass."

"Yes," he answered. "And before you ask, very, very high. Almost a certainty."

"They're talking about gnolls, but aren't those the hybrid human-hyena sort of things? I don't see them as much of a threat."

"Not what my simulation indicated, but not out of the realm of possibility, I suppose," he said thoughtfully. "Regardless, don't underestimate gnolls, Avery. They're nasty creatures when in their natural surroundings, which before you ask are grassy plains. Stay away from them."

"I'm not sure it's entirely within my control," I said, pointing out what I hoped was the obvious.

"We're almost out of time," Eldrin said rapidly. "Listen to me. Stay safe. Put extra people on watch, and contact me when you get to the village tomorrow so I know you made it."

The connection went dead. I stood for a few minutes listening to the wind blow through the grass accompanied by the increasingly ominous chords of the music. The plains were looking more and more threatening with every passing moment.

I walked back to camp. Everyone except Sam, who always turned in early to study his books, was gathered close around the campfire. If Valdara's story had been calculated to increase comradery through fear, it had worked. Even one to three of the gnomes were there. I could tell by the silhouettes of their pointy tasseled hats. I knew that I should sit down with the group and "bond," but I was thinking about Eldrin and hoping that he wouldn't be expelled come morning and feeling guilty about both him and Sam. I went into my tent.

I rolled into my blanket and closed my eyes. I shifted onto my right side, and after a time I shifted back to my left. I couldn't shut my mind off. The look on Sam's face accompanied with Eldrin's warnings kept replaying and echoing in my head.

I'm not sure how long I laid awake listening to the muted conversation of the others around the campfire and brooding, but most of them had drifted off to their tents and I was finally fading into a restless sleep when the music changed into a downright sinister key and then began to build to a terrible crescendo. My eyes shot open. I knew—I mean, I *knew*—what was going to happen. I gasped out, "Trolls!"

CHAPTER 14

TROLLS AROUND A CAMPFIRE

I threw off my blanket and scrambled toward the tent flap. Trolls were bad news. They were massive brutal blocks of sinewy muscle, mostly orange, with nasty crunching teeth and eyes like lanterns. There wasn't anything a troll wouldn't eat. They were worse even than goats. Pr Eldrin at the end of the semester.

"Trolls!" I shouted as I tried to clamber out of my tent. The music swelled dramatically at my warning. "Armor up! Draw your weapons! Ready your spells!"

One of the red shirts, who may have been Nigel, rose from where he had apparently been tending the fire with a stick. He looked at me dumbly. "What?"

"Trolls!" I responded.

A second red-shirted man, who I'll call Cameron,

stepped out of the high grass on the edge of camp. "What are you talking about? We haven't seen any—"

"Surprise!" boomed a deep voice as a large warty orange hand reached up from the grasses and clamped onto Cameron's head.

The troll stood up, revealing his colossal height. He was close to ten feet tall and just as wide. While keeping one hand locked onto Cameron and lifting him slightly off the ground, he swung an enormous spiked club into the middle of the man. I turned away as Cameron's screams were cut short by a nauseating meaty squishing sound.

As I was processing this first horror, a second troll emerged from the grasses on the other side of our camp and charged toward a still-unmoving Nigel—his arms outstretched. The monster leered and licked his lips, showing off pointed yellow teeth. "Ha, ha! We get to attack first! Pound them to mincemeat!"

A third troll with a higher voice, who we would later identify as a female, also rushed forward, screaming, "Leave a few of them whole for roasting!"

It was only now that faces began to appear at tent openings, blinking in bewilderment. It looked for a moment like our party was going to get slaughtered before it had a chance to wake up. And then Valdara arrived.

She sprung from her sleep, somehow fully armored and brandishing a sword in one hand and a wicked curved dagger in the other. She gave a high-pitched battle cry that made the hair on the back of my neck stand up and rushed at the troll that was holding Cameron's remains. Possibly inspired by her example, Seamus and Drake, still only half-dressed, charged out of their tents. I saw that Seamus had only managed one boot so he was running a little lopsided.

The dwarf raised his axe high and screamed, "For all the clans! Fight, lads and lasses! No mercy!"

I managed to pull myself free of my tent as Valdara vaulted onto the back of the troll with the great spiked club. She drove her blade into its back. The monstrous beast thrashed its arms about in a desperate attempt to dislodge her before dropping its club, staggering forward, and falling face-first into the campfire with a dying bellow. Valdara leapt from its back as a shower of flames and sparks enveloped the body.

Drake, leaning heavily on his staff, was facing off against the troll that had attacked Nigel. On the ground between them lay the man's mangled body. Seeing the unnatural way his limbs and head had been twisted, I hoped for his sake he was already dead. The creature roared defiantly and advanced. Drake made no move to retreat. Instead, he drew himself up and held his staff aloft.

"I defy you, foul creature," he intoned grimly. "Know that I am St. Drake, Vessel of the Seven Gods, and I call upon them to grant me the power to return you to the foul places from which you spawned!"

He struck the staff on the ground at his feet. For a moment it blazed with a pure, blinding radiance. The troll lurched backward, eyes wide with a fear that was matched only by Drake's own surprise. Then the priest's hand wavered; the light dimmed, flickered and went out. Evil laughter roiled the air.

Drake's eyes narrowed and his mouth twisted into a self-mocking sneer. "Never mind," he grunted, and in a motion as sudden as it was violent he thrust the tip of his staff into the monster's chest.

The blow seemed little more than a touch and the troll began to laugh again, but then a spasm of pain wracked its body. Wide-eyed, it tore at the staff, even as a blackness spread like a stain across its chest. The monster choked and yellow foam erupted from its mouth. It shuddered again and fell. The creature was dead before it hit the ground. As Drake withdrew his staff from the thing's body I saw the glint of a very thin blade withdrawing back into the wood. Whatever had killed the troll had nothing to do with blessings or gods.

All this went on around me while I stood rooted to the spot, unable to move. I admit, I was totally overwhelmed by the situation. Everywhere I looked there was blood and gore, and the intermingled bits and pieces of trolls and my former companions. It was only when Ariella and Sam rushed by that I realized how useless I was being. And it was not until Rook literally kicked me in the butt that I did anything.

With the dwarf shouting, "Do somethin', Avery!" I silently cursed my cowardice and took a few faltering steps toward the clearing where the remainder of the company (even one or two of the gnomes) had the last troll surrounded.

Although this one was not as big as the brute that Valdara had dispatched or as foul as Drake's foe, its desperation had made it all the more dangerous. The creature was cursing and lashing out with its long black talons looking for a way to escape. As it spun about, it kicked two of the three to five gnomes I could currently see deep into the dark grass.

Ariella screamed what sounded like, "Puddlestripe! Fizzwhistle!"

Without pausing, she drew back her bow and let loose an arrow into the crowded melee. Unfortunately, the bolt glanced off of Seamus's axe as he brought it high. I think Ariella muttered something about dwarfs as she nocked another arrow. The next shot struck the troll, but it only seemed to enrage the creature.

With a roar of pain and anger the troll charged through the chaotic melee toward Sam, who was wiggling his fingers and gesturing at the monster with a cricket. Whatever power level the troll was in Sam's magical system of accounting, it was too much for his spell, because the monster never broke stride. Knocking the wizard aside with a casual backhand, it rushed into the darkness of the night, Valdara at its heel.

The clamor of their passage faded. Nobody moved. With a start, I realized that Valdara was alone in the dark with an angry troll. I started to run after them, but Drake grabbed my arm.

"Valdara's alone," I shouted. "We've got to help!"

"She's going to be fine," he said, "but we have wounded and dying here."

I spun about and saw that Rook, Seamus, and Ariella were gathered in a solemn circle around someone. I rushed to their side. Sam lay on the ground in a twisted heap. His arm was thrust under his body at an unnatural angle, and a line of ragged bloody gashes ran down from his neck to below his ribs.

I turned back to Drake and asked, "What do you expect me to do? You're the healer! You're the holy man!"

He shook his head. "You saw what happened with the troll. We both know I can't help him. Not anymore." I started to protest, but he cut me off as, with a flick of his wrist, he extended the hidden blade in his staff. "Listen, kid, you are the leader of this group, and the leader is responsible for everyone, even a wizard he considers worthless like Sam. Now, you told Valdara and me that you were 'better' than any wizard we'd seen. Well, gods or no gods, holy or unholy, she and I have seen wizards that could work miracles. Now, work a miracle."

It was at this point that Valdara reemerged from the grass holding the head of the troll. She was breathing heavily, and her rent and torn armor was covered in blood, most of it not her own. There was something awe-inspiring and utterly terrifying about her. She threw the head on the fire next to the still burning body of the other troll and stomped over. "What's happening?"

Drake quickly retracted the staff's blade. "The kid was going to heal Sam. Weren't you, kid?"

Everyone turned to look at me. I did the only thing I could do; I nodded and knelt down next to Sam.

Classes in magical first aid are a mandatory part of the curriculum at The Mysterium University—of course, so is arcane algebra and at least one class in demonic cultures, so that doesn't necessarily signify anything. Nevertheless, what I told Sam was true: magic is magic and power is power, and there is nothing fundamentally different about using it to warp the reality of an object so that it is heated sufficiently above its flash point to create fire, versus using it to warp the reality of a person to heal wounds or cure disease.

This didn't mean I was particularly good at magical healing or that I had done anything but practice on the most rudimentary types of ailments, but in theory there was a nonzero chance I could help. The question wasn't *Could I*; the question was *Should I*.

In the larger scheme, Sam's death wouldn't matter. It wasn't that I wanted to see him or any of the others come to harm, but I knew that if I went back to Mysterium for a year or two, Sam and everyone else (except possibly Ariella with her elfin life span) would be dead. They were all ephemeral wisps, but Vivian was real, and if she made a mistake, that might be the end of Trelari. My goal, my only goal, had to be to build up enough power to stop her. The only way to do that was to follow the weave of the reality matrix spell to its conclusion. The question before me was whether Sam was meant to live or die.

As these thoughts swirled through my mind, Sam's eyes opened. "Sorry I failed you, Wizard, Avery. I guess I never really understood magic."

That helped make my decision. *To hell with the spell*, I thought.

I leapt to my feet and shouted for everyone to clear a circle around him. "I need him on bare earth and I need something to make marks in the ground with," I ordered.

In less than a minute, the dwarfs had stripped the ground beneath and around him for several paces of every blade of grass, and Valdara was thrusting the burnt end of a stick from our fire into my hand. The time had given me a chance to remember the basics of a healing circle, and I began to sketch it. Every moment, Sam's condition was growing worse. His eyes no longer opened, and his breathing now came in short, painful gasps. I was in a race against time, but the symbols had to be right, or the magic would kill him for sure.

It took me five agonizing minutes to complete the circle. When at last I was done, Sam was stretched out and centered on an elaborate series of interlocking ellipses each inscribed with symbols representing the major organ systems of the body. I gathered the power I would need, stripping it from the world around me. I don't think the others noticed, but the colors of things grew a bit duller and their edges less distinct. If I drew too much it was possible that things, objects, even people, might simply vanish—erased from existence. Thankfully, this was a relatively minor job.

When I had enough power I drew a deep breath and then unleashed the energy into the circle. It glowed like flame in the night and the air above rippled as reality itself was torn asunder. Where the tracings of fire met Sam's body, his flesh moved and was reshaped like soft clay. It was pretty ghastly to watch.

The magic took only a few seconds. It was a fairly straightforward procedure in the end, although I'm pretty sure that I unintentionally removed Sam's appendix in the process. I stepped out of the circle and felt my legs shaking with the effort. I frowned, because such a minor casting shouldn't have affected me that much, but I had little time for reflection because the entire Company of the Fellowship, including all two to three of the remaining gnomes, were standing in a semicircle staring at me. I heard Sam stir.

"He should be okay now," I said, and then remembered about his spell book and added, "But he needs to rest until morning so he can relearn his spells."

This pronouncement was greeted with silence.

Hoping to escape any questions, I said, truthfully I might add, "I'm a little tired now. I'm going to go lie down."

Without a word, the wall of people parted and I made my way back toward my tent. I was hoping that after a little breather the fatigue would lift, but my exhaustion seemed to be growing with every step. It was alarming actually. Something I definitely needed to talk to Eldrin about . . . in the morning . . . when I was fresher.

I had reached my tent when I felt a hand on my arm. I feared it was Drake again with his spikey staff and his general spookiness, but instead it was Valdara, a sweaty and gore-soaked Valdara.

"Nice job, handso—" She stopped herself. "Thanks, Avery. I have to be honest . . . I put you down as all talk. I thought I would join your group to get Drake out of that stinking bar before he drank himself to death, and then we would slip off before the Dark Queen made her first appearance. I'll admit, I was wrong."

She leaned forward and kissed me on the cheek and walked, in that lovely swaying way she had, back to the fire where the others were hefting the last troll onto the smoky pyre. Whether it was the magic I'd performed or the kiss or the fact that Valdara had left some entrails behind on my arm, my legs gave out. I collapsed to my knees and proceeded to vomit.

In my defense, I had never seen this much death up close. Even as the Dark Lord, up until the very end, violence was a remote thing: lines on a map, or specks on a battlefield miles away or hundreds of feet below.

After a few heaves, I crawled into my tent and felt Eldrin calling me. "Yes?" I said wearily.

"Good news," he said. "I managed to check out the teacher's lounge and it's clear, although there are certain signs Death Slasher was brought through there at one point. Also, Professor Bishop from the Department of Subworld Biology has some extremely disturbing eating habits. Oh, and I ran my simulation again. You are definitely going to encounter trolls."

I had just enough time to stick my head back out of the tent before I threw up again.

CHAPTER 15

A VERY BRIEF MEMORIAL

We didn't bury Nigel and Cameron until the morning, and we never could find one to two of the gnomes. Everyone was traumatized, but the deaths had hit a couple of the members of the company particularly hard. Ariella wept bitterly over the death of the gnomes, whom she saw as kindred spirits. In true elven fashion she recited a poem-song-thing she'd written the night before that might have been sad and touching except all the words were in elvish so no one understood what she was singing. Sam kept stumbling about saying, "I'm a terrible wizard," which even I could recognize wasn't good for his self-confidence. The NPC crowd was down to Paul and two new guys that Rook drafted out of the last of the retainers and servants. He had even thrust them into red tunics, which I hoped weren't the ones from Nigel and Cameron.

And then there was Valdara, who, despite her earlier disclaimer of all responsibility, was clearly taking each death personally. It was she that insisted we dig proper graves and erect proper memorials and not "dump them in a ravine" as Rook had suggested. I had to admit that while I appreciated his mania for efficiency, sometimes Rook came off as a bit disinterested in the health and safety of the rest of the company. In any case, everyone took turns digging. Even I pitched in. I wanted to help honor the dead and all that, but I also didn't feel I could refuse when Drake thrust a shovel in my hand and glowered at me meaningfully while tapping the end of his staff on the ground. At least, I didn't think I could safely refuse. In other words, it seemed like the right thing to do on many levels.

Another thing that was not helping with everyone's mood was the choking smoke from our fire. As I mentioned before, we—or rather, other members of the group and not me—had set fire to the trolls because someone (likely Ariella) had said it would be cathartic, and someone else (definitely Valdara) had said if we didn't the trolls might reanimate themselves. Whatever the reason, the bodies had gone into the fire where they continued to smolder through the night and into the morning. As a result, our camp was covered in a cloud of acrid smoke, the stench of which made it nearly impossible to breathe.

We had finished laying the last of the night's dead into the ground and my lungs were aching and my eyes watering from the smoke when Rook slapped me hard on the back. I bit my tongue to stop from yelping in pain as he said, "Laddie, you can't let these losses affect you so much. It's all part of the pattern."

This was *far* too close to what I'd been thinking myself. I knew it was long past time for me to have a heart-to-heart with the dwarf. "What do you mean by that?" I asked sharply, looking down at him.

"Just what I said, laddie. We've got to expect losses in an expedition like this. The Dark Queen plays for keeps. If we wallow in our defeats, we won't have the fortitude to do what must be done. If we try to save everyone, we will surely fall behind. Stick to the plan, that's the ticket."

"But you said 'pattern.' You said, 'It's all part of the pattern,'" I probed, suddenly uncertain if I was reading too much into his words.

"Did I? Interestin' choice of words. Don't know what I meant by that. Do you?"

"I'm not sure," I answered slowly, because I wasn't.

What followed was a silent staring contest—his washed-out gray eyes against my faded blue. I lost again, but to my credit there was a lot of smoke in the air and he is lower to the ground. Anyway, I wish I could say that I'm an excellent judge of character and that afterward I was able to tell, with absolute certainty, what and who Rook was. The truth is that I had no idea in that moment if Rook was another Mysterian infiltrating my subworld (in which case I was dead), a spy from Vivian sent to sabotage my attempted coup (again probably resulting in me being dead), or just a highland dwarf with delusions of grandeur (another good way to get killed). On the sole ground that there was nothing I could do about it, I decided to believe that he was on my side.

As soon as I blinked I felt his broad hand on my elbow guiding back to the graves. "Well, nothing for us to worry about today, laddie," he said. "Right now it's time for you to say a few words about our fallen comrades, and maybe even something about those that you chose to give a second chance to. Don't you think?"

He wandered off to gather the remainder of the Company of the Fellowship. As usual, Rook's efficiency was my undoing. I hadn't even begun to contemplate what I might say or how I might escape saying it when he was back, herding the group into a circle around the graves and me. There they stood, waiting. The music in my head had gone appropriately somber, which bothered me on several levels.

I looked around the group and saw a lot of tears and decided Rook was right. A few words couldn't hurt. Unfortunately, I was wrong.

"These things happen," I started. Angry looks snapped in my direction and I cursed myself for being an idiot. "But . . . but . . ." I continued hastily, "we shouldn't let them happen. Again. As their souls go to a better place, let us look to one another and promise ourselves that their deaths will not be in vain. We will stay unified in our purpose. When I look upon these faces and see Nigel and Cameron and . . ."

I hesitated as I realized that I had no idea whether I should even mention the one to two gnomes that had apparently gone missing last night. I started to say something generic about "the others," which admittedly would have been awful, when the wind shifted and a particularly noxious cloud of smoke sent me into a coughing fit.

"He is overcome," Rook said, stepping in front of me. "Let us have a moment of silence." He bowed his head somberly.

The dwarf wasn't kidding when he said "a moment," because less than a minute later he wheezed, "Right! Now, get to your packin'! We ride out before noon!"

I was saddling my horse and trying to wrestle the fifty-foot coil of rope back into place when Valdara walked up. Sometime in the night she must have cleaned her armor and her weapons, but she was not the glamorous post-battle warrior-woman I had always imagined. She had twisted her long red hair into a braid that ran down her back, her face was covered in soot, her hands and nails were caked with grime, and frankly she smelled like a charnel house.

"Can I talk to you a minute, Avery?"

I swallowed against my gag reflex and nodded.

She led me away from the rest of the group out onto the plains. Out here, at least, there was a stiff wind blowing so the smell didn't linger. We stopped on a low mound of dirt and stone, and she asked, "Why are we going to the Village of Hamlet?"

"It's our best chance to get information on the location of Justice Cleaver," I replied, a little disappointed that she had either missed or ignored my dramatic speech the very first day of our adventure.

"Yes, I know that's what you said," she said with a frown, and stared out at the mountains in the distance.

I've been called dense before and emotionally unavailable and a jerk, but even I could see she was worried. "What's wrong, Valdara?"

Ripping a long thin stalk of brown grass from the ground she began wrapping it around her fingers nervously. "Did you know that when we joined together to fight the Dark Lord I first found Drake in a bar, and then I met two dwarfs, and our adventure started at dawn, and we had an elf with us and a wizard, and we had eighteen in our group to begin with, and we ran into a trio of trolls on a barren plain on our way to the Village of Hamlet—" she paused and took a deep breath "—and five of us died before we made it to town? I have raised two burial mounds on the Sea of Grass, one we just came from and the other we are standing on."

I stumbled backward off the mound and said, "I don't understand," because I didn't.

She let her gaze rise to meet my eyes, and I saw that they were bright with tears. "Everything is happening as it did last time—everything!"

My initial thought was, *That's entirely possible,*

maybe even probable. However, I doubted that would make her feel any better. Instead, I settled on the safer and more academic gambit of arguing a technicality. "Not *everything* is the same," I said. "The town is only half a day ahead and we have only lost two."

"Four," she said raggedly. "Nigel, Cameron, Puddlestripe, and Fizzwhistle."

"Puddlewhat and Fizzwho?" I said before I could stop myself.

Her eyes narrowed in anger. "The gnomes!" she barked. "Berrycrank and I have combed the area around the camp, but they're gone. They were probably thrown into a ravine and carried away by gnolls. This plain is crawling with gnolls."

"I'm sorry. I didn't know," I said, still coming to terms with the idea that we had a party member called Berrycrank.

"I'm not surprised," she spat. "I know you never bother to talk to them, but you should at least learn their names." She was right, and defending myself by saying that I hadn't even been sure that the gnomes were real didn't seem likely to improve things so I said nothing. "The point is," she said, twisting the blade of grass angrily in her hands, "it's all happening again."

"Not exactly," I said brightly. "You said five died on the journey to Hamlet last time, but we will be in the village in a few hours and the plains have only claimed four of us."

She threw the mangled grass back to the ground. "That's what's worrying me."

I saw the merits in her concern. Silently I put odds on Paul or one of the gnomes, but out loud I gave her a confident smile and said, "Last time you didn't have me."

She put her head to one side and looked at me searchingly. "I know. That's the other thing I've been thinking about. Everything has been the same . . . except you. I was lying back in Blightsbury when I told you that we had two wizards last time. You were just so cocky and certain, and I wanted to contradict you. The fact is, we had one. He died in the troll attack. Last night Sam would have died save for you. Even before he fell from grace Drake would never have been able to do what you did."

I know it wasn't what she was intending, but Valdara was reawakening my earlier fears that I might have screwed up the pattern by saving Sam. "Should I not have?" I mumbled.

I meant it for myself, but she heard. She grabbed my hands in hers. "Gods, Avery, that's not what I meant. You were amazing. It's just that if you could change that, maybe you can change everything else."

Even with the smell it was nice being this close to her, and having her hold my hands, and having her tell me that I was amazing, but the direction the conversation was taking was alarming. "What do you mean?"

"Let's not go into Hamlet. Let's go directly after the Dark Queen. Maybe this time we can prevent the darkness from spreading in the first place. Maybe we can stop the killing before it starts."

We had officially entered the danger zone. I pulled away from her and said, "She's too powerful, Valdara. Sam and Ariella and the others aren't ready to face her."

"But that's the point. With your magic, my sword, Drake's staff, and maybe the dwarfs, we don't the rest. Don't you see, no one else needs to die, Avery!"

Her face alive with excitement at the possibility. In that moment, I wanted to say yes, but I knew what we would be facing when we finally met Vivian. Absent the full power of the reality pattern supporting us, it would be impossible to stop her.

I shook my head. "It's too dangerous. We need Justice Cleaver, which means we need Hamlet. Trust me, it's better this way."

She wrapped her arms around her body and turned away to look back out across the horizon. "You don't know Hamlet."

CHAPTER 16

THE VILLAGE OF HAMLET

I remained at Valdara's side for a time, but she would say nothing more. When I finally left her she was still standing quietly staring into the distance. I wondered what she was seeing. Maybe it was the faces of lost friends, or the Plains of Despair in those final days of the Dark Lord, or some other horror I had visited upon her. I decided that I owed it to her to do a little more research into Hamlet, which meant Eldrin.

"Eldrin? You out there?" I asked when I was safely away.

The response came back a little staticky. "Avery? I'm having some trouble. Give me a moment. Ah . . ."

I felt a popping in my head and the connection became stronger and clearer. "That's better," I said.

"No," he countered, "it's worse. Your subworld's frequency continues to change, which means that the world is continuing to shift. I should be at the observatory plotting your course instead of tracking down this stupid battle-axe of yours."

"Well, where's Dawn? I thought she was helping you."

"Student records," he said with a sigh. "I told her it was a waste of time to descend into the chaos of that bureaucracy, but she thinks she found some oddities in Vivian's stated home world. On that subject, did you know your girlfriend dots her *i*'s with little eyes? It is exceedingly creepy."

"She isn't my girlfriend," I growled. "She's my . . ." I could think of nothing better to call her. Instead, I said, "Never mind."

"That's what I thought," he replied. "Anyway, we are about to go dark so what do you need?"

"First, how much closer are we to Mysterium? When do you think other subworld astronomers will start to notice what's happening?"

I pictured him staring off at nothing as he thought it through. "Well, it is hard to be precise based only on the frequency shifts, but there are roughly fifty-two potential frequency shifts that your subworld could take on its way to harmonizing with Mysterium. In the best-case scenario we have months or even years Mysterium-time before the orbital decay becomes noticeable."

"Worst-case," which I though more likely, "the

shifting accelerates at some logarithmic rate, in which case we have about a week or so before your world collides with Mysterium, wreaking untold damage and guaranteeing your expulsion. In that case we have at most a day or two before every subworld astronomer worth his salt notices you. Unless . . ."

"Unless what?" I asked suspiciously.

"What?" he asked. "Nothing, just an idle thought."

"Is it important?"

"No," he said much too quickly.

"Eldrin . . ."

"I said 'no,' don't you trust me?"

"No."

"Well, lack of trust is an issue you need to take up with your therapist," he said. "Right now you're wasting time. Why did you want to talk to me?"

As usual, Eldrin's cavalier attitude about his own danger had distracted me from the entire point of my call: the village. "What can you tell me about the Village of Hamlet? Valdara seems to want to avoid it." I heard the sound of pages flipping. "Are you actually carrying around my DMG?"

"Of course."

"Has it been of any use?" I asked hopefully.

"Not really, but the selection of tables and statistics makes for amusing reading. Did you know you put in a table on 'Astral Color Pools' and another on, and I'm not making this up, 'Random Harlots'?" he said with a chuckle. I didn't recall the first and I'm still convinced he was making up the second. "I'm serious," he giggled. "In the table you have the odds of running into a slovenly trull, a brazen strumpet, a cheap trollop, a saucy tart, a wanton wench, an expensive doxy, a haughty courtesan—you even give a two percent chance of finding an aged madam, a sly pimp, or a rich panderer. Where did you get this stuff?"

Predictably my head was beginning to ache. "Can we get back to Hamlet, and why Valdara might not want to go there?"

"Yeah, we don't have much time left anyway," he said lightly. "From everything I can find, Hamlet seems perfect for your needs. Both Morgarr and the Heroes of the Ages came through the place during your reign as Dark Lord. It's proximal to any number of significant locations. The Castle on the Borderlands is nearby, which is famed for the Caves of Disorder. It's also an easy hike to the entrance of Darkunder where the Fortified Safe of the Dark Elves lies. Plus, you can reach the Cathedral of Compounded Chaos without too much effort. The vampiric stronghold of Crow's Attic isn't too far away, although I'd avoid it. It's rather spooky, and then there's—"

"Wait," I interrupted. "Why would anyone live in a village situated so close to so many different sources of death and destruction?"

"I know it sounds weird, not that anything in that subworld is what one would call normal, but it seems the village economy is almost entirely based around adventurer tourism."

"Adventurer tourism?" I asked in disbelief. "Hamlet is built around people exploring dungeons?"

"Exactly," he said as though the idea of a town built around groups of people going on legendary quests made any sense whatsoever. "By the way, I hope you have a lot of money. Prices will be pretty inflated."

I had no money, but before I could ask him what I was supposed to do about that, he said, "Well, I need to go. I have an exam to proctor, an observatory to sabotage, and Griswald's office to raid."

"Wait! What?" I shouted, but Eldrin had already disconnected. He was going to get himself expelled and there was nothing I could do to stop it. I punched the air in frustration and screamed, "ELDRIN!"

It was only then that I realized the entire company had been waiting for me and watching as I talked to myself. I took a few deep breaths, put the medallion back in my pocket, and marched silently back to the group.

We rode for most of that day and the beginning of the next as the flat plains began to roll into hills and trees began to appear in little clumps here and there. We reached Hamlet as morning was giving way to the midday. The town was nestled among the wooded foothills of the mountains, a little stream spilling down from the highlands wound into the village, around its handful of buildings, and then back out again as though it was satisfied it had seen enough. It might have been any place except for a large sign that had been erected by the side of the road next to a small wood shack just on the outskirts:

WELCOME TO HAMLET. KNOWN ACROSS THE GLOBE.

A man stepped out from the building as we came near. He was dressed in ruffles and hose. The music suddenly shifted. There was a swell of violins, and a classical, courtly melody began.

Valdara, who had ridden up on my right, muttered, "And so it begins."

I turned to ask her what was about to begin, and whether she also heard the music, when our greeter put one hand to his chest, stretched the other out to the side, and gave an elaborate bow. As he rose he proclaimed,

"Greetings, friends unknown.
I give welcome from the Village of Hamlet,
which may never be the Hamlet of Village.
Lest, in a tempest thou split the ears
of our fine citizens."

This speech finished, he crossed to the other side of the road, spun, and switched which of his hands was outstretched and which was crossed over his breast.

"For if adventure is thy goal today,
Then best to suit your actions to your words,
and your words to the action.
Honesty and honor are the virtues which
we hold dear, and doing else will make the
judicious grieve, and lead to censure.

Which, in our village, would overthrow all
that thou might attempt . . ."

Thankfully, Drake rode up at this point. "We aren't paying for the performance," he growled.

Rather than finishing, the man gave a grunt of disgust and ducked back inside the little house.

"What was all that about?" I asked, and from the looks of many of the others, they had the same question.

Drake shrugged. "Nothing. Just a little of the local flavor," he said. "They like to try to impress people by speaking iambic. Visitors sometimes throw money—I think mostly out of confusion or a desire to get them to shut-up."

"I told you we should avoid Hamlet," Valdara said wearily, taking a swig from a bottle of wine she'd produced from one of her saddlebags. "The place is strange and that's coming from someone that has been through the fire swamps, into the paths of the dead, and over the rainbow."

"She did warn you, Avery," Drake pointed out, and took the bottle away from Valdara. She glared at him, but said nothing as he began to empty it on the ground. "This place may have a lot going for it in the adventuring department, but it can be a little off-putting. I've always thought the problem was their proximity to all the seriously creepy things that live in the abandoned castles, ruins, and dungeons around this place. I still say that you can't live so close to so much downright weirdness without having it affect you."

"Does that mean we'll have to talk like that?" I spluttered.

"Nah," he said with a dismissive wave of his hand. "The greeter is just here to add some color and get a little extra coin for the town from the tourists."

"They are crazy about gold in this village," Seamus agreed.

"Thank goodness we have Avery here to bankroll us," Rook said, and fixed me with one of his single-eyed stares.

There was hearty agreement from all around at this. On that ominous note, we entered Hamlet. And as we rode down the hill into the town proper, there was much discussion as to how people were going to spend my money in the taverns (Rook and Drake and Seamus seemed eager to get hammered), and at the armorers (much to my dismay Valdara said she needed to repair several very attractive tears and holes the trolls had made in her leather and metal shirt), and bookbinders (need I say anything but Sam), and cloth dyers (Paul and the new members of the NPC crowd wanted to see if dyeing their tunics a color other than red would improve their chances of survival), and hatters (the two to three gnomes that remained seemed to think they needed black tasseled caps to mourn the deaths of their one to two friends), and we would need lodging and stables for the horses, and apparently I needed to pay Seamus back for all the equipment he'd bought back in Blightsbury, and so on.

I lingered in the back, trying to figure out how to delay as long as possible the very awkward conversation I was going to have to have with the rest of the company about the fact that I was literally penniless.

CHAPTER 17

THE MONEY PARADOX

The Company of the Fellowship had dissolved, at least temporarily. Members of the group scattered through the village. I sat on my horse in the middle of the town square taking in the scene. There was activity everywhere as adventurers of all stripes loaded horses and packs, picked fights with each other, and, if they were on their own, wandered about trying to get hired into a group. There were many shouts of "LFG!" which I learned later meant Looking for Group. Valdara was right; it was unnatural and disturbing.

Also unnatural was the sheer number of people on the street. If this volume of traffic was indicative of "normal," I could see why everything cost so much here. Hamlet was the only town within a hundred leagues. They had a captive audience, and as anyone that's ever been to a movie theater will attest, captives are always subject to ransom.

I began to wonder what I should be doing, and how doing whatever it was I should be doing would result in me becoming instantly very wealthy. I tried to contact Eldrin, which wasn't going to make me rich, but would make me feel less alone in not being rich, but either it didn't work or he wouldn't answer. I seemed to be at an impasse, an impasse that would not last much longer, because eventually people would start returning from their shopping adventures and want some of my nonexistent money. The music in my head became contemplative, which actually helped me focus on the problem at hand.

Oddly, my first coherent thought was, *What would the Dark Lord do?*

This is not as mad as it sounds. The Dark Lord had a rather large army to support and heaps of coin to support it with, because trust me, if there is one thing blood orcs like more than drums, it's gold. I recalled with fondness the vast vaults under the Fortress of Despair where I'd stored the mountains of gold coins and jewels and other wonderful objects of great value that I'd accumulated. The problem was that I had used the reality key to make all that lovely money last time and, as Valdara had reminded me, it was well and truly gone.

In fact, as the Dark Lord, I had relied rather heavily on the key for fulfilling my most exotic needs, like mountains of gold and thrones of skulls and whatnot. As getting the key was the entire point of my presence on this world and would have made every other question and problem moot, this was not a very helpful observation. Nor was my second observation, which was that the Dark Lord probably wouldn't have even bothered with mundane matters like getting sacks of gold, but would have delegated that to the dread necromancers of the Circle of Nine, my most trusted underlings. This observation was useless for at least two reasons: first I was no longer the Dark Lord, and second I'd atomized the Circle of Nine in a volcanic eruption about a week before the final battle.

Nevertheless, this very meandering train of thought led me to the conclusion that the answer to my dilemma lay in the appropriate application of magic. Now, having observed my work on Sam you may think that conjuring a little gold would be a trivial matter. It is not. In fact, it is devilishly hard to use Mysterium magic to make things appear out of thin air, and back home in the Mysterium's heightened reality field it is virtually impossible unless you have access to something like the Hexagramical Reality Collider, which is a magical pentagram about thirteen miles long on a side that was built at great expense to determine once and for all whether a god was a particle.

The reason that pure conjuration is so hard for Mysterium mages is that Mysterium magic is based on reason. And as anyone that has ever stared at the place where they know they put their keys down last night will tell you, having something appear out of nowhere, no matter how badly you want it to appear, is simply not reasonable.

If I had known the local magic, with all its wishy-washy mysticism, I might have been able to do it. After hearing Sam's description of how his sleep spell worked, I had become convinced that anything, no matter how ridiculous, might be possible. Unfortunately, while the DMG I'd written was chock-full of detailed explanations for the theoretical practice of Trelarian magic, I had never studied how you actually cast the spells. Besides, I'd probably need to have something to make it work like a bat's eye or a frog's hair.

I needed some time to think and a place to rest my aching blisters. Fortunately, there were four inns in the town, each basically identical, and each identified by a sign emblazoned with a dragon: one painted red (the Red Dragon Inn), one that had been impaled on a spear (the Dead Dragon Inn), one that was roaring and spitting fire (the Dread Dragon Inn), and one that looked like an oddly shaped baguette (the Bread Dragon Inn). Unfortunately, when I inquired at each they all required a deposit. Apparently, the innkeepers of Hamlet had long ago learned that giving credit to adventurers on their way to explore diabolically dangerous dungeons and fight absurdly vicious monsters was not the best way to stay in business. I couldn't blame them.

Having found no shelter at the inns, I pulled my horse into a small grassy alley between a weaver and a blacksmith's shop. There was a low branched oak tree here, and I slipped into the shadows beneath it so I could think. It was only after I'd made myself comfortable among the roots that I discovered that I was not alone.

"Sam!" I cried out in surprise.

A short distance away the young wizard was sitting cross-legged with his precious spell book closed on his lap. His red-rimmed eyes told me that he had been crying. "Oh hi, Wizard Avery," he said, wiping his face with the sleeve of his robe.

I began to rise, saying, "Sorry, Sam. I didn't know you were studying here. I wouldn't want to interrupt."

"Please stay," he said with a shuddering sigh. "I was working up the courage to come talk to you anyway."

For a few seconds I hovered in an awkward crouch somewhere between standing and sitting, trying to decide if I should continue my exit or stay. Looking into his thin young face and sad brown eyes, I knew I couldn't leave without giving him a chance to unburden himself. I took a deep breath and sat. "Sure, Sam. What's up?"

He gulped and closed his eyes. "I have decided to leave the company."

Okay, I hadn't known what to expect him to say, but among the options I'd been turning over, that had not been one of them. I asked the obvious question. *Why?*

A little voice in my head answered that this was the pattern at work, trying to correct my interference from when I'd saved him. I begged it to shut the hell up. Meanwhile, Sam threw his book to the ground beside him, shrugged, and said in a low, ragged voice, "Because I'm a burden on the company. Had anyone been depending on me last night they might have been killed. The magic I know is worthless, and I'm not even good at it."

You know that empty feeling you get in your heart when the consequences of your actions come home to roost. Add to it the fact that the music had suddenly dropped into a depressing minor key and I felt terrible.

I began to say something lame and untrue like, "You are a really great wizard, Sam," when the resolution to both my problem and Sam's attack of self-doubt came to me in a flash of inspiration.

I picked up the acorn that had just fallen from the tree onto my head and said, "I'm broke, Sam."

Like my surprise at his decision to leave the company, it was clear that however he had thought I might respond to his revelation this was not it. "What?" he asked.

"I don't have a coin to my name," I said, rolling the acorn around in the palm of my hand.

"But . . . but . . ." he stuttered. "You're a great wizard."

I shook my head. "Obviously, I'm either not a great wizard, or great wizards are not inherently rich, or both."

He spun as the full import of what I was saying struck him. "But the rest of the company is out buying equipment and supplies," he said, wide-eyed with horror. "What will we do? I have a little coin, but—"

"You've resigned from the company," I pointed out before he could complete the thought. "So, technically this isn't your problem."

"I suppose so," he said, but his brow was furrowed with concern.

We sat in silence for a minute or so and I let the tension build. Finally, I gave a dramatic sigh. "It's really too bad," I said. "I might have been able to conjure the money, but my spell requires two wizards to work."

Sam's eyes widened at this. "You can conjure money? My old master could conjure water and food, but he never conjured anything of value."

I almost pointed out that in almost all cases being able to create food and water out of nothing would be far more useful than creating bits of metal or crystalized minerals, but I managed to stop myself. Instead, I waved a finger at him. "But I can't conjure the money, at least not by myself."

"I don't understand how I can help. I don't know how to conjure anything. I'm useless!" he said with a cry as he slumped back against the tree.

"You keep saying that."

"Because it's true," he wailed, pulling at his stringy brown hair. "You said yourself that my magic makes 'no sense' and is 'hokey.'"

I flinched as he threw my words back at me, but I

let it pass and said calmly, "Just because I don't understand your magic doesn't make it worthless. It simply means that I'm ignorant. There are plenty of things that my magic can't do that your magic can, and there are plenty of things about my style of magic that are just as absurd as your crickets and daisy petals."

"Rose petals," he corrected.

"Forgive me, rose petals," I said, managing to keep a straight face.

"I don't believe it," he said bitterly. "You brought me back to life. With that kind of power, you could do anything. Name one thing that a wizard like me could do that you can't."

"I can't create food and water out of thin air. In fact, I can't create even the smallest grain of sand out of nothing."

"I don't believe you." I noted that this was said with a much reduced level of sulkiness.

"I'm being perfectly frank with you, Sam." And for once I was. "True conjuration, the creation of something from nothing, a task that your master could so easily accomplish with food and drink, is impossible for wizards of my order. In fact, the impossibility of performing conjuration is a well-known limitation of my type of magic. We call it the Adams Paradox. Would you like to hear about it?"

"I suppose so," he said uncertainly.

"I will take that as an enthusiastic 'yes,'" I said, and, picking up five acorns, began juggling them.

"Magus Adams," I began as I wove the acorns into

a series of interconnecting loops, "was one of the most famous wizards of my order, and his principal area of focus was true conjuration—"

"But you said that conjuration is impossible!" Sam protested.

"Are you going to interrupt me or let me tell the story?" I asked with a mild glare.

"Sorry," he said, and pinched his lips together.

I changed the pattern of the acorns into a single large circle and continued. "As I was saying, Adams was studying conjuration, which is the magic of creating objects from nothing. He worked on the problem for hundreds of years, but never could get it to work. His continued failure to conjure even the smallest somethings made him a bit of a joke among the other wizards in the School of Conjuration, each of whom conjured a number of somethings on a regular basis—"

"But how could there be a School of Conjuration if . . ." Sam started to say, but then stopped himself and put a hand over his mouth.

I raised an eyebrow and picked up the thread of my story again. "Adams, being as pompous as any other mage and so knowing that most if not all of his colleagues were far less talented than he was, began trying to reproduce their experiments and discovered that the mages in the School of Conjuration were not conjurers at all, but instead very talented subconscious teleportationists who had been unknowingly stealing items from other people for years.

"When his findings were released," I said, now juggling the acorns in a complicated figure eight pattern, "the other mages of my order came to believe that anything that had ever gone missing in their lives could probably be put down to a thieving conjurer somewhere and so demanded that the School of Conjuration be disbanded and replaced by something useful, like a bar. It was while sitting in this bar that a now unemployed Adams came up with his theory of the conjuration paradox, and simultaneously solved our problem of how to get gold for the company."

I glanced at Sam and saw that he was sitting up on his knees, hanging on to my every word. He was hooked. More importantly, the enthusiasm of the young mage I'd first met in Blightsbury had returned.

With a swipe of my hands I collected the flying acorns into my cupped palms. "The story goes that he was staring at his empty glass of beer, and trying to convince the bartender to serve him another even though he had no money, when one of the other patrons, who also happened to be an ex-colleague of his, shouted that in the old days they might have just conjured another pint. After the grumbles of agreement died down—the bar, you understand, had become the regular haunt of former mages from the former School of Conjuration—he explained that he could prove logically that it was, always had been, and always would be impossible to make something out of nothing. Needless to say, this got everyone's attention."

"I'll say," Sam agreed with a wag of his head.

"Legend has it that he walked behind the bar holding up his empty beer glass—" I pantomimed "—and asked if everyone could agree that to conjure something from nothing you must replace the nothing with the something."

"Makes sense," said Sam.

"I'm glad you approve," I said dryly. "As you say, Sam, this initial statement seemed noncontroversial so everyone agreed, and he took the opportunity to fill his glass. He then drained it and, gesturing at the again empty glass, pointed out that nothing obviously takes up no space, it being, at its core, nothing. Moreover, because it takes up no space, nothing is without a doubt infinitely small. This everyone also agreed must be the case."

"What's 'infinite' mean?" Sam asked.

"Without end," I answered. "He was saying that the 'nothing' is so small that no matter how small you think it is, it is smaller than that. Another way of saying this is to say that the smallness of nothing is without end."

The young man cocked his head to the side and thought about this.

"Adams then filled his glass again. Once it was full to the brim he asked if they would also agree that something, no matter how big, must take up only a finite, which means fixed, amount of space, else it would consume the universe. This also seemed to be a safe statement and so there was general agreement on it. He then drained his glass yet again and said, 'And there's the paradox.'"

Sam looked confused, which is funny because in the story that was also the reaction of the other patrons, well, confusion and anger from the barkeep, who was beginning to suspect that the entire lecture was a ploy to get free beer off of him, which it was.

"Seeing that his logic had confused everyone, Adams explained that if the smallness of nothing is inherently infinite, and if the space of any something is inherently finite, it would by necessity take an infinite number of somethings to fill any nothing, and thus no matter how many somethings you try to conjure you always need at least one more something before the nothing is full enough for the something to replace the nothing; *ergo* it is impossible to conjure something from nothing."

"That makes no sense!" Sam blurted suddenly.

He was right it was utter gibberish, but that didn't make it any less true.

"Why not?" I asked, eyes-wide in feigned alarm.

"It's nonsense," he complained.

"Not at all," I argued, and began to pour the acorns back and forth from one hand to the other. "If I had an empty room of endless dimension (which we will take as the nothing), and I tried to fill it with acorns (which we will take as the finite somethings we are trying to conjure), it would take an endless number of acorns to fill the room."

"No, no, no!" he shouted, and, standing, began to

pace about under the tree. "Nothing isn't an endless space. It is something fleetingly small, like a grain of the finest sand. So, any finite something should be able to instantly fill it. There is no paradox."

"That's not the way my magic works," I explained.

He stopped midstride and looked at me with dawning understanding. "Your magic makes no sense," he said in an awed whisper.

"Exactly."

"My magic also makes no sense!" he crowed with glee.

"Precisely."

"All magic is barking!" he concluded with a whoop of joy.

"Now you've got it," I said, pocketing the acorns and rising to my feet. "Let's use some of this nonsensical, barking-mad magic to get filthy rich just like Adams did."

"Deal," he said, and picked his spell book up from the ground where it had fallen. "How do we start, Wizard Avery?"

"We start with you not calling me Wizard Avery. We are both professional mages, so it is just Avery to you." I stuck out my hand so we could shake on it.

After a moment of stunned disbelief, a wide grin split his face. He took my hand and began pumping vigorously. "Deal again . . . Avery."

"Good," I said, and I did feel good, maybe for the first time since coming back. I had spent nearly all my time in Trelari worrying about the land, but ignoring the people. Whether it hurt or helped stop Vivian, this felt much better.

I was still mulling over my feelings when I noticed that Sam was staring at me expectantly. "What?" I asked, suddenly nervous that I had forgotten to say something else, and that he would burst into tears again.

"Getting filthy rich? Remember the rest of the party is out spending all your nonexistent gold," he prompted.

"Oh, right," I said, relaxing. "I thought there was a problem."

"But isn't there? I don't understand how two wizards can conjure gold if it's impossible for one wizard to do it."

"Ah," I said, extending a finger into the air and laying it aside my nose, "but then you didn't hear the end of Magus Adams's story in which he invented a remarkably useful spell, which in the right circumstances can turn anybody's pockets into an infinite source of money, and which led him to become the richest magus of his age."

I scratched my head, wondering where to begin this part of the lesson, since I would be making most of it up. "Where did I leave off?" I mumbled.

This was meant more for myself, but Sam answered eagerly, "Magus Adams had just proved it was impossible to conjure something from nothing."

"That's right," I said with a snap. "But you missed the most important part of that story. He did his explaining while drinking more than a half-dozen pints of beer."

"Well, why is that important?" Sam asked.

"Because the barkeep had been keeping a count, and also did not seem to appreciate the magical history that had been made in his establishment. He demanded that Adams pay at once for everything he'd drunk."

"Gosh!" Sam exclaimed with a whistle.

"Gosh is right," I agreed, "but the word Adams used was, I believe, a bit more profane. Fortunately, Adams was not a mage to let impossible situations get him down. After all, he'd spent a century or so trying to do the impossible. I will now show you how he got out of this particular jam."

I went to my horse and dug through my saddlebag. I needed a box or a bag or something. My hand fell on the belt pouch Seamus had given me that I'd had yet to wear. I pulled it out and held it up. "Here is our solution!"

"A pouch?" he asked skeptically. "I have one exactly like it. Seamus gave us those, along with a mess kit, and fifty feet of rope, and—"

"Yes, yes, and a ten-foot pole," I interrupted. "But this is not the pouch Seamus gave me."

"It sure looks like the same pouch," he said skeptically.

I leaned in close to him and whispered, "If you had a magic item that could transmute objects into gold coins, wouldn't you disguise it?"

"Golly, yes!" he said.

I rolled my eyes. "'Gosh' and now 'golly'? We'll work on your expressive vocabulary later. For now, let's get started on the spell." I put the pouch on the ground at our feet, making sure the flap that covered the opening was only open a crack. Then I plucked a thin branch from the tree. I stripped the leaves and began twisting it into a circle. "You will be the focus of the magic."

This made him stand up a bit straighter.

I positioned myself so my foot was on one of the tree roots and began drawing power from it. In the shadows it was difficult to see the subtle graying of the trunk. Harder to disguise was the yellowing of the leaves. To draw his attention away I began tracing the branch with my finger and filling it with energy. The circlet began to glow a brilliant green color.

Truth be told, the pattern I was drawing—called the probability distribution pattern—is exceedingly simple (consisting of a series of undulated wavy lines), and I could have done the magic without the branch. But probability bending, which is what I was going to attempt, depended entirely on belief or at least a willing suspension of disbelief, on the part of the subject. And given the fact that Trelari magic had all these weird material component requirements, I thought it would help Sam believe in the spell more if he could touch something.

I placed the circlet on Sam's head and said very

somberly, "I will now ask you to focus your thoughts on each of the acorns I pass to you. If the magic is working, they should begin to glow green like the circlet. Once they're glowing, slip each one into the pouch."

I pulled an acorn from my pocket and held it up in front of his eyes. This gave me a chance to examine the shimmering field of improbability that I'd cast on him. It covered him from head to toe and looked strong enough for me to make the attempt.

I passed the acorn to him and as I did so I pushed a little power into it so it glowed green. "Great!" I said with a clap. "It's working perfectly. Now, focus all your thoughts and energies on the acorn, and when you're ready drop it in."

With a trembling hand and almost maniacal focus he carefully slipped the glowing acorn into the top of the pouch and I shut the flap. There was a metallic ring, which made sense because I'd put the tin cup from my mess kit (another standard item Seamus had given me) at the bottom of the pouch.

However, the effect on Sam from this simple deception was dramatic. His eyes grew wide and he whispered, "It's working."

I held a finger up to my lips for silence. "Concentrate."

He nodded his head seriously. The next several minutes were spent in a solemn but ultimately ridiculous ritual where I would pass him acorns and he would place them surgically into the pouch, listening each time for the metallic ring that would indicate that a "transformation" had occurred.

I would have been just as excited had any magic actually been taking place, but it wasn't. Certainly transmutation wasn't happening. Transmutation of matter from one thing to another was only slightly less impossible using Mysterium magic than was conjuring something from nothing. It turns out it is really hard to alter each and every atom of an object from one type to another and takes enormous power to do so—world-ending power. In fact, over a hundred years ago Mysterium and the innerworlds signed the Transmutation Test Ban Treaty because mages kept blowing up subworlds trying to make solid gold castles and diamond encrusted towers. The truth was, all Sam and I were doing at this point was dropping acorns into a metal cup, and almost anyone can do that. The real magic was going to come next, and everything else we had done up to this point was designed to increase the probability that the most improbable thing would happen, which is that when we reached into the pouch we would find gold coins where, by all rights, there should only be acorns. This was the magic of probability bending.

Probability bending was devised on the very same night Magus Adams got drunk and came up with his conjuration paradox. The story goes that after Adams explained his paradox, the barkeep explained to Adams that, impossible or not, he'd better find a way to conjure up some money to pay his bar tab or he'd be introduced to the paradox of the five knuckles. Adams, in a fit of desperate logical brilliance, then came up with the single greatest magical parlor trick of all time.

It is said that Adams calmly explained that he could easily pay his bar tab with the coins in his own pocket. There was a lot of skepticism at this claim, because Adams was known to be fairly destitute at this point. He then pulled out a piece of fazestone chalk and drew around his barstool the probability circle I'd just placed on Sam's head. Addressing the bar he said, "I don't know with any certainty how many coins I have in my pocket today. It might be none, but then it also might be any other number. If we assign even odds to all possibilities, this means that there is one out of an infinite number of chances that I have no money, but an infinite number of chances that I have one or more coins. Logically, this means that it is far more probable that I have all the money I need to pay my tab than it is that I am broke." To the surprise of everyone, including himself, he proceeded to pull coin after coin out of his pockets until there was a fair mound of them on the bar. When the barkeep was satisfied, Adams gave an unsteady bow and staggered out into the street.

This is precisely what I wanted to happen here, absent maybe the staggering.

As the last of the acorns went into the pouch I said

solemnly, "The transformation is done. Reach into the pouch, Sam."

With trembling hand he did, and *voilà*—he was holding a glimmering golden coin. I will spare you the details of the next ten minutes, but at the end of it we had filled a substantial portion of my backpack with lovely spendable money. When we had enough I cut off the flow of power to the circlet. And not too soon either. My head was swimming at the effort of holding the probability pattern (another bad sign that Trelari was getting closer and closer to Mysterium), and the tree had begun to lose leaves at an alarming rate.

Sam noticed nothing. He was glowing with pride at this point. I gave him a pat on the back and smiled to myself. Given his credulous nature and his ability to believe the most absurd things, I had known that Sam would be a perfect candidate for Adams's probability bending spell. I myself could never make it work, because I was a natural cynic and usually never had enough money to get drunk enough to forget how little money I had, which is essential to the working of the spell.

"I can't believe you did it!" Sam crowed.

"We did it," I corrected. "Without you it wouldn't have worked. Now, let's go spend this, and remember we've got to keep this on the down-low or someone might try to steal the pouch."

"Right," he said solemnly. "This will be between you and me."

What I didn't add was that we needed to spend the money now before the improbability field associated with the coins' existence started to collapse and they began to disappear. Effectively, we would be stealing everything we bought.

CHAPTER 18

A LICENSE TO QUEST

For the next hour or so Sam and I ran through Hamlet paying for this and buying that like we were everyone's favorite rich uncle. I won't go into the total damage, but safe to say had we been spending real money and not stuff I'd conjured out of a fundamental misunderstanding of probability and statistics, I'd have been angry.

When at last we'd managed to track everyone down and had settled their debts, I offered to buy Sam a well-deserved ale. He would have none of it. "I can't," he said with an earnest shake of his head. "I haven't studied my spells all day, and I have to be ready if you need me again . . . Avery."

With a spring in his step, he headed back to the

tree beside the weaver's shop to read his spell book. I wasn't sure if Sam would ever be a talented wizard, but he was a good fellow and I was glad to see his spirits revived.

To revive my own spirits, I decided to retreat to a place where I could drink some spirits. I found Valdara and Drake in the common room of the Bread Dragon Inn and joined them. I know what you're thinking, *But, Avery, inns don't serve alcohol—remember!*

Apparently, this universal rule did not apply to Hamlet, as Drake patiently explained to me when I asked him about it. "Kid, you don't survive long in a town built on adventurers if you don't serve something that will get them drunk."

I was into my second ale, and starting to feel human again, when Rook bustled up, eyebrows bristling vigorously. "What are you all doin' sittin' around drinkin'?"

"Hoping to get drunk?" Drake answered for all of us.

The dwarf rolled his eyes. "No time for that, and probably not enough drink in all the town for you inebriates."

"Lighten up, Rook," I said in the expansive tones of someone that has a good buzz on. "We've been on the road for weeks. What will one day's rest matter?"

"It'll matter when we can't get a license for a quest and get stuck here for the next month waitin' for the Master to open up shop again," he rasped in response. "I thought you were in a hurry, but maybe I'm wrong."

I heard the words he was saying, and I understood them individually, but put together they had made no sense. "What are you talking about, Rook?"

"I've been askin' around, and the only way to get one of the quests around Hamlet is to buy a license from some fella named the Master of the Dungeons," he answered. "But he only issues them once a month—today—and it's already afternoon. All the other adventurin' groups got their licenses first thing this mornin' . . ." He glared at me. "Before dawn!"

I ignored the gibe. I had other things to worry about, like the Master of Dungeons. I had completely forgotten about him. He was a construct that I'd created in the early days of my experiment to help me regulate access to important items and quests. I had been worried that if someone other than the selected group of Heroes found a specific item or defeated a key monster that the entire spell pattern might be disrupted. I had no idea that the Master would survive the fall of the Dark Lord, much less that he would set himself up here. I began to understand why Hamlet was such a strange place. The Master is extremely powerful within his limited domain, and he could very well be warping reality around him. The expression "old sins cast long shadows" popped into my head. I groaned.

Rook cocked his head to one side and gave me a one-eyed squint. "That's right, laddie. I'm also worried. Worried that all the good questin' licenses are already gone."

A thought occurred to me and I turned to Valdara and Drake. "Did you two know about this?"

They didn't answer for a second and then Drake said quietly, "Yes. We ran into the Master back when we were looking for the Mage Staff."

"How could you not tell me!" I shouted, and slammed my tankard onto the table. "You know how important finding Justice Cleaver is and now you may have ruined our chances."

Drake had the decency to look abashed, but Valdara narrowed her eyes and said unapologetically, "I told you I didn't want to come to Hamlet. The entire place is corrupt and the *Master* is the worst of all."

I shot Valdara a glare, which she returned in kind. I was obviously going to get no apology from her, and there was no use arguing about what was done. I needed a plan. I rubbed my eyes and tried to think of something. "Could we join up with one of the groups that already has a license?" I asked Rook.

Rook shook his head and tugged at his beard irritably. "We might have been able to had we tried a couple of hours ago, laddie, but the groups have all gone off already. Haven't you noticed how empty the town is?"

I looked about the common room. He was right; apart from the bartender, we were the only people here. I hadn't noticed, but while we'd been drinking the village had emptied out. I banged my tankard on the table in frustration.

"Well, we'll just have to go to the Master now and see if there is anything left."

I stood and looked down at Valdara and Drake, dropping a couple of coins. "Drink up—it seems to be the only thing you two are suited for at this point."

I gathered the rest of the company together and we marched over to the Master's office. It turned out to be a relatively modest building in the center of town.

Rook paused before opening the door. "Now, when we get in there let me do the talkin'," he growled. "I don't want to risk our standin' with the Master by havin' one of you sayin' something stupid." He took a moment to glare about at us in warning, lingering on me a bit more than the others. When I nodded my agreement, he barked out, "Seamus, did you get the food like I asked?"

"Yes, Rook," Seamus said, holding up a couple of heavily loaded bags.

He nodded brusquely and opened the door. The room was dark as a cave and it took my eyes a minute to adjust. When they did I saw that the walls were lined with shelves loaded to the point of collapse with brightly colored books and boxes. In the middle of the room under a single lantern was a large table covered in maps and little figures. On our side of the table were set a half-dozen or so chairs. A foldable screen about a foot high blocked the view of the other side of the table, and it took me a moment to realize that the Master was sitting behind there. All I could see of him was his bald head, on which sprouted a few tufts of thin white hair.

Rook marched up to the table with the rest of the group shuffling in nervously behind him. I stayed purposefully at the back of the group. He'd never seen me in person, but I didn't want to bring too much attention to myself.

The Master remained unmoved behind his screen for close to a minute. The only sound was the scratch of his pen on paper. At last he peeked up above the edge of the screen. I saw two piercing brown eyes, a small nose, and a broad smile. "Hello, you may call me the Master . . . of Dungeons. What adventure do you seek?"

Immediately ignoring Rook's earlier warning, the entire company pressed in around the table. "Ask about the Fortified Safe of the Dark Elves," suggested Ariella.

With a shake of his head, the small man responded. "That is already taken. You would have needed to get here before dawn to get a license for a quest like that."

While Rook was glaring at me for the crime of wanting a full night's rest, Sam bent forward and asked, "Is the Hidden Tower of Loch—"

"Taken."

Seamus asked, "What about the legendary tunnels under Castle Grayfalcon? I think Valdara and Drake have been through there before . . ."

"Off-limits for restock and repairs," the little man barked, and then turned that into a cough when we all looked at him blankly. "I'm jesting, of course. We don't repair or restock the local dungeons. That would be preposterous."

The slip may have gone unnoticed by the others, but it confirmed for me Valdara's suspicions that something was rotten in Hamlet. While I was considering the question of how this strange adventuring ecosystem might have evolved out of the pattern of my spell, the others in the group were calling out names of other places: the Shrine of Tuo-Kua, the Temple of the Toad, the Ghost Tower of Inertness . . . Each time the Master had a reason we couldn't go there.

Finally, Rook banged his hands down on the table for silence. Everyone jumped, even the Master. "Pray, Sir, what do you have left?" he asked.

"Hmm," the Master said, peering at something behind the screen. "I have a set of mines. The Mines of—"

"Mines? You call them mines?" Seamus snorted. "I'll have you know dwarfs made those into a palace. That was a grand place."

The Master cleared his throat. "The Mines of Maria."

"Oh," said Seamus. "I thought you were talking about those other mines . . ."

"Taken this morning," the Master said, "but if history holds it will be available within the week. You could wait."

Rook and Seamus looked at me hopefully. I didn't want to spend another day in this crazy place, but I was also in no mood to go crawling about in a mine if it wasn't going to get us closer to the Dark Queen. "Do the Mines of Maria have any connection with the ancient weapon Justice Cleaver?" I asked.

The Master's eyes narrowed almost imperceptibly at me as I stepped forward. "Do I know you?"

"This is the Great and Powerful Wizard Avery," Sam said enthusiastically before I could put a hand over his mouth to stop him.

"He is, is he?" the Master asked, and the twinkle that came into them meant that the name meant something to him. "Well, Great and Powerful Avery, your name precedes you."

"It does?" I asked, and was proud that my voice didn't break.

There was no reason that the Master should know me, but my palms began to sweat nevertheless. Could he suspect enough to expose me as the former Dark Lord? I began to worry that I was a few moments away from being hacked to bits by my own company.

"Yes," he said with a confirming nod. "There are riders on the Sea of Grass seeking a wizard by that name."

Not sure what else to say I stuck with, "Okay?"

"Hooded riders," he added significantly.

Everyone around me gave a gasp. I looked about uncertainly. Why did it matter to everyone that they wore hoods? I mean, pretty much everyone who wore a cloak had a hood. I had a hooded cloak on right now. I put the hood up whenever it rained. I suppose someone seeing me on the road might also call me a hooded rider. Was this some message from the reality matrix that I was missing?

Instead of mentioning any of these questions, I said, "Thanks for the warning." See, I was getting smarter.

"Don't mention it," the Master said, and pushed the license across the table toward me. "I think the Mines of Maria will serve your purposes, Wizard Avery." He smiled at me again, but it lacked some of its earlier warmth.

I purchased the license for the Mines of Maria for fifty gold, two electrum, and three copper pieces. For the record, I'm not exactly sure anyone knows what electrum really is, but apparently it is slightly more valuable than silver and slightly less valuable than gold. It didn't matter; the pouch had exactly what we needed.

The other began arguing about what order the company should use when marching through the mines, but I wasn't in the mood to listen. I was brooding over a new thought I'd just had. When I was the Dark Lord, I'd had my Circle of Nine necromancers that I'd sent out on my most important missions. They had worn deeply cowled robes so no one could see that I'd not put in the effort to give them faces. If these "Hooded Riders" were Vivian's version of those guys, then we had more to worry about than the mines or the Master.

CHAPTER 19

THE MINES OF MARIA

We stabled our horses in the village and made our way to the mines on foot. A day and a few hours later, we found ourselves at the entrance to the mine, which the others kept calling a dungeon. I'd asked enough questions on the journey to know that when they said dungeon, what they meant was an underground complex of hallways and rooms, not a prison in the classic sense of the word. In any case, the mines certainly didn't look like a mine. There was no sign of mine carts, or slag heaps, or waste containment ponds, or anything else one would need to mine ore. I couldn't tell you what purpose this complex could possibly have served, or why this Maria would have wanted to construct such a place. However, everyone took it as perfectly natural that someone—they all conjectured an ancient wizard—would have built such a thing at some point in the distant past.

"It's time to make the tough choices," shouted Rook. "We need a marchin' order."

"And who's going to keep a map so we don't get lost," added Seamus.

The arguing, which had never really relented since leaving Hamlet, increased in fervor. I couldn't understand why some people insisted on being in the front and others demanded to be in the rear. No one wanted Ariella in the back because of her reputation as a rogue, although thus far she was the least roguish rogue I'd ever met. I rubbed my right temple with two fingers and stepped away as the debate continued, the volume and pitch increasing so that soon we were making enough noise to warn every monster in the place of our intentions, strengths, weaknesses, and stratagems. Actually, considering the violence of the debate, I decided that if I were a monster, I'd probably run.

I was doubly irritated because I suspected that I had a map of the mines in my DMG, but hadn't been able to get into contact with Eldrin since before Hamlet. This had been the longest time between our check-ins, and I was growing more and more anxious that something had happened to him. An anxiety that was only compounded by my absolute inability to do anything about it.

"Enough," I said sharply. "Here's what we are

going to do. Ariella's going to be the mapmaker, since she has experience writing and on the move." It was true that if she wasn't singing-saying songs, she was writing poetry. "And as for the group order—" I pointed at two of the people in red tunics (still red because although they had dyed them, the dye had only seemed to deepen the redness of the red), but I realized I didn't know their names. Paul could have been one of them, but I wasn't positive he hadn't died already "—you two go in front. Everyone else start lining up behind those two."

I spent the next half hour lining people up leaving only Valdara and Drake to their own devices. They shuffled to the back and seemed to have no intention of going anywhere else.

"All right," I announced from the middle of the line just in front of Drake and Valdara, and just behind Sam and Ariella. "Let's move out."

We moved down the staircase toward a heavy iron door. The background music became quieter and more somber, even a little eerie. As Paul or whoever it was in front got to the foot of the stair, the shadows to the right of him shifted and a woman with long dark hair held in a high, tight ponytail emerged. She wore dark silvery armor made of multiple plates that fitted like a second skin. I was pretty sure she wasn't a member of our company.

Paul shouted in alarm and made a swing at her with his sword. She parried it with her bracer-covered arm and backhanded him. Paul slumped to the ground and the other members of the red tunic brigade backed away.

"Sorry about that," she said. "I didn't mean to startle you. My group is camped nearby, and I was wondering . . ."

Rook stepped forward, brandishing our license, his eyebrows crashed together as he furrowed his forehead. "Listen, lady," he interrupted. "We've got the license for these mines. If you don't want the Hamlet town guards to get involved, you'll move along."

She held up her hands in a gesture of peace as Paul, I'm pretty sure it was Paul, moaned at her feet. "I'm not looking for trouble, and certainly not with town guards." An odd comment given that my initial impression of her was that she should be able to mop the floor with any two-bit hireling the Village of Hamlet might have at its disposal.

"As I said," she continued, "we are camped nearby. We are looking for an orc with a gold molar that is supposed to be in the mines. We've bought thirteen different licenses for the mines and haven't encountered him once. We need that molar so we can forge our paladin his mystic weapon." She gazed up and down our line. "I'm sure it wouldn't do you any good. It doesn't look like you have holy men of any stripe," she said as her eyes swept over Drake. "Anyway, we'd pay very well for it if you retrieve it for us, or if you'd be willing to sell us the license . . ."

I wanted to ask so many questions. If they needed gold, why not simply get some gold instead of prying a molar from an orc? Why would an orc have such a tooth? I'd seen plenty of the monsters in my time as Dark Lord and none of them were particularly interested in oral hygiene, or hygiene of any other kind for that matter.

As usual, Rook acted before I could reveal my ignorance. "Thanks," he said, "but we have this, lassie. We'll let you know if we see a beastie with a gold molar."

She stalked up the stairs toward the dwarf. "Wonderful. And the name's Zania."

Rook waited until she was out of sight and shouted, "Let's move out!"

"Halt!" called Seamus.

We all managed to stop without crashing into each other. "What?" Rook asked, bristling with irritation.

"Light sources. Torches or lanterns?" Seamus asked.

The entire group sighed. I'll save you from the debate that ensued, but in the end we used a combination of lanterns and light spells. I was rather pleased at how quickly we came to the decision, or at least as pleased as I could be considering we had been standing in front of the bloody door to the bloody place for what felt like an hour. At last, we descended into the depths.

"The stairway goes down to a room that is a thirty-foot square. We enter in the middle of the north wall. Directly across from the stair is a wooden door, which upon closer observation, shows multiple signs of attempts at being forced, including being chopped, burned, and possibly bitten," announced Sam. "We notice a few bits of bone in the northeast corner, along with something foul, but in the southwest corner, you see some bits of string."

Ariella scribbled hastily on her vellum, and then called out, "Got it!"

I started to ask Sam why he was describing the room in such detail when we could all look around and see it for ourselves, but before I could get the words out, Seamus announced, "We should search for secret doors."

The other members of the company began tapping on the walls and rapping on the floor. I wasn't exactly sure how to react. I moved next to Valdara and asked, "Why are they doing this when there is a perfectly obvious door right in front of us?"

"New groups always do this," she said with a shrug. "They'll tire of it by the third or fourth room."

"Did your last group do this also?"

Her face darkened at my question and she mumbled, "Yes, and there will also be death and sorrow and there is nothing I can do about that either." She brushed past me into the center of the room. "Everyone be careful," she announced. "The door into the dungeon is probably trapped."

"I'll handle it," declared a large fellow in a red tunic who I had put up near the front.

He looked like a barbarian of some sort. Rook had taken to calling him Red Four, and the other new member of the red tunic brigade Red Five. I don't know why, but they accepted the monikers without complaint. Anyway, Red Four gave the door a hard kick.

It didn't budge, and his face flushed red. "That's okay," he said, taking a few deep breaths. "Like my priest says, 'If you don't succeed, try again without head-butting anything.'"

He kicked it again. The sound of the impact echoed through the room. It still didn't budge. This time his face turned red and his mouth drew back exposing huge sharpened teeth. "I . . . am . . . in . . . control . . . of . . . my . . . anger. My . . . anger . . . doesn't . . . control . . . me," he said, grunting while kicking the door with each word.

Nothing. The door might have been solid stone. Red Four's face turned purple and veins bulged in his neck. He gave a bloodcurdling scream. "Head-butt time!"

With a terrifying noise, his unhelmed head smashed into the door. When it didn't give way immediately, he tried again, shouting, "Head-butt! Head-butt!" as over and over he slammed his head into the door. As long as I live, I doubt that I shall ever see anything so pointlessly violent.

We all sprung forward to pull him away from the door, but were too late. He fell backward, blood streaming from his forehead. He was out cold, knocked unconscious by the force of his assault. The group fell silent. I'm not sure anyone knew what to say.

I finally spoke. "Drake, can you help him?"

The priest coughed. "No, kid. There's really no help for someone willing to slam their head into a door that many times. It would take years of counseling. All I can do is bind his wound."

As Drake knelt over the fallen barbarian, Ariella made a squeaking sound. "I figured it out. We need to pull the door open, not push it."

A quiet sense of embarrassment fell over the company. "Okay, everyone," said Rook. "We never speak of this. What happens in the Mines of Maria stays in the Mines of Maria." For once, the entire group agreed.

After that, the door was opened without incident and Sam immediately began commentating again. "There's a ten-foot-wide corridor beyond that extends south sixty feet to another door. Unlike the first door, this one is already open."

"Got it!" shouted Ariella, who was sketching again on her sheet of vellum.

Sam's weird need to describe everything was getting to me. "Sam, why are you—" I started to say.

"On further inspection," Sam shouted, cutting me off, his voice strained with fear, "you can see an orc staring at you with wide eyes!"

"What was that?" I asked.

"Orc!" shouted Rook.

"Attack!" yelled someone in red (I'm pretty sure Red Five) who then charged down the hall, his sword slashing. Several people drew bows and started shooting arrows down the hall right at his back. I cringed, but by a miracle the shots missed the man. Unfortunately, they also missed the orc, who, showing remarkable cool under fire, simply shut the door.

Heedless of marching order, or any other order, the rest of the group rushed after Red Five and smashed its way through the door into the room beyond. I found myself alone with Drake. Down the hall someone yelled, "More orcs! Kill them all!" Drake and I exchanged a glance and ran toward the mayhem.

While I might not have agreed with all the tactics, or more accurately lack of tactics employed, I couldn't disagree with the results. By the time Drake and I entered the room, six orcs lay sprawled on the ground, two with arrows in them, one with burns from a magical spell (I wondered if Sam had been holding out on me or if the multitalented Ariella had some undisclosed tricks up her sleeve), and the other three were cut into pieces (given the stains on Valdara's sword and armor I suspected that was her doing). Everyone and every surface in the room was covered in blood and bits of organ. The smell. Oh gods, the smell. No one else seemed to notice.

"We got them!" yelled Paul or Red Five.

"Yeah!" said Red Five or Paul. They high-fived, sending a spray of blood out across the room.

Even Ariella seemed unaffected by the abattoir atmosphere. She was very calmly kneeling over the orcs' bodies going through their pockets.

"Can we get out of here?" I asked, swallowing the gorge rising up my throat.

Sam nodded and cleared his throat. "The orcs are dead. You are standing in a twenty-by-twenty-one-foot room that—"

"Wait!" shouted Seamus. "There's something terribly wrong here." He reached into a pocket on his kilt and pulled out a roll of string.

He measured the room for five to ten minutes and then said, "Rook, look at this measurement: twenty-one feet."

"Ahh," Rook said inscrutably, and nodded. "Yes, twenty-one feet." His eyes shifted back and forth in confusion almost like he wasn't certain how to react.

"I put it down to shoddy construction," grumbled Seamus.

"What is it?" I asked, feeling that I was missing the significance of this one extra foot. "Does it mean that there's a secret door or something?"

Seamus stared at me as though he didn't understand the question. At last he said, "No, secret doors could be anywhere." The others looked about at the walls as though one of these doors might spring out at them. "It's . . . it's just eerie," the dwarf continued. "Everyone knows that all dungeon rooms are built around ten-foot squares. Sometimes there's a five-foot one, but that's rare."

"I'm not even sure how to draw twenty-one feet," said Ariella.

A shiver went down my spine as I realized that the limitations of the graphing program I'd used to render all the maps for the important locations in Trelari might be responsible for this quirk. So many unintended consequences. I closed my eyes and sighed.

Sam patted me sympathetically on the back. "It's okay, but it is obvious that, whatever the legends say, dwarfs didn't make this so-called mine. They would never make such a mistake."

"No, we wouldn't," agreed Seamus. "It's a sign of sloppy documentation and construction, and it only augers trouble in the future."

Many heads around the room nodded in somber agreement with this pronouncement.

Despite my new noninterference policy on things like this, I didn't want us to be slowed down by things that didn't matter. I decided I needed to clear a few things up. I stepped into the middle of the room and held up my hands. "We need a company . . . of the Fellowship conference. There are a lot of things that we are doing that are only slowing us down. First," I said, pointing a finger at Sam, "you don't need to describe every room in such excruciating detail. We can all see the size of the room and the doors and the monsters in them."

"But how will the mapmaker know what to draw?"

"Can't she see what the room looks like with her own eyes?" I asked in reply.

"I suppose so," Sam said, a bit chastened.

I spun to Seamus. "The extra foot doesn't really matter, does it? All we need from the map is sufficient detail not to get lost. We are two rooms into the mine, for the sake of the gods."

The dwarf grumbled over this and Rook joined in for moral support. I caught words like *negligent*, *slipshod*, and *haphazard* in their mutterings.

I ignored them and addressed the entire group. "And what about this obsession with marching order? As soon as we met an orc, the order, which we spent so long arranging, went straight to hell. Let's stop with all the nonsense."

By the end I was raving and waving my arms about.

It was at this point that Valdara and Drake grabbed me, one on each arm, and began dragging me back down the hall. "We need to talk to Wizard Avery," Drake said. "Why don't you all start looking for secret doors, particularly around that area with the extra foot?"

Behind me I heard Sam announce, "The orcs are dead, and we are standing in a twenty-by-twenty-one-foot room . . ."

CHAPTER 20

RED FOUR

As soon as we reached the entry chamber, Valdara turned on me and shook a finger in my face. "Who the hell do you think you are?"

"What? You mean what I said back there?" She stared at me. Her eyes glittered dangerously. "But you have to know it's all ridiculous. You've been through this before. You said yourself that checking for secret doors was pointless."

"I didn't say that at all. I said that they would grow tired of it after three or four rooms. I didn't say that we should stop them doing it. I will do anything I can to keep their minds off the fact that many of them will die on this quest." She pointed at Red Four, who was still out cold, lying in the middle of the floor where we'd left him. "Do you think he's going to make it through the mines? He barely survived the first room, and there was nothing in here. So, I ask again, who the hell do you think you are?"

"That's monstrously unfair, Valdara. You think I don't know what's at stake? I understand how dangerous the Dark Queen is, apparently better than you two do. Absent me dragging you both out of that two-bit town, you would still be wallowing in self-pity and doing nothing to stop her. Do you think I did that, that I put this group together for fun? I don't need to be here. I'm doing this for you and everyone else in this sub—" I stopped myself just in time. I took a deep breath and mumbled, "I just want to get to the Dark Queen before she can hurt more people. Forgive me if that's too much to ask."

"What's his name?" Valdara asked, pointing again at Red Four. I looked down at the man and away again without answering. She leaned in close and shouted, "What's his name!"

"I don't know!" I shouted back. "Happy? I don't know everyone's name. I admit it, but that doesn't mean I don't care."

"Doesn't it?" she asked.

I thought about it, but too long. Valdara threw her arms up in frustration and stalked out of the room, slamming the door behind her as she went.

I turned to Drake, who was leaning on his staff. "Drake, don't *you* see that it's getting to the end, to the Dark Queen, that matters? That's all I want."

"His name is Barth Hammerarm," Drake said in reply, in what I imagine must have been the voice he'd used as a priest at one time. It was calm, measured, and infinitely solemn. "He has seen twenty-four summers, and was born on the steppes of these mountains, not far from Hamlet. His grandfather and father both fought and died in the war against the Dark Lord. When the Dark Queen rose, his village was one of the first that orcs overran. He lost a wife and two children to their hordes. He does not have any hope of killing the Dark Queen. He has come on this quest to die with honor so that he can join his family in the beyond. The end doesn't matter to him."

I looked down at Barth. I had never given a moment's thought to his life's story, or any of the others' life stories for that matter. I cared about what they represented to the spell, and I had gotten sick when some of them had died, particularly when the visceral parts of them splattered on me. I liked Valdara and Drake. I felt a special affection for them, if I'm being honest. But if I was being perfectly honest, I couldn't say that I felt the same way for them as I did for Eldrin.

We were taught from early on that beings of lesser reality were like drawings on a piece of paper. They could be shaped and discarded and altered with magic. Erased or touched up, as you will. Time flowed so fast on some of their worlds, especially the outer ones, that they could die in the time it took you to grab lunch back in Mysterium. I knew they had their own reality and their own worth, but I had never considered how that should be reflected in my own behavior. Something about Drake's description of Barth made me question all of that.

I don't know when Drake slipped out the door to rejoin the group, but I stood for a long time staring at Barth. My mind was filled with images of the Armies of Light and Dark fighting beneath the walls of the Fortress of Despair. I saw again those white lines charging and faltering and falling back only to regroup and try again, like a foaming wave crashing and receding on a coast of black rock. How many died that one day, and all the other days that preceded it? How many Barths had I created?

As I watched this man breathe and bleed, I had a thought that sparked a feeling that ignited into an obsession. I became determined that, whatever else I did, Barth Hammerarm would not die. Not here. Not today. Not while I still walked this world. I bent down to pick him up, but the man was enormous and the weakness that had been growing on me since my return made it impossible for me to do more than drag his body into the center of the room.

If will make him safe, I pledged silently.

I spread my feet wide and raised my hands. I drank in power from the world around me. Colors faded and the mass of string in the corner disappeared. I continued to draw. The door Barth had battled flickered and then vanished. Still I drew. I drew energy until I was fairly bursting, and then from the tip of my finger a line of pure white light shot forth. Using it like a blowtorch I burned a circle of protection into the stone around Barth's unconscious form. Reality screamed and crackled at my spell. The very walls around me wavered for a moment like they were made of water. The air grew thick and viscous and I felt Vivian's presence in the room. I knew she could feel my touch and was looking for me. I did not care.

"Let her come. Let her touch this circle," I said to no one, to the walls, to Vivian. *Let her feel what a true mage of the Mysterium is capable of,* I thought.

With the reality key perhaps she could break through the circle I was forming, but it would require her to tear the world apart in the attempt. Absent that, Barth Hammerarm would remain perfectly preserved in his slumber. He would be untouched by the ravages of time and hunger and violence; he would rest until the Dark Queen was no more, or Trelari ceased to exist.

When at last the circle was complete, the weight of what I had done hit me. Tears burned in my eyes as I fell to my knees gasping, then the world room spun and I blacked out.

I was not out for long, or at least it did not seem like that long. I came to with Drake kneeling beside me, splashing water onto my face. "Hey, kid, you still with us?"

I nodded groggily and sat up. "I'm fine. Just a little tired."

"What the hell happened in here?"

"I wanted to protect Barth," I said slowly, trying to find my way to the words. "I needed to protect him."

"Right. Barth looks fine. Not that I can get within three feet of him, but what happened to the door, and why does it look like the walls have been melted?"

I looked about. The room was clean, not swept clean or mopped clean, but surgery room sterile. Every surface was brilliant white and looked to be made of wax. Rivulets of solid stone had dripped down the sides of the walls and gathered in smooth stone pools around the edges of the room.

"The spell may have gotten away from me a bit," I said as he helped pull me to my feet.

"Does this happen often?"

I shook my head. "No. I was—" I tried to think about what to say "—upset," was all I could come up with.

He never said anything, but I saw in his eyes a larger question, the question Valdara should have asked earlier: "*What* the hell are you?"

CHAPTER 21

POLYGON MADNESS

We rejoined the group, and I braced myself for Drake to tell them what I'd done, and for the inevitable and impossible-to-answer questions that would follow, but he said nothing except that I had cast a protection spell on Barth so we wouldn't have to worry about him.

Valdara would not look at me, but Rook nodded his approval. "Good thinkin', laddie. Draggin' a body around a dungeon is a nightmare."

And with that rather unsentimental observation, we were off.

There were no secret doors in the twenty-by-twenty-one room (not surprisingly), and so the south door was where we went. Sam continued to describe as we explored the mines. Ariella continued to map. The searching for secret doors lasted one more chamber before it was dropped by silent consent. I kept my mouth shut except for asking Red Five his name: Luke. I also asked the two gnomes who were with us what their names were: Spryspindle and Berrycrank.

I'll leave out much of the next several hours. We traveled around randomly. There were long periods of boredom when all we did was listen at doors and check for traps or locks and things of that nature, punctuated by mayhem when we encountered a group of kobolds or a pack of bugbears or a group of skeletons. I omit the details partly because everything seemed so random and pointless, and partly because my memory of it is foggy. I was in a daze formed of a noxious mixture of fatigue and self-loathing, contributing little or nothing to the group's efforts. Not that I had much left to give. I'm not sure I could've focused enough energy to light a match.

Eventually we rested for a few hours, something Rook called a "long rest," which was to be contrasted with a "short rest," which was only ten minutes or so. Everyone told me I would feel better after a long rest, and I was surprised to find they were right. It made no sense, but for once I was managing to keep all my questions to myself, and I had a lot: How do all these creatures live, in many cases right next door to each other, without killing one another? How do they find food and water? Where do they go to the bathroom (a problem I was always having), and why doesn't the mine smell of untreated sewage?

It was obvious that the world was playing by a set of rules that didn't have to make logical sense, as long as it maintained an internal coherence. I knew this because I recognized that many of the "rules" I was having trouble understanding had been drawn up by a smug adept—me—who couldn't be bothered to think about the people that would have to live in accordance with his edicts. So, yeah, I was pretty down.

At some point in our wanderings we found ourselves standing in front of a door, deep within the mines, that led into a natural cavern.

Sam said, "You push open another door."

"We already pushed open the door, kid," said Drake.

We were all getting tired.

Sam yawned and nodded. "Right, okay, then," he said, peering into the gloom. "The room before you is cavernous—the walls are natural and unhewn, unlike the chiseled stone found in the rest of the dungeon. A pale turquoise fungus hangs on the east wall and a corridor winds away to the southeast. It's noticeably damp."

"How do I draw that?" asked Ariella.

"I'll do it," said Sam, taking the quill.

Paul went over to the fungus. I noticed a sudden change in the music. It was building to something.

I put up my hand as a warning. "I wouldn't touch that."

"Why?" asked Paul, wiping his hand across it. "It's

blue. It's harmless. If it were a slime, that would be one thing, or perhaps an ooze. But a blue fungus should be harmless."

This had become Paul's MO since we'd entered the mine. The man seemed to be existing in a fugue-like state where he had accepted that it was his fate to die and was trying to get it out of the way as efficiently as possible. I hadn't been sure what to do to help him except to put him in the back and get him out of that red tunic. I'd insisted on both, but he kept slipping forward, and somehow, despite my orders, he'd donned another red shirt.

"I don't know, lad," said Rook. "Looks greenish to me."

"My eyes are blue," said Drake, "and that's not the same color as my eyes."

"Don't you mean your eyes are bloodshot?" suggested Valdara.

"So we have a sense of humor again?" Drake said sardonically. "How wonderful."

"Listen here," said Ariella, "I'm an herbalist . . ."

"When did that happen?" I asked.

She thrust her chin up and said defensively, "I've been studying herbalism at least as long as I've been studying crystal dowsing." Another skill I hadn't known she had. "Anyway, we herbalists know about fungi, and that's definitively—"

Paul screamed as his body shuddered and the turquoise goo engulfed him. We watched in horror as he melted into a puddle.

"—dangerous," finished Seamus, slamming a meaty fist into his hand.

"What can we do?" said Luke (Red Five as he was previously). "Can you heal him, Avery?"

I stared between Luke and the puddle, dumbfounded. All I could think was, that's the end of Paul, red tunic and all. A wave of nausea swept over me and I threw up.

Seeing that I was occupied, Luke turned to Drake. "What about you, St. Drake?"

"Look, kid, I'm not a saint anymore, and even if I were there's no cure for someone being melted."

Valdara held up a hand. "Listen, I hear something." She turned her head left and right before pointing to the southeast exit where Spryspindle and Berrycrank were standing. I became aware of a rumbling noise. It reminded me of the sound that a stone might make rolling downhill.

As we watched, a massive shape rolled out of the opening and squashed Berrycrank. I should say, it seemed to start absorbing him. Whatever it was, it was about ten feet high and had no limbs, eyes, mouth, or other identifiable body parts. It was also translucent, which only amplified the horror, because it meant we could watch as Berrycrank struggled briefly within the thing's body, grew still, and then began to dissolve. I screamed in terror and threw up again.

"It's a gelatinous sphere!" said Seamus as he pulled his axe from his belt.

"Don't be ridiculous," Rook barked, also grabbing

his axe. "A sphere is a round solid figure with every point on its surface equidistant from its center. That obviously has a number of different facets like a gem."

"Gods save us, it's a gelatinous polyhedron!" shouted Sam, who was digging desperately through the pouch at his side. He pulled out a twig and began to gesture at the thing with it.

Absorbing Berrycrank had only slowed the thing's progress briefly. Already it was rolling after Spryspindle, who was sprinting back towards us as fast as his tiny legs could carry him. It became quickly obvious that Spryspindle had no chance to outrun the monster.

Ariella screamed the gnome's name and fired arrow after arrow at the pursuing creature. Her aim was true, but the gelatin never slowed as the missiles were simply absorbed and digested.

I recovered enough from my nausea to set a spell pattern in my mind, but when I tried to draw energy to activate it my head began to spin and my legs gave out beneath me. I fell to my knees and watched as the gnome drew his daggers and spun to confront the monster.

"For Berrycrank, for Puddlestripe, for Fizz—" came the voice of the gnome before the thing hit him.

I closed my eyes as the monster hit the gnome with a loud smack. When I reopened them, the Spryspindle's body was half-inside the creature. The gnome twitched as his lower body was smashed into the floor and then the wall. And that was the end of the gnomes. There was no time to vomit.

"It's coming this way!" shouted Seamus. "Run for it!"

Everyone made for a small crevice in the cavern wall that was barely an arm-span wide and about twenty feet deep. Everyone that is except Sam. While we squeezed into the narrow gap, he stood his ground, gesturing wildly with his twig.

A burst of blue magic like lightning erupted from the end of the stick and arced through the dark of the cavern striking the gelatin. The shape crackled, before splitting in half. We all gave a shout of joy, which turned to horror as we watched the two halves reformed into new shapes and begin again to roll about the cavern. Our problems had doubled.

Sam sprinted to join us in the crevice. "Lightning doesn't work," he panted.

Thud. Squish. The polygons smashed into the wall just behind him, but the opening was too small for them to reach us.

"Really?" Rook asked. "How could you tell?"

"Because there are two of them now," Sam answered seriously.

Rook slapped a hand across his forehead and opened his mouth to say something else, but Valdara cut him off. "Leave it, Rook."

"Remind me later to work with you on sarcasm," I whispered to Sam while the others were debating our next move.

Thud. Squish. Thud. Squish. They kept relentlessly impacting the opening. We were trapped.

"What are we going to do?" Luke wailed.

"Maybe we could use fire," Seamus suggested.

"Are you mad?" asked Valdara. "Fire is for slimes, not gelatinous polyhedrons. You hit that thing with fire and it'll swell up at least twice its size. We're going to have to get physical with it." She tried to draw her sword, but there was no room in the tight confine of the crevice.

"Won't work," Drake muttered. "It'll just suck in our weapons or split into more pieces."

"Can someone cast a spell that isn't lightning or fire?" asked Valdara.

"Possibly," I said, not sure if I could in my weakened condition, or safely do so with all these people around. If my concentration slipped for even a second, I might erase one of them right out of existence. "Before I do anything though, I need to know what that thing is—exactly."

"It's a gelatinous polyhedron," Rook barked. "We established that already."

"What kind?" I asked sharply. "It matters."

Sadly this was true. It made no sense, but it was true. This whole time I had been desperately trying to remember what I had written in the DMG about these creatures. Please understand that the whole section on slimes, molds, oozes, and whatnots with all their different colors and shapes was a confusing mess. Most gelatins were tetrahedrons or at most cubes. They moved slowly. All you needed to do was not walk into them. Unfortunately, we were dealing with higher order polyhedrons, which were significantly more dangerous. They were fast and unpredictable, and these also seemed angry, which, given that they had been split in two, I could understand.

Rook squinted between Sam's legs and through the opening as the gelatins continued their assault. "They could be octahedrons. They have pointy bits here and there."

Thud. Squish. Thud. Squish.

"Now who's being ridiculous," I shouted at him. "They at least have more sides than a pentagonal trapezohedra, otherwise they wouldn't be able to roll that fast."

"I still say they're dodecahedrons," Sam said, peering through the crack.

"That would make sense," I replied. "I thought initially that the creature looked like an icosahedron before you split it in half, but it could easily have had twenty-four sides, which would naturally mean that it would form two dodecahedrons when split."

"Naturally," Sam agreed.

"The real question is," I said, rubbing my chin, "was it a tetrakis hecahedron or a deltoidal icositetrahedron?"

"Would that matter now?" Sam asked.

I looked at him seriously. "I have no idea."

Thud. Squish. Thud. Squish.

Did I mention that they were very determined?

"All right!" Valdara shouted. "So it's a dodeca . . . whatever. What does that mean? What do we need to use?"

"Cold," I said calmly as my memory finally recalled the table.

"Cold?" Valdara asked. "Are you sure?"

I nodded.

There was a sickening slurping noise as the gelatins abandoned their attempts to batter their way to us and instead began to squeeze their bodies into the crack.

"They are getting really close," Sam squeaked, and inched backward, packing us more tightly together.

I saw the bladed tip of Drake's staff pass over my head and poke at the thing. It squealed at the touch and pulled back out of the crevice.

"What the hell was that, Drake?" Valdara asked with obvious sharpness.

"Later," he growled. "It didn't work anyway."

He was right. Whatever was on Drake's blade may have stung the thing, but that had only served to make both the gelatins angrier. Now they were slamming into the wall of the cave with terrifying ferocity.

"Do any of our wizards know a cold spell?" Valdara asked.

"No," said Sam, "and even if I did I'd need one of Rook's long rests to learn it."

I had been trying to remember my elemental control spells. If I could manage the power drain, I thought I could make an attempt to drop their temperature and freeze them, but they would have to agree to hold still so I could draw a circle around them, and given the way they were still rolling about I doubted they would be amenable. "No," was all I said.

Ariella sighed, "Wizards!" Then she waved her hands and gestured. I shivered as the world went cold and blue light swirled around the gelatins. In an instant they grew more opaque and then froze solid. The next time they hit the wall, both of them shattered into thousands of frozen pieces. There was a mad scramble to get out of the crack and back into the open.

We all stood for a moment looking at the fragments of the creatures and trying to catch our collective breath. There was no sign of the gnomes or their bodies.

"Poor Spryspindle and Berrycrank," I murmured.

"Who?" asked Rook.

"The gnomes," I said, surprised as I had thought I was the only one that hadn't known everyone's name.

"We should say something," Ariella said, gesturing at the scattered remains.

"What's the point?" Valdara asked bitterly. "There's nothing left to say words over."

"Excellent point," Rook said brightly and rubbed his hands together. "No use standin' around. The treasure will be somewhere in all these bits. Let's see what we got for all our trouble."

Ariella shot the dwarf a side-long glare, which he ignored as he began picking through the frozen pieces of the gelatins. After an awkward pause the others joined in.

There were fragments all about and many of them held things that had been sucked up in the thing's body over the years: coins, a sword, a ring, but it was obvious that Rook and Seamus were looking for something bigger. Eventually, amid a pile of debris, Sam found a small locked chest. We gathered around as Ariella tried to pick open the lock.

After watching her fumble for a few minutes, Rook muttered, "Have you ever done this before, lassie?"

"No," she said and began humming a little tune as she twisted a small piece of metal in the keyhole.

The dwarf grunted, "Do you have any idea of what you're doin'?"

"Not a bit." She smiled. "But I'm a quick study."

After this confession we did the only sensible thing, and smashed it open with a rock. In the remains of the chest was a rolled-up piece of parchment.

"One scroll! That's it!" Rook shouted. "What a rip-off."

"Maybe it's a map," suggested Ariella. "It could lead to a bigger treasure."

"What does it say?" asked Drake.

Sam's hands were shaking, and his face was white as a sheet as he read, "'It has come to our attention that License No. 05309 to the Mines of Maria was purchased using conjured gold. The bearer of this scroll is ordered to return to the Village of Hamlet, there to present himself to the Master of Dungeons for judgment.'"

Every eye turned to me.

"Avery!" shouted Valdara.

I briefly considered concocting a lie about how I

must have grabbed the wrong bag, or that they must have confused our payment with someone else's. Sam scuttled those plans. He fell to his knees, the scroll forgotten in his hand. "It's not his fault. I did it."

"Sam!" Valdara shouted again, but with less venom. "I expect that behavior from Avery, but not from you! I have never been more disappointed . . ." There were tears in the wizard's eyes as she berated him.

I am a lot of things. I like to cut corners, like using Mysterium magic to create the core element of the reality matrix for my spell, and that sometimes leads to complications, like Death Slasher. I sometimes bend the rules, like taking my world's key with me on a night out, and that sometimes comes back to haunt me, like Vivian becoming the Dark Queen. But one thing I will say for myself, and I know it isn't much, when I cut corners and bend rules and it hurts my friends, I always come clean.

"It isn't his fault," I said, stepping between Valdara and Sam. The murderous look she gave me did give me second thoughts about whether it was wise to do what I was about to do, but I did it anyway. "Sam thought we were using real gold that we had transformed from acorns. He didn't know it was conjured."

In a smooth, lightning-fast motion, Valdara drew her sword and swung it at my throat. I have no idea if she would have followed through with that blow or not, and thank the gods I never had to find out, because halfway between her and me the blade ran into Drake's extended staff. Blue and white sparks flew as the weapons connected. Their eyes met and the intensity in that gaze was enough to know that they were in love, although not what they felt about being in love.

"Leave the kid alone, Valdara," said Drake. "He did what he thought he had to do. We need to go back and see what we can do to make it right."

"People died," insisted Valdara. "For nothing."

Drake shrugged. "As you've pointed out before, there was a risk we weren't going to survive from the moment each of us decided to join this quest."

A look filled with conflicting emotions passed between them. Valdara's body slumped; her arms went slack. She sheathed her weapon. "Seamus, see how much we can get from the gelatins. Maybe it'll be enough to pay what we owe."

The others, who had been struck motionless with shock as the struggle between Valdara and Drake played out, now bent to the task of gathering and sorting through the things we'd gathered from the slain gelatins. It took some time, but finally Seamus announced, "Thirty-seven gold pieces, sixty-two silver, and eighty-five copper, a semiprecious gem worth about twenty-seven gold, a few bits of string, and . . ." He paused dramatically and held something small and gleaming up to the light. ". . . a gold tooth."

"If we can strike a good bargain with Zania, it may be enough," Drake said.

Valdara shrugged and walked back the way we came without a word. The rest of the party followed after her. Nobody acknowledged my existence except Rook, who marched up and kicked me in the shin.

"Ow!"

He waited until the rest of the company was well out of earshot and then drew his ax. "You deserved that, laddie, for lyin' to *me*." He ran a finger along its edge. "In the future you'd best remember to tell me if you deviate from the pattern. Right?"

I nodded and continued to nod until he was out of sight. I had to figure out who Rook was, and why he seemed to lie outside the rules of Trelari, or at least to be aware of the contours of those rules. As usual, now was not the time. I scurried after the others, chasing their light as the shadows closed in around me.

Following Ariella's map and the bloody remnants of our passage, we made it safely back to the entrance chamber. There was Barth, just as I had left him. A glowing white aura surrounded him that no one, not even me, could approach.

"Can you undo the spell so we can get him out of here?" Valdara asked after several unsuccessful attempts were made to extract the man.

The answer, of course, was no. If I'd made it possible for me to undo it, then it would have been possible for Vivian to undo it, and at the time I hadn't been thinking about what happened after we were done exploring the mines. This is because I wasn't thinking at all at the time. I said none of this, sticking with a simple: "No."

"So, instead of us being able to take him with us, you've trapped him in this forsaken mine, potentially forever. Is that about it?" she asked savagely.

"Yes," I answered.

Drake very kindly and incorrectly explained that I had placed him into a suspended animation, because he was close to death, and that I thought this would be the only way to keep him alive until a better healer could be brought back to revive him. I don't know if anyone bought the story. However, whether they did or didn't mattered little. This new revelation changed nothing. Valdara looked at me in disgust and walked away, and the rest of the company took their lead from her. No one had been speaking to me before, and no one spoke to me now.

It was the deep of night when we emerged from the mine. Our first order of business was to find Zania and present her with the tooth. I prayed she was still around, and that she had been serious in her offer so some reward would come of this mess.

We soon found what we assumed was Zania's camp nearby. The group's bedrolls and backpacks were still lying arranged around the dying embers of their campfire, but there was no sign of them. Valdara tried to look for tracks that would indicate where they might have gone, but the ground had been trampled by a troop of horses. The only thing she could discern in the confused muddle of hoofprints was an ominous patch of discolored dirt.

She dropped to the ground, ran her finger through the stained earth, and brought it to her lips. She spat. "It's blood."

Silently, Valdara signaled for us to form a defensive perimeter around the remains of the fire. Then she and Drake disappeared into the darkness. Despite the horrors we'd faced in the mine, I had never been more scared. There was something eerie about how quiet the woods around us were. Nothing moved or made a sound, not even the wind in the trees. The minutes ticked by and a bead of sweat dripped from my brow. Finally, Drake and Valdara returned.

"We couldn't find any trace of them," Valdara said. "There are hoofprints coming in from the west and riding off to the east, but there are too many for this group."

"They might have been attacked by orcs or something else that came out of the mines while we were down there," Drake suggested. "Whatever it was is probably long gone by now."

Valdara considered this for a moment. "Possibly," she said, but didn't sound convinced. "Whatever happened I don't think they're coming back. Let's search their gear and take what we can use, and then let's get out of here. Whether it is orcs or brigands, I don't like the feel of these woods."

I was in total agreement with her. The company made quick work of the search. Soon a mound of gold, silver, and copper coins, gems, jewelry, books, scrolls, and potions was laid out on the ground. The sight of all the treasure was unnerving.

"Not brigands, then," Rook growled.

"Nor orcs, nor kobolds," Seamus added in his own low grumble.

Valdara stared at the pile of glittering objects like she might divine the tale of what happened if she studied it long enough. The muscles in her jaw clenched and unclenched. "Everyone take a portion and let's get on the road. I want miles between us and this accursed place before morning."

I was never happier to hear that I would be marching through the night.

CHAPTER 22

RULES LAWYERS

Our journey back from the Mines of Maria was uneventful and lonely. The company's collective opinion of me did not improve the day after our flight from the mines nor the day after that. No one spoke to me except Drake, but I wasn't sure if that was because he counted me a friend, or didn't care enough to be angry with me. Only Sam showed any sign of regret about my treatment, just not enough to do anything about it.

I had hoped things might improve when we got back to town, but if news travels fast, bad news must fly on wings of eagles, because when we arrived at the gates of Hamlet, every merchant we'd paid using the fake gold was waiting for us. They wouldn't let us pass until we'd squared our bills, plus interest. I won't say what the rate was that they charged, because this is a family book and it was indecent.

When we settled our accounts with the town merchants, the crowd melted away, but still our way was blocked. Not by angry citizens or merchants, but by two stone-faced nightmares dressed in gaudy costumes. I recognized them at once as golems, yet another of my creations. They were enormous, at least eight feet high and almost the same length wide. If you ignored their size, they might have passed for misshapen men except for their faces. Expressionless doesn't do them justice. Their features, rough as they were, were frozen into permanent glares. I had brought them into existence during the early part of my time in Trelari to guard me and frighten away anyone that might have tried to meddle in my affairs. I thought they'd been destroyed.

The thought came to me that Vivian might have reanimated them. The background music changed, becoming more sinister. *Has she found me at last?*

I ran forward and put my body between the golems and the rest of the company. Whatever happened here, I was not about to let my companions suffer from another one of my mistakes. "Don't touch them," I shouted, and began to pull energy from the ground beneath my feet for whatever was going to come next. I swayed at the effort, but managed not to collapse.

I felt a pull on my arm. Valdara was beside me. "What are you doing, Avery?"

"Stay back, Valdara. I know how to handle these monsters." I tried to push her behind me, but she didn't budge.

"Those monsters are the town guards," she said in a low voice, "and I'd advise you not to antagonize them."

"She's right, kid," Drake said, pulling at my other arm. "Fighting monsters in dungeons is one thing, but no one picks a fight with the Hamlet town guards."

"The what?" I asked, looking between the two of them. "Those are the Hamlet town guards?"

They both nodded. I looked back to the creatures. Their dreadful, unblinking gazes were directed at me now. "You tried to trick the Master," they both said in monotone voices. "You must come with us."

It was bewildering to be standing in this quaint if weird little town with these nightmares. It wasn't right. I had to get these things away from the company, and then I needed to talk to Eldrin. None of this was right.

I held up my hands in a gesture of peace. "I will come with you, but my companions had no part in my deception. Let them stay behind."

"Avery, no," Sam called out, but he was the only one.

"It's okay," I said, turning to give him my best smile. "I'm sure the Master and I can work this out. Get us lodging at one of those dragon inns. I'll catch up later."

The guards' expression didn't change. "Come," they uttered.

I went.

I glanced back to see the rest of the company staring after me. Their faces were somber, almost funereal. Oddly, I did not share their fear; instead, I was angry. I had to know why the Master of Dungeons, someone I'd created to be a guide for the original Heroes, someone that was supposed to be a good guy, was using Dark Lord golems to guard his town.

"It wasn't supposed to be like this," I said to no one in particular.

The golems led me to the door, but remained outside as I entered. The Master of Dungeons was still at his table, but he'd moved his screen to one side. He sat calmly, hands folded in front of him, a smile on his face. But this was not the calm, cheerful smile of my last visit. This one was cruel and calculating.

"Greetings, Wizard Avery. It seems that we have a problem," he said cheerily.

I walked over to the creepy little man and dropped the coins, clattering, onto the table in front of him. "Here's your money, Master. Count it if you'd like, but it's more than enough."

He didn't even glance at the money. "Yes, certainly. I believe that should be sufficient to reinstate the license. The other members of your company are released to continue their journeys and adventures, and even to stay here in Hamlet if they choose." He waved a hand absentmindedly, and I knew that it was done. "But what do I do about you?"

Here it came. Whatever the Master wanted, it

wasn't money. I decided to play innocent. "What do you mean?"

"You have violated the rules, Wizard Avery. This isn't something I am allowed to take lightly. If everyone violated the rules, then where would we be?" He tilted his head and spread his hands wide at the possible implications. "There would be mayhem, groups fighting each other instead of monsters, new parties being ambushed on their way out of the gates . . ."

I was tired of whatever game he was playing. "Can you get to the point?" I sighed.

The Master raised his eyebrows. "Very well. *You* know better than most what happens to those who violate the rules. I'm afraid that *you'll* have to suffer the penalties. *You* have tied my hands."

The stress on each "you" sent chills along my spine. With sudden clarity, I understood that the Master knew who I really was. I didn't know how; perhaps he recognized the feel of the spell I'd cast in the mines. In the end, it didn't really matter, because the question wasn't how he knew, but what he was going to do with the knowledge. By obtaining a license and entering the mines, I had placed myself directly under his control. The Master would know this. He had been created to understand the rules of this world with precision. I'm not sure I breathed, but I am sure that I turned several shades whiter.

His smile disappeared. "Let us play no more games, Wizard Avery, or would you prefer Magus Avery? That is the proper title for your kind, is it not? I presume you have returned to fight the Dark Queen, just as you intervened to help defeat the Dark Lord."

I relaxed a little. At least he didn't know I was the Dark Lord.

He stood and faced me across the table. "Did you think I wouldn't recognize my creator when in his presence? I am not some mindless golem. You created me to have great power and intellect, and that has consequences. Unfortunately, you also constrained me with limitations on my power that have confined me to this dreadful place. I have chaffed beneath your restrictions for years, and I have been waiting and hoping for this day almost from the moment of my creation. I was surprised that you would place yourself under my control for so small a prize as the Mines of Maria. But here we are, and you *are* under my control."

He gestured with one hand and my throat tightened until I could barely breathe. "What do you want?" I choked.

"I want what everyone wants," he answered in a toneless voice. "To control my own destiny."

I clasped my hands to the table to stop them from shaking and gasped, "I can't." Nor was I lying. I'd used the reality key to create him and the golems and all the other horrors that surrounded the Dark Lord.

"Oh, I know that, Magus Avery," the Master said, and he smiled at me with that cruel, clever smile. "The power that created me has been passed to another. It is she I will be dealing with. I have already made my bargain with her. Her servants are nearby and will be coming soon to retrieve you. Until then I am allowed to entertain myself as I wish."

He tightened the grip and the edges of my vision began to darken. In desperation, I formed the spell of return in my head and tried to gather enough power to activate it, but the magic kept slipping away. It was impossible to focus while fighting for breath. As my consciousness faded, strange thoughts raced through my mind. All I had wanted was to save one subworld from extinction. What had I accomplished? Look at the misery I'd created for Drake and Valdara, at the golems patrolling the local villages, at the Master plotting with the Dark Queen. The irony was too rich. Someone was laughing hysterically. I was alarmed to find that it was me.

I was on the edge of passing out when there was a loud bang from the doors behind me. I heard Ariella shout, "Release him! We have a violation of the rules to discuss with you."

The Master cleared his throat; I still hovered, caught in the grasp of his power, a few inches above the floor. "Come back later. This is a private matter between Wizard Avery and myself."

"But the rules violation relates specifically to the license you issued to Wizard Avery and the Company of the Fellowship," she replied with a steely resolve I had never associated with her before.

"Guards!" the Master called out.

"Oh, they won't be responding," Valdara said grimly.

"You . . . you defeated the golems?" he asked, for the first time showing some uncertainty.

"More or less," Rook grunted.

"We filed a formal protest with the town council," Ariella said briskly. "They felt there was enough merit in my complaint to grant us this hearing. They also instructed the town guards to make no attempts to bar our access to you."

"In fact," said a voice I didn't recognize, "we have taken a direct interest in this matter, Master. A very serious breach of your ethical duties has been alleged."

"Fine," the Master said between clenched teeth. "It appears that I must consider your protest." He snapped his fingers and I felt the grasp of power release. I fell to my hands and knees choking and sputtering. The Master sat down and drew his screen in front of his face. "State your case, and be quick about it."

I managed to rise to my knees as Ariella approached the table and laid a piece of paper on it. "I am submitting this original copy of License 05309 for this tribunal's attention." The Master waved a weary hand for her to continue. "Do you, Master of the Dungeons, acknowledge that you sold License 05309 granting access to the Mines of Maria to Wizard Avery?"

"Yes, of course!" barked the Master. "And let me remind everyone that he—" at this point, he pointed directly at me "—paid for his license, and many other items from our local merchants, with gold that by his own admission was conjured, and which fades mere hours after its creation. As such, he threatened the stability of the Village of Hamlet. While post-violation compensation has been made, and accepted in the case of his less culpable companions, we have determined that further punitive consequences are in order."

"Don't you think killing him is a little drastic?" came a woman's voice.

I had regained enough of my wits to look about, and I saw that in addition to the entire Company of the Fellowship, three elderly citizens of Hamlet were also audience to my hearing. It was one of these, a thin, gray-haired woman with a determined look in her eyes, that addressed the Master now.

The little man banged his hand on the table, knocking his screen over and revealing mounds of paper, several bottles of drink, plates of food, and innumerable models of gelatinous polygons. He hastily set it back up and then pointed an accusing finger around the room. "We cannot have adventurers undermining the lifeblood of the town. If they do, the entire basis of our economy will suffer. No one will stay at the inns. Life insurance policies and final will and testament writing will suffer. Not to mention the markups that we make outsiders pay on food and supplies . . ." His voice trailed off.

He cleared his throat. "Anyway, this is beyond the purvey of the town council. This is a violation of the rules of the dungeons. According to my mandate—" he held up a battered scroll that I recognized at once as the one on which I'd written my original parameters for the Master "—I have absolute power over any and all adventurers that purchase a *bona fide* license to a dungeon or other adventure under my control."

"Aha!" said Ariella, raising a hand in the air. "I object."

"What?" gasped the Master.

"Did you or did you not say that you have power only over those individuals that purchase a *bona fide* license?"

"I did," he said with a shrug. I wasn't sure where she was going with this argument either.

"Do the Mines of Maria have any connection to the mystical weapon called Justice Cleaver?" Ariella asked casually.

"Of course not," he said dismissively, "but I don't see the relevance—"

She interrupted his explanation with a curt, "Do you know where Justice Cleaver lies?"

The Master's eyes glittered dangerously as he answered. "Of course I do. I am the Master of Dungeons. Justice Cleaver lies in the Tomb of Terrors, and is guarded over by the dread semi-lich. Again, I question the relevance of this line of inquiry."

Behind her the council members shuffled nervously. Ariella herself seem nonplussed as she asked, "Do you recall the day that Wizard Avery purchased License 05309?"

"Yes, of course," the Master growled. "It was less than a week ago. How long must I put up with these irrelevant questions?"

"We would beg you to hurry," pleaded one of the

town council, a short, fat man who was sweating profusely. "The Master is very busy."

Ariella nodded graciously. "I am almost there, esteemed council member." The fact that he'd been called "esteemed" seemed to mollify the councilman considerably. She turned back to the Master. "Do you recall what Wizard Avery asked when you offered him the license to the Mines of Maria?"

The Master thought for a moment and his eyes grew wide. He licked his lips nervously. "Well . . ." he began.

Ariella gave him no room for maneuvering. She leaned forward. "Did he or did he not specifically ask you whether the Mines of Maria were 'connected in any way with the mystical weapon Justice Cleaver'?"

"I . . . I don't . . ." the Master spluttered.

"Answer the question!"

"Yes! Yes, he did!" the Master shouted, his face growing red and flushed.

"And did you not specifically tell him that the 'mines would serve his purposes'?"

"Yes," he said more quietly, and his arms dropped to his sides.

Ariella turned back to face the town council. "I submit to this body that License 05309 was offered under false pretenses and so the sale was null and void at the moment of the offer. That Wizard Avery purchased the fraudulent license with conjured gold is entirely beside the point, because the entire transaction was void *ab initio*, in accordance with laws long established in El Drin's Guide to Universal Constants." She dropped a long sheet of velum on the table that was filled with line after line of her inordinately neat script. "I've written up a summary of my arguments. Oh, and I've included a recital of my personal background. I was raised by elves and there are a number of tragedies and unusual coincidences and circumstances in my childhood that I would like to place in the official record. I've indexed a list of encounters with monsters and portents in the back. I assure you that you will find everything in order."

The Master looked up with an empty expression. "What manner of elf are you?"

"Among other things," she answered with an upturned chin, "I'm a rules lawyer."

His expression darkened and he waved his hand again. I felt his power lift from me. "The case is dismissed. Wizard Avery is free to go."

There was a roar of joy from my group. Ariella had done it. In that moment I regretted all the disparaging things that I had thought about her, from my annoyance at her poetry to the tedium with which she insisted on mapping everything to her overly elaborate life story. I was still contemplating the wonder that was this elven woman when many hands gripped my body and began carrying me from the room.

We were at the door when the Master called from behind us. "Before you leave, would you like to know who, or should I say, *what* you just saved?"

He was smiling again; his preternatural calm had

returned, but now the insanity beneath it was exposed. The effect was ghastly.

"Shall I tell them, Magus Avery? If I don't, you know that the Dark Queen will, if your pets survive long enough to meet her. I think it would be a kindness to let them know now so they can decide for themselves whether they wish to continue their "Fellowship" with you. He stared at me coldly.

There was an uncomfortable silence as everyone looked back and forth between me and the Master. Rook was the one that broke the tension. "No thanks, laddie," he growled, and spat on the floor. "Oh, and we want a refund."

He marched to the table, scooped the coins I'd dumped there into his pouch, and walked back out the door. Without a word, the rest of the company fell into order (marching order) behind him.

CHAPTER 23

HELLO, MY NAME IS AVERY . . .

Our feel-good unity lasted until we got out of sight of Hamlet. We were barely two leagues down the southern road that would take us to the temple when Valdara, who had been silently leading since our departure, reined to halt and spun her horse about to face the rest of the group.

"Before we go any further, I want to know the answer to the Master's question. *What* are you, Avery?" she asked, folding her arms.

No word was spoken, but the others spread out in lines on either side of Valdara so that I was alone, facing them all.

"I am not sure what to say," I answered honestly.

"Why don't you start with the truth?" Valdara suggested.

I know she didn't mean the remark to be helpful, but I doubt she realized how unhelpful it was. I was fairly convinced that telling them the whole truth about my history with their world, including the part about me being the Dark Lord, would be fatal. A conclusion I had come to repeatedly over the last weeks. And for as much as I had grown attached to the members of the company, I was still not keen on dying for them, or at least not at their hands. A partial truth would have to do.

"I am a wizard . . ." I began, but was immediately interrupted by Sam. "Not one with powers like I've ever seen before."

I cleared my throat and said, "Correct, Sam. What I should have said, is that I am a wizard from another world, one beyond the confines of your reality. There we are called magi. I have been sent here to help the people of your world defeat the Dark Queen. This is why my powers operate in such an unusual way, and it is also why I am so focused on our getting to the Dark Queen."

I expected some kind of a reaction to this announcement—gasps of alarm, shouts of outrage—but that wasn't what I got. Instead, Rook rasped, "That makes sense." The others nodded their agreement.

Drake raised his eyebrows and said, "It does explain a lot, kid. Like how you recognized me as St. Drake straight-away. I'd been perfecting my drunk reprobate for months."

"So that was an act?" asked Ariella.

"No," he said, "but there's always room to improve."

Drake's comment seemed to lighten the mood, and soon everyone started chattering to each other about quirks of mine that had given them clues that I was different, and when they'd figured it out. Seamus and Luke talked endlessly about how clueless I was about the most basic of things, like the importance of establishing a marching order and having a ten-foot pole when you go questing. Sam and Ariella spoke avidly about the strange spells I cast. Rook just kept looking at me, stroking his beard, and chuckling to himself.

Only Valdara was silent. She sat, staring at me with those piercing eyes until I could no longer meet her gaze. She let the group banter for a few minutes and then put two fingers in her mouth and let loose with a piercing whistle. In the silence that descended she asked, "Why?"

Thankfully, Rook answered for me. "Why not?"

She turned her gaze on the dwarf and frowned. "I can think of any number of reasons why not. It is harder for me to understand why a magus that can travel to any world he chooses would choose to come to our world."

"Maybe there aren't that many worlds," Sam suggested.

"Or maybe our world is special," Ariella added brightly.

Valdara dismissed both answers with a derisive snort. "If that were the case," she countered, "then why would they only send Avery to save us?" She walked her horse forward toward me. "Why not send a whole army of magi to make sure of the Dark Queen's defeat? And why involve . . . what did the Master call us . . . pets in their battle against the Dark Queen? Surely, we are vastly inferior to the warriors such a powerful race could employ. And why send a magus now? Why wasn't one on hand when we were fighting the Dark Lord?"

The volume and cadence of her questioning had increased as she moved closer. Now that she was directly in front of me, her voice dropped to a murmur only I could hear. "Or was there a magus here when the Dark Lord reigned?"

"Last time was—" I struggled to put into words that there was something bigger at stake. I never did find them "—it was different."

"But you were here," her voice creaked. In her eyes tears were gathering.

"I was here," I said, and I wanted to look away, to not see the pain I was causing her, but I couldn't.

"What did you do?" she hissed. "Because you weren't there when my father died under the blood orcs' swords, or when Drake's village burned from their torches, or when the thousands perished at the walls of the Dark Lord's fortress."

I hadn't even been in Trelari when the blood orcs had first arisen, but the guilt for all those that had died by my hand or command welled up in me. In a better person the guilt would have turned to remorse, but I'm not a better person. I'm just Avery. Instead, it turned to anger. I'd saved this world from breaking into shards of subether dust. Everyone would have died. Everything would have been extinguished. *I saved everything*, I wanted to shout. But I didn't.

My jaw clenched in the effort to stop the outburst. "I am not all-powerful, Valdara," I said, spitting out each word in my frustration. "By now you should know that."

"What did you do!" she shouted, the tears now rolling down her cheeks.

"I made sure that you won!" I screamed back at her. "I made sure that when you faced the Dark Lord you had everything you needed to destroy him."

At some point Drake had ridden up to join us. "Val," he said, and, taking hold of Valdara's arm, tried to draw her away.

She shook his hand off without taking her eyes from mine. "Are we supposed to thank you?"

"Did I ask you to?" I said, still screaming and shaking. "All I want, all I've ever wanted, is to defeat the Dark Queen and go home!"

"No matter the cost?" she asked, and her voice had regained its usual steel.

"Yes," I admitted with a shudder of emotion.

Her eyes held mine, but despite the outward appearance of defiant strength, for the first time since I'd known her, I sensed a fragility in Valdara. Perhaps she also felt it, because she looked away as she said, "Then I wish you the best of luck in your quest, Magus Avery."

She spurred her horse away from the road and off to the west across the open country. Drake looked after her and sighed. "Sorry, kid," he said in that now familiar gravelly growl. "I would have followed you to the end, but my course lies with her."

He extended his arm. I took it and we shook, and then he gave his horse a nudge and soon disappeared over the crest of a hill. I don't know how long I sat there, staring after them, wondering what I might have done or said differently, but somehow I knew that this was just the inevitable end to choices I'd made long ago.

Sam broke my depressing reverie by asking, "Now what do we do?"

I turned back to the group. He had clearly spoken for everyone. They were all staring at me with varying levels of dismay and shock. I should have said something inspirational to rally the troops and all that. Again, that isn't me.

"My plans have not changed," I said wearily. "I am going after Justice Cleaver and then whatever's after that until I can find and face the Dark Queen. Anyone that wishes to join me is welcome. I will understand if you don't."

Without another word, I urged my horse into a slow trot and, passing through the remaining company, continued along the road to the temple. Behind me, I heard Rook growl, "Remember the marchin' order, people," as the others fell into line.

CHAPTER 24

AND THEN IT DAWNED ON ME . . .

At the end of the day, we found ourselves traveling through a steep-walled pass that Seamus said would take us through the mountains and out onto a wasteland where we would find the tomb. He knew this, and I'm not making this up, because he'd bought a map in town entitled Jennifer's Guide to Hamlet's Top Ten Most Hideous Dungeons. When he told me this, I knew it was time to stop for the night.

Seamus's guide raised many questions: Who was Jennifer? Had she personally adventured in all the dungeons around Hamlet so she could make such an authoritative guide? If she had, why had we not hired her to join us? All of these questions led to my real question: Why in the name of the gods was Trelari so bizarre? And the corollary to that question: Why had I never noticed how bizarre Trelari was? And the natural follow-up to that corollary: Had it only just become this bizarre? And the obvious extension to the natural follow-up to the corollary: Was I to blame for all the strange weirdness?

With so many questions flying around my head, I wasn't able to fall asleep. I tossed and turned for an hour or so, and then decided if I was going to be awake anyway, I might as well do something useful. Despite the awful precedent it might set, I went out and relieved Luke from watch duty.

Sitting in the dark, staring at the vast emptiness of space, I thought about Eldrin. I pulled out my communication medallion and gave it a swipe. It had been close to a week since we'd spoken, but it might have been only a couple of hours of Mysterium time. I wanted to do the calculation, but with all the shifts that had occurred, I had no clue what to use as a conversion factor. Either he would answer or he wouldn't.

"Avery?" It was Dawn.

"Hello, Dawn."

"Hello, Avery," she said with a yawn. "Do you know what time it is?"

"Let's not start that again," I said, and then thought about the potential significance of the time to Dawn's presence with Eldrin. "But out of curiosity, what time is it?"

"Late or early," she said, "depending on your perspective."

"Is Eldrin there with you?" I asked suggestively.

"Yes. He's asleep," she answered, and then added sharply, "And before you ask, it's none of your business."

"Fair enough."

She yawned again and made the kind of groaning sound you make when stretching. "I don't mean to be rude, Avery, but I'm really tired. What do you need?"

I wanted to say that I just needed to talk to someone, but I didn't know her well enough. Instead, I stuck to the facts. "I was checking in on your progress. I know you were looking into Vivian. Any news on that front?"

"Only that she's not from around here."

"What's that supposed to mean?" I asked. It really was a meaningless statement. Almost everyone at The Mysterium University was from elsewhere.

"She's not from Mysterium," she began, and then added significantly, "or any of the innerworlds."

"But that would mean . . ." I started.

"Yup, she's a subworlder," Dawn confirmed.

It was hard to believe. The Mysterium University has very strict rules about admission, and one of the primary requirements is that the person has to be from Mysterium itself or one of the thirteen innerworlds. And they don't take your word for it. As part of the admission screening, they put you in a reality scale, which is a chamber that precisely measures the density of your reality. This sounds scientific, and it is, but it isn't enlightenment scientific; it's more medieval scientific, because if your reality isn't dense enough the measurement can be fatal.

This all raced through my mind before I gasped out, "That's impossible."

"Funny," she said with a giggle. "That's what Eldrin said also. I've always thought that someone clever might manage it. Of course, the morality of keeping people out of Mysterium just because they are from more remote worlds and therefore theoretically less 'real,' whatever that means, is highly questionable. Professor Piers in the Department of Magical Ethics has written a fantastic monograph on the subject . . ."

I groaned. "I thought you wanted to go back to sleep."

"Okay," she said sullenly. "No ethics lectures."

"I don't know what to do about Vivian being from a subworld," I admitted.

"Neither do we. For now we are ignoring the fact."

Trying to move away from this disturbing revelation, I asked, "Well, are you two any closer to tracking down Death Slasher?"

"We are," she answered. "In fact, we know exactly where it is."

"What?" I jumped to my feet and started pacing. "That's great news! How?"

"Oh," she drawled lazily. "Eldrin came up with a very clever scrying spell that can detect the peculiar magical emanations of the battle-axe by—"

"You can skip the technical details," I said, cutting her off.

"Thank the gods," she said with a relieved sigh. "I would have been making most of it up anyway."

"So when will you get it?" I asked, thrilled by the idea that at least their half of the plan was going according to, well, plan.

"Well, that could be tricky," she said cautiously.

"Why?"

"A professor has it," she answered, and then added, without preparing me at all, the part she should have told me as soon as we started talking, "Your professor."

"What, Griswald has . . . has . . ." I couldn't bring myself to finish the sentence.

"It appears so," she said, and then added, "Sorry."

I found myself sitting on the ground and wasn't sure how or when I got there. Griswald had the battle-ax? What did it mean? What could it mean? Like everything else it made no sense. I sat there alone with my thoughts until I remembered that I wasn't alone, not really, and that Dawn was still talking to me.

". . . Eldrin says not to worry about it, Avery. He has a plan," she said in a voice I think was meant to be calming, but that I knew it was meant to be calming only made me more nervous.

Of course he did, I thought.

"He's very clever," she said.

Of course he is, I thought.

"Do you know he managed to do something to the main scrying scope at the subworld observatory so that it can't scan your sector of subspace? Don't ask me to explain—it was all a lot of gibberish. And there's the spell he used to sneak into the faculty lounge. Did he tell you about that? Well . . ."

She talked on and on about Eldrin, and there was a pride in the way she talked about him that confirmed more than the time of night or day that I should think of Eldrin and Dawn as Eldrin & Dawn, and not Eldrin . . . and . . . Dawn. This led me to something else I'd been considering from the first moment Eldrin had put Dawn on so many weeks ago. I realized that now was the time to stop considering and start doing. Too much was happening back in Mysterium that could turn bad for the two of them. Griswald had Death Slasher, which meant my deception was almost certainly known to him, and if even one of the things Dawn had described them doing was traced back to either one of them . . . It didn't bear thinking on, and my academic career wasn't worth it.

"Dawn?" I said. interrupting the very detailed description she was giving me about how Eldrin had managed to transport her into the filing room of the notoriously well-protected Records Department undetected.

"Yes, Avery?" she replied, clearly annoyed at my interruption.

"I . . . I know you don't owe me anything," I began hesitantly, "but can I ask you to do me a favor?"

"Depends," she answered suspiciously, which was fair enough.

I paused briefly, and then said in a rush of words, "If you think Eldrin and you are in danger I want you to go to your advisor or Griswald or Mysterium security or whoever you feel comfortable going to, and turn me in. It's the only way to be sure that the two of you and Vivian come out of this safely."

"What? Why me?" she asked.

"I can't ask Eldrin, because he won't, but you don't know me, and have no reason to like me or lie for me," I answered bluntly.

"I don't know—" she began.

I cut her off. "Dawn, we both know that Trelari—"

"Where?" she asked.

"The subworld I'm on," I snapped, and then inhaled deeply to calm my uncalled for irritation at her question. "The point I'm trying to make is that if Eldrin's calculations are correct, and it is always a bad idea to bet against Eldrin's calculations, this world is moving closer to Mysterium. That means that reality here is going to get stronger and stronger, which means that I am going to get proportionately weaker and weaker." I took in another breath and let it out in a stuttering hiss. "I . . . I am not sure I'm in control of the situation anymore, and I will be progressively less and less in control as things move along."

What I didn't say was that this had been happening for some time. The drink at the Badger should never have affected me so much. Conjuring the gold in Hamlet should have been a snap, and not something that nearly made me pass out. In the mines I should have been able to lift Barth's body with ease. At some point, I was going to become a liability to the group.

"I understand that," she said. "What I don't understand is why you don't come back now and turn yourself in."

I had been hoping to avoid this question, because I knew that returning to Mysterium is exactly what I should have done almost as soon as I got to Trelari. One doesn't travel through a world as long as I have and not know the feeling when things aren't right, and things with me hadn't been right here from day one. I felt weaker than I ever had before and I had lost the sort of detachment a magi needed to make clear-headed decisions. But having lost my ability to remain aloof I also couldn't help worrying about what would happen if I did go back—to me, but more importantly to Valdara and Drake and the others.

All I said to Dawn was, "I can't."

"You mean the return spell won't work?"

"No," I said in a voice that was almost a whisper, "I mean I can't bring myself to do it. I know what returning will mean for Trelari, and I can't. That's why I need your help. Please promise me you will do this, and that you won't tell Eldrin."

She paused before saying, "I promise."

I knew I had her, because she was a student of magical ethics, and that meant that she had to be ethical. Her word was her bond. It was only much later that I learned that studying ethics and being ethical are two totally different things.

CHAPTER 25

THE TOMB OF TERRORS

By this point in my chronicle, I would hope that you, the reader, would see the manifest and many reasons why I would make a terrible leader. Well, add to those the fact that I had grown increasingly impatient to get to Vivian, while at the same time becoming increasingly more pessimistic about our chances to take her down when we got there, and that I had become even more sullen and ill-mannered as a result, and I think you will begin to see why three days into the journey I stopped speaking altogether. This forced Rook to take command. When you also hear that he did this without any complaint and that everyone accepted the new situation without protest, you will have the full picture of why I was so out of sorts.

Almost.

There was one more reason that I was in such a pensive and foul mood: there were Hooded Riders following us. (Yes, I know I capitalized Hooded Riders even though a few chapters ago I derided the fact that everyone was so afraid of riders simply because they wore hoods. What can I tell you? I'm a fickle storyteller.) My opinion changed the moment I saw one of them.

It happened at the end of another long day. The road we'd been following was climbing through a series of sharply rolling hills that lay in a low point in the mountains. As we crested a particularly burdensome rise, I happened to look back. Atop a far distant ridge, silhouetted against the evening sky, was the dark, distorted shape of a Hooded Rider. I only saw it for a moment and then it was gone. When I told the rest of the company about it they chalked it up to a trick of the light, but that one glance put a fear in me that I couldn't shake. From that day on I felt that there were always eyes at my back, and I kept imagining the sound of hoofbeats coming along the trail behind us. I was seriously creeping everyone out.

I think in this one instance I would have been happier if I had been going crazy—gods know I had my reasons to go crazy. Unfortunately, three days later, as we were breaking camp, we saw "it" again and another "it" for good measure. They were sitting motionless atop their horses several leagues away. At a distance they looked like little more than shadowy fingers—an unfortunate bit of imagery that I shared with the rest of the company, and which made everyone jumpy.

This explained why seven days out of Hamlet I found myself crouching next to Rook behind a pile of rocks, staring at a rather nondescript pile of earth that rose out of the blasted wasteland of a valley to which the road had led us. The mound was no more than half a mile from where we sat. By all rights it should have taken fifteen minutes at most to get there even on foot, but deciding on how we were going to get across the waste had already consumed three hours.

"There it is," said Rook, stroking his beard.

That was the third time he'd said it. I was beginning to suspect that he wanted me to say something back. I decided to humor him. "Yes," I said. "I know."

"Well, what's the plan?" he asked, still staring at the low mound and still stroking his beard.

"I guess we go out to it?" I said, but made it a question because it seemed too obvious.

"We could do that," he said doubtfully. "But we'll be exposed out there."

At this point Seamus popped out of nowhere and said, "Sitting ducks for the Hooded Riders!"

I jumped with fright and my heart followed suit, skittering a bit before settling back into a chest-pounding rhythm. "Don't sneak up on me like that, Seamus!" I shouted.

"Quiet, laddie," Rook cautioned with a stern bristle of his brow. "You keep makin' noise like that and it'll be the riders that sneak up on us. It's like a game of chess with these mysterious Hooded Rider types. Cool heads and clear thinkin', that's what'll win the day." Had I mentioned that everyone was really nervy?

"I still say that we should wait till dark," Seamus opined as he ran a rag over his bare head.

It was considerably hotter in this valley than it had been in the mountain pass, and we were all beginning to feel the effects of the sun.

"I'm not entering a place called the Tomb of Terrors at night," I said for the fifth time in the last twenty minutes. "That's just asking for trouble."

"We should vote on it," Seamus said cheerfully.

Both Rook and I groaned. Seamus had started this whole "vote on it" thing after Valdara and Drake left and, to be fair, after I refused to step up as company leader. Like elections everywhere, it was a torturously slow process, involving multiple ballot proposals, speeches in support and against, caucuses, and round after round of votes and vote counts. All I can say is thank the gods the Hooded Riders showed up. (Wait, I can't believe I just wrote that.)

"Hooded Riders!" shouted Sam, who had been on Hooded Rider watch.

The entire company rushed over to him, weapons already drawn. Sure enough, on the top of a hill no more than a mile away were *three* riders, their shapes bending and twisting in the midday heat. "What do we do?" Luke asked, his eyes wide as saucers.

"There's no escape," Ariella wailed.

"She's right," Rook growled. "If we make run for it, they'll cut us down like dogs in the wasteland, and if we stay here they'll just wait till dark and gut us like fish." He punctuated this speech by gruesomely pantomiming his guts falling out.

"Why don't we vote!" shouted Seamus.

At that moment the riders began to advance toward us. I pointed and cried out, "No time! Here they come! Leave the horses and grab your packs. We're going to make a run for the temple. Maybe we can seal ourselves in."

It is a testament to how terrified the company was of the Hooded Riders that the idea of sealing themselves into a crypt with something called a semi-lich sounded like a great idea. Nevertheless, soon we were all sprinting down the hill and across the desert toward the mound.

I was sure we were going to be cut down halfway across the waste (this conviction being helped along by Sam, who stated it as definite fact every minute or so during our flight), but we made it, sweating and panting, to the top of the mound as the riders reached the edge of the waste.

"The riders will be on us in minutes!" Luke shouted.

"Well, stop starin' at them and look for an entrance to the tomb!" Rook shouted back.

We all scrambled about, but there was not much to see of the dreaded Tomb of Terrors except a circular disc of stone lying on the ground at the mound's center. It was about six feet across and had some indecipherable symbols carved into its face.

"There's no way in," wailed Sam, who I think was being really negatively affected by all the doom and gloom.

"It's a trap!" cried Luke.

"No," Seamus said as he ran his sleeve over his head. "I think the stone is covering the entrance."

Rook and Seamus, who had both somehow managed to carry their ten-foot poles and fifty-foot lengths of ropes with them across the waste, set to work at once on moving the stone. They pried at it with their poles. They yanked on it with their ropes. The disc wouldn't budge.

I stared back out at the wasteland. An approaching cloud of dust marked the progress of the riders. Rook was right; they really would be on us in minutes. I walked back to the dwarfs as they took turns hacking at the edge of the disc with their pickaxes. "Keep at it," I said, trying to be calm and failing. "We will try and hold them off as long as we can."

"Aye, laddie, we'll fight to the end," Rook growled defiantly.

Seamus rose and grasped my arm in his hand in what I had learned was a traditional dwarven farewell. "But between the three of us, our fates are sealed and we all know it." Rook nodded his agreement.

On that optimistic note, the rest of us formed a circle around the base of the mound and waited for the riders, who were now no more than a hundred yards or so away. The dust obscured them, which made facing them a little easier, but the drumbeat of their horses as they charged, and the unholy screams and shouts they made, were enough to frighten the bravest of men, and I think we've established that I'm not the bravest of men. I was petrified.

Fortunately, we had barely gotten into position when the dwarfs called out, "It's open!"

I turned to see that they had somehow managed to rotate the stone covering to the side, revealing a man-sized hole. We all rushed over and stared down into a pit of utter darkness.

"It's funny actually," Rook was saying as he scratched the top of his head. "It opened quite easily."

"It even had instructions," Seamus added, wiping the shine from his head.

"Well, now what?" Ariella asked.

"We go down the hole," I said, and made a welcoming gesture in case anyone wanted to take the lead.

"Shouldn't we be worried about getting ambushed when we go down there?" Sam asked reasonably.

We were all pondering this when the thunder of hooves reminded me what else we were up against. "It's either the pit or the Hooded Riders!" I reminded myself and everyone else with a shout, and jumped into the hole.

It was only as I was descending through the darkness that I heard Ariella say in her usual bright tones, "Anyway, Sam, the semi-lich doesn't ambush people.

I'm not even sure that he has monsters in there with him. It's the traps that'll get you."

Hearing this I had a number of thoughts as I fell. I will place them in the order in which I had them for your amusement.

Traps! That would have been nice to know before I leapt into the hole.

If this semi-lich is known for his traps, then he's bound to have put a really good one at the entrance.

I hope it isn't a pit of snakes. I hate snakes.

Although spikes would be worse. I hate being impaled even more than I hate snakes.

This fall is sure taking a long time.

What if this is a bottomless pit of some kind?

The real question is how do you die in a bottomless pit? Starvation? Dehydration?

Probably dehydration.

I wonder if I brought any water with me.

I was feeling around for my water skin when: Thump! My feet hit the ground. There were no snakes or spikes, just ground—solid ground. I looked up and saw Sam and Ariella peering down from the hole, which was about five feet from the top of my head.

"Seems fine," I called up, glad that the darkness hid the blush of my embarrassment.

The concealment did not last long. The others began to jump down behind me. When Sam landed, he pulled a glass orb from his pouch (a purchase he'd made in Hamlet that he was excessively proud of) and with a flick of his wrist and a couple of muttered words it was glowing like a hundred-watt bulb. It was a clever bit of magic that I wished I could duplicate with as much facility, but the last few times I'd tried to use Mysterium magic to do something even moderately simple, like lighting a fire or summoning a fresh pair of underwear, I had either almost collapsed from the effort or nearly blown a hole into reality. I had tried to learn how Sam worked his spell, but it was like trying to speak a foreign language with a lot of those little symbols above the letters; my accent wasn't right.

The dwarfs came last. "They're nearly at the mound, laddie," Rook panted as soon as he'd landed.

"With us sitting down in this hole and them up there, it'll be like shooting swamp rats in a barrel," Luke cried out.

Seamus, who had wandered over to one of the walls of the chamber, raised a finger. "Or we could pull this lever that says PULL TO CLOSE."

"What's the use of that?" Sam asked. "They'll just open it again."

"Possibly," Seamus said calmly. "But we could lock the door."

"How?" Rook asked, tapping his foot irritably. Overhead I heard the hoofbeats of the riders' horses on the mound.

"Well, the sign also says TWIST HANDLE TO RIGHT TO LOCK."

A shadow fell across the opening.

"Just do it!" everyone shouted.

From above a shrill, almost inhuman voice screeched, "Stop . . ."

Seamus threw the lever and the disc swiveled smoothly into place, silencing the cries of the Hooded Rider. Then he gave the handle a sharp twist to the right and there was a satisfyingly solid *clunk* as of a bolt sliding into place. Everyone gave a cheer.

"Now we're safe!" I said with a contented sigh, and then remembered where we were. "Sort of."

Despite the fact that we were now locked in a crypt with a semi-lich, everyone seemed much more relaxed. We looked around at our new refuge. The chamber was a rough cylinder about ten feet high and thirty feet across. A single doorway led off into the darkness. The only notable feature, apart from the lever Seamus had manipulated, was that every inch of the walls was covered with writing and pictograms.

Ariella pointed at it and read: "'I am the Semi-Lich Aldric. Welcome to my Tomb of Terrors. Within the chambers and corridors below lie the incalculable riches and treasures that I have gathered, including many artifacts of the Dark Lord himself. However, if you enter, you will face not only the power of my dark magic, but also my genius. I will be waiting and watching . . . and laughing. Enjoy!'

"It repeats the message over and over again in every language that I know and a number that I don't," she said.

I was reading it along with the others when I saw

something scrawled in fine print right at the base of the wall. I read it aloud without thinking.

"'Entrants take all responsibility for any instant annihilation, sudden gender changes, asphyxiation, drowning, bludgeoning, burning, evisceration, decapitation, extreme frustration, or sudden and unexplained death. Adventurers should be in extremely good health before entering this tomb and free from high blood pressure, heart, back or neck problems, motion sickness, or other conditions. Expectant mothers should not enter this tomb under any circumstances. No eating or drinking outside food or beverages within the tomb. Note, management is not responsible for lost, stolen, or damaged property.'"

For reasons that should be self-explanatory, this warning seemed to take the shine off of our escape. The wonder and relaxed calm of moments before was replaced for most by abject terror.

"S-so where's the semi-lich, do you think?" Sam stuttered.

Rook seemed to be the exception. He had promptly reverted back to his normal unflappable self. "Hidden at the center of his maze of traps," he said with an unfortunate amount of enthusiasm. "They are supposed to be devilishly fiendish."

"Well, which . . . which way do we go?" Luke asked.

"I'd wager he's in that direction," Rook said, pointing his finger at the one door in the room.

Something suddenly struck me about this quest

that I was surprised we'd never discussed. "Before we go on, does anyone know what the semi-lich is besides a lich?"

The question seemed to confuse everyone. "What da ya mean, laddie?" asked Rook, giving voice to the puzzlement of rest of the company.

"Well, if the lich . . ."

"Aldric," Ariella supplied helpfully.

"Yes." I nodded with a roll of my eyes. "If Aldric were all lich, then he would just be called a lich."

"True enough," Rook agreed.

"But he calls himself a semi-lich," I pointed out, by actually pointing at the word on the wall. "This would mean that he is only half or partially or almost a lich, but not a full lich."

"I thought semi-lich was a kind of rank," Sam said. "You know, that he was a lich, but sort of an inferior lich."

"Rot!" Seamus shouted. "Anyone that's ever seen the semi-lich will tell you he's inferior to no lich."

Sam looked a bit crestfallen at this rebuke. Ariella put an arm around him and said, "I think you're thinking of a demi-lich, not a semi-lich, Sam. A demi-lich is by definition an inferior or diminutive lich, like a demigod, which is a being that is godlike, but not quite as godlike as a god. On the other hand, a semi-lich, as Avery suggests, would be a partial lich, like a semicircle is partly a circle and partly not a circle. Being a semi-lich doesn't mean that he is necessarily less powerful than a full lich though. For example, a semi-lich could be partly a lich and partly a god, which would actually make him more powerful that a full lich."

"Technically, wouldn't a half-god/half-lich be a semidemigod?" Rook asked.

Ariella shook her head. "I think the proper term would be a demisemigod, like a demisemiquaver."

She sung a note that I supposed must be a demisemiquaver, and then all three of them turned to me as though their exchange had answered my question. I explained to them patiently that it hadn't, which meant I shouted, "So, do any of you know what the semi part of the semi-lich is?"

"Nope," said Luke.

"Sorry, laddie," replied Rook. "Accordin' to Jennifer's map, no one's ever seen him and survived."

"We will be the first!" Ariella stated optimistically. The rest of the group nodded their agreement.

"Wait. That's not possible!" I shouted.

"That's bein' a little pessimistic, don't you think, Avery?" Rook said, giving me a sideways look.

I wanted to point out the irony of that statement given everyone's recent behavior, but thought there was a good chance it would lead to a long argument over the difference between irony and situational irony, and so I gave it a skip. "No, no," I clarified. "I don't mean that it's not possible that we are going to survive meeting the semi-lich. Although I think our chances would be improved if we knew whether he was a half-lich/half-god or a half-lich/half-squirrel. I mean how is it possible for anyone to know anything about the semi-lich if no one's ever seen him and survived? If no one has seen him and survived, how does anyone know that there's a semi-lich here at all?"

There was much head scratching at this. Finally, Seamus pointed at the wall and offered, "Well, it does say that there is one right there on the sign."

"He's got a point," agreed Rook.

I gave up. It didn't matter whether there was a semi-lich or not. I needed to retrieve Justice Cleaver, defeat Vivian, and stop this world from colliding with Mysterium. Oh, and save my dissertation! "Let's go," I said wearily, and began walking toward the door.

"Wait a minute!" Seamus cried.

"What now?" I asked. "We've argued about how to get to the mound, how to get into the mound, how to close the door to the mound, what a semi-lich is, and whether it does or does not exist. What else could we possibly argue about?"

"Marching order!"

Everyone groaned.

CHAPTER 26

IT'S A TRAP

As we lined up, it suddenly struck me how few in number we were. At one point, I couldn't keep track of all the members of our group, but now we were six: Seamus and Rook, Ariella, Sam, Luke, and me.

I hadn't had much time to reflect on what we'd all been through. The argument over marching order gave me that time. I missed Drake and Valdara. Not just because having them would have meant more swords and staves to bring against the semi-lich, but because I missed their company. I missed Drake's gravelly voice and his animated eyebrows. I missed Valdara's cool competence, her fierce devotion to her companions, and of course her body-hugging armor. Hell, I even missed Barth and the three to five gnomes.

I missed them, but even if we survived this and won a great victory over Vivian, all of them would be dead in two years. I began to understand why some magi drank so heavily.

I was still wandering through these gloomy corridors of feeling when I realized that Rook was trying to get my attention. "Avery?" he said, waving a hand in front of my face.

"What?" I asked, blinking at him.

"You're behind Seamus and Luke," he said, pointing to the line that had formed in front of the door.

As soon as I was in place Rook, who was in the rear, barked, "Forward!"

Immediately, Sam began narrating. "The group leaves the round entrance chamber and starts walking down a ten-foot-wide corridor that extends into the darkness at least sixty feet." I found his voice strangely comforting.

What was not comforting was the background music. Moments ago it had been a chorus of sad violins as I thought about the ephemeral nature of these people; suddenly it dropped to an ominous growl. That got my attention. "Be careful, everyone!" I shouted.

There was a loud metal on stone clang from somewhere near the front of the line that nearly made me jump out of my clothes.

"Pit trap!" shouted Luke.

"Good thing we brought these poles," Seamus said, and gave a stern glance back at me.

"Watch everything," Rook shouted from the back. "Traps could be in the ceilings, the floors, the walls, everything and anything."

"Um, I have a spell for revealing traps," Sam said, holding up his book. "Would that be helpful?"

Everyone glared at him.

"Why didn't you mention that before, laddie?" growled Rook.

"I haven't had it long," he explained with a sheepish grin. "It seems to have written itself into my spell book last night."

"It what?" I asked.

"Last night I was reading my spell book," he said unnecessarily, since he did this every night, "and then I turned a page it was there."

"Seems a little convenient to me," Seamus said suspiciously.

The others began to argue about whether it would be possible for the semi-lich to insert a false spell into Sam's book to sabotage our attempts to get to him. My mind was spinning along other avenues, like whether this was my spell at work again or the simply the inherently goofy nature of Trelari magic and, if it was my spell, whether it was a bad sign that it seemed to be increasing the obviousness with which it was influencing events. I had written the spell to try and conceal its actions through implausible coincidence, but this went well beyond that.

"Well, Avery, should I cast it?" Sam asked, and I

realized everyone was waiting for me to decide the question.

I nodded. It was almost certainly the spell trying to help us; what it's lack of subtlety meant for our chances of surviving were a worry I wouldn't burden them with.

Sam gestured and threw a handful of sand down the hallway. The length of the passage suddenly lit up with traps. There were pits outlined in the floor, glowing trapdoors in the ceiling, loose stones vibrating in the walls.

Seamus made his way forward. "This is dwarf work. You ready, Rook?"

Rook's eyes went wide, but he nodded and joined his compatriot at the front of the line. The two dwarfs held their poles out in front of them and began triggering every trap in the corridor.

Sam began narrating faster and faster, trying to describe how each of the pits full of snakes *and* spikes sprung open, how every one of the trapdoors full of boiling oil or falling rocks or burning acid dropped out the ceiling, and how every poisoned dart or spear or spinning axe blade popped out of the wall. In a hundred feet, we saw more devilry and cunning than I care to mention. It was obvious that the semi-lich had some serious privacy issues, even for someone who was partially undead.

Finally, when the last of the traps had been triggered, Sam took a long drink from his waterskin and said, "After an exhaustive effort, the group comes to a strange door with carven images of leering demonic faces surrounding it."

"Got it," said Ariella beside him. "This is one of the most dramatic mapmaking efforts I've ever attempted. Look at all the markings for traps."

Everyone gathered around and started making appropriately impressed noises. For myself, I was staring at the demonic faces, which were staring back at me by the way. "What about this door," I asked.

"My spell didn't detect a trap, so it must be an innocent door," Sam said confidently.

"But look at these creepy demons," I said, pointing at one of the heads that was winking most suggestively at me. "They don't look innocent."

Rook looked up from Ariella's map and frowned. The faces were now doing their best to look casual, but they kept breaking into silent giggles at the effort. "Laddie's got a point, laddie. Just because your spell didn't detect anything doesn't mean we shouldn't be cautious."

Seamus started poking at the door with his pole. The demons didn't like this at all and began making extremely rude faces at him. This only made Seamus mad, and he did everything he could short of tearing the door apart to find a trap. Finally, he nodded to Rook and Rook nodded back. "It's safe," they announced.

One of demons stuck out its tongue at them. With

a muttered curse Seamus stepped into the room. We all followed.

"The group enters a thirty-foot-by-twenty-foot room," Sam said, which was true enough. "There is a door opposite the one they entered," he continued to narrate, which was also true.

I was examining the floor in detail, which I'd taken to doing ever since I saw that it was possible to have a pit with both snakes and spikes in it, when Sam said, "Suddenly, as the last party member steps inside, stone slabs fall into place, blocking the entrance and exit. There is the sound of rushing water and . . ."

I looked up. It was true. Water had started pouring from small holes in the ceiling and the walls. "In the name of the gods," I shouted, interrupting him. "The room is filling up with water!"

Sam pursed his lips in irritation. "I was going to say that."

"Let's just hope the walls don't start closing in!" said Luke.

"If you three are quite done," said Rook with a wet tap of his foot. "Would one of you wizards like to use your unearthly powers to help us out?"

Sam shrugged. "Last night I memorized my trap spell, my sleep spell, and a spell that makes me light as a feather, and then I kind of fell asleep."

The water had risen to the toes of our shoes.

"Your problem is that you procrastinate too much," Ariella said with a shake of her finger.

"That's not fair," Sam said defensively. "I needed to trim my toenails and reorganize my backpack."

"Third night in a row you've reorganized your backpack," muttered Seamus.

"No one else has to read *every* night," he whined.

"Great," Rook groaned. "We're goin' to die because of your bad study habits."

The water was at our ankles now. Everyone turned to look at me.

"I . . . um . . ." I said.

"That's not very helpful," Rook growled, which was true.

The truth was that I didn't know exactly what to do, and I was slightly panicked at the thought of the room filling up with water. I know I've told you about the thing I have about snakes and impalement, but I also have this thing about drowning. In fact, if I'm being perfectly honest, I have a general horror of my own death no matter the form. The result in this case was to drive every good drying spell I knew for dealing with spills and the like straight from my mind.

"Wizards," Ariella muttered with a roll of her eyes. She gestured, and the same freezing blast of air we'd felt when she stopped the polygons shot from her hands. The sound of running water turned into the crack and pop of ice forming.

"You did it!" Sam shouted with a whoop. "All the water in the room has turned to ice."

It was true; the floor had been converted into a

glittering mirror of frozen water and great icicles hung from the each of the holes in the ceiling.

"Of course I did it," she said smugly. "I am a direct descendent of a frost fairy, as any of you would know had you bothered to read my background."

"Yeah, great, lassie," Rook said with a tug of his beard. "Now we just have to chip ourselves out."

This was also true. The water had frozen around our ankles, encasing all of our feet in ice. The next half hour was spent chipping at our feet and then at the stone slab blocking the door, while Ariella told us all about her various fairy descendants. The relief, both at being free from the room and from Ariella, was palpable. Everyone rushed into the corridor beyond.

We were all so relieved that Sam even forgot to narrate the next forty to fifty feet of our exploration. It was the strange silence that made me realize that there had been no traps. The background music had become soft and mysterious.

"Has anyone noticed that there haven't been any traps lately?" I asked.

"Or descriptions?" Ariella said as she glanced up from the sketch of the corridor she was making in her map.

Sam looked around with a guilty start. "Sorry about that."

"Don't apologize for the lack of traps, laddie," Rook said, and slapped him on the back. "I know it's not as excitin' to describe, but this is good also."

Sam and I stared at Rook like he'd just said that

he wouldn't mind having the Dark Queen around for tea, which would have made more sense.

"At least, I think it's nice," he said defensively when he saw our expressions.

We kept staring.

"If you two like traps so much you can have them," Rook muttered into his beard.

"Door!" cried Seamus from the front of the line.

Unlike the last door, this one was utterly without ornamentation. The fact that it was such a plain, ordinary-looking door, the kind of door that let onto a broom closet or a tax preparer's office, made it creepier. Although part of that for me could have been that the music was getting more and more ominous.

I mentioned my feelings about the door, but needn't have. Everyone felt it. Seamus, Rook, and Ariella all took turns examining it for traps. There either were none, or the mechanism was one of those "devilishly clever" ones that the guide map Seamus purchased had warned us about. In the end, we could find nothing and, cringing against the coming acid or spike or poison or whatever, Seamus turned the handle and shoved the door open with his pole.

Behind the door was a square room, maybe thirty feet to a side that was whitewashed floor to ceiling and entirely featureless except for an open archway directly opposite our own through which a hallway beckoned.

We all gazed at the empty room, each of us experiencing a sense of dread. Mine being heightened when there was a crash of cymbals and the background music went silent. After spending my time in Trelari with some kind of music playing softly in my head, the silence made what I saw even more unnerving.

Rook, Seamus, and Ariella all stepped away from the door and looked back at me.

"Who . . . who should go first?" Ariella asked.

When no one said anything, Luke stepped forward. "I'll do it," he declared. "I've walked across plenty of rooms back home even plainer than this one."

I saw the fear in his eyes and remembered all the other men in red tunics that had died for my quest. I couldn't let him do this. I held out a hand. "Luke, you don't have to—"

He shook his head. "This is my destiny."

Throwing out his chest, he stepped inside. As soon as his foot touched the floor the room began to shake and emit an evil-sounding hum. Now, I don't know how best to describe an evil-sounding hum, but if you had heard it you would also know that it did not have our best interests at heart.

Shaking, he pulled his foot back. "I don't have a good feeling about this."

"I don't either, laddie," Rook said. "That hummin' is downright sinister."

We all nodded our agreement. It was obvious that this was the worst trap yet. We decided that what was needed was study. We would examine the room further to find out what gruesome fate awaited us inside. Sam and I both tried to sense any magical residue, but we found nothing. If it was mechanical, neither of the dwarfs could find any sign of trigger plates, trip wires, or other malicious mechanisms. Ariella suggested throwing something in and so we threw things—gold, string, sand, food, a ten-foot pole, Seamus's entire pack—through the door. Nothing happened, except that the floor of the room became less featureless as the pile of junk grew larger.

How long we spent staring into the room and discussing every feature of its featurelessness I don't know. How many plans we proposed and discarded, and the absurdity to which we reached in plotting our stratagems I hesitate to describe. We made any number of different attempts to cross the room. Luke stepped in another three times. Ariella put a foot in once. Sam scampered in on his hands and knees with a rope tied around his waist. Whenever a person entered, no matter how they entered, the room shook and hummed.

I don't know what happened to me, but at some point I lost my patience. If this room did lead to a horrible end, then how could I ask anyone else to suffer it for me? This whole affair had gone terribly wrong, and it was all my fault. I was the Dark Lord. Without warning, I bolted across the room.

Unfortunately, I should have been looking at where I was going, because halfway across I tripped on the pile of debris we'd created and stumbled forward uncontrollably, my arms windmilling as I tried to catch my balance. As I lurched toward the opposite door, the room quaked like the walls would collapse and the humming grew so violent it sounded like thunder. And then I was through the archway.

I lay panting on the floor of the hallway as the room fell silent behind me. "I made it," I gasped.

"Look at that!" Rook cried with an odd mix of wonderment and disgust. "Nothing happened!"

I stood up and looked back across the room. "What do you mean, nothing happened?"

"It didn't do anything," Seamus said.

Rook, looking madder than I'd ever seen him before, stalked across the room, with the rest of the group in tow. The humming grew louder and the room shook, but nothing happened. I went back in and helped them gather our things, and we left.

"Hell," said Luke as we gathered outside, and that about summed it up.

Somehow we all knew that the semi-lich had been watching us the whole time, and as he'd told us he would be, he'd been laughing. I stared back into the white featureless room and hated it. "We are going to find this semi-lich and teach him we are not to be trifled with," I vowed to the others, and then I slammed the door shut.

There was a sudden hissing sound and the entire corridor began filling with a noxious green cloud. My lips went numb.

"Gas trap!" gasped Sam, and began fiddling in his pouch before folding in half and slumping to the floor.

A little further down the hall I saw through the

haze Ariella begin a complicated series of gestures. "Antidotious Univer—" she began to say and then she also collapsed.

At the far end of the corridor the dwarfs and Luke were battering at a door. I watched as they each dropped one after the other. Rook was the last. He looked back down the hall at me, shrugged, and then slumped slowly to the floor

I took a deep breath and held it. My Mysterium constitution would allow me to hold out longer than the others, but I needed to act fast. I fixed the spell pattern for purification in my mind and I held it there. I threw my arms wide searching for power to energize the spell. Wherever we were, magic was scarce. It was like trying to find water in a desert.

The effort was enormous, and already my lungs were beginning to burn and my legs to shake. There simply wasn't enough magical energy to create a spell field. The pattern flickered. I focused all my concentration on trying to stabilize it, but it was fading. In desperation I poured all the energy I had into it, draining my own reality to feed it, but it was too late. My lungs were bursting for air. I found myself on my knees, my head spinning. Reflexively my mouth opened and I gulped in the gas.

The last thing I saw was the door at the end of the hall open. A tall, deathly white figure stepped through. He was laughing hideously. I had failed everyone. Again.

CHAPTER 27

THE SEMI-LICH

Drip. Drip. Drip.

Those were the first sounds I heard as I started to wake, and I was glad to hear them because not long ago I hadn't thought I'd be hearing anything ever again.

Drip. Drip. Drop.

The second time around the sound wasn't nearly as pleasant; this was less about the sound and more about the fact that the last drip, or rather drop, had landed with a cold splash directly in the middle of my forehead. Also at this point, my brain registered that my wrists and ankles were burning with pain. Instinctively I tried to move my arms and legs, but they were held fast by something hard, cold, and metal.

Drop. Drip. Drop.

I opened my eyes as two more drops hit my forehead. The normal course of action would have been to look and see why I couldn't move, or what was dripping on my head, or whether the rest of the company was with me, but the sight that greeted me made me forget about my companions, the sound, the water, the fact that I seemed to be chained spread-eagle to a wall.

I was in an enormous circular chamber that vaulted upward in a series of tiered rings. Countless candles illuminated the room, some in odd iron brackets like grasping hands that stuck out at random from the walls, some in man-high candelabras standing here and there about the room, and some in great ringed chandeliers that hung down from the heights. The candles did not give off a warm natural light, but burned a deep red so that it looked like the air was filled with dancing drops of blood. Directly across from where I was chained, a set of wide steps rose to a dais on which coins and jewels and strings of pearls and ancient armor and weapons were piled in heaping mounds, and which reflected the crimson light with obscene decadence. Before this glittering backdrop stood a high-backed throne of black wood and red velvet, and on this throne sat the semi-lich.

He wore a robe made of a dark material richly embroidered in gold. Two gloved hands adorned with numerous rings rested on the arms of the throne. A pointed crown set with glowing rubies rested on his head, but beyond this I could say little. His face was hidden by the shadows and I could see nothing of his features save a vague pale outline. It was so bizarrely theatrical that I almost laughed, but another drop came at that moment and spoiled my mood.

The semi-lich laughed. "You are finally awake, Avery. Excellent!" His speech was an odd mixture of deeply resonant vowels and hissing consonants. Somehow it suited him. "I am the semi-lich Aldric. I have enjoyed watching you traverse my maze of death."

He gestured casually at an ornate stand to his right on which stood a gilt framed mirror. The shining face of the glass clouded, and wavering images of the entry hall and the flooding chamber and the humming room flashed one after the other.

"Your solution to my water trap was particularly engaging. I don't think I have ever been more amused than I was watching you chip your ankles out of the ice." He laughed again, a dry, uncomfortable sound.

"I'm glad you got your money's worth," I said with way more defiance than I felt. And looking left and right to confirm that the others were there, which they were, I said, "Since we've served our purpose, why don't you let me and my friends go?"

He dismissed the notion with a wave of one of his ringed hands. "Not a chance. I have a hideously evil reputation to uphold and letting people go would set a bad precedent. Besides, I will enjoy slowly torturing you all to death."

Drop. Drop. Drop.

"Ugh!" I said with disgust. "Well, if the dripping water is part of your program of torture you're off to a great start."

"No, no," he said bitterly, "that's a plumbing issue. The drain from my water trap room keeps backing up into the main line. If I ever get my hands on the contractor who installed it, I will teach him the meaning of the words *back pressure.* I told him repeatedly to put in a backflow preventer or at least an air gap and a check valve. Did he listen to me?"

"No?" I answered, at a loss as to what he was talking about, but happy that we now seemed to be discussing someone else's torture and death, and not my own.

"Of course he didn't," Aldric spit. "But I know his game. He created this problem on purpose. He thinks he'll be able to come in here and charge me double-rate for an emergency job, and his stone contractor will be in on it with him, because inevitably they're going to need to open up the walls. I wasn't born yesterday . . ."

"I didn't think liches were born at all," I said aloud before I could stop myself.

"What?" he barked, seeming to suddenly remember that I was there. "Of course liches are born . . ." He paused and thought about it for a second. "Well, technically we aren't born . . ." he corrected, then stopped again and threw up his hands. "It's complicated."

"I think I understand," I said, because I had taken

three semesters of necromancy before switching majors. "A lich is typically a mage that decides to become immortal by embracing the dark powers of necromancy and converting himself into the undead. This means that while the lich itself is not born, but rather made through dark and demoniac rituals, the man that becomes the lich is born like any other man."

Aldric gave a gasp of disbelief and his entire manner changed. "You have it exactly," he said with some excitement. "Do you know how many times I've tried to explain that to other captives?"

"Laymen," I said in disgust. "I did study necromancy, although obviously I never went as far as you did with the subject."

"Be thankful," he said with a tired sigh. "Being a lich isn't all it's cracked up to be. First you research for years trying to uncover the secret to eternal life only to discover that you have to kill your body and trap your own soul to accomplish it, which is a bit of downer, I can tell you. And don't get me started on the up-front costs."

He gestured at his glowing crown. "There's the phylactery you need to make to confine your soul. That's not cheap. You also have to find someplace to set up shop, and it can't be an ordinary graveyard or a haunted mansion. No, you're expected to maintain a certain 'lifestyle.'" His gloved hands made eloquent little air quotes as he said this. "Add it all up and you barely manage to make enough to build even a modest treasure horde."

I didn't think it was the right time to point out that he was sitting in front of several kings' ransoms worth of loot. *Then again,* I thought as another drop of water landed on the bridge of my nose, *I don't know how much this plumbing rework is going to cost him. This is a pretty bad leak.*

"Whine, whine, whine . . ." came a voice like deep thunder that echoed about the chamber.

The semi-lich turned to me, his eyes blazing like deathly blue flames in the shadows. I tried to put my hands up in a gesture of bafflement, remembered I was chained, and beseeched, "I swear that was not me, O Great Semi-lich Aldric. I would never try to minimize the pain of your eternal existence."

"I know it wasn't you," he moaned. "It's . . . it's . . ."

"The greatest and most powerful—" the rumbling voice began.

"Silence!" Aldric commanded. I felt a rush of mystical power come with the command. I expected to suddenly lose the ability to speak or to hear, but I didn't. I realized that he had cast the spell on the area behind the throne where the piles of treasure lay.

"Who was that?"

"No one important," he said, and then turned his head and shouted back over his shoulder toward the treasure pile, "Not the least bit important!" He turned back, but he was clearly shaken. He put a gloved hand to his head and gave a groan. "You don't know what it's like, Avery. To live forever with that voice. It's enough to drive me even madder than I already am."

After saying this he seemed to forget I was there, and sat mumbling curses under his breath. I used the time to look at my companions. There was another possibility to mind—to consume my own reality—but I was hesitant to implement it since it would require me to die.

I was still pondering this unhappy option when Aldric sat up and said brightly, "Let's talk about something more cheerful, like how I'm going to torment you and your companions for the next several months or maybe even years."

"Or you could tell me, one student of necromancy to another, what a semi-lich is?"

"Behold," he said ominously.

He turned sideways so that he was facing to the right and leaned forward out of the shadows. His face was little more than a bleached skull with purple flickering shadows flowing over it. In the socket where his eye should have been, burned a ghastly blue flame. He then very deliberately removed the glove from his left hand, and showed that it also was nothing but bones knitted together by those strange purple shadows.

"You look like every other lich I've seen." I left off mentioning that all of those had been in textbooks.

"Ahhh," he said with a skeletal smile, "but you haven't seen the other side. Would you like to?"

I had to admit, despite the peril of our situation, I was immensely curious. I had always enjoyed necromancy as a subject, and if I ever managed to escape all this, I thought I might be able to include a chapter on the semi-lich in my dissertation, as a case study in subworld biodiversity. I nodded vigorously.

With a flourish he quickly spun to face toward the left, revealing his right side profile. The contrast was stunning. He had glossy black hair and smooth ghost-white skin. His eyes still danced with an unholy light, but the red lips and the hint of fangs left me no doubt.

"Seriously, you're a vampire-lich?!" I sighed in admiration. "That is so cool! How did you do it?"

"You really want to know?" he asked with a raised eyebrow.

Intellectual curiosity had gripped me with both hands. I could try and tell you that I was stalling him in order to gain time, but I really wanted to know how a half-vampire/half-lich came into being. I hadn't even minded the last two drops of water, that's how distracted I was.

"I guess it wouldn't hurt to talk about it," he admitted, and sat again so that his vampire side was visible. "I was Aldric the High-wizard, master of everything magic and occult. This was before the Dark Lord, but as you probably know, the world had been falling into ruin for some time. My tower was in the Sea of Grass and I became convinced that a band of marauding gnolls were going to devour me."

"Why gnolls?"

He shrugged. "It's silly, but I've had nightmares about gnolls since I was a child. I think when I was young and heard stories about them, I confused them with knolls. I'd always imagined them as large rolling hills with eyes coming to eat me. Utterly terrifying."

"That actually would be terrifying," I agreed, and added a confession of my own. "For years I thought a gazebo was a type of dread monstrosity."

"Completely understandable," said Aldric. "The word sounds like one of those part-this and part-that creatures, like a merlion or a cockatrice . . ."

I nodded along and added, "Or a griffin or a hippogriff."

He paused at this and asked, "What's the difference between a griffin and a hippogriff anyway? Aren't they both part eagle?"

"Yes," I said slowly, trying to remember my basic magical zoology class, "but one is half-eagle and half-horse and the other is half-eagle and half-lion."

"That's odd don't you think?" he asked after a moment's pause. "Some wizard must have spent years making the griffin or the hippogriff, whichever came later, when there was a perfectly acceptable eagle chimera already at hand."

Having known mages that had spent lifetimes perfecting magic considerably less notable I simply shrugged. "That's the nature of magicians, I suppose. I've never known one to be satisfied with someone else's magic, or at least who wasn't certain that he could improve that magic if he only set his hand to the task."

Aldric frowned. "As you will see," he murmured,

"your words could apply equally well to my own circumstance."

He began pacing back and forth across the dais, shifting from showing me his vampire side to his lich side and back again. "Back in my tower on the Sea of Grass, after long meditation on the subject, I came to the conclusion that the best way not to be killed by the forces of evil was to become an evil undead myself. I did my research and weighed my options. I wrote a long list of pros and cons. It was a difficult decision as I was not completely satisfied with the forms of undead that were available to me."

He stopped pacing with his vampire side to me. "Initially vampires seemed to be an attractive option. They don't look like a rotting corpse or smell bad or anything like that, and they seem to be the subject of a lot of romantic literature, so becoming one of those wouldn't necessarily be fatal to my love life. As an added advantage, you can turn into a bat or wolf, which is pretty cool. On the other hand, I was concerned about their vulnerability to common everyday things like sunlight, running water, stakes, and whatnot. Then there's the whole blood thing." He turned to face me full-on, which I wish he hadn't done because the effect was ghastly. "To be perfectly frank, Avery, that's why I left you all alive. I do need fresh blood periodically. Sorry."

I didn't know what to say to that, so I said nothing, but I did feel that I had to get some resolution on the whole "killing us" thing soon. Another drop of water landed on my face. Or at least get him to move me out from under this damnable leak.

"In any event," he continued, "I couldn't get over the fact that I would thirst for blood. I was always a touch squeamish when it came to blood and drinking it seemed out of the question." He pivoted to display his lich side. "On the other hand, liches are the ultimate undead. They are surpassingly fearsome and have limitless power. They can drain a man's life essence with but a touch and cast spells of such potency that entire kingdoms crumble before them."

"Kingdoms?" I raised an eyebrow.

He shrugged. "I exaggerate. The point was, I could see myself being a lich. I just hated to lose the romance of the vampiric lifestyle."

"So how'd you manage to make yourself both?" I asked.

"Pure accident. Imagine if you will the following scene. I am casting the unlife spell. The candles are flickering. The spirits of the dead are swirling all about. The time comes for the final proclamation, and at that crucial moment, I knew I had to be a li . . . mpire." He sighed. "Anyway, I'm not sure it came out exactly like that. I might have said vampich."

He sat down on the edge of his throne and, shrugging, gestured at his body. "The end result is what you see. A complete monstrosity." He slumped sadly.

I rolled my eyes. "You should have taken better notes."

"Avery!" Ariella said sharply, although a bit groggily, from my left. "Leave the poor semi-lich alone. He's obviously been through a lot."

"Lass, he's gonna kill us," Rook growled from my right. I glanced that way and the dwarf looked to be completely recovered. I got the sense looking at him that he'd been faking unconsciousness for some time. The others, as far as I could tell, were still out cold.

Seeing other people awake brought Aldric back to himself with a start. He sorted his face into a nasty sneer and turned so that his lich side was showing, and then thinking better of it he pivoted back to the vampire side. Once he was sure he was in a properly gruesome pose, he said, "Good, you are finally awake! Now I can begin the slow process of killing you all."

Rook rattled his chains as though trying to break free.

"Don't try to resist," Aldric said with a cruel chuckle. "I have rendered you all completely helpless. Your arms and legs are bound. Your weapons and magical constructs have been seized. You are totally under my power. All that is left for you to do is wail and despair as I . . ."

Ariella was raising and waving a finger in question.

"What is it you want, my dear?" he said irritably. "Is the incredibly attractive vampiric side of me making you fall in love?"

"Two things," she said, holding up a second finger. "First, why does your ceiling leak so much?" Aldric frowned and began muttering to himself again. "And second, how could you have seized my pouches? I had dozens of cloves of wild garlic in them!"

"Because you are a lady, and we vampires have a soft spot for the fairer sex, I will answer your questions before I destroy you." He raised an eyebrow at her suggestively, but when she made no reaction he hurried on. "One of the advantages of being a half-vampire is that garlic doesn't bother me. Shallots on the other hand . . ." He shuddered. "As for the ceiling." He turned back to the lich side. "That is only a portion of the torment I intend to deliver to you as I slowly drain you of your sanity and life." He laughed so hideously it made my skin crawl.

"Aldric," I said plaintively. "I thought we'd made a real connection."

"I am sorry, Avery, but this is what a semi-lich does," he said, and at least he did sound genuinely sorry.

"You thought you could reason with a semi-lich?" Rook barked out. "Yer as daft as he is. There's a reason they put the best treasures down here in the tomb. This guy's bat-crazy!" Aldric glowered at him, but didn't dispute it.

Around me I heard the stirrings from Luke and Seamus and Sam beginning to stir. Aldric paced in front of us, chuckling evilly and rubbing his hands. I had hoped that Ariella or Sam might be able to do something, but their hands were chained. They both needed to make complex gestures to complete their castings, and Sam needed his little pouch. It was up to me, but I was still having no luck summoning up any magical energy Whether Aldric had set magic protections on the room, or whether it was simply the natural consequence of his half-lich nature, there was no power for me to use.

Another drop of water fell right on the bridge of my nose. I couldn't even stop that—how could I take down a semi-lich? It was hopeless. I would either have to drain the life of one of my companions or myself. I slumped in my chains and muttered, "All I needed was Justice Cleaver. That's all."

Suddenly Aldric was in my face, his undead eyes blazing like never before. "Did you say you came here for Justice Cleaver?" he asked. "To be clear, if you got Justice Cleaver, you would take him away from me . . . from here?" His hands, both skeletal and vampiric, were shaking with excitement.

"Yes," I said irritably. "Our plan was to take it with us and use it to destroy the Dark Queen."

Aldric fell to his knees and raised his hands to the sky. "I knew there must be at least one of the gods dedicated to looking out for the hybrid undead. This is wonderful news."

He stood and with a snap of his skeletal fingers our manacles fell away. "Sorry about all this. We've just had a misunderstanding. No hard feelings. Look, all your things are—" he snapped again and our equipment appeared on the ground in front of us "—right there. Please let me get you what you've come here for."

I wasn't sure what to say. Everyone else seemed to be in shock as well. We got our gear back on while he crashed through the treasure area behind the throne, muttering about all the clutter and throwing aside bits of magical armor and great piles of coins and gems.

"Here it is!" he screeched, and came scampering back carrying a double-bladed battle-axe wrapped in leather. He thrust it at me. "It's all yours."

"Wait a minute." Rook stepped in between me and Aldric. "Why do you want to get rid of that thing so badly?"

"I just like to be helpful," he said in a disastrous attempt at an innocence. "You know, helpful is my middle name."

"What happened to 'draining us of sanity and life' is just what a lich does?" Ariella asked suspiciously.

He looked around at the doubt in our faces and his shoulders slumped in defeat. "Okay, can I be perfectly honest with you?" We all nodded. "I've been a semi-lich for a long time. I've had a lot of powerful magic items come through the tomb. Never have I had a problem with any of them until this Justice Cleaver came along."

"Is it c-cursed?" Sam asked, and everyone, including me, took a step back.

"No . . ." Aldric began, and then stopped. "Not really. He just won't shut up. If I didn't cast a silence spell on him every day, he would happily talk about how great he is and how he's being wasted in here and so on without end. It's been driving me mad for months."

"Months?" Sam asked. "But I thought Justice Cleaver had been down here for eons."

"News to me," Aldric said. "If it were true I really would be mad." He gave a hysterical little giggle after this that made everyone genuinely uncomfortable.

I was getting nervous about the direction this conversation was taking. To end the debate I stepped forward and took the battle-axe from him. It felt heavier than I thought it should. "Whether the battle-axe is cursed or not," I said, "it is what we need to complete our quest, and I thank you, Aldric."

"No, thank *you*." He reached out with his lich hand to shake.

As we grasped hands, I felt the icy sting of death. My arm went numb.

"Ooops! Sorry about that," he said and quickly let go.

Aldric apologized repeatedly and profusely. And then when we'd gotten all of our things back on and together he gave a little bounce on his feet that didn't seem in keeping with his lich persona and said eagerly, "Well, I know you must be anxious to go and destroy that awful Dark Queen." He gestured and part of a wall slid back to reveal a stair going up. "Let me show you the way out. Your friends are waiting."

"Friends?" I suddenly remembered the Hooded Riders and took a step away from the stair.

"Out you go!" he commanded, and a rush of powerful magic came on us and we found ourselves on the stair, and then up the stair, and then into the open air. There was the noise of a stone being rolled into place and when I turned all that remained was the featureless mound.

"What just happened?" asked Sam.

"I don't know, laddie," Rook said.

Over the dwarf's shoulder I saw two figures in dark cloaks rise from the ground and rush toward us.

"The riders!" I managed to shout.

Everyone spun around, reaching for their weapons. Without thinking, I took a defensive posture and raised the wrapped battle-axe before me.

CHAPTER 28

NOT IN KANSAS ANYMORE

The sun was in our eyes, and we blinked as the riders came up the side of the mound toward us. Rook and Seamus had their own axes at the ready, Ariella had her daggers out, and Sam had pulled his little bag of sand from his pouch and was beginning an incantation. Luke held a sword and closed his eyes as if he were trying to focus.

Despite my recent failures, I fixed a pattern in my mind that would form a wall of fire between us and them and began to draw in the power I would need to energize it. I knew that something was wrong at once. A feedback of magical energy seemed to run through the air around my body, and a jolt of pure magic raced through my hand to the battle-axe. A brilliant white light burned through the wrappings that had been covering the weapon and shooting into the sky like a beacon. Above our heads came a mighty peal of thunder.

When the light finally died away, the covering had been reduced to ash. I found that I was holding Death Slasher's twin, save that this one was made of brightly polished silver instead of pitted black metal, and where the evil battle-axe had an eye that always watched, this one had a symbol of the scales of justice etched into its handle.

"I, Justice Cleaver, am come!" said the battle-axe in a voice that shook the ground beneath my feet.

I had no time to ponder the fact that I was holding a talking battle-axe, because at the same moment I felt the reality of the world jolt as though it had been struck by a tremendous force. A hot wind came howling across the wasteland and swirled up the mound. It tore at my clothes and rose into the sky in a whirlwind. My vision blurred, the background music swelled and then suddenly stopped. Not silenced momentarily for dramatic effect, but really gone. I knew at once that Trelari had now shifted perilously close to Mysterium. I sagged to my knees, the battle-axe forgotten in my hand.

A dark figure loomed above me. I started to lift Justic Cleaver. "A simple hello would have done," said Drake in his so familiar gravelly rasp.

"Drake?!" I shouted with joy, and soon everyone took up the cried of "Valdara!" and "Drake!"

Valdara ignored the cheers and came straight to my side. She stood above me, staring down at me in silence. "You survived the semi-lich. And I see that you found Justice Cleaver."

From her tone I wasn't sure if she was happy about either, but there was no time for a proper explanation, her words brought everyone's attention back to me and the battle-axe. All eyes were fixed on the weapon. Above our heads dark black clouds massed. Inside those clouds, flash after flash of lightning could be seen.

It was in this solemn and eerie moment that Justice Cleaver thundered, "I know, there are not words. You are all in awe, which is only right and understandable. I'm certain that none of you have beheld another battle-axe nearly as impressive as I am, and you can't even begin to comprehend even half of what I can do. Fix the memory of this moment in your mind, because you will cherish it for the remainder of your life. Your descendants may choose to sculpt you in this exact position, because today is the day the greatest weapon for justice in the history of time was unleashed upon the world. Let us have a moment of silence to properly honor this occasion and give your followers a chance to note where they stood for posterity."

This speech, as ridiculous and ill-timed as it was, was exactly what we needed to break the tension.

"Someone thinks a little much of himself," Seamus snorted.

"Dwarf," Justice Cleaver boomed. "Do not be

downcast. Though your own axe is but a child's plaything compared to me, the mightiest battle-axe in history, as a friend and companion of the wielder of Justice Cleaver, I will defend you against all foes. All will fall before my justice."

"I think I can see why Aldric wanted to get rid of the thing," Rook said, eyeing the battle-axe with distaste.

Justice Cleaver shook in my hand. "Aldric knew that his evil would eventually falter against my virtue. In time my will would have bested his and he would have dedicated himself to the cause of justice. What a brilliant pair we would have made! No one could have stood before a half-vampire/half-lich champion of righteousness!"

"Can you shut that thing up, kid?" Drake asked.

"I . . . I don't think so," I said honestly. I looked at the battle-axe and said, "Justice Cleaver, could you give us a second?"

"None can silence Justice Cleaver!"

"I'm not trying to silence you," I assured it. "I just need to talk to Valdara and Drake for a moment, and then I promise we will discuss your greatness and what enemies we need to defeat and all the rest."

"We will interrogate them together. Even the wicked fear to lie when faced with the might of my splendor!"

I shook my head in frustration, took off my pack, and shoved Justice Cleaver into it. Dropping the bag at the feet of Rook and Seamus with strict instructions to watch it, I led Valdara and Drake down the mound away from the rest of the group. The violence of the wind lessened as we descended and was just a memory of the earlier torrent when we got to where they had their horses picketed. We stood in silence for a few moments.

Drake spoke before I could gather my thoughts. He looked up at the clouds, which still hung heavy, and said, "I take it that the light show wasn't your doing."

I had no idea. It might have been. Perhaps trying to use Mysterium magic with the battle-axe in my hand had yanked on the connection between the worlds. Perhaps I had, once again, made things worse. Eldrin would have known. I didn't. I shrugged my shoulders. "I don't know," I admitted, "but it wasn't my intention."

Valdara, who had said nothing for a while, threw her arms into the air in disgust. "Intention, intentions, who cares about intentions, Avery," she said sharply. "This is what has troubled me about you from the beginning. All that matters are your actions—what you do, what you have done, and what you will do."

I looked to Drake for support, but he fixed me with his dark eyes and said gravely, "No one thinks that they are evil, kid. Even the Dark Queen probably thinks she's doing good."

I wanted to argue that intentions did matter. I wanted to tell them that I had come to Trelari for the best of reasons. I had selected this place because it was already aflame with violence and chaos. Everywhere people lived in terror from the monsters of their nightmares. A band of these blood orcs had killed Valdara's family and burned Drake's village years before I had even conceived of the Dark Lord. I unified the forces of darkness; I moderated and weakened them so that ultimately the forces of good could defeat them. If I had not come, civilization, likely all life, and possibly the reality of Trelari itself, would have been wiped out. My intention was to stop that, and to make a golden age on Trelari. That was my intention now also. But the music was gone. We were nearly out of time, and here we sat arguing about intentions. Besides, Drake had struck too close to home with his comment about Vivian.

Frustration rose in my breast. "All I want to do, Valdara," I snapped, "all I have ever wanted to do, is find the Dark Queen and stop her from bringing ruin to the land."

Her eyes burned into me. "I asked you once before, and I will ask you again: Why?" I pointed to the sky for an answer, but she shook her head. "Who is the Dark Queen to you, Magus?"

"She's . . ." I began, but couldn't finish. I didn't want to answer that question. Even now I couldn't bring myself to speak the whole truth. That I was responsible for everything that had happened after the fall of the Dark Lord. "She . . . she's a threat to everything you and Drake and everyone else in the Army of Light fought for," I stammered, "and every moment we bicker here the danger grows greater."

"Always you deflect and deny, Avery?" Valdara said. "Answer one question truthfully for me: Why does that battle-axe make the world tremble and the sky boil?"

I started to answer. I honestly don't remember what I was going to say, but it wasn't going to be the truth. Before I could speak she held up a hand and said, "Avery, know that I forgive you for every mistake you have made. I believe, important or not, that intentions do matter. But no more lies."

She sounded like a queen, the queen I had hoped she would become, but now she was judging me and finding me wanting, and I felt rather small. "Fine," I said chastened. "No lies."

I told them to wait and then retrieved my pack and brought it back down to where they stood. With a deep breath I opened it. Justice Cleaver shouted, "AHA!"

"Be quiet," I commanded. The battle-axe quivered, but did not respond. Perhaps I did have a level of control over the thing.

As I pulled it forth, there was another peal of thunder and the wind whipped around us, throwing up a cloud of sand. I felt the hairs on the back of my neck rise and a chill run up and down my spine. I gazed up at the sky. The clouds were churning again and growing darker and more sinister with each passing second. Butterflies twisted in my stomach. This whole experiment had gone so terribly wrong, and every time I held Justice Cleaver it was only further confirmation that my original sin, using Mysterium magic, still haunted Trelari.

I held Justice Cleaver up before them. "I told you before that I am from another world." They nodded in response. "For reasons I don't fully understand—" and the gods help me that was the real truth "—my world and this one are affecting each other. It is my belief that the battle-axe we recovered from the tomb and the one you fought against are responsible."

"Do you mean Death Slasher, the axe of Morgarr the Slaughterer?" She spat both names.

"Yes." I really hoped that this wasn't going to end with Valdara leaving again. "I've got to reunite Justice Cleaver with Death Slasher. I don't know what will happen when I do that, but I do know that if I don't, and if I don't do it soon, terrible things will happen. I'm not sure what, but this world could be destroyed."

"That's a lot of 'I don't knows' and 'maybes,' Avery," Valdara said.

"You wanted the truth." I let the axe drop to my side. "The truth isn't always neat or sure."

"Kid's got a point there, Valdara," Drake said, raising one eyebrow.

"Okay," she conceded. "So, we need to get you to Death Slasher, but it was lost when the Dark Lord was defeated. Do you know where it is now?"

"My world," I said without explanation.

Her face stiffened and she locked her eyes onto me. Questions lay behind her gaze. Questions about Death Slasher and the Dark Lord and their connection to me. If she had asked I would have answered—no lies—but somehow I think she knew that the answers to those questions might mean making an enemy of me, not that I would have considered her an enemy, but that she would have felt compelled to count me as one.

A sad smile turned the corners of her mouth. "After the world is saved there will be a time for questions and answers, and consequences. Right now I believe that your intentions are good, and I will let it pass." She exchanged a look with Drake, and something unspoken passed between them, like an agreement had been reached. "Return to your world with the battle-axe, Magus," Valdara finally said. "When you are done come back and help us defeat the Dark Queen."

"Just like that you would send away your best weapon for defeating the Dark Queen?" I asked.

"Now who's getting big in the head," Drake said in his best growl.

"That's not what I—"

"Stop teasing him," Valdara chastised as he chuckled. "Can't you see he and I are trying to have a meaningful and significant conversation about significant and meaningful things?"

Drake snapped his mouth closed and crossed his fingers over his heart.

Here was the thing. I had been thinking about this possibility since I'd learned about the connection between the battle-axes. As Dawn reminded me in our last conversation, I have the ability to cast my return spell at any time. I could take the battle-axe, return to Mysterium and be done with this whole damned adventure. But I knew I wouldn't.

The question had never been about getting home; the question was what happened when I got there. I would never be able to cast the spells necessary to destroy the battle-axes without telling Griswald everything, which meant getting magi from Mysterium involved. They would destroy the axes. They would send in a squad of disciplinary magi to stop Vivian. It goes without saying that my dissertation would never be accepted, and that I'd probably get banished from the university entirely. Yes, I was selfish enough that my academic career often entered into my internal debates.

To my credit, my very little credit, had those been my only considerations, I probably would have gone back home anyway. But something had happened to me while in Trelari: I had fallen in love. Not with a woman, although I had great affection for Ariella and Valdara. I had fallen in love with this land. I loved the place and all its infuriating quirks, and I hated what I had done to it. I had come to Trelari with the inherent belief in my own superiority, and it led me to create the Dark Lord, and Death Slasher, and the Master, and the golems, and all the other monstrosities that continued to haunt the world. I hadn't brought peace. Vivian or no Vivian, things were already bad when she arrived. In short, I had come to the conclusion that I couldn't be trusted to save Trelari, and the reason was because I thought like a Mysterian. This also meant that I couldn't trust anyone else from Mysterium to save Trelari.

I was a symptom of a broader problem: a fundamentally flawed view of what was real and what had value. I had to face the possibility that if I went back to Mysterium now, they might determine, in their wisdom, that Trelari represented a real and present threat to the stability of the Mysterium and/or the innerworlds, and that would be that. No further hearing. No appeal. No more Trelari. Subworlds were inferior realities. They were expendable. It was what you were taught from day one. If my original goal had been to save Trelari from itself, now my goal was to save it from Mysterium.

"Tempting" is what I said as I tucked the battle-axe into my belt. "But we need to stop the Dark Queen first. With Justice Cleaver we should be strong enough to resist her power." I realized with my new no-lying policy that I should moderate that a bit. "At least possibly?"

"Possibly?" Drake said, and cocked an eyebrow.

"Possibly," I repeated.

Drake shrugged. "I always like playing the long odds anyway."

"It is a certainty," boomed Justice Cleaver.

"But I could learn to bet the favorite," Drake amended with a twisted smile. "What about you, Val?"

She tapped a finger to her chin and then tucked her arm in his. "I have nothing else going on today."

"Wait," I said, holding up my hand. "Before we go on, why did you come back?"

Valdara half smiled. "Well, we were on our way home when Drake reminded me that the Dark Queen still needed stopping."

I was pretty sure she was kidding. I took a deep breath and looked between the two of them. I felt tears in my eyes. "It's good to have the two of you back."

Drake gave me a pat on the shoulder. "In all seriousness, kid, you know we've been trying to catch up to you for a week. We even hired a tracker, but you guys never slowed down, even on the mound when we were shouting at you to stop."

"I understand that now," I said a bit sheepishly. "We got it in our heads that you were Hooded Riders."

The both looked at each other and then back to me. "Well, technically I guess we were," Valdara said. "We were wearing hoods, but it was only to keep the sun off our heads."

"You can get a bit paranoid if you ride all day through a wasteland with the sun beating down on you, kid," Drake advised about a week too late.

I cleared my throat and tried to change the subject. "Since time is pressing, shall we be off?"

"Be it known," Justice Cleaver intoned significantly. "Whoever you need to battle, whoever you intend to defeat, they will be mine!"

"Thanks, JC," Drake said with a chuckle.

We wandered back up to the top of the mound and called the Company of the Fellowship together. I knew that this was the sort of moment where a real leader would say something to rally the troops. I held my hand aloft dramatically and began. "Company of the Fellowship, I call you here at the beginning of the last leg of our journey. We have been through many hardships—"

"I thought you said time was of the essence, kid," Drake interrupted.

"Well, I did," I said uncertainly, "but I thought that we should tell everyone that we've decided to go after the Dark Queen."

"We're going after the Dark Queen?" Sam asked eagerly.

"We're with you, Avery!" announced Ariella and Luke in an attempt at a combined pledge.

"About time," Rook huffed, and pointed to the sky. "I'm gettin' tired of this mound and this awful weather."

I followed his gesture up; the clouds were beginning to spin and coil together in a great funnel, and lightning was streaking outward from the maelstrom in flashes of red and blue. I didn't have the heart to tell Rook that this was not weather; it was the reality of Trelari fraying and flying apart, and that as long as we had Justice Cleaver with us it was unlikely to get better.

"How do we get there?" I asked Valdara and Drake in the hope that they would know.

"We could go back the way we came," Sam suggested. "That's the quickest route."

"I don't think so," said Valdara with a shake of her head. "According to our tracker the Dark Queen's armies marched in behind us. The land near the village will probably be an armed camp now, and hooded riders . . . real Hooded Riders will be patrolling the Sea of Grass day and night. We'd never survive that way."

"That's okay," said Seamus. "We can go the overland route. You and Drake know it pretty well. At least that's what the legends say."

"The legends are all true," Drake drawled, and, pointing a thumb at himself, boasted, "Particularly this one." Valdara rolled her eyes at him.

"Can I ask a question?" said Luke.

"Wait a bit, kid," said Drake. "Let me tell everyone about the route. First, we go through the Forest of the Lost."

"Isn't that the mazelike wood with paths haunted by fairies and spiders?" asked Sam, who was taking notes on the back page of his spell book.

"That's right, the leaves in the forest are so thick on the branches that even light can't penetrate down to its paths. They say monstrous mushroom men lurk in the forest too, but I can't say we ever saw any," Drake said, then casually pointed up into the sky and added, "The upside is that the canopy is so thick that it should protect us from the rain if these storms don't let up."

I closed my eyes, trying to imagine how hard it would be to make it through the Forest of the Lost.

"Sounds pretty sketchy, but I'm sure we can get through the forest and make it to the Dark Queen's fortress." I had to say it twice because the winds were beginning to howl rather loudly again.

"Whoa, kid," Drake said when he finally understood what I was saying. "Don't get ahead of yourself."

"That's just the first couple weeks of the journey," explained Valdara, speaking more loudly to account for the crashes of thunder. "After the Forest of the Lost, we have to venture through the Swamp of Mire, a foreboding dark fen inhabited by poisonous frog people and giant crocodilians."

"Wait, I've heard of those," said Sam, jotting quickly in his book. "Don't they keep giant killer freshwater eels as pets?"

"And lumbering bog beasts!" interjected Ariella. She nearly jumped with excitement. Her long dark hair was whipped back in the wind. "I've heard that rare flowers grow on their backs. There's one potion recipe that I've been dying to try out if we can find enough of them."

"I still have a question," said Luke.

"After we are done figuring this out, kid," said Drake, who was nearly shouting to be heard over the storm. "The real issue in the mire is the quicksand and the mosquitos. Both of them will eat you alive."

Valdara, who was clutching her cloak close around her, glanced doubtfully at the dwarfs. "The water can be pretty deep as well. You wade through most of the mire."

Drake nodded. "It's a foot killer to be sure. We want to make sure we have extra shoes and socks."

I felt flushed. We'd have to get through this swamp after the forest. Maybe we could build a raft? I hoped the winds would die down soon as I was having trouble concentrating on what everyone was saying with all the dust whipping through the air.

"And climbing gear," said Valdara. "We'll need climbing gear for the Cliffs of Madness."

I didn't want to know, but still I found myself asking, "The Cliffs of Madness?"

Drake rolled his eyes. "Yes, Avery. Everyone knows that the Cliffs of Madness mark the end of the Swamps of Mire."

Rook muttered. "Avery's not from around here."

"Oh, right. Sorry about that, kid," said Drake.

"Hold on." I was determined to retake control of this conversation. "So, with the forest and the mire and the cliffs, how long will this journey take?" I asked, and stumbled a bit as a particularly violent gust nearly lifted me off my feet.

Valdara answered in a full throated shout as the winds seemed to be screaming around us. "It depends on whether the disease hawks, blood vultures, or vile harpies attack us on the ascent. One to two months, generally, assuming you can find a ledge and there's nothing lurking in the Caves of Corpses . . ."

"Which there always is!" barked Drake.

She nodded at this assessment and continued. "But that'll be nothing compared to the time it takes to cross the Eerie Wasteland, not to mention the Magma Pits of the Ragelords."

"I'm actually pretty excited about this journey," said Sam. "I've always wanted to see the Glacier of the Gods and make my way through the Impassable Passages of the Minotaur King . . ."

"Not meaning ta be a stickler there, Sam," interrupted Seamus, "but I hear he calls it the Labyrinthine Labyrinths now. It came out in a royal bull."

They both chuckled.

"Can I ask my question now?" said Luke.

"Calm down, kid," Drake sighed. We all huddled together in a circle to hear each other better. "Valdara, have you heard whether the bridge over the Chasm of Calamity is still standing?"

"I think so," Valdara answered. "We just have to hope that the guardians will let us pass."

This was completely out of control. I had visions of long treks through forest and mires and up cliffs and along winding hallways and labyrinths, of being frozen on glaciers and having my eyebrows singed off by the heat from magma flows. "Please stop," I pleaded, half to the party and half to the incessant winds. "I just want to know how long it will take to reach the Dark Queen."

"Six months to a year?" suggested Valdara with a slight shrug.

"Give or take," agreed Drake.

"Six months!" shouted Rook before I could.

"To a year . . ." Drake reminded him.

I paced and Rook paced with me. "What are we goin' to do," he muttered.

"Maybe if I could find a way to reunite the battle-axes . . ." I suggested.

Justice Cleaver made a sound like it was clearing its throat, which seemed odd as it had no throat. I pulled it from my belt and held it to my ear so I could hear what it was saying. "Maybe you should ask someone that is the world's greatest expert on magical battle-axes?"

"I don't have access to anyone like that," I snapped.

Justice Cleaver sighed. "Really? Okay. Fine." It almost sounded like it was sulking.

That's when we heard Sam scream, "Hooded Riders!"

He pointed out across the wind-whipped waste. From each point of the compass, both cardinal and ordinal, came a gaunt black-cloaked rider on a night-mare stead. Despite the sandstorm swirling around them, they galloped on, heedless of the growing cata-clysm.

"What do we do?" Sam shouted.

Valdara, Drake, and I looked between ourselves. I could see that they had as many ideas as I did—none.

"I don't think we're going to have to worry about them," said Luke with wide eyes.

We all turned to look at him. I screamed, "These aren't hooded riders, Luke. They are Hooded Riders. They are the real deal."

"Yes, I know," he roared, and he really had to

roar to be heard now because the sound from the winds and the thunder and blowing dust was deafening, "But so is my question." He pointed to the sky. "What's that flashing?"

I looked up and gasped. It was there, a thing of magical legend: a dimensional tornado, a towering column of pitch-black reality filled with red, blue, and purple lightning that reached up as far as the eye could see. The energy within it was incomprehensible. It had been growing above our heads as we talked, unnoticed by everyone but Luke, and it was descending out of the sky toward us at an incredible rate of speed. I wanted to run, but all I could do was stare in awe and wish Eldrin were here to see it.

"This is worth a paper all by itself," I said to myself, even as I tried to recall any spell or bit of Mysterium magic that would have any effect on it. I had nothing.

In the next moment, it was on us. It centered on me and Justice Cleaver. I caught a glimpse of my reflection in the battle-axe. My reflection was smiling back at me and winking.

"Don't forget that I tried to help you," said Justice Cleaver.

I started to shout that he had done no such thing, or had done so in such a passive-aggressive way as to make no difference, but we were torn from the ground and swept into a sky full of multicolored lightning before I could get the words out. Below us the Hooded Riders had reached the mound. They stared up impotently as the storm carried us away.

CHAPTER 29

THE DARK LORD RETURNS

I spun uncontrollably through the raging storm, clinging to Justice Cleaver with both hands. I thought I could see other bodies whirling in the vortex. There was a streak of red that could have been Valdara's hair, and I kept hearing snippets of cursing that certainly belonged to Drake or Rook or Seamus . . . or all three.

Most of my time falling through space was spent praying to anyone who might be listening to let us live. I wasn't only worried about physical dangers like one or more of us being impaled on a tree or smashed into a mountain or any of the other mundane ends that could befall someone in such a storm, falling hundreds of feet to your doom being the most likely, I was worried that reality itself might have given way and that we were being flung through subspace, possibly lost in the uncharted infinity beyond imagination. Overly dramatic? Perhaps, but that's what was passing through my mind.

I had this vain hope that Justice Cleaver would protect me—somehow. Even though it was unclear how a battle-axe could be of any help in these circumstances. All I knew was that it was the only solid thing around me so I kept holding on. Unfortunately, holding Justice Cleaver also meant listening to Justice Cleaver.

"Don't worry," he said reassuringly. "You are holding the most powerful battle-axe in the known universe. You are invincible. Now, if you were holding a more mundane magical weapon, like a mystic sword, I wouldn't like your chances. There are so many magical swords. The good ones that glow when orcs are about, and the black menacing ones that moan and eat souls, and then there are the disreputable ones that loaf about, stuck in stones or at the bottom of lakes. Have you ever seen a knight in full armor wade into a lake to try and get a sword? Technically, neither have I, but the mental image is ridiculous enough to put a sane person off swords altogether."

Aldric had certainly not been exaggerating about Justice Cleaver's lack of an inner monologue. It never shut up. It carried on and on as we spun around and around. Now, I complain, because at this point you are sort of expecting me to and I feel like I need to live down to expectations, but the truth was, after a time, it became comforting to hear its voice. I closed my eyes and hung on as Justice Cleaver explained about the proper care and storage of a battle-axe of his pedigree, and I continued to hang on as he recounted the sloppiness with which Aldric had kept his treasure chamber, and I almost let go as it began to detail all of its best qualities.

Then, Justice Cleaver fell silent. My heart beat two or three times and I opened my eyes, just to make sure we were still whirling about in the storm. We were.

"Got you!" Justice Cleaver said with an overhearty laugh. "I needed you to open your eyes so you could see how I gleam when all this multicolored lightning flashes off of my blades. This moment should be captured for posterity. I'm thinking a painting would be the right way to go. Any thoughts?"

"I'm just hoping we survive," I yelled over the winds.

"I certainly will. I'm an unbreakable artifact tied to the very fabric of this world. I'm not as sure about you—you are a bit squishy. This is my advice: when we land, try not to land on your head, and when you're lying there gasping in pain, don't sit up too quickly. Oh, and if you need to throw up, don't do it on me."

"Thanks," I said with as much sarcasm as I could muster given the way my head, and all the rest of me, was spinning.

"Don't mention it. I am the greatest giver of advice

in this or any other world," he confessed grandly. I would later learn that Justice Cleaver did understand sarcasm; he just never thought it applied to him.

As abruptly as we were taken from the semi-lich mound, we landed. To my surprise, we didn't slam into the earth or plummet to the ground. In fact, we landed rather gently. I actually touched down on my feet, but was so woozy from spinning that I fell to my knees. Apart from the nausea brought on by all the spinning, I was fine. I heard Rook curse and Seamus grumble nearby. Luke moaned.

"We're alive!" said Sam.

"How fun!" Ariella squealed as only an elf can squeal, and began to dance around. "Did anyone else see the pegacorn flying around up there?"

"I saw nothing," said Drake. "I think I need to start drinking more."

"Hardly," replied Valdara as her horse landed on its feet, apparently unflustered, next to her. Without blinking at this incredible occurrence she reached out and grabbed its reins.

The winds whirled about for a time, swirling dust and debris around and obscuring what lay beyond their margins. Soon enough the whirlwind began to die down, or at least to draw back up into the sky. As it rose, remnants from our journey—sand, the odd rock and bush, a bicycle with a basket—began falling to the ground.

I looked about at our surroundings. We were in a vast courtyard of hewn black rock. Overhead, the dark clouds still clashed and crashed in flashes of lightning. The storm obscured whatever sun there might have been, if it was even day. In the dim and indifferent light, I could make out black walls rising up to ragged heights. The battlements were pocked here and there by doors and barred windows that looked out like dead eyes. A great iron gate was at our back and another before us.

There was a beat or two of utter silence and then a mighty clanking boom and a groan, and the iron gate we were facing swung open. A mass of blood orcs, fiend trolls, and beastlings marched out in a ragged formation. At the front of the group was a woman in a black robe holding a crooked staff. She was tall and had a drawn face. She might have been pretty were it not for the green tinge of her skin and her haughty expression. She struck her staff on the ground and the army fell out around her in ranks three-deep and surrounded us. We closed in around Valdara's horse and drew our weapons.

"I am the High Witch of the Fortress of the Dark Queen, interlopers. Despite your unusual means of transport, your intrusion will not go unpunished! I will take great joy in dragging you before the queen herself. You may surrender of your own accord, or you will be slaughtered where you stand."

She gave a terrible high-pitched shriek of laughter. All around us the army echoed her. If you've never heard a mixture of orcs, trolls, and beastlings laugh, you are fortunate. It was horrible.

I was all for surrendering, but Justice Cleaver chose this moment to shout, "Raise a hand against us and it will be the last thing you do, witch scum!"

"Oh," she said, staring straight at me. "You dare to challenge me?" She took a step forward and lifted her staff to the sky. A ball of black energy began to swirl at its tip. "Now, fools, feel the full power of—"

With a terrible crash and a crunch of timber, a house plummeted out of the sky and landed on her.

There was a beat of silence before a disappointed Justice Cleaver said, "I had hoped to do the slaying myself. Well, the important thing is that we are one for one . . ."

While he explained that the next logical move was for us to single-handedly destroy the army, I did the only actually logic thing and looked up. Everyone else—dwarfs, humans, elves, orcs, trolls, and beastlings—were doing the same thing. There were some flashes of colored lightning high up in sky, but lower down there were dozens of enormous dark shapes falling through the void toward us.

Valdara shouted, "Run!" Then she leapt atop her horse and galloped toward the open gate, slashing a path through the creatures with her sword.

Not that the High Witch's army was in much of a mood to stand before her. In fact, they seemed to take Valdara's shout as a kind of order and began scattering in all directions. The company followed through the chaos and confusion of her wake toward the distant gate.

We were halfway to the opening when things started to land, or should I say crash violently, around us. A windmill shattered among a group of blood orcs to our right, instantly crushing a dozen or more and then pummeling the rest with its still-spinning sails. A herd of cattle, like gigantic fleshy missiles, began exploding amid a rank of trolls to our left, sending them howling toward the shelter of the walls. Nor were we safe, but found ourselves dodging hay bales, three or four wagons, a stand-up piano, and innumerable spinning blades and farm implements. I saw a squad of dead beastlings that had been peppered with hundreds of roofing nails.

There were many other things dropping around us, but I tried my best not to look. I kept my eyes focused on Valdara's back, and now and then up at the sky. But nothing I could do would silence the screams of terror and agony from all around.

By some miracle and no small amount of luck, we made it to the gate. But blocking our way was a double line of orcs that had not broken in panic. They were under the command of an enormous hobgoblin, and from the way the orcs kept glancing nervously at him, I knew there was nothing that could fall from the sky that was as frightening to them as he was. There was no time to consider our options, we charged at them.

The hobgoblin gave a terrible smile, showing row upon row of sharpened teeth. He raised a wickedly curved sword. "Regiment! Attack . . ." he began to shout, when there was a whistling noise and a black mass came hurtling out of the sky and took his head off with a metallic clang.

"An anvil! Did you guys see that?" Sam asked.

"We know, kid," said Drake in a sickened growl that matched my own feelings.

The orcs had seen it also and needed no further encouragement to dive through the gate into the shelter of the fortress. We followed on their heels, cutting them down as we came. In our pursuit we passed out of the courtyard and found ourselves in an arched chamber of such a scale that its only possible purpose could have been the mustering of armies. A forest of mighty pillars soared into the gloom of the high vaulted ceiling above. The few orcs that remained from the gate guard that had not been slain in our assault went screaming and shouting down side passages and were gone.

Seamus and Rook immediately went to work turning the great wheels that were used to close and open the vast iron gates. In no time they banged shut with an echoing clang, sealing the army out and us in. We were, momentarily, alone.

We explored the great room briefly, but only far enough to confirm that no stray orcs or goblins remained in the shadows. At last we were able to regroup and make sure that everyone was okay. Most of the company huddled together and compared notes on the storm and what they'd witnessed during our flight to safety. Valdara took her horse to a deep corner of the chamber and tied it to a pillar there. She stayed with it for some time, stroking its ears and whispering to it. I found myself wandering through vastness of the chamber in a fog of terrible déjà vu.

The design of this hall, and in fact the entire fortress, was almost an exact duplicate of the Dark Lord's fortress, my old home. I recalled that I used to have a standing army of skeletons lined up between the arches in this room, and that it would have been through that large archway that my army would have marched out to meet Valdara and the Army of Light. My hand started shaking violently and I leaned against one of the pillars for support.

I was still focusing on not passing out when there was a popping in my ears. *Eldrin was calling! Maybe he'd managed to find Death Slasher. If he had, then maybe I would get out of this mess, with all the Company of the Fellowship, Vivian, and Trelari intact.*

I touched my medallion. "Eldrin? Please tell me you have Death Slasher. We're in Vivian's fortress, but reality is going to hell around us. Don't geek out at me too much, but we were literally transported here in a T.O.R.G. storm. I'm betting it's all because of these damned battle-axes. You were right from the start. I should never have made that thing."

"Avery Stewart?" The voice didn't belong to Eldrin. It belonged to Griswald. I suddenly hoped another storm would strike.

"P-Professor Griswald? What a surprise!"

"Don't even start, Mr. Stewart!" he roared. "You may be a brilliant student, but I should flunk you back to freshman year for the stunt you've tried to pull. It's one thing to not shut down your experiment correctly. Every subworld adept student has tried it at one time or another, but having Eldrin try to break into my office? What the hell were you thinking?"

"This is all my fault, Professor. Please don't blame him," I urged, suddenly far more worried about the trouble I may have gotten Eldrin into than the fact that I was about to confront a Mysterium magus with a reality key.

"Funny," Griswald barked. "He said the same thing."

Not for the first or last time, I thanked the gods for giving me such a cool friend.

"So," he drawled. "Are you going to explain why you're worried about battle-axes, why you've been studying tornadic omnidimensional rotating gyres, which are way outside of the purview of your research project, and why I found your friend ransacking my chamber?"

I knew that there was no way I had the time or wit to answer any of those questions. "It's complicated," I said lamely.

"Would it be helpful if I told you that it is way more complicated than you know?" he asked, with none of his usual growl or grumble.

"What do you mean?" I asked, not sure where this was going, but happy he'd stopped yelling at me.

"It would seem . . ." He cleared his throat uncomfortably. ". . . that I may be partly responsible for Vivian being in your subworld."

I am not sure what I expected him to say, but I know it wasn't this. I lost all ability to think for at least a minute. "Avery, are you still there?" I heard Griswald ask for what I realized was the third time.

"What . . . what do you mean, you're responsible?" I asked in a voice at least two octaves higher than normal.

"She and I are part of an organization, and she may have gotten it into her head to use your experiment to further our goals," he said evasively.

I asked, "What kind of organization?"

"I can't tell you everything, Stewart," he said, reverting back to his grumbly professorial voice, "but there is more at stake in your world than just your dissertation. There is a group of professors and students here at the university that have been secretly fighting for years to win rights for subworlds: self-determination, free travel, freedom from interference, and so on. We have been stymied time and time again. One of our members in Vivian's program had a vision that the completion of your experiment represented an opportunity to fundamentally shift the balance of power between Mysterium and the other worlds, and that getting the reality key and sending a magus into your world was the initiating event."

"You set me up?" I asked, both angry and amazed.

"No," he drawled. "We thought it was too dangerous, but Vivian is young, and she must have decided to go on her own. I'm not sure. Absent your roommate's ill-advised attempt to turn burglar I never would have known what she *or you* had been up to."

I didn't want to believe him. "How could she know that my experiment ended early?"

"Regrettably, I may have let it slip," he said, and I knew it was the closest thing to an apology I was going to get.

"How did you know?"

"Stewart," he said sternly. "I'm a professor. I've dealt with hundreds of students in my day. I'll tell you a secret. We always know. Sometimes we choose to look the other way, but we always know."

"Oh," I said, feeling far less clever.

"The big surprise for me is that you decided to try and deal with this problem yourself. I thought you were just playing truant. Had I known what Vivian had done, had you confided in me, I might have been able to help. Instead, you've managed to get you and your friend into deep trouble."

"Deeper than you know," I confessed.

It was his turn to say, "What do you mean?"

"Trelari, this world, is moving toward Mysterium," I said simply, and let the full import of that statement sink in.

The "*What!*" that followed was deeply satisfying. He followed that up with an explosive *"That's impossible!"*

"Not really," I explained. "Eldrin can do the subject more justice, but effectively I've recreated the Palantir Effect. It has to do with the kernel to my reality stabilizing pattern. I tried and tried, but I couldn't make it work purely with subworld reality . . ."

This next bit was likely going to get me expelled, but as he'd said I was in deep anyway.

". . . so I made the kernel using a combination of Mysterium reality and subworld reality. That kernel is a battle-axe called Death Slasher that I brought back with me to Mysterium when I returned, and that Vivian stole from me and must have slipped it into your things at some point. Somehow the battle-axe is serving as a Palantir and is drawing this world toward Mysterium. I'm afraid Vivian is in real danger."

"You both are!" he barked.

"Sorry, Professor," I said, and I truly was.

"Quiet, Stewart! I need to think."

He muttered to himself for a while.

"Professor?" I urged as gently as I could.

"It sounds to me," he lectured, "that you have woven yourself too tightly into the fabric of that world. I warn students every year that simply because a reality key can do something doesn't mean that doing it won't have consequences. What was the primary solution to your catastrophe equation?"

"The Dark Lord needed to be destroyed," I answered quickly.

"What is the first law of Tolkienian physics?"

"An artifact with the essence of an evil being will maintain the evil of that being unless destroyed."

"Which means?"

"The artifact and the Dark Lord are insuperably tied to each other."

It was like I was sitting in his office while he puffed on a pipe behind his desk and peppered me with questions. And he had fallen into the familiar pattern too.

"Precisely," he said proudly. "But you ripped the artifact out of reality. It's like an open wound. This whole time the world has been trying to replace it *and you.*"

Eldrin and I had sorted out the first part of Griswald's conclusion, but my eyes opened wide as I understood the significance of what he was saying about me. "So, when Vivian came with the reality key, it reactivated *everything* from the reality pattern, recreating Death Slasher by forging Justice Cleaver, and using her to fill the gap for me?"

"Yes," he grunted. "It seems that Vivian may have gotten more than she bargained for when she took your place. I bet she's had a hell of a time trying to maintain control of the situation."

It made sense, but one oddity immediately struck me. "If the spell was trying to duplicate the two of us, why is Justice Cleaver good?"

In response he asked, "What should the result of your experiment have been?"

"Peace and stability," I mumbled bitterly.

He thought about this for a second and then said, "Sounds like your subworld wants to reach that endpoint. In Tolkienian terms, it must destroy the last piece of the Dark Lord, and has formed a weapon to do that. Now it is moving itself toward Mysterium so a final battle can be waged. The only way to prevent a collision of realities is to get both artifacts back into your subworld."

It fit with Eldrin's ideas, but I couldn't help feeling that there was a piece to this we were all missing. I started to ask him another question when a ringing boom reverberated through the keep. Something was hammering at the gates.

"Can you throw it back through the portal?" I asked.

"I could, but with the subworld moving as it is I don't know where it would end up, or what condition it would be in when it got there," said Griswald. "It's a puzzler. I think a casting involving a multiworld ritual could work. It is brutally complicated, but if we triangulate the combined powers of three circles of nine magi, each spread across three equal points around the . . ."

Another shock ran through the floor as the battering continued. I heard footsteps coming rapidly toward me. I had to go. "I think I've got this, Professor," I lied and then compounded that lie with another absurdity. "Don't worry."

"Wait, what?" he started to ask.

I broke the connection and spun about to find Valdara watching me. My heart froze. How long had she been standing there, and what had she heard? A sickening feeling of guilt more dreadful than I'd ever felt in the storm vortex roiled my stomach. Under the force of her gaze I had an urge to tell her the truth.

That had been my promise: no more lies. What a joke, when the biggest lie remained. Still, my tongue clove to the roof of my mouth.

Her eyes narrowed, but she asked no questions. Finally, when I said nothing, she turned her back on me and returned to the rest of the group. She made no pause but, sword in hand, proceeded up a massive set of stairs toward a pair of arched double doors on the opposite end of the great chamber. Without a word, we followed.

Maybe she didn't have to know, I told myself. Maybe none of them had to know. What I did know was that this wasn't the time or place. Frankly, I wasn't sure that there would ever be a good time or place.

"Fear is for the weak," Justice Cleaver said, as if he could read my mind.

With that, we opened the doors and peered inside to find an elaborately vaulted entrance hall of black marble and high columns. It was identical to the one I'd had, but what really drew my attention was the rank upon rank of armored hobgoblins arrayed down the center of the hall. I had always stationed terror trolls here myself.

The front ranks of hobgoblins parted and a large reptilian figure in a black cloak and matching scaled armor stepped forward. It was General Cravock. He had clearly come up in the world and was now an imposing figure and not the cowering snake I'd recalled.

He ran his eyes up and down our group. "Lady Valdara and Ssst. Drake, ssso niccce to sssee you after sssso long. I know that you wisssh an audience with the Dark Queen, but unfortunately ssshe isss indisss-possed" he hissed. "Perhapsss my men and I can entertain you until ssshe is free."

His forked tongue darted out at his little joke and he began to laugh sibilantly. Then he froze and, turning his pointed head, regarded me. More deliberately he extended his forked tongue, tasting the air. His yellow eyes grew wide, and he started twitching. I realized that he was shaking with fear.

"You." He pointed a clawed finger at me. "I have not tasssted your ssscent in a long time. Asss you can sssee thingsss have changed."

Damn lizards. He knew exactly who I was. My appearance may have changed, but my scent had not. The only way I was going to get through this was to be the Dark Lord. I made myself as tall as I could, fixed my gaze on him, and used the voice I had practiced for so long. "Take me to the Dark Queen. Now, General Cravock!"

He thought about it, hissing and sputtering to himself. I raised Justice Cleaver and let the reflection from its blade strike his eyes. That was too much for him. He nearly squealed in terror, and bent his body over almost in half. Suddenly, he was my Cravock again. I winced as I realized that the pathetic subservience I had remembered had been as much a performance as was the commanding general he was playing at now.

He turned back to his soldiers and commanded,

"We take him and hisss companionsss to her now. No quessstionsss if you value your soulsss."

The army of hobgoblins seemed shocked, but General Cravock was undeniably their leader. The army parted down the middle, forming a passage to another even more ornate door at the far end of the hall. No one moved and I stepped forward. Cravock's gaze fell on me again. I nodded my approval, even as I felt the eyes of my group on my back.

"No lies?" whispered Valdara from right behind my right ear.

"It is the only way," I said softly in response. "I'm sorry." I didn't know whether I was apologizing for the danger I'd led her into, or the lies, or the pain I knew the inevitable truth was going to cause, or all of them. I was past certainties.

"It's just like I remember," mused Drake on my other side. "Except now we have an escort."

General Cravock led us through the ornate door and then stepped aside. We were in the innermost chamber of the fortress. Before us stood a throne of skulls—my throne of skulls—and on the throne sat Vivian. She was clad in a long black gown with a crown of spiked black iron atop her head. In her hand she held a long elegant staff of iron that was cleverly shaped to look like the braided tendrils of a rosebush. She had foregone make-up, which I wished I had done as the stuff used to make me break out in the worst way. Still, the contrast between the black dress and her pale skin and corn-silk hair was stunning. She looked every inch the Dark Queen.

"Vivian . . ." I began, but she interrupted me.

"Welcome, Avery," she said in a voice that was more commanding than I remembered. She rose elegantly, almost sensuously, and extended a hand in greeting. "I was wondering when you would finally get here. I've been having simply the worst time trying to figure out all this Dark Queen nonsense. Now that you're here, Dark Lord, you can help me."

My heart stopped beating.

CHAPTER 30

THE DARK QUEEN

"Oh, I'm sorry, Avery," Vivian said, placing a theatrically dainty hand in front of her lips. "Had you not told them that you are the Dark Lord?"

Is she insane? was my first thought. My second thought is unprintable. My third thought was *She must have a plan.*

Whatever her game, I could not believe that the woman I knew, okay, the woman I had met, the woman Griswald had confided in, would purposefully expose me as the Dark Lord for no reason. Perhaps she was being threatened or held captive. The way she was lounging so languidly on the throne seemed to belie the idea that she felt unsafe, but perhaps she was a drama double-major. She had certainly fooled me back in Mysterium. The only course was to go along with her and see where it led.

"I had not," I said stiffly.

"Well, I always think it's important to get these little things—" she raised a pale hand and wiggled her fingers at my companions "—out of the way. Don't you?"

"No!" Luke shouted. "That's not true! It's impossible."

She laughed and it had some of the warmth that I remembered, but was tinged with something else. Something like madness. A chill ran over my body as I realized that I might be dealing with a crazy person.

"It's true," tittered Vivian. "He was the Dark Lord. Isn't it marvelous?"

"Say she's lying, Avery," Luke said with a gasp.

I didn't have the words to say anything so I stayed silent, and searched her face for some sign of sanity. Didn't she understand the danger she was putting me in? Didn't she see the pain she was causing my companions? Was this all a joke to her? Anger welled up inside of me. Well, *anger* may not be a strong enough word. Rage, blinding rage, filled me as I began to suspect that it would not be me rescuing Vivian from a situation that had spun out of her control, but me trying to keep Vivian from destroying everything I'd worked so hard to create.

A rumble of thunder echoed through the fortress. The storm was building again. There was no time for this. I had to get the key. I had to summon Death Slasher.

"Enough!" I shouted, which only made her laugh all the more.

Beside me my companions finally seemed to understand what I was confessing. I turned my back on Vivian and faced them. I saw a kaleidoscope of emotions from confusion to disbelief to anger. Only Drake and Rook could I not get a read on. Drake because he wore the same bored expression he'd had since I met him in the sty in Blightsbury, and Rook because he was looking down at his boots, muttering and shaking his head. But it was the disappointment in Valdara's eyes that hurt the most.

"Why?"

She only said the one word. It felt more like a command than a question. Maybe she thought this was part of my plan and that I was pretending to be the Dark Lord to deceive Vivian. Maybe she knew I was the Dark Lord but wanted to hear me say it before she cut me to ribbons.

I started to say something and stopped. No lies. I owed her that. I worked up just enough courage to look her in the eye and told her the truth. "Good intentions."

The room shook as three successive crashes of thunder echoed through the fortress. Valdara's hand went to her sword and I saw it clench and unclench on its hilt. I tensed in the expectation that I would feel the bite of its blade between my ribs. I might have welcomed it at that point, but nothing happened. I exhaled in relief.

There was a sudden blur of movement on my right and something hard slammed into my jaw. I fell back and sprawled to the ground, tasting blood. A series of hard blows struck my body. Drake was standing over me kicking and screaming.

"You bastard!" he shouted over and over again as his boot connected with my ribs.

Rook finally dragged him off me. I think the others would have gladly let him continue. Sam and Seamus were staring at me with utter hatred. Luke and Ariella just looked lost. I lay, curled in a ball at the foot of Vivian's throne, panting for air and groaning in pain.

Drake was still struggling and cursing. "Let me go! He's the Dark Lord! He must die. Valdara!"

His cry woke the dormant fury in her. In a flash, Valdara was standing above me her blade pointing at my heart. "This time, Dark Lord," she spit, "I won't use a piece of glass atop a fake staff."

Her eyes shone with such a hatred as I had never seen before. I understood the fear her foes must have felt before they died. Desperately, I tried to form the recall spell, but my head was still spinning from Drake's beating and there was no time. I closed my eyes as her arm drew back.

"Stop!" Vivian shouted.

Everything stopped.

I looked about, the entire company, except for me, was frozen in place. Valdara, her face twisted in a tormented combination of anger and sadness, was tensed to strike. Drake and Rook were locked together as they struggled—Rook's body still wobbling a bit in the awkward position he was trapped in. Luke, Sam, Seamus, and Ariella were all standing, wide-eyed with shock, a silent scream trapped on Ariella's lips, as they watched Valdara's attack from across the room. They all still breathed, and their eyes still blinked and looked about, but they could not move.

Vivian laughed cruelly. In her hand, she was holding the key, and it was blazing with white-hot intensity. A malicious smile crossed her face as she sprawled back onto her throne, putting one of her legs over one arm of the chair and leaning on her elbow on the other arm. Her eyes twinkled with mischief.

I stood painfully, grabbing at my battered ribs. "What are you doing, Vivian?"

"I am saving your life, Avery," she said with a giggle. "No thanks are required."

"You know what I mean," I said, gesturing at the throne of skulls and my frozen companions. "I know this isn't why you came to Trelari."

She frowned at this. "You've been talking to Griswald, haven't you? And worse, he's been talking to you. Naughty boys."

I couldn't understand why she was doing this, but I could hear the storm outside. It was intensifying far more quickly and violently than the last one had. If I did not get the key soon we might all be killed. "Yes, we have been talking, Vivian. He told me you came here to make life in the subworlds better, but what you're doing now isn't right. Give me the key—this can all be fixed."

"Fixed?" she said, tapping the key to her chin and puzzling over the word. "But I don't think I want this to be fixed. In fact, I'm sure I don't." She stood and ran her hands over the black dress and touched the iron crown. "In case you hadn't noticed, Avery, I'm the Dark Queen."

"Yes, like I was the . . . Dark Lord," I said, the confession coming no easier the second time. "But that isn't who we are, Vivian. Those are roles we play to give the Heroes of Trelari—" I gestured at Valdara and Drake and the others "—something to defeat. They need an evil to unite and inspire them, but that's not who we are. Try to remember, you're from Mysterium."

"No!" She stood, her whole body shaking with anger. "I am not! You may be from Mysterium, Griswald and all the other busybodies in the Sanctum may be from Mysterium, but I'm not. I came from a subworld not unlike this one. A subworld that was studied by magi and ruled by magi and ultimately destroyed by magi when they'd done with it. *I am* the Dark Queen, and I will bring peace and stability to Trelari or all will perish!"

My blood ran cold as the last piece of the puzzle fell into place. Vivian was from a subworld. Eldrin and Dawn and I had been so focused on finding Death Slasher that we had failed to see the importance of this revelation, but it explained everything that had happened since Vivian's arrival in Trelari. Whereas a magus from Mysterium could stand outside the effect of my spell as an observer, she could not. From the moment she'd arrived on-world, the spell had been weaving her into its pattern. Vivian really was the Dark Queen. That meant that she was not in control, and everything—the citadel of darkness, the blood orcs, her madness—all of it was my responsibility. I had to get that key.

I took a step toward the throne, holding my hands before me in a gesture of peace. "Vivian, you aren't yourself. Give me the key. I don't want to hurt you."

"Hurt me?" She giggled again. "How could you hurt me, Avery?"

At my side Justice Cleaver quivered, and I put my hand on the battle-axe to quiet it. Vivian saw the movement and her eyes narrowed.

"I do not want to have to do anything to your friends," she advised. "But if you force me . . ." She gestured at Sam and I saw his body began to bend slowly backward. If she kept going his back would snap. "A girl must do what a girl must do after all."

My hands leapt away from my side and the shaft of Justice Cleaver. "Please stop hurting him."

"Good," she said, and Sam's body straightened again. "Because I have a better idea. Join me, Avery. Become the Dark Lord again and we can rule this world together."

Maybe, if I can keep her talking, I thought, *I can grab the key from her hand.*

There was a double blast of thunder that made me stumble and the throne shake. Dust and small bits of stone fell from the ceiling. I ignored it and took a few more steps forward. "How would that work? What about the key?" I had a foot on the lowest stair now.

"What about it?" she asked, and lowered her hand with the key to her lap.

I mounted a few more stairs so that I was closer. "Well, we can't both use it at the same time."

She cocked her head to one side and glanced down, considering. I saw my moment and I lunged. Just then the room gave a shake as though it had been struck by a mighty force. I fell off balance. Time seemed to slow. Vivian's eyes grew wide as she realized that she had been tricked. My hand stretched out. There was a bang and a terrible flash of white light issued from the key, and I felt myself thrown backward. I hit the ground hard and all the air went out of me.

Looking down from her high throne, Vivian sneered. "Liar! You lie to everyone, don't you? You lied to your 'friends' about who you are. You lied to me about why you came here. You were never interested in helping this world. You only wanted to feel what it was like to have absolute power. Now feel what it's like to have none."

She rose and pointed the key at me. A ragged whiplash of energy issued from its end and struck me. Blinding pain coursed through my body. I screamed and the lash fell again and again and again. How long she tormented me I'm not sure, but at the end my throat was raw and my body burned all over.

When I finally caught my breath, I gasped, "I swear, Vivian, it wasn't meant to be like this. You are caught in the spell's weave. Give me the key and I can free you from this madness."

She threw back her head and laughed dreadfully. "I think not, Magus. If this is madness, then I will take it over your Mysterium version of sanity." She sat again on the throne. "As I see you have no intention of listening to reason, I have no wish to speak to you further."

"Cravock, summon your men," she commanded. She looked at me and her eyes flashed and her smile twisted cruelly. "The Dark Lord and his companions have overstayed their welcome. See to it that they never see the light of another dawn."

Cravock bowed in hissing supplication, and stepped outside. Through the open door I could hear the roar of the winds and the crash of the thunder, which was almost constant at this point. I had to try and bring Vivian to her senses, even if that meant risking her wrath again.

"It . . . it is time to put an end to this, Vivian," I said with a grunt of pain as I rolled onto my knees. "Being in this place has twisted your mind. Give me the key and we can return to Mysterium . . ."

"Where they will lock me away as a deviant?" she thundered. "Maybe if I'm lucky they will banish me to an outer subworld to live out what remains of my life." She sneered at the thought. "No, those fates are reserved for my betters. For me, a mere subworlder, they will put me in a stasis pattern and study me like a curiosity, and when they've learned all they want they'll unravel my reality one strand at a time."

She was probably right. Mysterium magi have little patience for subworlds, much less subworlders that threatened them. Of course, I wasn't going to tell her that. "It doesn't have to be like that," I said as with a grimace I rose, shaking, to my feet. "There is still time to set things right, but not much."

Cravock returned and bowed low. "The army ass-sembles, Dark Queen."

Vivian gave no indication that she'd heard him. "Your problem, Avery, is that you were never committed to the cause of darkness. Take poor Cravock there. When I found him, he was a pathetic wretch. Useless." I saw the lizardman's body tense like he'd been struck. Vivian did not appear to notice, but continued. "You had instilled no discipline in him, no drive. But with some training and a free hand with the lash, I have been able to bend him to my will and reshape him into what you see today: my loyal pet You have no idea what is possible if you let go of the constraints of Mysterium's rules and give yourself over to the multiverse."

From beyond the closed doors there was a rushing sound and a groan of metal as though the storm was battering at the gates of the fortress itself. I decided to try one last attempt. I fell to my knees I supplication. "Dark Queen, I do not care what becomes of me. Lock me in your dungeons. Execute me if you wish. But I beg you, before it's too late, use the key and summon Death Slasher. Trelari will soon reach the innerworlds—you must feel that, you must feel reality beginning to solidify around you. What do you think the Mysterium mages will do then? They will pull this world to pieces around you. Save this world even if only for your own dark purposes."

Her body shook with hideous laughter. "Do you think I care if this world comes apart around me? I am eternal!"

There was a hissing intake of breath from Cravock, and I saw in his expression a reflection of my own thought. *She really is mad.*

"But, Vivian . . ." I began to say when she gave a sudden shout of surprise.

I looked up from where I was kneeling and saw that somehow Rook had broken free from his paralysis. In the confusion, he had slipped unnoticed behind the throne, and now he and Vivian were struggling for control of the key. They both had one hand on the key, which was flashing and strobing like a thing possessed. With their unoccupied hands they tore and clawed at one another. While the dwarf was stronger, Vivian had the advantage of height and was bending him backward so that he teetered on the brink of the stairs.

I sprang to my feet and rushed at them. From across the room Cravock did the same, his reptilian body crouched low to the ground so that he was running on all fours. I was halfway to them when Rook gave a mighty shout and twisted Vivian's hand downward so that it slammed against the arm of the throne. The blow jarred the key from their grasp and it went clattering down the stair and skittering across the stone floor of the chamber. Vivian fell back into the seat with a cry as Rook tumbled off the side of the dais.

In an instant, the paralysis lifted from the group. Valdara lunged at the thin air as Luke stretched out his hand toward the emptiness where I had lain. Ariella screamed, Sam and Seamus shouted. Drake toppled to the ground in a confusion of limbs. Only Cravock and I were in any position to reach the key. Cravock was faster.

With a hiss of victory, he snatched the key up. I lie at his feet. I seemed to be doing that a lot lately.

"Cravock!" Vivian commanded. "Bring that to your queen."

"You know she's mad, Cravock," I whispered.

Cravock gave a barely perceptible nod of his head. His fork tongue extended and he hissed softly. "Before, were you ssspeaking of Death Ssslassssher, the weapon of Morgarr?" I nodded. "And all you need to sssummon it isss thisss key?" he hissed. I nodded again.

"Cravock!" Vivian shouted again, a little more desperately. "I command that you obey me."

Cravock flicked his tongue in thought. Then I saw a light come into his eyes, a devious and greedy light, and I knew that I had made a terrible mistake. I started to rise to my feet but Cravock's tail lashed out and struck me in the face, sending me, once more, crashing to the ground.

"No, missstress!" he shouted in his sibilant reptilian voice. "Now, I have the power!"

Too late the others sensed what was coming. They rushed him, but he held the key aloft and roared, "Death Ssslassher, I sssummon thee!"

There was a great cracking and the stone of the ceiling was swept away. Above us a storm of flashing lightning ten times the size of the one that carried us from the Tomb of Terrors swirled and crackled. For a moment only, the center of the maelstrom seemed to open into a long passage. Something black swirled down that passage toward us and then the opening drew closed.

Above me Cravock stood, the key in one hand, and Death Slasher in the other. For the first time I saw the lizardman's real persona, not the subservient wretch he had been when he served me, nor the commander of armies that Vivian had created, but he himself. My soul shuddered.

He looked down at me through those reptilian eyes. "Don't fear, massster. You will not have long to sssuffer. I'll take your head and give the tasssk of bowing down before me to your lifelessss body."

Through the doors behind him, the massed armies of the Dark Queen, now Cravock's armies, entered.

CHAPTER 31

PURE CHAOS

Okay, let me start by saying that, purely from the standpoint of spectacle, the scene that was playing out before me was awe-inspiring. Vivian, the insane Dark Queen, was slumped in a sort of faint on the seat of her skull throne. Around the edges of the chamber, rank upon rank of hobgoblin axe-men and bloody orc swordsmen stood forming a rough circle around the Dark Queen and the rest of us. Above the roofless chamber a terrible storm of swirling reality and flashing lightning roiled and boiled. In the very center of the room stood the reptilian General Cravock. He held the key to Trelari's reality in one hand and the dread battle-axe Death Slasher in the other.

Opposed against him and his army were arrayed

the Heroes of Trelari: Sam, master of the mystical forces; Ariella, archer and sorceress scion of the fairy elves (also herbalist, rogue, rules lawyer, among other titles); Seamus and Rook, dwarf lords of the smithy clans; Drake, fallen priest of the Seven Gods; Valdara, legendary swordswoman of the fighting lands; and Luke, who was, um . . . Luke. Oh, and me, I suppose.

Like I said, pretty spectacular if you didn't have to be there yourself. Unfortunately, I was there, and I was overwhelmed. Overwhelmed here meaning scared to the point of paralysis. Fortunately, the other members of the company were made of sterner stuff.

Valdara, Drake, Luke, and the dwarfs all charged Cravock with simultaneous shouts of challenge. With lightning-fast speed, Ariella had a bow in her hand and an arrow on the string. Sam, meanwhile, had pulled his glass orb from his pouch and a pulsating blue light was building within it. None of them would reach me in time.

Cravock, still holding the reality key above his head, swung Death Slasher down at my neck. I tried to scuttle back like a crab, but there was no way to avoid the blow. I watched that evil eye glitter in anticipation of feasting on my soul. Then there was a rush of air and a blur, and Cravock screamed. His blow went wide and struck the stones beside me in a shower of sparks. Ariella's arrow had struck him in the wrist of the hand that held the key, which went flying from his grasp and fell to the stones behind him.

The pain distracted Cravock long enough for me to roll away. I struggled to my feet, and did what anyone would do when facing a terrifying lizard monster with an artifact battle-axe. I screamed. After that, I shouted, "The key!"

The rest of the company closed in on Cravock. I was still rising as the dwarfs, Luke, Drake, and Valdara surrounded the lizardman and began to attack. By all rights, it should have been a short fight. The five warriors were experienced and deadly, but Cravock had Death Slasher, and with it he became a whirlwind of mayhem. With a backhand, he struck Rook and Seamus with the flat of the blade, sending them flying into Luke. Then he spun and parried Valdara's sword thrust, and drove the butt of the battle-axe's hilt into Drake's chest, who fell onto his back with a grunt. Swirling and slashing, he pursued Valdara around the throne. No matter what she tried, Death Slasher forced her into the defense, and it was quickly clear that she was using every bit of her skill to keep from being cut in half.

Cravock pointed at Valdara and roared to his army, "I have her! Kill the ressst!"

They hobgoblins and orcs surged forward like a living wall of death. We put our backs to the throne and faced the advancing host. Ariella was a blur, sending spells flashing and arrows flying into the hordes in a futile effort to keep them at bay. I could not find Sam, but I did see his flashing blue orb as it bobbed and weaved amid the chaos.

"Why are we watching?" Justice Cleaver urged. "How many times do I have to remind you that I am the world's greatest battle-axe? This is what I was made to do."

I tried to assume a defensive posture and started to weave a spell around the throne dais, but the battle-axe would not be denied. Somehow, and I still do not know how, Justice Cleaver was in my hands, and I was charging toward Cravock. I'm fairly sure that the battle-axe made me do it, although perhaps I had gone mad. Regardless, I found myself in the middle of the fight. Unfortunately, I was still me. I had no idea what I was doing.

Cravock saw me holding Justice Cleaver, and a light of vengeance came into his eyes. "You are not a warrior, masssster," he hissed. "Now, it isss my time. There will be no more Dark Lord! No more Dark Queen! No more sssniveling! I am Cravock the Terrible and no man can defeat me!"

Whether you think he'd gotten a big head or not, he drove Valdara back, and then, swinging Death Slasher in spinning circles above his head, he slashed at my neck. Had it only been me fighting, the story, or at least my part in it, would have ended there. But I felt a jerk in my arms and Justice Cleaver blocked the blow. The parry saved my life, but the shock of its force jarred the battle-axe from my grasp. It fell to the ground at the feet of Valdara.

"What are you doing?" Justice Cleaver shouted. "We're in a duel for all existence, battle-axe versus battle-axe. If my wielder loses, I lose. Someone pick me up!"

Thankfully, and I mean everyone in Trelari should be thankful, I never got the chance. Valdara grabbed Justice Cleaver. She whirled it through the air, getting a feel for its weight, testing its balance.

"Thank goodness!" said Justice Cleaver. "You should have been holding me in the first place. Now, let's see what the world's greatest warrior can do with the world's greatest magical weapon."

"Agreed," she said with determination.

"Prepare for justice, lizard!" shouted Justice Cleaver.

Valdara took the offensive, swinging the battle-axe back and forth, in tighter and tighter arcs, giving her larger foe little time to adjust. Despite his reptilian strength, Cravock was slowly being driven back. I nearly cheered and then realized he was retreating right into the teeth of his army. As good as Valdara was, and as powerful as Justice Cleaver claimed to be, there were too many of them.

I ran to Vivian, who still sat stunned on the throne. "You've got to stop this," I shouted, shaking her. "This is your army. Order them to stand down."

"I want to," said Vivian in a dazed, almost drugged voice. "But I can't, Avery. I don't want to. I think maybe that I've lost my mind." She began laughing hysterically while tears streamed down her cheeks.

I turned back to the battle. It was not going well. With the army at his back, Cravock was pushing forward against Valdara. The company had formed a tight circle on the lowest stair of the throne. The orcs and hobgoblins were paying a heavy price for each foot they gained, but still they advanced. Ariella, who was standing below me, had exhausted her supply of arrows and had taken to casting her cold spell, freezing groups of the enemy in place. But the potency of each blast was growing weaker. The time had come for me to do something; I just didn't know what. I knew a lot of spells I could cast, but my education had never included combat. I was out of my depth. I was still considering what to do (perhaps a wall of flames) when there was a blue flash at the edge of the throne and about a half-dozen blood orcs toppled over. Sam stepped through the hole created in the lines.

"I found the key!" he shouted, and to my wonderment he held aloft the silvered key of Trelari.

I ran to him. "Sam, let me have it," I said, grasping at the key in his hand.

He pushed me back and shook his head. "I can't trust you, Avery."

"Sam, I need that key," I pleaded. "I can stop all this." I held out my hand. It was shaking.

"You're right not to listen to him," Vivian said in voice that was sweet and reasonable compared to mine. She had come down the stairs and was standing to my right, looking more like the girl I'd met in Mysterium than the Dark Queen. "He is the Dark Lord, the Father of all Lies, and he has lied to you from the first. Give the key to me and you shall rule beside me for all time."

Sam looked at us both with disgust.

In dismay I saw the company retreat another step up the stairs. I considered trying to wrest the key away from him, but I couldn't bring myself to do it, and wasn't sure I'd win the fight anyway. "Please, Sam. I only became the Dark Lord to bring peace and stability to this world."

"As did I!" Vivian said, and she lunged at him, snatching at the key.

Sam pulled a pinch of sand from his pouch and blew it in her face. Her eyes rolled back in her head and she toppled forward, unconscious. Seeing her on the ground, her expression frozen in a twisted mask of desperate need and her grasping hand still outstretched like a claw, I realized she was right. There was no difference between us. I understood at last what Valdara meant when she said that intentions didn't matter.

"You're right not to trust us," I said, and sat down heavily on the stair.

The clanging of battle-axes reminded me that Valdara was still dueling Cravock, and the screams of the company and guttural shouts of the blood orcs reminded me that there was still a battle going on, and that we were losing. An idea came to me.

I sprang back to my feet and shouted, "You need to use the key, Sam!"

He considered for a moment and asked, "How?"

"All you have to do is imagine an effect and will it to happen."

I hoped I was right and that he could. Normally someone from a place like Trelari wouldn't have the reality density needed to use the key, but with Trelari having moved ever closer to Mysterium, I wondered if there was that much difference between us anymore.

He pointed the key at a group of hobgoblins that were pressing hard against Seamus and Rook. There was a flash and the hobgoblins froze in place. "Wow!" he said, a reasonable reaction in my opinion.

"Now, expand the effect . . ."

He was already way ahead of me. I saw him close his eyes. The key glowed, and the hobgoblins and orcs disappeared entirely. At least, I thought they'd disappeared until I saw the tiny piles of ash scattered about the throne room floor.

The larger war may have been over, but the duel between Valdara and the lizard raged on. The battle-axes sparked as they crashed together. "Great work, Sam!" I shouted. "Now get Cravock!"

Sam shook his head and tucked the key back into his pouch. "Valdara doesn't need this," he said. "She is the best among us."

"She is, but what if something happens?" I pleaded.

Sam locked eyes with me. "Sometimes we need to fight our own fights, Avery. Believe in her. You should too."

He was right, of course. It was precisely my own desire to help that had given rise to the Dark Lord, and it had been Vivian's desire to do the same that had transformed her into the Dark Queen. It was well past time for Mysterians to give the people of Trelari a chance to fight their own fights.

And so I watched as Valdara and Cravock continued their deadly dance. At the outset it seemed that Sam's faith was well placed. She had backed the lizardman up against a wall. But just as Valdara seemed to be about to end the duel, he lashed out with his tail, wrapping it around her leg, and pulled her to the ground. In a blur, she rolled out of the way of his descending axe and jumped to her feet. Cravock charged, Death Slasher held high overhead. She spun to the side, and with a brilliant backhand stroke, Valdara sliced through Cravock's neck. His head tumbled to the ground, wide-eyed with disbelief. As the lizard's body fell to the ground, I felt myself relax. It was done and no one had died . . . ignoring Cravock and the hundreds of orcs and hobgoblins that had been massacred of course.

"And so," said Justice Cleaver, his voice echoing in the now near empty throne room, "once and for all, I have proven that I am the greatest battle-axe in all history!"

"Are you always going to talk?" asked Valdara still breathing heavily from the fight.

"Yes."

She sighed. And then she was engulfed by the embraces of the others.

I sat alone on the throne next to the unconscious

Vivian. I was happy for them, but overhead the storm continued to build. Through the upper windows, I could see lightning streaking across the sky as thunder shook the keep.

That's strange, I thought. *The storm should have ended.*

Across the room, Death Slasher's eye stared at me with the same malevolence I remembered from my days as the Dark Lord.

That's even stranger. Death Slasher should have ceased to be.

For some reason we hadn't won yet, and I didn't know why.

CHAPTER 32

THE FINAL SACRIFICE

"Um, guys," or something of the sort was the first thing I said, but I said it way too softly for them to hear. Looking back that was probably by design, because I wasn't sure what I was going to say after that, and after a moment's consideration, I was thankful that they hadn't heard me. In fact, I was so uncertain about what to do or say about what hadn't happened with Cravock's defeat that I sat next to the unconscious Vivian and stared up at the storm and I thought for a while as the others told their versions of what had happened and what they had done, and began the wonderful process of making it all grander and better.

My thoughts took me back to the beginning, back to my closet of an office in the sub-basement of the

Subworld Studies building where I had first conceived of the reality matrix spell. As with all really good ideas, it came from having no clue about what to do for a dissertation research project.

It was afternoon and I was tired, and found myself staring at a wonderful picture of deep subworld space that Eldrin had taken it a few days before. I wasn't really thinking anything specific when the beauty of it all struck me, and it made me sad. I'm sure someone at some point has made the connection between beauty and sadness, and made it eloquently. I'm not going to do that except to say that seeing all those lovely swirls of light got me to thinking about the paper I was supposed to be studying, a copy of which was sitting unread on the desk in front of me.

The paper was a dry statistical analysis of subworld extinction rates by aura color. I can't explain it, but the author had some weird theory about burnt-umber having some significance to predicting stability. I remember nothing of the paper, which may be because I only ever managed to get through the abstract, but I do remember feeling sad that so many of Eldrin's swirls were going to vanish. That got me wondering about why they vanish, and that eventually led me to Professor Griswald's survey paper on the subject. I was hooked.

What I found most interesting was that while there was a lot of literature on subworld extinction—the numbers and the possible whys—there was next to nothing on intervening in such extinctions. What was more, most previous attempts to prevent the collapse of a subworld had met with failure. In a flash I had my dissertation topic; now all I had to do was come up with magic that could do what had never been done before.

As my knowledge grew deeper I began to notice patterns in extinction events. One that intrigued me was the fact that worlds that disintegrated released huge amounts of reality energy. (Sometimes it is helpful having a roommate who is a bit compulsive about observing subworld collapse.) My original theory was that if you were able to etch a magical construct into the reality pattern of a world that allowed the world to use the energy of its own decline to renew itself, you would have a world that could exist, in theory, in perpetuity.

And so I set out to create what I call a reality matrix that would do just that. I would set an end point (peace and stability), and as the decay energy increased, the reality matrix would redirect that energy back into the world's own pattern in a positive feedback loop that would ultimately lead to stability. On the ground what that meant was that the forces of decay and decline would have to be accelerated and concentrated so that they could be converted, in that final moment, into a world stabilizing force. What I termed a *golden age*.

Great theory, but as I have revealed previously, in practice I found it impossible. The power of the world on its own was simply not strong enough to etch the new pattern. So I cheated. I created a spell kernel out of Mysterium magic (Death Slasher). Then to make sure the pattern was fully and truly etched into reality, I myself oversaw the initial formation of the reality matrix as the Dark Lord. This meant . . .

I sat up with a start. The truth was staring me in the face, and so were Valdara and Drake and the rest of the Company of the Fellowship.

"Why is the battle-axe still here?" Valdara asked.

"Because I am eternal!" declared Justice Cleaver.

"Not you," she barked. "I'm talking about Death Slasher." She pointed across the room, and the evil battle-axe glared back at us.

"He is as nothing," Justice Cleaver assured her. "You can ignore him now."

Everyone was waiting for me to answer, but I was trying to wrap my head around what my revelation meant.

"Maybe it's because Vivian is still alive," Sam suggested, and nudged her with his foot to make sure she wasn't dead.

Drake picked her up by the front of her dress and growled, "It wouldn't take much to snap her neck."

I looked at Drake, St. Drake the Pure, now suggesting that they snap the neck of a woman who was defenseless. I couldn't help but think of how he, of all people, had gone wrong after the "defeat" of the Dark Lord. And that, by the way, segues nicely into my epiphany: The Dark Lord had never been defeated. Not really.

Drake knew he hadn't defeated the Dark Lord. That was what had broken his faith and sent him down a spiral that had changed him into the man he was now. If Drake knew, then the reality matrix certainly knew. I was the key to everything, because I was the Dark Lord. I had woven myself into the experiment and thus into the story of Trelari. The reality matrix could not be complete until I was destroyed.

I had to die.

Because I've been trying to be completely honest with you, I have to tell you that my immediate reaction was *To hell with that.* To my credit though, my very next thought was *Coward*.

If I lived, then every Trelarian, and because of how she'd been caught by the reality matrix spell, Vivian herself, was going to have to suffer. Trelari would not stabilize. Its reality pattern would fray and the world would march from cataclysm to cataclysm and terror to terror until at last its pattern disintegrated and the world vanished from creation. I really had to die. Which was heavy.

"Drake, please let her go," I said before I had fully come to terms with my decision. "She's not to blame, and killing her wouldn't solve the problem."

"And remind us why we're listening to you, Dark Lord?" Seamus snarled.

There were nods all around at this question, and it was a fair one. "Because I'm going to tell you how to get rid of Death Slasher and the reality storm, and it will cost you nothing of value."

"No lies?" Valdara asked, or maybe it was a command, because she was pointing Justice Cleaver at my throat.

I chuckled bitterly. "If only."

There followed a moment of silence while they waited for me to say something else, and during which my courage failed me—repeatedly.

"Okay, kid," Drake said finally. "You've got our attention. Are you going to tell us your plan, or are you going to make me beat it out of you?"

I looked at him and sighed. I hoped when this was all over that he would find his faith again. Because he was a miserable drunk. I locked my eyes on his and said, "You have to *really* defeat me."

Drake's eyes narrowed briefly at that and then his eyebrows shot up in shock. His expression told me that he understood completely. He dropped Vivian and took a stumbling step backward like I'd struck him.

If Drake understood, the others were still confused. "And what happens when you're defeated?" asked Seamus.

I blinked. "When I am defeated everything will be set right. The fortress will fall. The armies will be swept away. The storm will clear. Death Slasher will be no more. A golden age will begin."

"So, surrender yourself, laddie," barked Rook.

"It's . . . it's not that simple, Rook," I said, unable to stop the catch in my voice.

Valdara's green eyes had never left my face since we'd started talking. Now she too seemed to understand, although she was uncertain. She walked over to where Death Slasher lay and picked it up. I could see Justice Cleaver quivering with rage at this. She deposited the weapon at my feet.

"What if we fight?" she asked, and twirled Justice Cleaver in her hands. "If I disarmed you . . ."

"No." I shook my head. "I just need you to . . ." I looked up at her and pleaded silently that she not make me finish.

"No," she choked.

"You have to," I said. "I'm sorry."

"Can someone tell me what he's talking about?" Sam shouted.

Valdara's voice was full of anger and frustration. "He wants us to kill him."

"Avery?" Ariella asked.

"Well, 'want' may be too strong a word . . ." I said, because I can be sort of an ass sometimes.

The entire group started speaking at once. Seamus and Rook began arguing about the real meaning of "defeat." Seamus seemed to be pro-killing and Rook anti-, but I can't be sure because there were so many dwarf curse words thrown in it was hard to follow. Ariella and Sam were shouting about different spells that they had heard of that might place me in a death-like state. Luke put his head in his hands. "I wish I were somewhere far, far away." Drake and Valdara stood in a silent embrace.

I marveled at these people. Whereas a few minutes ago the entire company, almost without exception, would have gladly sliced me from throat to belly, now that I was giving myself to them of my own accord they seemed determined to find any other way out. And that, I reflected, is why they're heroes.

I let them argue for a time until a streak of lightning caught my attention. I looked up. The storm, which had been unhappily spinning above us, had now begun to descend in a swirling vortex. Reality was not happy. I slowly picked up Death Slasher, avoiding the eye's gaze. I did not want that to be my last vision.

"For obvious reasons, I really hate to cut your discussion short, but . . ." I pointed up at the sky.

"Avery," said Ariella, "I won't pretend to understand, but there has to be another way."

"No, Ariella. The Dark Lord has to die. It will break the pattern."

"What about the key?" said Sam, holding it up. "Can't we just—"

"Sorry, Sam," I said. "This is something that imagination and will won't fix. I would ask though that once I'm gone you give the key to Vivian and let her go home. I promise you that she's an innocent." I reached over and brushed a few strands of hair out of her eyes. "She's actually a lovely person when you get to know the real her."

I thought of one more thing. "Because that part of the pattern will be burned out, she probably won't remember much of what happened while she was here. Please promise me you won't tell her what happened to me. She will learn soon enough, but I'd rather she be at home among friends when she finds out." I glanced at the silent faces. "You can tell her I left her behind." I gave a short self-mocking laugh. "She'll believe it."

I stroked Vivian's cheek one last time, and then stood and walked down the steps to a place on the floor of the throne room that was relatively clear of orc ash. I went to my knees and grasped Death Slasher. The group followed me down and stood in a circle staring down at me.

I looked at Valdara. "Whatever you choose to do, it is going to have to be Justice Cleaver that makes the last stroke."

Valdara was not able to meet my gaze. "I can't do this, Avery. I'm a warrior, not an executioner."

"Look at me, Valdara," I pleaded. She did and I saw the unshed tears in her eyes. "You are not an executioner. You are a savior to your people. Whatever happens, never forget that you are removing a great evil from your world. *You* are killing the *Dark Lord*." She looked away for a moment and ran a finger across her eyes. "And, Valdara?"

"Yes?" she said, looking back.

"You are one of the most amazing people I have had the honor of knowing." I looked about. "All of you are. And I want to thank you for the chance to know you." I couldn't help adding, "If it's any solace, if this works, it will prove the thesis of my dissertation."

With that, I closed my eyes and lowered my head.

A strange sense of peace came over me. For once in my life, I knew that I was definitely doing the right thing. I had a brief thought that it was a shame that it was the last right thing I'd ever do, and that I hadn't had a chance to say goodbye to Eldrin, but who dies without a few regrets?

I took a few breaths—savoring them. The time passed and I wondered how many breaths I would have to savor before she finished me. When more time passed, I opened my eyes and looked at Valdara. She was staring down at me with a cunning smile.

"The storm really is going to be bad when it gets down here," I said, and as the funnel was at the top of where the roof to the throne room had been, that wasn't going to be very long.

She ignored me and began barking orders. "Rook! Bring Vivian to me! Sam! Give me the key."

"I told you already," I said, slightly frustrated. "She's not to blame and the key won't work. Destroying me is the only way."

"I'm not going to kill her, I'm not going to use the key, and you are not as clever as you think, Avery," she said with a wink.

Rook laid Vivian's sleeping body on the floor next to where I kneeled and Sam placed the key in Valdara's hand. She nodded in satisfaction and then dropped the key on the floor. Before anyone could react, she took Justice Cleaver and sliced the key in two. I felt the impact on a mystical level more than a physical one. My mind echoed with the force of the blow. In an instant I heard the music again, loud and bright. It was a song of freedom, the essence of a world unleashed. Reality energy twisted around Justice Cleaver and Valdara. She glowed with power, a goddess of light and justice.

"Do you think I'm a complete idiot, Avery? Do you think I could have traveled with you this long and not have some understanding of how your magic works?" She pointed Justice Cleaver at me. "Dark Lord, by all the powers of this world, I condemn you and the Dark Queen and all of your kind to eternal exile."

Her words felt like an incantation. She meant to seal me and Vivian and every other Mysterium magi out of Trelari. With a great slashing motion of Justice Cleaver she rent a hole in reality. A portal, like a tear in a tapestry, opened and through it I could see Mysterium. It had worked! I realized with a sudden rush of joy that I wasn't going to die.

With a laugh I jumped to my feet, and then it struck me that I was being banished—forever. A deep sadness stole the laughter from my lips and the joy from my heart. For the last time I looked about at the people I had fallen in love with, drinking in every detail. There was so much that I wanted to say, but there was no time. The portal was already beginning to shut and the storm was now close enough over our heads that its winds were beginning to whip up the ash and debris in the room. It was time to go.

Holding Death Slasher in one hand, I bent and lifted Vivian in my arms. I turned about so I could look at them all one last time. "Thank you, for everything. I love you all . . ." I said, and then lied to them for the last time. "And hope never to see you again."

With that rather cheeky goodbye, I stepped through the portal. I felt Death Slasher fade from my hand first. I never knew if it was aware of what was coming. The petty part of me hopes to the gods that it did. Vivian transformed next, losing the iron crown as the portal began to close behind us. I turned back at that point and watched as the fortress walls dissolved and beams of sunlight cascaded down on the group, *my* group.

The golden age of Trelari had begun.

CHAPTER 33

ABD

People say that you can never go home. I don't know who these people are or where they live, but they're full of it. I made it home just fine, thank you. Granted, the portal let Vivian and me out in the middle of a Magicology final, but that class is worthless so the students undoubtedly learned more about magic from our appearance than they had the previous fifteen weeks of the semester.

Anyway, after escaping the proctors, I dropped Vivian in her room—literally. I dropped Vivian on the floor trying to carry her to her bed. Not my fault. The room looked like it had been ransacked, and I tripped over a stack of old class notebooks and a hair dryer before I'd made it two steps through the door. I didn't know it then, but I would never see Vivian walking through those halls again, but that story comes later and I'm already way over my page count.

Once I had her off the floor and into her bed, I made my way back to McKinley and my crappy dorm room. I opened the door. Let me repeat that. I opened the door! Apparently, Dawn fixed the doorknob in about five minutes with a couple of screws and a screwdriver.

Eldrin and she were sitting on the floor, heads bent together over an enormous glowing map of Trelari. By the way Eldrin was rocking and shaking; he was upset. She had her hand on his back and was whispering to him. It was an intimate moment I wish they'd been able to have without me barging in, except of course I was the reason he was upset.

It turns out that to follow my progress through Trelari, Eldrin had invented an incredibly powerful and complex scrying spell (that he has decided not to publish because of the privacy implications). When Valdara's portal sealed behind us, my signal went blank, an indication in Eldrin's mind that the entire world, and presumably me with it, was gone. I'm not sure that *sorry* covers something like that, but, Eldrin, when you read this, I'm still sorry.

After the apologies and the inevitable good-natured insults that followed the apologies were done, we ordered a pizza and I got the whole story of how I came to be talking to Griswald and not Eldrin in those desperate last moments.

"I'd been working on the new monitoring spell for a while." Eldrin gave a furtive and haunted glance at the map he'd been examining when I entered. "Anyway, I'd tuned it for Death Slasher . . ."

"Wait, how'd you do that?" I asked, snagging the last piece of pizza.

"Simple," he snorted.

"Don't show off, Eldrin," Dawn said.

"It was," Eldrin protested. "How many things in the multiverse are a mixture of Mysterium reality and 2A7C?"

"Trelari," I said firmly. "The world is called Trelari."

He nodded, but I could see he didn't understand. Why would he, after all?

"The point is, the only thing I know that has that composition is your stupid battle-axe. The spell found it right away and in five minutes it was clear the weapon was in Griswald's office. The only question was when to get it."

Dawn rolled her eyes, which showed the classic signs of someone that has studied arcane morality for a number of years: pitch-black pupils surrounded by brilliant-white whites. "He means that he was delayed for a day or so because he was engineering a fault in the subworld observatory so no one would be able to track 2A . . . Trelari's approach." She turned to him and scolded. "By the way, I heard that they are going to need another month to fix the thing and that you also sabotaged the auraometer, which you only did to get back at the magus in your department that likes to look for burnt-sienna worlds."

"It's burnt-umber and he's an ass," grumbled Eldrin. "All I wanted was five minutes on the auraometer to see if it could tell me anything about Trelari's stability state and he refused because it was 'reserved'."

"It's still mean," she said, but then casually rested her hand on top of his and intertwined her fingers with his.

He glanced down at her hand and then up at me and blushed. In the future I would definitely need to give them lots of privacy.

Pretending not to have noticed anything, I asked, "And Griswald?"

Eldrin shrugged. "After the observatory, I cast an imperception field on myself and staked out Griswald's office until he'd left for the evening. It should have worked perfectly, but I forgot about his stupid imp. Anyway," he said, looking at me through his bangs. "I don't know why you're always complaining about Griswald. The guy was pretty cool about it, although he has some messed-up ideas about subworld quantum orbitals."

This reminded me that Professor Griswald had been very cool and very helpful, and that I hadn't checked in with him yet. So, after a shower, which was blessed, I headed over to the Subworld Studies building. It was the middle of the day and Griswald always had office hours at this time.

After waving my hellos to a few of my less-prickish classmates and picking up my mail, which was all junk, I made my way to his office. On the third floor, where the tenured professors live, there is always a hush to the air. The professors themselves are typically hiding from students behind closed doors, and the students won't dare come up unless driven by desperation, because the typical professor's answer to any question is extra work for the student. This made the fact that I found Griswald's door partially open extremely unusual.

I put my ear to the opening and could hear his imp wheezing away within. I knocked lightly and waited for an answer. When none came, I called, "Professor?" Still nothing. I pushed the door open and peered in.

His office looked almost normal. The shelves that lined the sides of the long room still groaned beneath the weight of the papers and books that covered them, most of which hadn't been read in thirty or more years. Beside the door, his blackboard was still covered with arcane magic circles, symbols, and equations, each one written erased, revised, and rewritten until what remained was an incomprehensible blur. The broad window behind his desk was open to catch the afternoon air, as it always was unless it was raining. And on a stand beside the desk sat his imp, a kind of part orange-haired monkey and part something you would expect to get if a witch doctor shrunk a grumpy old man down to around two feet tall. The imp stared at me and wheezed. That was normal. But two things about the room made me pause on the edge of the threshold.

The first was that Griswald was not there. He was always there at this time. I don't mean a kind of sometimes always, but an *always*. You could set your watch by Griswald's schedule—secondhand included. Still, I might have been willing to overlook that oddity had it not been for his desk. After years of sitting across from professors as they hunted around for some vital piece of paper or a pen or paperclip or glasses or anything else, I can say that their desks are never clean. In fact, I am convinced that they are enchanted so that once a thing is placed on their surface it can never be removed again, which would explain why the quantity of things on a professor's desk only increases over time. All of which is to explain why I got a sick feeling in my stomach when I saw that Griswald's desk was bare save for an envelope, a single bound manuscript, and a small wooden box.

I walked over to the desk and stared at the pile of things. There was a glow of magic around them. I looked at it out of the corner of my eye, which is the proper technique for examining such things. It was a personalized concealment circle, which are devilishly tricky to cast. A personalized concealment circle will reveal whatever it is concealing only to the desired person, but more than that, an advanced circle like this one actually makes the concealed items only exist for that person. This meant that I was the only one that could see and touch these things. To everyone else Griswald's desk would be empty . . . unless he had other concealment circles meant for other people, but let's not get lost in semantics.

A note was stuck to the top of the box. It said, "To Avery Stewart, Congratulations and best of luck, Professor Griswald." And in tiny lettering on the bottom: "3L9E." It was the coordinate to a world.

I tucked the note in my pocket and picked up the box. Something knocked about inside. I tried to find a lid, but after a few minutes I became convinced, despite the rattle, that it was made from a solid block of wood. I'd have to figure it out later, or more likely I'd get Eldrin to open it. He was mad about puzzle boxes.

I took up the manuscript next and had to catch the edge of the desk to keep from falling. It was my dissertation! I flipped open the cover and found Griswald's signature. I'd graduated! And there was another wonderful surprise. Paper-clipped to the inside cover was a letter from the editor of the journal *Majic* indicating that not one but two chapters from my dissertation would be published in next month's edition, and one would be the cover article! I was a full magus and had a publication coming out in the most prestigious journal of magic.

There is the joy of love at first sight and of seeing your child being born, but slightly below that and to the left (not that I have a child) is the feeling of completing your dissertation. If you have four or five years to spare I would highly recommend it.

My elation lasted until I opened the envelope, which also bore my name in Griswald's slanty scrawl. Inside was a short letter from my former professor that would change my life and the history of The Mysterium University, but let's not get ahead of ourselves. This was what the letter said:

Dear Avery,

I'm sorry I cannot be there to celebrate the completion of your dissertation. It was either leave in the middle of the night (or midmorning as it were) or be taken away by force. It may not have been the courageous choice, but I chose the former.

I am afraid that Vivian's decision to enter your experiment has put you and her in grave danger. Had we known she was a subworlder we never would have shared the information we did with her. But we did and it nearly got the two of you, and many other innocent people, killed. For that, and many other things, I want to apologize. Only know that we have always had the best of intentions.

While I have been able to cover up much of what happened in Trelari, there are those within Mysterium who know, and who will not like it. I have done my best to make it difficult for the university administration to discipline you by approving your dissertation (the easiest decision of my career), and by ensuring the publication of your results in a high-profile journal (although, truth be told, most of the credit for that goes to your exemplary work). I have also made my recommendation that you be put up for my (now vacant) position within the faculty in the Department of Subworld Studies. It would be unprecedented and cause an enormous ruckus within the faculty if they were to refuse that request. I hope this means that you will have additional good news soon, but do NOT relax and be careful!

As you will soon find out, if you haven't figured it out already, not all is as it should be in Mysterium. I hate to be dramatic, but there are dark forces at work within the university and they are not a group that you should trifle with. And yet I would urge you to do just that. Trifle! I've spent the better part of my career working with a group of triflers and I wouldn't go back for any reason. In time, one of my trifling colleagues will contact you. You will have to decide your own course. All I will say is that Mysterium is wrong, but it will be up to you to discover why for yourself.

Assuming my plans work and you become a professor, you will have a great deal more free time. That is one of the best perks of the job. Use that time to think. The more time you spend thinking, the more you will come to realize how wrong Mysterium is. I had my own epiphany while sitting on the quad one day watching a group of novices playing invisible plasma Frisbee. Never forget to go and sit in the quad now and then. It's really a lovely place.

Enjoy whatever comes next. I doubt that we shall see each other again. It has been a privilege and an honor being your mentor.

Warmest regards,

Prof. Eustace K. Griswald

P.S. Please take care of Harold for me. He is too set in his ways to want to leave the university. He is a good imp, and only bites when he's hungry. I've left his asthma medication in my top left-hand desk drawer. A final tip: butterscotch candies—he loves them.

EKG

P.P.S. Make sure you open the top left drawer only!

EKG

P.P.P.S. I know that you may not have particularly fond feelings for her at this moment, but please look in on Vivian. She's a good egg and this could cause her no end of trouble.

EKG

I read the letter twice through, and then folded it up and put it in my pocket next to the box and the note. By all rights I should have been happy. A faculty position at The Mysterium University was not something that came along every day. In fact, since the professors had a tendency to live for hundreds if not thousands of years they came along exactly never. But I looked at Griswald's empty chair and would have given anything at that moment to have him back, puffing on his pipe, and growling at me again.

The room was a little dusty and my eyes were tearing, but I was absolutely not crying. I walked across to Harold, still blinking. He was staring blankly across the room at the blackboard.

"Sorry about this, old ch-chum," I said, my voice catching . . . from all the dust of course. "I know I'm a poor substitute, but if you'll have me I can assure you that you'll not want for trouble."

I held out my arm to him like I'd seen Griswald do so many countless times. The imp stared up at me somberly, gave a great wheezing sigh, and climbed from his perch across my arm to sit on my shoulder. I walked to the door of the office, took one last look around. Through the open window I could hear the sound of the novice and acolytes celebrating the last day of exams. I smiled and pulled the door closed.

EPILOGUE

After I got Griswald's letter I ran back to Vivian's place. She was gone. She has been gone ever since. Eldrin has tried his scrying spell with no luck. He says that if she's in Mysterium, she's in a place that's impenetrable to detection, which he doesn't think is possible. I have a tendency to agree.

Vivian's disappearance, following so quickly on the heels of Griswald's own departure, made me more than a little paranoid. (I took to hiding in the defective void space in our room whenever someone knocked on the door.) Every day I expected the jackbooted thugs of Mysterium security, or at least the weaselly dean of students to bring the hammer down on me for what happened. But nothing ever did.

I was put up for Griswald's old faculty position and was accepted after an interview that, admittedly, bordered on the inquisitorial, but was no more intrusive that I'd been expecting. Even Eldrin escaped his extracurricular activities undetected and unscathed, except that he and Dawn had a knockdown about whether his sabotage of this guy Johnson's experiment was ethical or not. They eventually made up, but Eldrin mooned about and wrote bad poetry for a week or so before she forgave him.

With the "big" bucks I was making as a very junior professor, and the extra money Eldrin picked up fixing the subworld observatory, which I will remind you he was responsible for breaking, we were finally able to move out of the dorms. We picked the East Village in New York, because the Indian food is great, we couldn't afford London, and even Eldrin admitted that Hylar would be way too frolicky for us. It turns out I kind of like my old home world, although visiting family is still a tribulation. There's even a convenient door to Mysterium near NYU in the old Fire Patrol No 2 building, right across the street from what is left of one of Edgar Allan Poe's many former homes. The only downside to moving out of the dorm is that, as expected, we lost our deposit.

First day in my new office, which by tradition was Griswald's old office, I was visited by the chair of the Subworld Studies Department. He informed me that Trelari (he referred to it as 2A7C, of course) was off-limits. This was not surprising. I did protest, but only because I felt like he would expect me to. The fact is, I know better than anyone how off-limits Trelari really is to me and everyone else in Mysterium. He also gave me my teaching schedule, which as the most junior member of the faculty was . . . what's the word I'm looking for . . . HELLISH!

After several months working on lesson plans and lectures I began to wonder when all this wonderful free time Griswald had talked about was going to show up. And then it happened. One day Harold and I found ourselves at the far edge of campus sitting on a bench in the summer sun staring down a little path that disappeared into the shadows beneath an avenue of ancient-looking oak trees. Our being here was not all that random. I came here often to think and fiddle with Griswald's little box. (Eldrin had not been able to open it. A source of near constant frustration for him.) Nor was my choice of this bench as my regular place of repose random, because at the end of the little path, somewhere beneath those ancient trees lies the entrance to Trelari.

As an explanation, because of all the shifting Trelari now sits directly on the border with Mysterium. It has not been officially recognized as an innerworld, but only because no one from Mysterium can get into it. A fact that really, really annoys the otherwise all-powerful magi.

The funny thing about the path is that if you walk down to the end you find yourself right back at the beginning. In fact, some undergraduates had begun using it as a convenient jogging trail, because apparently it is exactly a quarter of a mile long.

Anyway, there we sat, me staring down the path at the mists that always swirled among the trees and wondering what and how Valdara and Drake and all the rest were doing, when a jogger came by. At first was not paying much attention except that I had a vague sense that something about him was odd. I glanced up from the box and saw that the fellow was short, really short, dwarf short. And he had a shock of bright orange hair.

As he disappeared among the trees, I shouted, "Rook!"

He either didn't hear me, or didn't want to be caught, because he kept going. I dropped the box, jumped to my feet, and sprinted down the trail after him. Exactly a quarter of a mile later I found myself back at my bench. Harold was still there, sleeping. I did this three more times before I gave up.

This was probably (certainly) the most exercise I'd gotten in a month and so I was a bit winded. I sat down to catch my breath and wonder at what this all meant when I noticed that Harold was awake and had the box in his lap, and that the box was open and that the box was empty.

"How?" I asked.

Harold turned and stared at me with those rheumy eyes of his and wheezed, "Sorry, I got tired of watching you muck about with it. Here you go."

He held up a key, not just any key, but a reality key. I took it and cradled it in my hand. I wondered what world it fitted to. Maybe the one Griswald's note had referenced. Maybe even Trelari itself! My heart raced at the possibilities it represented.

I was on my feet and several steps under the trees before I knew what I was doing. I stopped and stared down the path and thought about Trelari and her people and my friends and everything that had happened. And that's when I had my epiphany. I saw the flaw in Mysterium. The wrongness that hid in every crack and behind every shadow.

I laughed. I laughed at myself and all the other magi, but mostly at myself. Then I put the key in my pocket and turned about.

As I passed the bench I put my arm out and Harold scrambled back onto my shoulder. I gave him a hard candy from my pocket—butterscotch—and asked, "How long have you been able to talk?"

ACKNOWLEDGMENTS

We'd like to thank everyone. Here is our best attempt.

Harry would like to thank Zu, Kayla, Cathy, Josh, and Andrew and everyone at Unboxed for the unending support. John would like to thank Oliver and Taba for reading this when it was not ready to be read, and to DCon, Aaron, Patrick, and all the other friends of fantasy he's met and made in California.

We'd like to thank our fellow Harper Voyager authors, especially Bishop for being slightly taller than Rook and for listening to the original story at NYCC 2014.

We want to thank the staff at Harper Voyager, from the cover designers to the people we have never met who made this book happen. We'd especially like to thank Kelly and Rebecca for being the original editors, and Anna for being with us at the end. Jessie is a phenomenal publicist, too! You are all amazing.

We'd like to acknowledge everyone who gamed with us at American University—you know who you are. And we hope you remember Justice Cleaver. He is the world's greatest battle-axe.

Harry would like to thank his family in Georgia, Tennessee, North Carolina (yes, that means Butterworths!), Virginia, California, and New Jersey for their ongoing support, especially the Curatola clan who endured the family reunion weekend coinciding with edits. Andrea, I owe you. Kathy, thank you for the setup and the quiet room. Gary, your encouragement means the world to him. Mark, Michael, Tony, Betty, Eric, Lindsey, and Brad, you are all wonderful. And the kids are amazing.

John wants to give a special thanks to Bill and Susan for always being there for his two most precious things. Everything would be harder without your support and love. The rainbow-kitty-corn loves you, too!

Thanks to Evan for showing off the Legos and his map of Royaume. This is a different series, but your enthusiasm for Charming means the world to both of us.

To Kelly and the entire staff at Fountain Books—your store is something truly special. Thank you for all you do for authors. To the Hanover Writers Club and the Paragon City Writers, we appreciate all the feedback. To anyone that has visited our website at www.jackheckel.com or found us on Facebook, thank you! We especially appreciate our reviewers. You make us better.

Most of all, if you are holding this book in your hands or looking at it on your e-reader, you are why we write.

ABOUT THE AUTHOR

JACK HECKEL is the name of the writing team of John Peck and Harry Heckel. College roommates and fellow gamers. One day they were reminiscing about late nights role-playing and debating their favorite authors, and decided to write books together. They are the authors of The Charming Tales series as well as *The Dark Lord*, and, given the chance, plan to write too many other novels to count. Harry lives in Virginia with his wife, daughter, and two cats. John lives in California with his wife and son and a menagerie of four-legged creatures and one snake. They both have other jobs and enjoy envisioning a day when they sell their movie rights and become full-time writers living somewhere like Kauai or Vermont. To find out more about their works, visit them at www.jackheckel.com.

